HA

GANZ BROKE FROM the mass first and charged the dais. Lowenhertz was behind him, with Drakken and Gruber. He reached the stone steps of the dais. Above him the hooded figure threw off its robes and laughed down at him. Volcanic flame-light from behind made the Templar armour it wore glow as if it were red hot. One pink eye gleamed. The commander of White Company saw how the Wolf armour it wore was rusting and beginning to moulder. The flesh of its grinning face was greenish and starting to stretch. It stank of decay, of the grave. It held out its hand to him.

'Call me by my real name, Ganz. Call me Barakos.'

Ganz didn't reply. He flew at the monstrosity, hammer swinging in a wide, sidelong arc. But the decaying thing was faster – terrifyingly fast. It smashed Ganz aside with a fierce blow of its warhammer. Ganz fell hard, clutching at his dented breastplate and the cracked ribs beneath. His vision went bright and hazy, and there was a coppery taste in his mouth.

Barakos took a step towards him.

'I should have killed you in the cellar,' he panted.

'You cannot kill what has no life.' The liche's voice was hoarse and dry, but there was a depth to it, an inhuman grumble that curled the edges of the words, like age-mould curling the edges of old parchment.

A WARHAMMER NOVEL

HAMMERS OF ULRIC

By Dan Abnett, Nik Vincent & James Wallis

A BLACK LIBRARY PUBLICATION

First published in Great Britain in 2000 by
Games Workshop Publishing
Willow Road, Lenton,
Nottingham, NG7 2WS, UK

10 9 8 7 6 5 4 3 2 1

Cover illustration by Martin Hanford

A CIP record for this book
is available from the British Library

ISBN 1 84154 033 1

Set in ITC Giovanni

Printed and bound in Scotland by
Caledonian International Book Manufacturing Ltd., Glasgow

See the Black Library on the Internet at
http://www.blacklibrary.co.uk

Find out more about Games Workshop
and the world of Warhammer at
http://www.games-workshop.com

Jahrdrung

A Company of Wolves

IT WAS, TO no one's great surprise, raining in Middenheim that day.

Spring rain, fresh as ice needles, spattered down on that vast old city which sat brooding atop its granite crag, gazing down across the dismal forests around it. Another long winter season was slowly thawing, and the city, and everyone in it, was cold and wet and miserable to the bone.

In a puddled yard behind the Spread Eagle tavern, Morgenstern carefully adjusted a line of plump turnips he had arranged along the flagstones, each one sat on an upturned pail. Then he walked to the end of the yard, belched delicately with a hand to his mouth and little finger cocked, then spat on his meaty palms and hefted up the great warhammer leaning against the slimy bricks.

He began to spin it, crossing his grip deftly, looping the mighty head back and forth in a figure of eight around his shoulders. *Whoooff! Whoooff! Whooooff!* it hissed as it circled. But Morgenstern was standing a little too close to the back wall and, after another circuit, the hammerhead struck against the stonework. Several bricks shattered and dropped out, and the warhammer bounced to the ground.

Morgenstern swore colourfully, and wobbled slightly as he stooped to retrieve his weapon, rainwater dripping from his vast shaggy beard. Then he wobbled some more as he stooped to retrieve his tankard. He straightened up and supped from it. Then he tried unsuccessfully to replace the bits of brick, fussing as if somehow no one would notice the dent if he smoothed it over. Several more bricks fell out.

Giving up, Morgenstern turned back to his row of buckets and started to spin the hammer again, this time checking he had swinging room.

'Is this going to take much longer?' Aric asked from the tavern doorway. He stood leaning against the doorjamb: a tall, powerfully built young man not yet twenty-two, with a mane of black hair and bright blue eyes. He carried the gold-edged plate armour and the snowy pelt of the White Wolf Templars well.

'Hush!' said the older knight, concentrating on his swing and not looking round. Morgenstern adjusted the fall of his own wolf-pelt so it did not constrict the movement of his armoured limbs. 'Behold, my young friend, how a master of the warhammer displays his skill. See! Before me, the heads of my foes!'

'The turnips on the buckets?'

'Quite so. That is indeed what they represent.'

'These foes are what? Lying down? Buried up to the neck?'

Morgenstern smiled patiently. 'They are large and able-bodied warriors, Aric. I, however, am on a horse.'

'Of course you are.'

'For the purposes of this demonstration, imagine I am on a horse.'

Still spinning the hammer, Morgenstern began to prance back and forth on the spot like a hobbyhorse mummer in a Mystery Play. He made clip-clop noises with his tongue and occasionally admonished 'Steady there! Whoa, girl!'

Aric closed his eyes.

'Yah-hah!' Morgenstern barked suddenly and lurched forward, head back, as his imaginary horse bolted.

His great, thundering, armoured mass, with the hammer swooping about him in a vast circle, drummed down the yard, spraying up water and dislodging flagstones as he charged the buckets. His initial swing smashed the turnip on the first bucket, then, without breaking stride, he galloped in and out of the remaining buckets, decapitating each turnip in turn, slaloming between the rows, swooping and crossing the hammer with astonishing precision.

Aric by then had reopened his eyes. For all the pantomime idiocy, for all the drunkenness, for all the fact that Morgenstern was at the wrong end of his fifties and two hundred pounds too heavy, Aric was still impressed by the big man's weapon skill.

With a bellowing flourish, Morgenstern elegantly took out the last of his foes, bucket and all, crushing both with a blow that lofted them over the gable end. Then his boot slipped on the sheened cobbles, he stumbled at full pelt and went headfirst into the stables. Through a door he hadn't opened first.

Aric winced. He turned and went back inside. It was going to be a long day.

INSIDE THE Spread Eagle, he rejoined Anspach, Gruber and von Glick at the small table in the corner.

'Did he do it?' Gruber asked.

Aric nodded. 'All of them.'

Anspach chuckled his dirty, melodic chuckle. He was a handsome man in his late thirties, with devilish eyes and a smile that could charm chastity belts into spontaneous release. 'That's six shillings from each of you, I fancy.'

'By the Wolf, Anspach!' von Glick grunted. 'Is there nothing you won't wager on?'

Anspach accepted his winnings. 'Actually, no. In fact, that reminds me, I have a bag of gold riding on a certain goathead going the distance at the Bernabau this afternoon.'

Von Glick shook his head in dismay. A veteran Wolf of the old school, von Glick was a slender, angular man of sixty years. His grizzled hair was long and straggly, and his chin was shaven to pepper stubble. He was stiff and disapproving about all things. Aric wondered if there was anything von Glick couldn't complain about. He somehow doubted the prim old man had ever had the passion to be a noble warrior.

'So where's Morgenstern now?' Gruber asked, toying with his tankard.

'Having a lie down,' answered Aric. 'You know, I think… he drinks too much.'

The other three snorted.

'Brother Templar,' Anspach said, 'you're too recent an addition to this noble order to have witnessed it, but our Morgenstern is famous for the prodigious scale of his imbibing! Some of his greatest victories on the field of combat… like those orc-scum he took at the Battle of Kern's Gate… such feats have been fired by Ulric, and fuelled by ale!'

'Maybe,' Aric said doubtfully, 'but I think it's getting to him. His reflexes. His co-ordination...'

'He killed the turnips, didn't he?' von Glick asked.

'And the stable door,' Aric said darkly.

They fell silent.

'Still, our Morgenstern...' Anspach began, 'I'll wager he could–'

'Oh, shut up!' growled von Glick.

Aric sat back and gazed around the smoky tavern. He could see Ganz, their new, young company commander, sitting in a booth side, with the hot-blooded Vandam talking eagerly at him.

'What's that about?' he asked Gruber. The white-haired Gruber was deep in thought and snapped up with a start as Aric addressed him.

He looked almost scared just then, Aric thought. *That's not the first time I've caught him lost in thoughts he doesn't like.*

Gruber was the most respected of the Company's men, a veteran like Morgenstern and von Glick, who had served with old Jurgen from the beginning. His hair was thin, his eyes pale, his papery skin almost translucent with age, but Aric knew there was a power, a terrible force inside that warrior.

Except now... now, for the first time since he joined the Company eighteen months before, Aric sensed that Gruber's power was waning. Was it age? Was it... Jurgen? Was it something else?

Aric gestured again over at Vandam and Ganz. 'What's Vandam bending our commander's ear about?'

'I hear Vandam wants to transfer,' von Glick said quietly. 'He's a glory-hound. He wants promotion. Word is, he sees our company as a dead end. He wants to move to another mob. Red Company, maybe.'

The four of them grunted their disapproval and all took a drink.

'Don't think Ganz will let him. Ganz has barely had time to make his mark in command since the... since that business. He won't want to lose a man before he's had a chance to prove something.' Gruber looked thoughtful. 'If they ever let us prove anything again.'

'It's not long till Mitterfruhl,' Anspach said. 'Then the campaign season really starts. We'll get something... a good raid into the Drak. I bet you.'

Aric was silent. Something had to happen soon, or this particular brave company of White Wolves was going to lose its heart entirely.

THE GREAT TEMPLE of Ulric was almost empty. The air was still and cold and smelled of candle smoke.

Ganz walked in, and reverently placed his gloves and warhammer in the reliquary in the entrance hall.

The acoustics in the vast, vaulted chamber were superb, and Ganz could hear the precise intonations of four knights who were whispering prayers on the other side of the high altar, kneeling, heads down. He could also hear the faint squeak of lint as a Temple adept polished the brass finials of the lectern. The great statue of Ulric himself rose up like a thundercloud to block the light from the high windows.

Ganz bowed his head and made his observance, then crossed the chamber and knelt before the Sacred Flame.

He was kneeling there when he felt the hand on his shoulder. Ganz looked up into the face of Ar-Ulric, the High Priest himself, his craggy, bearded features catching the flame light.

'We should talk, Ganz. I'm glad you came by. Walk with me to the Regimental Chapel.'

Ganz got up and fell into step beside the venerable warrior. He saw the four knights were leaving, casting curious glances in his direction.

'I came to seek… guidance, High One,' Ganz began. 'This season will be my first as a commander of men, and already, I–'

'Do you lack confidence, Ganz?'

'No, lord. But I lack experience. And the men are… listless.'

They walked down a short flight of steps and reached an iron cage door where a Templar of Grey Company stood watch. He saluted the High Priest respectfully, and undid the padlock so that the cage door could swing open. Ganz followed Ar-Ulric through and they entered the smaller, warmer interior of the temple's regimental chapel, decorated with standards, banners, trophies and the honour roll of memorial slabs.

Both men bowed briefly to the great wolfskin pelt on the wall, and to the snarling, silver-inlaid treasure on a raised plinth beneath it. The Jaws of the Wolf, the Temple's most precious icon.

The High Priest bent before it for a moment, murmured a blessing to Ulric and to Artur, then rose and turned to Ganz. His eyes twinkled like the first frost of a hard Jahrdrung. 'Your company is more than listless, Ganz. There was a time when White Company was the finest and best this Temple could field, performing deeds that the riders of other Wolf Companies like Red or Grey could only dream of. But now it is weak – it has lost its way. This whole winter they have idled here in the city, wasting their health and money and time. Several have become noted drunkards. Especially Morgenstern.'

'It is easy to exaggerate–'

'He relieved himself in the font in the Temple of Verena,' the High Priest said with great and sad certainty. 'During High Mass. And then he suggested to the priests that the Goddess herself was a "piece of all right" who could really do with a good… what was it again?'

Ganz sighed. 'Man in her life, High Priest.'

The High Priest nodded. It seemed to Ganz he was almost smiling but that could not be so and his tone confirmed it. 'Morgenstern is a disgrace. And Anspach. You know about his gambling? He owes a large amount to the stadium brokers and to various less-official wager-takers. And I have had audiences with that hotblood Vandam twice now to hear him petition me for a transfer to Red Company. Or Gold. Or anywhere.'

Ganz hung his head.

'There are others with problems too… each to his own. I don't pretend your job is easy, Ganz, taking command of a demoralised mob like this. And I know everything stems from that one incident last summer in the Drakwald. That beastpack got the better of you. They were strong. Sometimes, Ulric save us, the evil ones do win. It was a tragedy White Company lost so many good men. And to lose Jurgen. It can't be easy for you to take his place.'

'What can I do, High Priest? I don't command the respect Jurgen did. How can I rally White Company?'

The High Priest crossed to the far wall and lifted down the standard of Vess. It was old and tattered and stained with ancient, noble blood. It was one of the oldest and most revered battle standards of the Wolf Companies, carried at some of the Templars' greatest victories.

'You will take your company out, into the forests, beneath this old and venerable standard, and you will destroy the beastpack that broke your honour.'

Ganz took the shaft of the standard with amazement. He looked up and met the steely gaze of his old commander, Jurgen, the newest of the graven memorials on the wall. For a long while, Ganz stared into that marble face, remembering the long white beard, the hawkish look, the famous studded eye-patch. Ganz knew the High Priest was right. It was the only way.

IT WAS A cold dawn, and raining once again. The fourteen brothers of White Company assembled in the stable block behind the Temple, adjusting the harnesses of their warsteeds, grumbling in low voices, their breath steaming the air.

'A raiding party? Before Mitterfruhl?' Morgenstern complained, swigging from a flask in his saddlebags as he pretended to check them.

'A drink? Before breakfast?' von Glick sneered quietly.

Morgenstern laughed at this, booming and hard, but Aric knew it was sham good-humour. He could see the pale strain in Morgenstern's pallid face, see the way his great hands shook.

Aric looked about. Vandam was resplendent, his face flushed with determination. His white wolf pelt hung just so across the shoulders of his gold-chased plate armour. Gruber looked far away, distant and preoccupied as he fumbled with the harness straps of his stamping steed. Einholt, the old, bald warrior with the facial scar and the milky eye, looked tired, as if he hadn't slept well. Aric felt sure some old dream chased the veteran Einholt each and every night without fail.

Anspach laughed and joked with his fellows. Von Glick scowled at him. Ganz looked grim and quiet. The others began to mount up, exchanging jokes and slurs – haggard Krieber, stocky Schiffer, the blond giant Bruckner, red-maned Kaspen, the whipcord Schell, and Dorff, whistling another of his tuneless refrains.

'Aric!' Ganz called, and Aric crossed the yard. As the youngest of the company, it was his privilege to carry the standard. He was amazed when Ganz placed the precious Standard of Vess into his mailed hand. Everyone in the yard fell silent.

'By the decree of the High Priest himself, we ride under the banner of Vess, and we ride for revenge,' Ganz said simply and swung into the saddle.

He turned his steed about and the company fell into step behind him, riding out of the yard into the streets and the rain beyond.

THEY CAME DOWN the western viaduct out of the city, in the shadow of the great Fauschlag Rock. High above them, the craggy walls and towers of Middenheim pushed their way up into the cold, friendless skies, as they had done for two thousand years.

They left the smoke and stench and clamour of the city behind, moving past trains of laden handcarts bound for the Altmarkt markets: strings of cattle from Salzenmund, the piled wagons of textile merchants from Marienburg. All pulled themselves to the sides of the sixty-foot wide viaduct to let the Wolf Company pass. When a party of Ulric's best rode out, only a fool got in their way.

White Company left the viaduct and joined the Altdorf road, cantering into the damp woodlands, and followed the forest track for six hours before stopping to water their horses and eat at a village by the way. In the afternoon, the sun came up to glint off their grey and gold plate mail. The heat drew mist out of the wet trees, and they rode as if through smoke. In each village they passed, the locals came out to see a brave and feared band of Templars, singing a low battle hymn as they rode along.

They slept the night in a village longhall above a waterfall, and they rode at dawn into the darker paths, the long tracks of black mud that ran down into the oily darkness of the Drakwald Forest, a region that lay across the land like the fallen cloak of some black-hearted god.

IT WAS NOON, but a pale, weak noon, and chill rain pattered down through the naked branches of black elms and twisted maple. The ground beneath them was coated in a stinking, matted slime of dead leaves that had fallen the autumn before and now lay rotting back into the dark soil. Spring would be a long time coming here.

There seemed no sign of life except for the fourteen riders. Occasionally a woodpecker would hammer in the distance, or some loon or other bird would whoop. Aric saw cobwebs in low branches hung with rainwater like diamond chokers.

'Smoke!' von Glick called suddenly, and they reined up, sniffing the air.

'He's right!' Vandam said eagerly, sliding the long haft of his warhammer out of his saddle loop.

Ganz held up a hand. 'Steady, Vandam! If we move, we move as a company or not at all. Aric, raise the standard.'

Aric edged alongside the leader and pulled the old banner upright.

With a nod, Ganz led off and the column moved two abreast through the trees in the direction of the smoke, hooves splashing through the leaf slush and rot.

The clearing was wide and open – trees had been cleared for it and now the wood was being burnt on a stone slab set before a crude statue. Five shambling, hairy forms were worshipping at the fire.

'For Ulric! Wolves! Ride!' Ganz yelled and they broke into a gallop, tearing down the slope into the clearing itself, exploding water from the marshy ground with their heavy hooves.

The beastmen at the shrine looked round in horror, baying and breaking for cover.

At the back of the file, Morgenstern turned from the charge and looked to Gruber, who had reached a dead stop.

'What's the matter?' he bellowed. 'We're missing the fun!'

'I think my steed has thrown a shoe,' growled Gruber. 'Go on, you old fool! Ride on!'

Morgenstern turned again after the main charge and took a deep pull from his saddle bottle. Then with a huge cry he charged down the slope after the main party.

The low branch took him clean out of his saddle.

The rest thundered out across the clearing, Aric bellowing as he held the banner high. Three of the beastmen broke and fled. Two snatched up pikes and turned to face the charge, shrieking in a deep, inhuman way.

Vandam was by now leading the charge. His swinging mallet-head destroyed the skull of one of the defenders, smacking the goat-headed aberration back into the ground.

Ganz, just behind him, overshot the other and tried to wheel around. His horse lost its footing on the wet leaves and slid over, spilling him off.

The beast turned to capitalise on this but in a moment Aric and Krieber had run it down between their horses, smashing its bones.

Anspach galloped past the shrine after one of the escapees, whirling his hammer. Von Glick was close on his hind.

'Ten shillings says I make this kill!' laughed Anspach.

Von Glick cursed and tried to pull level, but Anspach hurled his hammer and it went spinning off after the fleeing creature. It decapitated a sapling and missed the beast by ten yards. Anspach swore and reined in his charge.

'Gods help you that you ever win a wager!' von Glick cried as he carried on and caught up with the beast at the tree line. He swung two blows which both missed, but the creature doubled back and was driven into the aim of Dorff, who crushed its brain.

The other two fled into the trees. Vandam, without breaking stride, galloped after them.

'Back! Vandam! Back here!' bellowed Ganz as he got up and righted his shaken horse.

Vandam paid no attention. They could hear his whoops echoing into the forest.

'Schell! Von Glick! Go and round that idiot up!' Ganz ordered and the two riders obeyed. Everyone else had galloped to a standstill around the shrine. Ganz looked back and saw that Gruber had dismounted at the edge of the clearing and was helping to prop Morgenstern against a tree. Morgenstern's horse was trotting around, with its reins trailing.

Ganz shook his head and spat an oath.

He strode up to the shrine and gazed for a moment at the crude statue. Then he swung his hammer and smashed it into splinters.

Ganz turned back and looked at his men. 'Now they know we're here. Now they will come looking for us and our job will be easier!'

'VANDAM? WHERE are you, you idiot?' bawled von Glick as he rode slowly through the dark glades beyond the clearing. Dark meres stood stagnant between the filthy trees, and brackish water trickled down the slate outcrops. Through the trees and the mist, von Glick could make out Schell, riding a parallel course, yelling out 'Vandam! Come around the back or we'll leave you out here!'

Von Glick heard movement in the trees nearby and raised his hammer ready. Vandam rode out of the trees.

'Trust you to come looking for me, von Glick!' he snorted. 'You mother-hen the whole company! You're so stiff you wouldn't know valour if it came knocking!'

Von Glick shook his head wearily. He knew too well his own reputation with the younger members of White Company: stiff, inflexible, an old bore who nagged and complained. Jurgen had once told him he was the backbone of the company, but von Glick had a suspicion the commander had been trying to make light of von Glick's attitudes. Von Glick hated himself for it, but he couldn't help himself. There was no discipline these days. The young Templars were reckless bravos, and Vandam the very worst of them.

'Ganz ordered me to find you,' von Glick said sharply, trying to hold his anger. 'What sense is it to ride off alone like that? There's no glory in it!'

'Isn't there now?' Vandam smirked. 'I ran one to ground, broke his back. The other slipped away though.'

That was the worst of it... Vandam's arrogance was matched only by his skill as a warrior. Damn his eyes! thought von Glick.

'We'll ride back. Now!' he instructed Vandam, who shrugged mildly and turned his horse around. 'Schell!' von Glick called. 'I found him! Schell!'

Von Glick could still make out the other rider, but the mist and trees were deadening his voice.

'Go on,' von Glick told Vandam. 'I'll fetch him.'

He spurred up along the edge of a mere in the direction of Schell who saw him at last and began to ride over. Von Glick turned his horse back.

The beastman came out of the bushes with a feral scream. Driven, hounded by Vandam, it had hidden, but von Glick had passed close by its hiding place and panic had galvanised it into fierce action. The iron barb of the spear took the old Wolf through the right hip. He bellowed in pain and the horse reared. The beastman clung on, shaking his weapon, which was wedged fast in the bone and meat and armour. Von Glick screamed, hooked like a fish, pushed back in the saddle by the spear so far he couldn't reach his warhammer.

Schell bellowed in dismay and galloped in.

Vandam, hearing the commotion, turned and looked in horror. 'Ulric's bloody fists!' he gasped. 'Oh lord, no!'

The spear broke. Freed, von Glick tumbled from the saddle and landed in the shallows of the mere. The beastman lunged forward.

Schell's horse leapt the mere at the narrowest point and the warrior swung the hammer spike down on the creature, killing it instantly.

He leaped off his horse and ran to von Glick, who lay on his side in the pool, his face pale with pain. It looked like his red and gold armour was leaking into the black water.

Vandam raced up.

Schell looked up at him with fierce, angry eyes that blazed from his lean face. 'He's alive,' he hissed.

GANZ STRODE ACROSS the shrine clearing to where Morgenstern was picking himself up.

'Let's talk,' he said. 'Away from the others. I'm sure you don't want them hearing what I'm going to say to you.'

Morgenstern, who had twenty years more service to the Temple than Ganz, looked sour, but he did not disobey. Talking low, they moved away across the clearing.

Aric joined Gruber, who sat to one side on a fallen log.

'You okay?' he asked.

'My horse was wrong-footed. Thrown a shoe, I thought.'

'Looks fine to me,' said Aric.

Gruber looked up at the young man, his lean, lined face hard but not angry. 'What's that supposed to mean?'

Aric shrugged. With his long dark hair and trimmed black goatee, he reminded Gruber of the young Jurgen himself. 'Anything you want it to mean,' he said.

Gruber steepled his hands and thought for a moment. Aric had something, a quality. One day he would be a leader, a lot more effortlessly than poor Ganz, who tried so hard and was liked so little. Aric had natural command. He would be a great warrior for the Temple in time.

'I…' Gruber began. 'I seem to lack the fire I once had. At Jurgen's side, courage was easy…'

Aric sat next to him. 'You're the most respected man in the troop, Gruber. Everyone acknowledges that, even bluff old warhorses like Morgenstern and von Glick. You were Jurgen's right-hand man. You know, after Jurgen's death, I'll never understand why you didn't take the command when it was offered you. Why did you hand it on to Ganz?'

'Ganz is a good man… solid, unimaginative, but a good man. He'd paid his dues. I'm just a veteran. I'd be a poor commander.'

'I don't think so,' Aric said with a shake of his head.

Gruber sighed. 'What if I said it was because Jurgen was dead? How could I take the place of that man, my sworn commander, my friend? The man I failed?'

'Failed?' Aric repeated in surprise.

'That dreadful day last summer, when the beastpack fell on us out of nowhere. We stood together as a company or we fell, each man watching the other's back.'

'It was hell, all right.'

'I was right by Jurgen, fighting at his right hand. I saw the bull-man swing in with the axe. I could have blocked it, taken the blow myself, but I froze.'

'You weren't to blame!'

'I was! I hesitated and Jurgen died. If it hadn't been for me, he'd be here today.'

'No,' Aric said firmly. 'It was bad luck and Ulric called him to his hall.'

Gruber looked into the younger man's face. 'My nerve's gone, Aric. I can't tell the others... I certainly can't tell Ganz... but as we rode in to the charge, I felt my courage melt. What if I freeze again? What if it's Ganz who pays the price this time? You? I'm a coward and no use to this company.'

'You are no such thing,' Aric said. He tried to compose an argument to snap the veteran out of his grim mindset, but they were interrupted by shouting. Morgenstern strode back into the clearing, bellowing, with a stern-faced Ganz in his wake. The big ox reached his horse, pulled three bottles from his saddle bags and hurled them at a nearby tree, smashing them one by one.

'Satisfied?' he bawled at Ganz.

'Not yet,' Ganz replied stoically.

'Ganz! Ganz!' the shout echoed round the clearing. Schell led von Glick's horse back to them, the old warrior slumped in the saddle with Vandam riding alongside to support him.

'Oh great God of the Wolf!' Gruber cried leaping up.

'Von Glick!' shouted Morgenstern, pushing past the dismayed Ganz.

They lowered the wounded man down and the company stood around as Kaspen, who had studied with a barber-surgeon and an apothecary, treated the ugly wound.

'He needs a proper surgeon,' said the thick-set, flame-haired man, wiping blood from his hands. 'Wound's deep and filthy and he's lost blood.'

Ganz looked up at the sky. Evening was slipping down on them. 'We'll return to Middenheim tomorrow. First light. The fastest will ride ahead to fetch a surgeon and a cart. We–'

'We will not,' von Glick said, his voice thin and bitter. 'We will not go back on my account. This mission, this undertaking, is a holy cause to refound the strength of this company and avenge our fallen leader. We will not abandon that task! I will not let you abandon this!'

'But–'

Von Glick pulled himself up to a sitting position, wincing. 'Promise me, Ganz! Promise me we'll go on!'

Ganz faltered. He did not know what to say. He wheeled on Vandam, who stood to one side. 'You bloody fool! This is your fault! If you hadn't been so impetuous, you'd never have led von Glick into that!'

'I–' Vandam began.

'Shut up! The company stands together or it falls! You betrayed the very foundation of this brotherhood!'

'He's not to blame,' von Glick said. His eyes were glittering with strength born out of pain. 'Oh, he shouldn't have broken from the pack and ridden off alone, but I did this to myself. I should have been wary, I should have been looking. I dropped my guard, like any old fool, and paid the price.'

Silence. Ganz looked from one man to another. Most looked uncomfortable, awkward, disconcerted. The company spirit had never seemed so deflated, not even after Jurgen's death. At least then there was anger. Now, there was just disillusion, a loss of faith and comradeship.

'We'll make camp here,' Ganz said finally. 'With luck, the beasts will come for us tonight – and we can finish this.'

DAWN CAME, cold and pale. The last shift of watchmen – Schell, Aric and Bruckner – roused the others. Morgenstern poked the fire into life and Kaspen redressed von Glick's wound. The old warrior was as pale and cold as the morning, shivering with pain. 'Don't tell Ganz how bad I am!' he hissed to Kaspen. 'On your life, swear it!'

Anspach was going to water the horses when he found Krieber. At some time in the night, a black-fletched arrow had skewered his neck where he lay sleeping. The Templar was dead.

They stood around in silent mourning, more sombre than ever before. Ganz boiled with rage. He strode away from the group.

At the tree line, Gruber joined him. 'It is bad luck, Ganz. Bad luck on us, bad luck on poor Krieber, Ulric take his soul. We didn't deserve it, and he deserved a better end than this.'

Ganz wheeled round. 'What do I have to do, Gruber? For Ulric's sake! How can I lead this company to glory if we don't get a chance? I destroyed their shrine to bring them to us, to make them angry and drive them into a frontal attack. A pitched battle where we would shine! But no! They come back all right, and with typical beast cunning, they harry us and kill us as we sleep!'

'So we change our tactics,' Gruber said.

Ganz shrugged. 'I don't know how! I don't know what to

suggest! I keep thinking about Jurgen, and how he kept command. I keep trying to think the way he did, to remember all the tricks and inspiration. And you know? *I can't remember a thing!* All those great victories we shared, and I can't recall the plan behind a single one of them!'

'Calm down and think, Ganz,' Gruber said, sighing. 'What about Kern's Gate? Remember? The winning stroke there was to swing around behind the orcs.'

'Yes, I remember it. Sound tactics.'

'Exactly!' Gruber said. 'But that was Morgenstern's idea, wasn't it? Not Jurgen's!'

'You're right,' Ganz said, his face brightening. 'And it was the same with the siege at Aldobard... there it was von Glick who suggested a two-pronged attack.'

'Yes,' Gruber agreed. 'Jurgen was a good leader all right. He knew a good idea when he heard it. He knew how to listen to his men. The company is strength, Ganz. We stand together or we fall. And if one of us has a good plan, a good leader knows not to be too proud to adopt it.'

'So?' Ganz said, trying to sound lighter than he felt. 'Any ideas?'

Late winter wind sighed through the elms. The company coughed and shuffled.

'I bet I know–' Anspach began.

There was a general groan.

'Let's hear him out,' Ganz said, hoping he was doing the right thing.

'Well, myself, I like a wager,' Anspach said as if this were news, getting up to address them. 'So do many folk – the chance to win something, something important and valuable, something more than you normally get a chance at. These beastmen are no different. They want revenge for the smashed shrine, but not so much they're going to risk their stinking hides in a frontal assault on armoured cavalry. Who would give them good odds on that? They'd rather live. But if we tempted them with something more – something they might feel was worth risking their necks for. We could lure them out. That's my plan, a tempting wager for them. And I'll bet it works.'

There was some nodding, a few sneers. Dorff whistled aimlessly. Morgenstern turned a belch into an approving chuckle.

Ganz smiled. For the first time there seemed to be a slight sense of union, of all their minds working as one.

'But what do we offer them?' Kaspen asked.

Anspach shrugged. 'I'm working on that. We carry gold and silver, between us probably quite a lot. Maybe a pot of coins…'

Vandam laughed. 'You think they'd care? The beasts don't value gold much.'

'Well, what else have we got?' asked Schell, scratching his sinewy cheek thoughtfully.

'We have this,' Aric said and lifted the standard of Vess.

'You're mad!' cried Einholt. A quiet, reserved warrior, he seldom said anything. This outburst startled them all. Aric wavered, looking into Einholt's scarred face, wishing he could read anything except scorn in the man's one good eye.

'Think! Think of the prestige, the glory they would achieve amidst their foul kind to capture this. Think of the victory it would represent,' Aric said at last.

'Think of the disgrace if we lose the bloody thing!' scoffed Vandam.

'We won't,' Aric said. 'That's the point. It's precious enough to lure them out en masse…'

'And precious enough to make damn sure we fight to the last to keep it,' von Glick finished for him. 'A good plan.'

Ganz nodded.

'So,' Dorff asked, 'do we just… leave it out in the open for them?'

'Too obvious,' Ganz said.

'And I won't leave it,' Aric said flatly. 'It's my duty. I cannot abandon the standard.'

Ganz paced the circle of men. 'So Aric stays with the standard. The rest of us lie in cover ready to strike.'

'Aric can't stand alone,' Gruber began.

'It'd still look too obvious,' Anspach added. 'Someone has to stay with him.'

'I'll do it,' Vandam said. There was ferocity in his eyes. Ganz knew the young warrior was eager to make amends for his earlier rashness.

He was about to nod when von Glick spoke up. 'A brave offer, Vandam. But you're too good in the charge to waste. Let me stay, Ganz. We'll stay with Krieber's corpse and it'll look like the standard bearer has been left to watch the dead and the dying.'

'That would be more convincing,' Anspach said.

'I'll stay too,' Gruber said. 'They'd expect at least two men. And my horse has thrown a shoe.'

Ganz looked around at them all. 'Agreed! Let's do it! For the glory of Ulric and the memory of Jurgen!'

The ten riders mounted up and thundered off across the clearing to disappear into the dark woods. Ganz paused before he rode. 'May the wolf run beside you,' he said to Aric, Gruber and von Glick.

Aric and Gruber made von Glick comfortable by the shrine. They covered Krieber with a saddle cloth, tied the horses off to the west, and lit a fire. Then Aric planted the standard in the clay soil.

'You needn't have stayed too,' he told Gruber.

'Yes, I did,' Gruber said simply. 'I need to do this very much.'

EVENING SLOPED down on them, speckling the heavy sky with dark twists of cloud. Rain lanced down, slantwise, and a wind picked up, lifting the ragged hem of the old standard and swishing through the miserable forest.

The four remained by the fire – the two living warriors, the dead man and the man half way between.

Von Glick's eyes were clouded as dark as the heavens. 'Ulric,' he murmured, gazing up at the cold sky. 'Let them come.'

Gruber reached out and pulled at Aric's arm. This message needed no words. Stiff from the cold, the two men lifted their warhammers and rose, standing by the guttering ashes of the fire, looking across the clearing.

'By the sacred flame, Aric my brother,' said Gruber, 'now we'll see a fight.'

The beastmen attacked.

There were perhaps four score of them, more than Aric remembered from the pitched battle the previous season when the beastmen had caught them by surprise and Jurgen fell. The misshapen monsters were clad in reeking pelts, their animalistic heads crowned by all manner of horns and tusks and antlers, their skins scaled and haired and furred, bald and muscular, diseased and slack. They bellowed as they charged in from the eastern tree-line, their foul collective breath gusted before them, eyes wild like insane cattle, wet, drooling mouths agape to expose ulcerated gums, black teeth and hooked fangs. The ground shook.

Aric and Gruber leapt onto their horses, and galloped around to stand between the charge and the lonely standard.

'For Ulric!' yelled Aric, his hammer beginning its swing.

'By the hammers of the Wolf!' raged Gruber, holding his horse steady.

'For the Temple! *For the Temple!*' came a third voice. The riders glanced back. Hammer in hand, von Glick stood beside the standard, supporting his weight against the haft.

'For the Temple!' he screamed at them again.

Their battle roars as feral as the beasts, Aric and Gruber leapt their horses into the front of the pack as it came to them, giving themselves momentum and meeting the charge head on. The hammers swung and flew. Blood and spittle sprayed from cracked skulls. The hooves of the warhorses tore into flaccid flesh. Spears and blades thrust at them. The war cry of the two wolves echoed above all. Aric rejoiced. He had almost forgotten the ecstasy of combat, of the raging melee. Gruber laughed out loud. He had just remembered.

Von Glick stood his ground by the standard, despite the blood that leaked down his armour from the broken wound, and slew the first beast that charged him. The second fell, its skull cloven. The third rocked back, its ribs cracked. Now there were three, four around him, five. He was as deep in the fight as Aric and Gruber.

Aric struck left and right, blood painting across his grey armour, foam flecking back from the frenzied mouth of his steed. He saw Gruber laughing, striking…

Falling.

A lance thrust took down his mount. Gruber fell amongst the howling beasts, his hammer swinging in furious denial of the end.

They heard the thunder.

Above, in the sky as the storm broke.

Below, on the ground as the Company of Wolves charged in behind the beastpack.

Inside, in their hearts, as Ulric bayed the name of Jurgen.

THE KNIGHTS OF the White Company charged in line abreast, with Ganz at the centre, flanked by Vandam and Anspach.

'God's teeth, but I need a drink!' shouted Morgenstern as they swept in.

'No, you don't! You need this kind of courage instead!' rallied Ganz.

They hit the beastpack as it turned in confusion to meet them, ploughing over ranks of the fierce creatures, toppling and trampling, warhammers raining down as furiously as the downpour from above. Lightning flashed on the grotesque mayhem. Blood and rainwater sprayed into the air. The baying creatures turned from their original targets and swept into the fight with the cavalry force. Aric rode forward across the corpse-strewn ground and helped Gruber to his feet. The older warrior was speckled with blood, but alive.

'See to von Glick and watch the standard. Give me your horse,' Gruber said to Aric. Aric dismounted and returned to the banner of Vess as Gruber galloped back into the brutal fray.

Von Glick lay by the standard, which was still stuck upright in the earth. The bodies of almost a dozen beastmen lay around him.

'L-let me see...' von Glick breathed. Aric knelt beside him, and raised his head. 'So, Anspach's bold plan worked...' breathed the veteran warrior. 'He's pleased, I'll wager.'

Aric started to laugh but stopped. The old man was dead.

IN THE THICK of the combat, Morgenstern wielded his warhammer and drove his horse through the press of bodies, swinging left and right, destroying the enemy as easily as if they had been a row of turnips on upturned pails. He laughed his raucous laugh and set about himself. Nearby, Anspach saw his display and joined the laughter, smashing down with his own hammer.

At the heart of the fight, Vandam, the fiercest of all, glory singing in his veins, destroyed beast after beast, three times the number of any of them. He was still slaughtering the monsters as their spears cut him down.

In the tumult, Ganz saw the great bull-man, the pack leader, the beast that had slain Jurgen. He charged forward, but his hammer was dragged down by the weight of creatures on him. The bull-man swung to strike at him.

The haft of Gruber's hammer blocked the axe. Gruber, yelling the war cry, rode in on his commander's right hand, guarding his flank. Ganz pulled his weapon clear and, before the massive bull-head could swing again, drove its snout back into its skull in an explosion of blood.

'In the name of Ulric!' Ganz screamed, rejoicing. The heavens thundered their applause.

SMOKE ROSE FROM the storm-swept field, smoke and the steam from the blood. The Wolf Templars dismounted one by one amidst the carnage and kneeled in the mud to offer thanks to the raging sky. Fierce rain washed the blood off their armour as prayer cleansed their spirits. Of the beastman horde, not one had survived.

Ganz walked quietly to view the fallen.

Von Glick, at Aric's feet. Ganz was sure Aric was guarding the old man's body more than he was guarding the fluttering banner.

Vandam, skewered four times with crude lances, twisted at the top of a mound of dead.

'He has found his glory,' Morgenstern said. 'He's transferred to that better company. Ulric's own.'

'May the wolves guard his brave soul,' said Ganz.

Across the bloody, torn-up field, Dorff began to whistle a tune that resembled a battle hymn. Anspach caught it up and began to sing, making a shape and melody out of Dorff's notes. Einholt joined him, soft and low. It was a mourning song, of victory and loss, one of old Jurgen's favourites. Within three bars of it, all the other voices had joined the song.

THEY CAME BACK into Middenheim three days later. It was raining then too.

Mitterfruhl was almost on them all, but the High Priest came away from the preparations at the Temple, drawn by the excited whispers. He and his entourage were waiting for them in the Temple Square as White Company rode in, eleven riders, proud behind the fluttering banner of Vess, three noble dead lashed to their steeds.

Ranked in honour behind the motionless priest, Red, Grey, Gold and Silver Companies, the fighting packs who, with White, made up the Templar force, raised their voices in a throaty cheer.

Ganz, tall on his horse, gazed down at the High Priest.

'White Company has returned to the Temple, lord,' he said, 'and the heart has returned to White Company.'

The Dead Among Us

THE GOD OF DEATH stared down on me as I prepared the corpse for burial. His hooded eyes were not visible but I could feel his gaze on my hands as they moved over the cold body before me, and he saw that the work was good. The atmosphere in the vaulted room beneath the temple was quiet and damp, smelling faintly of mildew, ashes and of the thousands of the dead of Middenheim who had passed through here on their last journey.

I chanted the words of the ritual under my breath, my mind aware of nothing but their rhythm and the power they held, my hands moving in the sacred patterns of the ceremony. I had done this many times before. The body before me was nothing but a carcass, its soul already blessed and freed and fled to the afterlife. My job now was to seal the corpse, to make sure that no other entity could move in and take possession of this empty shell.

A footfall on the stone steps intruded upon my concentration and broke the spell. Morr was no longer watching; the carving of the patron deity above the altar was just a carving again. The footsteps stopped for a moment, then came on down into the Factorum. The tall, well-aged frame of Brother Gilbertus blocked out the faint light for a moment as he passed through the doorway. I knew it would be him.

'I'm not disturbing you, am I?' he asked.

'Yes,' I said plainly. 'You are. That's the third Funeral Rite incantation you've interrupted this month, brother, and as penance you will take my place to perform it. This body goes out to be buried in the forest at noon today, so I suggest you start the ritual as soon as you've finished telling me why you're here.'

He didn't protest. Instead he said, 'They've found a body.'

'If you hadn't noticed, brother, this is the temple of Morr, who is the God of Death. We are priests of Morr. Bodies are what we deal with. One more corpse is hardly a reason to barge into the Factorum while another priest is performing a ceremony. Clearly your apprenticeship in Talabheim has taught you little. I may have to give you more lessons.'

He stared at me blankly, my sarcastic tone unnoticed or not understood. I stared back at his greying forelock and the furrows of age around his eyes, and thought for a moment how old he was to be a new priest. But then I had joined the temple late in life as well. Many did.

'It's a woman,' he said. 'Murdered. I thought you'd want to know.'

I blinked. 'Where?'

'Through the heart. With a knife.'

'Where in the city, dolt?'

'Oh. The alleyway behind the Drowned Rat, in the Ostwald.'

'I'm going out.' I pulled off my ritual robes and flung them into the corner of the room. 'Start that Funeral Rite now and you will be finished by the time I get back.'

A COLD JAHRDRUNG wind whistled over the slated rooftops and between the bleak stone buildings of Middenheim. If there had been any leaves on the few trees that grew on the heights of this rock, the pinnacle in the air that men called the City of the White Wolf, they would have been ripped off and hurled into the sky. But it was the last days of winter, the festival of Mitterfruhl was not passed, and the spring buds were not yet beginning to show. There would be no new life here for some time.

The wind cut through my thin robe as I strode up across Morrspark, the frosted grass crunching under my feet, and out into the streets, which grew narrower and less well-kept as they led south-west into the Ostwald district, crowded with early morning bustle. It was bitterly cold. I cursed myself for not putting on a cloak before leaving the temple, but haste was more important than my comfort. Rumours and falsehoods spread fast in a city as compact and tight-knit as Middenheim, and where an unexplained death was concerned, anybody speaking ill of the dead would only hinder my work.

The alley behind the Drowned Rat was narrow and sloping, stinking and crowded. A couple of members of the city watch were trying to keep onlookers away and not doing a good job of it, but the gawpers drew back slightly as I approached. The dark robes of a priest of Morr will do that, and it's not out of respect. Nobody likes being reminded of their own mortality.

As the crowd moved apart to let me pass, I saw the bald pate of Watch Captain Schtutt standing beside the corpse. He looked up, saw me and smiled in recognition, his face creased by middle-age and good living. We'd known each other for years, but I didn't smile back. He started to say something by way of a greeting, but I had already crouched down by the body.

It was a woman – or it had been. Probably turned twenty; probably beautiful. Dark brown hair with a wave to it. Something about her face said she had Norse blood, although with one eye and most of a cheek missing it was hard to tell for sure. She had the most delicate ears. Her clothes, gaudy but cheap, had been slashed all ways with a blade of some kind – a hunting knife or dagger, I guessed – before the fatal blow had slipped between her ribs and into her heart. This had been a competent murder, and someone had tried hard to make it look like something less polished. Her left arm was missing, and someone had thrown a rough brown blanket over an object a couple of feet from her. Blood from the cobbles had begun to seep into its fabric.

She wasn't Filomena. Filomena had been blonde.

I REMEMBERED where I was, and looked up at Schtutt. 'What's under the blanket?'

He muttered, 'Don't lift it,' and there was something nervous in his voice. Then he turned to the pack of vultures and gossip-seekers and spoke loudly: 'All right, bugger off the lot of you. Nothing more to see. Constable, get them out of here. Give the priest of Morr room to do his magic.'

I wasn't planning any magic but the suggestion of it, together with the taint of death in this narrow place, was enough to clear most of the crowd away quickly. Good old Schtutt.

He looked down at me for a second, his expression filled with some stress I couldn't identify, then bent down and raised one corner of the blanket. Underneath was something not human: a limb, maybe four feet long. It had no hand or bones, but large cup-like suckers along the underside. It smelled of decay and something bitter and sharp, like wormwood and stale wine.

It startled me. I felt Schtutt's gaze on my back, and that of the other watchmen too. Were they looking at the thing under the blanket, or watching to see how I'd react to it? I realised I was breathing fast, and steadied myself. Deep breath. Priests of Morr don't panic. They must not. They cannot be seen to.

'Right,' I said, and stood up. Be firm. Decisive. 'We need a cart to get all this back to the temple. High-sided if possible.'

'I saw a soil-collector's wagon on the way here,' one of the watch suggested.

'That'll suit. Go and fetch it.' I waited until he had gone, then gestured down at the blanket. 'How many saw this?'

'Two or three.'

'Make sure they don't talk about it. Harass them, put the fear of Ulric in them, anything short of cutting out their tongues. The last thing we need is a panic about a mutant in the city.'

'Mutant,' Schtutt said. His voice was flat, like an echo. It was as if he hadn't dared to use the word until I'd spoken it out loud, confirming his worst fears. A tentacled limb? Well, it hadn't been hacked from a bog-octopus or a kraken from the Sea of Claws, not in an alley in the Ostwald. But now he'd said the word, I had to stop him saying it again where people might hear.

'There'll need to be a full investigation. A dissection. If it is a... well, we'll burn it quietly. For the sake of Ulric, don't go talking about mutants around the city. Even among the watch. Keep it to yourselves. But circulate the girl's description: age, height, dress, everything except the arm.' I rubbed my hands; they were freezing. 'We've got to get the body back to the temple so I can start. Where's that bloody wagon?'

It arrived, and the body was loaded unceremoniously into the cart, the soil-collectors not too happy about having their work interrupted. Nobody wanted to touch the thing under the blanket. Eventually I bundled it up in its covering and dropped it beside the corpse, in the back of the stinking wagon, then stood back so I could wipe my hands on my thin robe where Schtutt wouldn't see me do it.

The drayman flicked his whip, the elderly horse strained at the traces and the cart rumbled slowly down the filthy cobbles of the slum-streets towards the open space of Morrspark and the temple at its centre. Schtutt and I walked behind it.

'Any idea who she was?' I said.

'Apart from being–' Schtutt caught my glare. 'No, we don't. She was dressed like a tavern wench or maybe a night-girl, but she couldn't have got work with an arm like that. Although maybe she disguised it with magic. She could have lured someone into the alley, dropped the disguise, and then he killed her out of horror.

'Or maybe it was a cult killing. They say there's powerful cults of Chaos-worshippers in the city. We do find sacrifices. Cats, mostly.' He shivered. 'If I thought there was going to be trouble with Chaos, I'd take my family and leave Middenheim. Go north. My brother has an estate about thirty miles away. Would thirty miles be far enough, you think? To escape the Dark?'

I didn't reply. I was following my own thoughts. Schtutt seemed happy to continue talking without a reply.

'We shouldn't have to wait for them to act. We should track them down and burn them. Burn their homes too. To the ground,' he said, and there was a certain relish in his voice. 'Get some witch hunters to come and investigate. Remember those two who came up from Altdorf? Seventeen Chaos-worshippers found and burnt in three days. That's the sort of men we need. Eh? Dieter?'

That broke my concentration. Nobody called me Dieter these days – not in eight years, not since I'd entered the Temple. I looked across at him, meeting his gaze in silence. After a moment he looked away.

'Ulric's beard,' he muttered. 'You're not the man you were. What have they done to you in that temple of ghouls?'

I could think of a hundred replies but none of them fitted the moment, so I said nothing. Silence is the first thing a priest of Morr learns. I had learnt that lesson well. A wordless void stretched between us, until Schtutt filled it.

'Why do you do it?' he asked. 'That's what I don't understand. I remember when you were one of the best merchants in Middenheim. Everyone came to you for everything. You weren't just rich, you were–'

'I was loved.' Schtutt went silent. I continued, 'Loved by my wife and son, who vanished. You know that. Everyone knows. They were never found. I spent hundreds of crowns, thousands, looking for them. And I neglected my trading, and my business failed so I gave it away, and I joined the Temple of Morr and became a priest.'

'But why, Dieter?' That name again. Not mine, not now. 'You can't find them there.'

'I will,' I said. 'Sooner or later their souls will come to Morr, and be received by his hands, and I will know it. It's the only certainty I have any more. It was the not knowing that was killing me.'

'Is that why you do it?' he asked. 'Investigating the unexplained deaths? In case it's them?'

'No,' I said. 'No, it just passes the time.'

But I knew I was lying.

THE CART TRUNDLED across the hard earth of Morrspark, still too solid for burials, and stopped outside the temple. The dark stone of the building and the bare branches of the high trees around it were silhouetted against a sky that was grey and heavy with snow yet to come, like outstretched hands offering a closed box to an unseen god.

Schtutt and his deputy carried the body down the stone steps into the vaulted gloom of the Factorum while I followed, the blanket and its unpleasant contents in my arms. There was no sign of Gilbertus, or the corpse he had been preparing for burial. Good.

The girl's body was laid on one of the grey granite slabs, and I placed the tentacle next to it, still wrapped in its blanket. The stench of the soil-wagon clung to the corpse's clothes, but there was another odour, bitter and unpleasant.

In the quiet and the semi-darkness she could almost have been any beautiful woman lying asleep. I stared at her still form. Who was she? Why had she been killed so deliberately, so coldly, and the deed disguised to look like something else? Did she have a powerful enemy, or was she dead for another reason? Was she more important dead than alive? The arm…

Schtutt shuffled his feet and coughed. I could sense his uneasiness. The bodies on the other slabs could have had something to do with it.

'We'd best be going,' he said.

'Yes,' I said abruptly. I wanted to be alone with the body, to try to get some feel for who or what had killed her. It's not that I like dead people. I don't. I just prefer them to the living.

'We'll need an official report,' he said. 'If it's mutant business the Graf will have to be told. You'll dissect her today?'

'No,' I said. 'First we do the rituals to rest her soul.'

No, not 'we'. I would do the rituals personally.

'Then we do the dissection – for the records, and for the Graf's precious paperwork. Then, if we can't find a next of kin, she gets a pauper's funeral.'

'Off the Cliff of Sighs?' Schtutt asked, shock in his voice. 'But surely mutants must be burnt? To cleanse them?'

'Did I say she was a mutant?' I asked.

'What?'

I grasped the section of tentacle that had lain beside the corpse, and shoved it at him. It felt cold and rubbery in my hand, and damp. Schtutt recoiled like a slapped dog.

'Smell it,' I said.

'What!'

'Smell it.' He sniffed at it, cautiously, then looked at me.

'Well?' I asked.

'It's… sour. Bitter. Like something stale.'

'Vinegar.' I put down the unclean flesh. 'I don't know where that came from, but I do know it wasn't attached to anyone who was alive this morning. The damn thing's been pickled.'

SCHTUTT AND HIS man went eventually, promising that they'd try to find out who the girl had been. I almost asked them not to. The last way you're going to learn anything about a death in the Ostwald, with its twisting alleys and shadowy deals, is to have heavy-booted watchmen asking questions with all the subtlety of an unwashed ogre. Even if they got an answer it wouldn't do any good. I still wanted to find out who the girl was, but the more I thought about this, the more I suspected that it was her death, not herself, that was important. Someone had wanted to convince people that there were mutants in the city, and they would have managed it if the investigation had been left to the likes of Schtutt.

He wasn't a bad man, I reflected as I prepared the ritual. We'd known each other quite well in the days before I joined the temple: he'd been a young merchant trying to muscle in on trade franchises held by families much older and more powerful than his. He hadn't done well, but he hadn't given up, I'll say that for him. Then the Sparsam family had framed him for evading taxes, and part of his punishment had been a month with the city watch. And that was that: he found his niche in life there, and he was a much better watch captain than he'd been a merchant. Which didn't mean he was much of a watch captain.

I lit the last of the candles around the body, sprinkled some blessed water over the body with the appropriate ritual gestures, breathed deeply, and began the deep, slow chant of the Nameless Rite. Inside, I was waiting. The spirit of Morr moved over me and through me, within the patterns I had created with my hands and my mind, and flowed out from me to encompass the body of the woman before me, to bless it and protect it from evil.

And stopped. Something was resisting.

The energy of the Lord of Death hovered in me, waiting for me to use it. But I felt as if I was trying to force two lodestones together: the harder I pushed, the closer I came to the body, the greater was the repulsion. I kept chanting, drawing more of Morr's energy to me, trying to spread it out over the corpse, but it slipped away like rain off oiled leather. Something was wrong, very wrong. But I wasn't going to give up. I chanted on, summoning all my force, pushing Morr's power out over the corpse. The nameless resistance pushed back. I couldn't break it. Impasse.

One of the candles guttered and snuffed out, burnt down to its stub. It had been three, maybe four inches long when I'd started the ritual. Hours must have passed. I let my chanting cease and the divine power slipped away, taking the last of my energy with it. My knees felt like green twigs, and I felt myself swaying with exhaustion. Alone in the shadows, I stared at the body. The Factorum was absolutely quiet except for my own faint panting, absolutely still – but not tranquil. It was tense, as if waiting for something. The chill of the spring and the cold stones stuck needles through my robe and I shivered. For an instant I felt what the normal people must feel in here: the terror of being surrounded by the dead. The terror of not understanding.

I snuffed out the remaining candles between my fingers and hurried away, upstairs, to the comparative warmth of the main body of the temple, and felt my momentary fear fade as I did. For a moment I considered visiting the main hall and praying for a while, but instead I slipped in through the side entrance that led to the priests' private chambers, headed down the narrow stone corridor, and knocked on the door to Father Zimmerman's room. I felt uneasy about having to do this, but sometimes the only way to deal with a problem is to kick it upstairs.

There was a shuffling from within the room, a muffled voice, and then the door opened part-way from the other side and

Brother Gilbertus squeezed out. I was reminded of a cat moving through a small space, or a snake. He smiled his bland smile at me and disappeared off towards the refectory. I pushed the door fully open and entered. Father Zimmerman was sitting at his writing desk. It looked as if he had been drafting a letter. Ink stained his fingers, and there were broken quills on the floor. He turned around and I saw there was ink on his white beard too.

'What is it?' he said. There was irritation in his voice: not, I guessed, from having his meeting interrupted. It probably had more to do with the fact that he didn't like me. That was fine by me. I didn't like him either.

'There's a new body in the Factorum, father.'

'Bodies are our stock in trade, brother. You may have observed that in the years you have been working here.' I thought of my words to Gilbertus earlier that day, and cursed the Talabheimer. He'd been here, telling tales of my disrespect for the dead, no doubt.

'I've been trying to bless it for burial,' I said. 'The blessing won't… won't take. It's as if something is resisting it.'

'This would be the mutant girl?'

Bugger the Talabheimer, and bugger him again. 'Yes, but she's not–'

'You waste too much time with street-scum and the dregs of life, brother. It's not a good attitude for a temple such as ours, with a certain standing in the community. You should think of other things, and spend more of your time on the good works that I have suggested you pursue.'

'I don't work for you. I work for Morr.'

'Perhaps you would be happier working for him with a solo ministry? We have been asked to establish a shrine in one of the Wasteland towns to deal with their plague victims, you know. I could recommend you for the post.'

He gestured to the writing desk. Obviously matters of transfer and administration were on his mind, but then he'd always been a petty status-minded pen-pusher, more concerned with appearances than with the real business of Morr's work. I hated him, but I realised that I wasn't going to get what I needed without an apology, so I gritted my teeth and backtracked.

'I'm sorry.' A breath. 'But we have a corpse down in the Factorum which I can't cleanse and prepare for burial. I don't know if it's enchanted or what else, but I thought you might know, and I thought you'd want to be told about it.'

'And you thought that I, being an older, more experienced and more powerful priest, might perform a Purification Rite on it for you? You did.'

I did, so I nodded – and saw his expression change, and instantly knew I'd made a mistake. It was the answer he'd wanted. He glowered at me. I could feel his dislike now, and I'd given him an excuse to vent it.

'You thought,' he hissed, 'that the senior priest of the temple of Morr in Middenheim has time to sully his hands blessing the corpse of some street tart?'

'I didn't–'

'You presume to ask me to waste my time with one of your low-lifes, and a mutant to boot? You dare to come in here and insult…'

I lowered my head and let the words wash over me. It was nothing I hadn't heard before. The antipathy between Father Albrecht Zimmerman and me was the main reason I was still only a second-tier priest after eight years in the temple, and was unlikely to rise higher. I'd accepted that. The father might be close to retirement but I knew his place would go to someone who acted like he did, thought like he did and disliked me as much as he did. Probably Gilbertus, who might be new but who seemed to be doing a lot of wheel-greasing recently. Ambitious, that Gilbertus. That letter on the father's desk was probably about him.

Eventually the words slowed and stopped. A new paragraph was about to begin, so I started paying attention again.

'As penance, I want you to go to the Cliff of Sighs, where you will find Brother Ralf, who is due to officiate at a funeral. You will take over for him. Then come back here and pray to Saint Heinrich that your good intentions do not overcome your common sense. Pray hard, brother. Pray until the tenth bell. That is all.'

I left.

IT WAS NIGHT. I lay awake on my hard, narrow bed and stared at the pattern of the moonlight as it fell on the stone wall of the tiny window of my tiny cell, the harsh brightness of Morrslieb's aura slowly eclipsing the warmer glow of Mannslieb. My body was completely exhausted, drained from the energy of the ritual I had performed that day, but I knew I would get no sleep tonight. It was too cold for a start, spring or no spring, and my single blanket did a bad job of keeping me warm enough to get comfortable. Besides, my mind was filled with the dead girl.

Who had she been? Where had she come from, to die so ignominiously on the streets of Middenheim? Had her death got anything to do with who she was, or had she simply been in the wrong tavern, with a kind word for the wrong man, who had led her into a dark back alley as dawn approached and stuck her over and over again with a short knife, carefully angling his blades to make the attack look frenzied. And then cut off her arm, to replace it with something inhuman, hiding her real one – he must have had a bag with him, probably a big one, watertight perhaps – and sneak away.

I could visualise the sort of man he must be, but right now I wasn't interested in him. I wanted to picture her.

She had been beautiful once. Perhaps she had been beautiful last night: what was left of her complexion hadn't had the blowsy gin-blossoms of an old street-walker. Laugh lines had creased the fresh skin around her mouth and eyes, and she wore no cosmetics. This was not a woman who had relied on her physical charms to earn a living. Not for long, anyway.

What had brought her, this Norse beauty, to Middenheim? The Norse were too pragmatic and down-to-earth to believe the old stories of the cliff-top city with its streets paved with the gold dug from the mountain below. Something other than dreams of foreign places and easy fortunes brought her here. It was probably the arm of a merchant or traveller – possibly Norse but probably not: they were loyal to their own, particularly abroad – who had abandoned her when she made eyes at another man or got pregnant, or any of the thousand other reasons that men break their promises to women.

How long had it been since the stability and love she had thought were hers had been revealed as a hollow joke? Her clothes had seemed quite new and probably too expensive for the sort of woman who drank in the Drowned Rat, so she probably hadn't been on the streets too long. Unless she had robbed someone recently. No; people can disguise themselves in life, but a dead face reveals the true character behind it, and I had seen nothing of the petty criminal in what remained of her features. There was nothing of the ground-down, hardened street-walker there either. She'd been new to the idea of having to rely on her charms and a low-cut dress to earn a living. Or new enough that she didn't yet know how to spot the sort who would be good to her, and the sort who hated her kind and wanted nothing but ill for them.

Someone in the city had to know who she was, and I wanted to bless her with her real name when I buried her. Someone knew. It might be the person who had killed her, and that meant I had to find him. Nobody at the Drowned Rat would admit to remembering a thing about last night – it was that kind of a place, and not even the fear of Morr would persuade them to talk.

There was a faint sound, a sudden vibration that seemed to run through the temple building. It came again a few seconds later. Then a pause, and a third. From somewhere further down the corridor came a scrape of wood, and the thud of a thrown-open door. Running footsteps. I thought briefly about getting up to investigate, decided that I was still too tired from the failed ritual, and rolled over. Let Zimmerman sort it out. If he was so protective of his status as head of the temple, let him take some of the responsibility that came with the position. I went back to my thoughts.

That arm – the arm that wasn't hers. It all came down to that. There are easier ways to spread the fear of Chaos and mutation around a city like Middenheim than faking the murder of a mutant in an alley. So why? The only other reason I could think of was that a dead mutant would spark an official enquiry. Lots of paperwork. Probably a promotion for someone in the Watch. Maybe a witch-hunt, and a couple of old women burnt. And the temple would be involved, because we'd have to dissect the body and make the official report. Which meant that the first place the corpse would be brought was here. But why? And why the corpse of a tall, fair-skinned Norse beauty, as nameless as me, instead of some local good-time girl?

There was a scream, and I jolted to full consciousness. – I must have dozed off. Someone pelted down the corridor outside my room, shouting something. There was a distant crash.

Trouble. I dashed outside, tugging on my robe as I went. It was dark and I couldn't see anyone in the faint moonlight, but there was a lot of noise coming from the main hall of the temple so I headed that way. Unsteady light and shouting told me I was going in the right direction. The connecting door was open – no, it was ripped off its hinges and lying on the floor. I jumped over it and arrived in the main hall.

It was mayhem. A tempest had been here. Everything was smashed. The Flames Eternal had gone out again, but in the faint light from the night-lamps on the pillars I could see three priests, two with makeshift weapons – a broom, a rod of office – circling but keeping well back from someone. It was her.

IT WAS HER. The face I'd been imagining as I lay in bed smiled dully, deadly. She looked like hell, as you would if you had been murdered a day ago. Her movements were jerky, abrupt, and there seemed to be no sight in her eyes or expression on her face except a blank grin. With her one arm she clasped the torso of Brother Rickard. The rest of him lay a few yards away. As I watched, she dropped the body and began to cast her head from side to side, as if trying to feel for something with some strange inhuman sense. It was like… I didn't know what it was like.

'Stay back!' It was Father Zimmerman. I doubted that any of us had any intention of getting any closer. He struck a stance and began to chant. From the sound of his syllables it was a ritual, but not one I recognised. The dead woman's head snapped upright, as if she had found what she was searching for. Then she took a slow, stiff step towards him.

'Father! Move!' I yelled as I looked desperately for a weapon to defend myself. The cult of Morr has never been big on armaments, and its temples aren't exactly prepared for battle. The corpse took another step towards the father. He kept chanting, faster now, and there was panic on his face. I could have run in to pull him to safety but I didn't; instead I ran away, up towards the high altar. The flattened disc of the great bowl lay there, its gold plate and the heavy liquid in it gleaming slickly in the low light. Behind me there was a scream, high like an old woman.

I reached around the rim of the bowl and lifted it with both hands. It was heavy with the liquid, which sloshed between the shallow rims. As I turned with it, I heard the snap, and an instant too late saw Father Zimmerman die, his spine broken like an autumn twig. The dead woman dropped his body and it hit the floor, twitching.

I took measured paces across the marbled tiles. The liquid slopped in the great bowl, a little spilling out with each step. The puppet-corpse was casting its head around, looking for a target as I drew closer to it. The other two priests backed away from us both. She was fifteen feet away. Ten. Her head turned in my direction, and her slashed face bared its teeth at me in a dead smile.

I flung the great bowl at her, its contents flying outwards in a wild shower. Not holy water but oil, blessed for the anointing of mourners. It covered her, soaking the remains of her once-fancy clothes. The bowl hit the floor edge-on with a clang and spun away. I leapt backwards, grabbed a night-lamp from its niche on the nearest pillar and flung it at the sodden abomination.

It was like a flower blossoming, or the sun breaking through clouds. The temple was filled with the light from the burning woman. She blazed. Something in her must have sensed what was happening as she slowly began to flail against the flames. She fell over. Her body crackled. There was a smell of roasting.

The other two priests – Ralf, I could see now, and Pieter – stood in shock and watched as the body and the temple burned. I didn't have time for that; I headed for the main doors and outside into the fierce chill of the night, my mind working furiously as I went. Dead Norse women. Missing arms. Animated corpses. On the steps I saw Gilbertus coming up.

'Where are you going?' he said.

'To raise the alarm.'

'I've done that. What was it?'

'An animated corpse. Someone was controlling it. The father is dead.'

'Ah.' He didn't seem surprised. 'Are you coming back inside?'

'No,' I said. 'For one thing it's on fire, and for another I know who killed that girl.'

'Oh. Who?'

'A necromancer,' I said. 'A necromancer with a grudge.'

IF YOU WANT to know about grudges, you have to talk to a dwarf. I didn't relish the idea of having to go and see this particular dwarf at this time of night, not because he'd be in bed – I knew he wouldn't – but because of where he'd be. The Altquartier area was unpleasant enough during the day, but past midnight it was at its worst: the cheapest tarts, the pettiest criminals and the most desperate people. And at its heart lay the Bretonnian House.

Lit by harsh moonlight, the place looked just as tattered as I remembered it: an old, small tavern, its front black-painted, with cracked panes of glass in the windows and the stale smell of boiled cabbage seeping from the cheap eating room above. It looked closed but I knew it wasn't; places like this were never closed, if the patron or a regular owed you a favour. In years gone by I'd had some good evenings, some useful tip-offs and two fights in here. I hoped that the latter wouldn't be repeated tonight.

I knocked on the door, and after a few seconds it opened a crack. 'Who's there?'

'I'm looking for Alfric Half-nose,' I said.

'Who wants him?'

'Tell him…' I paused. 'Tell him it's the man who was Dieter Brossmann.'

The door closed. I could imagine the conversation that was happening on the other side. After a long minute it opened, to reveal a short, scrubby man with a pudding-bowl haircut. 'Enter,' he said.

I did. There's a trick with long robes and dresses that all high-born ladies know and all priests should learn: keep your steps light and short and silent, and if you do it right it looks like you're gliding, not walking. With the black robes of a Morr worshipper, it can look very eerie. The place had fallen silent as I came in, and the quiet lay over it like a blanket of cold dew as I moved across the small room. There were maybe ten people in, from cheap hoodlums drinking cheap beer to the less disreputable with glasses of wine or absinthe in front of them.

A man in a flat black Bretonnian hat, seated at the bar, nodded and raised a glass to me. His face was cracked with age and hard living like an old painting, and his eyes looked like blood-shot poached eggs. I recognised him from the old days, but couldn't remember his name. He probably had several.

There was a sound from one of the booths at the far end of the room. Nobody looked that way, so I knew it was what I was after and glided over to it. The great bulk of Alfric was squeezed in there, with one of his henchmen and a fat human in opulent robes sat opposite. The table was covered with empty tankards on the dwarfs' side, and gold coins. Alfric looked up. There was more grey in his beard than I remembered, and the scars around his ruined nose were a flaming red: a sure sign he'd been drinking heavily. But it would be unwise for me to assume he'd be drunk, or unobservant.

'Good evening, brother,' he said. 'Sit down. How may I be of service to the Temple of Morr this evening?'

I didn't sit. Instead I said, 'Alfric Half-nose, whose family name is Anvilbreaker, I am here to restore the balance of honour between our families.'

'Oh yes?' Alfric didn't look as if he was interested. The fat man was sweating, I noticed. He wasn't a merchant, or at least not a good one: he clearly didn't have the nerve for negotiating tricky deals. Idly I wondered who he was, and what had made him so desperate he'd come to see Alfric after the second bell of the night. He looked worried, but his problems were his own. I had mine to deal with.

'Five years ago,' I started. 'I... Oh sod it, I'll cut the formalities. You owe me a favour from the time I burnt the body of that storekeeper your grandson shot. I'm calling it in.'

'So I do, so you can.' Alfric took a swig from his tankard. 'You always were impatient. Always wanted things done your way. Your name and your taste in clothes, are they the only things you've changed since your family disappeared?' I said nothing. 'You haven't found them yet, then? Well, if you need some help, you know where to come.'

I knew he was trying to needle me, to show how displeased he was that I'd interrupted his business, so I didn't answer him. Instead I said, 'The temple was attacked this night. Someone animated a corpse against us. It looked like it was sent to kill people, not do damage, but it did a lot anyway. And Father Zimmerman is dead.' It was the second time I'd said that, but the first time I understood it. Suddenly I felt very tired. There was a spare place on the bench next to the merchant, and I sat down.

Alfric watched me, his dark eyes glinting like wet stones in the faint lamplight. 'Sounds like a necromancer's work.'

'I thought so.' A pause. 'Are there any of... such a calling in the city?'

'None that I know of. And that means probably not.' He paused for another swig. I trusted his word: Alfric's eyes and ears were everywhere in Middenheim. The dwarfs had built the place and their tunnels still pervaded it, like woodworm in a rotten cabinet. Alfric and his informants knew them all, and from listening at their secret entrances and watching at their spy-holes, he knew all the city's comings and goings. Best informant and biggest blackmailer in town, Alfric Half-nose.

'So who could have done this? Do you know of anyone with a grudge against the temple?' I asked.

Alfric swilled the beer around his mouth and swallowed. 'Shut up. I'm thinking about necromancers.' He took another slow mouthful and savoured it thoughtfully.

Necromancy, I thought. If it was a necromancer then asking about grudges was pointless. Necromancers hated priests of

Morr as much as we hated them. Both sides dealt in death, but we saw it as a passing, a stage in a process. They saw it as a tool. We were interested in freeing souls; they wanted to enslave them with their dark, unholy magics. Of course they'd have a grudge against us. Of course any ambitious necromancer would want to destroy the power of the local Temple of Morr, and if that meant killing its priests – well, like us, bodies were their stock in trade. But there was something about the way the girl's corpse had moved, something about the way it had sought out Father Zimmerman… I grasped for the idea, but couldn't catch it.

Alfric's voice broke my thoughts. 'One of your own corpses, was it? Corpse in the temple?'

'Yes,' I said. 'And there was something–'

'I'll know how that's happened, brother,' and he leant on that last word. 'That new priest of yours, the one from Talabheim…'

'Gilbertus.'

'Gilbertus. He's sloppy. Doesn't do the blessings properly. In too much of a hurry, like you. You should watch him at the Cliff of Sighs sometime. Goes through the motions all right, enough to fool the mourners anyway. But mark my words, those bodies are going over the cliff unblessed. Careless. Dangerous too, if there's a necromancer around: unblessed corpses, ready to be raised. Now if there is a necromancer in town – and I'm not saying there is, mind – then be careful. Nasty, necromancers. My grandsire tangled with one. They're fast. If they start to chant at you, count to five, he said. You'll never reach six. You'll be dead by then.'

Something, some idea about necromancers and the Temple, was forming itself in my mind, trying to push its way through the day's exhaustion. I stood up. The thoughts would take a while to clarify and it'd be morning before I'd know if I had heard the answer I needed, but the long cold walk back to the temple would help. 'Thanks, Alfric. The debt is cleared. I'll leave you to your business.'

He looked surprised for a moment, but it took more than that to ruffle his scarred composure. 'Good seeing you again, Dieter,' he said, and turned back to his sweating customer without another word.

I walked to the door and out into the cold night. It had started to snow, and I pulled my robe closely around myself. It was only as I turned the corner away from the Bretonnian House that I realised he'd called me Dieter, and that I had forgotten to ask him anything about the dead girl. A brief image of her burning face with its dead smile flickered in my mind. Somehow her identity didn't seem so important now.

THE CLIFF OF SIGHS is a place where contradictions meet. From its edge you can see the whole of the Middenland stretching away as far as the Middle Mountains: hills, tiny towns and the vast green carpet of the Drakwald Forest with the Talabheim road winding its way through it. In the days when I could still appreciate beauty, I thought it the most romantic and lovely place in the city. Step closer to the edge, look down and you see the shattered ruins of the coffins, the shrouded bodies spread across the rocks or hanging in the branches of the trees after being dropped, and sometimes the unconsecrated corpse of a suicide or murder victim as well.

Or you could have done if it wasn't snowing so damned hard. I wrapped my cloak more tightly around me, and watched the mid-morning funeral party. Gilbertus's voice was muffled by the snow but I knew the sombre incantation he was chanting so well that I would have noticed the slightest error. So far he had-n't put a syllable wrong. Around him, the mourners huddled to protect themselves against the cold, and against their mutual grief and the fear of death. The bare pine coffin sat on its bier at the edge of the cliff. This was not an opulent affair.

Gilbertus turned slightly and I pulled my head back out of sight around the corner of the building. It was bloody cold and the sharp wind was turning my feet and fingers numb, but to move too much would give away my presence. Instead I stood, a silent shivering statue, and listened to the chant.

There.

He'd missed something. Nothing as obvious as a dropped word or missing line: just a subtle change to the rhythm of the incantation. Two lines later: again, and quickly again. Then a whole section I didn't recognise.

This wasn't some mis-remembered lesson. He was changing things. I didn't understand the language of the sacred chants – almost nobody did, we just learned them by rote – but I could tell that there was something wrong here. Fear crawled slowly up my spine, and I would have sweated if it wasn't for the cold.

A final blessing was said, the bier was pushed to the edge of the rock and tipped, the coffin slid off it and into space, and the mourners were ushered away from the cliffside before the crash echoed up from below. They didn't hang around, the party dispersing quickly, eager to get away from this place of death, into the warm, to console each other and start on the funeral meats, I guessed. Gilbertus lingered a moment, and I stepped out to meet him.

'Well met, brother,' I said.

'Aye, brother. Cold.' He stamped his feet. 'Are you here for a funeral?'

'In a way,' I said. 'But I want to talk to you about the attack last night.'

'Yes,' he said. 'Unpleasant affair. You've been told there's a meeting after supper to discuss who's to be acting head of the temple?' Something in his tone, his whole stance, had changed. His voice wasn't the voice of an apprentice any more. Yesterday he had spoken to me with respect. Today it was arrogance. He paused and turned away, and I wondered if he didn't want me to see his face as he spoke again.

'Last night you said you thought you knew who was behind the attack. Do you still know?'

'I was wrong last night,' I said.

'Oh yes?'

'Yes,' I said. 'I thought it was a necromancer with a grudge. It's not: it's a necromancer with ambition. Do you feel ambitious, brother?'

'When it's cold, I feel cold,' he said. A new tone, half-way between fear and aggression, had entered his voice. 'Why don't we find somewhere warm to discuss this?'

'I'm happy here,' I said. 'This won't take long. I've only got four questions. First, if you'd gone to raise the alarm last night, why didn't I see your footprints across the frost in the park?'

'Because I went a different way to you, clearly. What's the second question?'

'How did you know the dead girl had been stabbed through the heart?'

'A watchman told me. Next?'

'Where did you get the tentacle?'

He whirled to face me and I thought he was about to cast a spell. I did nothing. For a moment he paused, then let his arms drop slowly to his side. He was frightened, I could tell. Frightened but still confident.

'What do you know?' he asked.

'That you're not going to leave this cliff without killing me.'

I stepped towards him, my hands slightly raised, palms and wrists exposed. Merchant's trick. Makes you look vulnerable, unthreatening. He didn't react, or at least he didn't try to move away, which was good.

Instead he said, 'Apart from that.'

'You arrived here six months ago, disguised as a junior priest from Talabheim,' I said. 'We were expecting a Brother Gilbertus to come from there, so I imagine you killed him and took his place. You've spent six months making sure that there are a lot of unblessed corpses buried around the city which you could use your magic to reanimate later.

'Yesterday morning you killed a girl behind the Drowned Rat, enchanted the corpse, and then made it look like a mutant so it would have to be brought back to the temple for an investigation, and so there wouldn't be too much surprise when I couldn't perform the ceremony of Nameless Rite on it. You also persuaded Father Zimmerman that I was wasting the temple's time, so the corpse would lie in the Factorum all night, unblessed, ready for you to reanimate. When I met you outside the temple, you'd been there all along, controlling the dead thing.'

'You know all that?' he said.

I moved closer to him. Only a few feet separated us. Behind him, the edge of the cliff dropped away into eternity.

'It's mostly guesswork,' I admitted.

'So much guessing… for a ruined merchant still obsessed by the loss of his family. I am impressed.' The disguise had dropped completely now: he wasn't Gilbertus any more. He'd never been Gilbertus at all, except in the minds of some too-trusting priests. If any of them had been around, they wouldn't have recognised this sarcastic arrogant who dared to taunt me with my grief.

But there was no one else: the Cliff of Sighs was deserted. Just us and the swirling snow: he with his plan and his magic, I with a new-kindled memory of Filomena, and the sadness and anger that it brought.

He smiled again. 'So, brother, why would a priest of Morr – or even a necromancer – do what you've described?'

'Because,' I said, and I didn't try to keep the bile out of my voice, 'because you're ambitious. Because there would be no more powerful position for a necromancer than leading a temple of Morr. All the corpses you need, brought to your doorstep by the good citizens of Middenheim. You probably have some scheme for taking over the city in a couple of years.'

'Perhaps.' He was close to me now, and he wasn't smiling any more. His face was set cold and hard against me. Snowflakes whirled in the space between us. 'And your last question?'

'I was going to ask who the girl was,' I said. 'But it's not important any more.'

'She was young. Strong. Susceptible to my magic. A potential tool. We're alike, you and I, brother. I had no interest in the girl when she was alive, and neither did you. All the suffering, all the pain in this city, and you only have use for them when they're dead. We could work together. We could learn a lot from each other. And I could use a man like you. What say you? Join me. Come back to the temple. I'll tell you about the girl there.'

'I said it wasn't important.' But his suggestion had thrown me off-guard. Were we similar? Had I the seed of necromancy in me? Then he started to chant: high-pitched and fast, and my fate suddenly became a lot more short-term.

Count to five, Alfric had said. Five seconds to survive.

One. I moved forward two paces.

Two, and I was in front of him, the dagger drawn out from under my cloak.

Three. I plunged it deep into his stomach. Blood gushed onto my hand, hot over my numbed fingers. I raised my face to his, and our gazes met. His eyes were full of horror.

Four. A long second passed. He didn't stop chanting.

Five. I twisted the knife hard, my fingers slipping against the blood. Gilbertus gave a pain cry. The chant was broken, his spell useless. He paused for an instant, then launched himself at me. The snow-covered ground slid under my feet and I went down.

He landed on top of me, grasping at my neck. I tried to roll away, but he pinned me to the ground. He was bleeding to death, but he was still larger and stronger than me: at the very least he could take me with him.

His fingers found my neck and squeezed, twisting my head to one side. Snow covered my face, filling my eyes and nose with gritty cold. I could feel the warmth of his blood on my stomach, and the hilt of the knife in his wound pressed itself hard against my kidneys. My mind fogged with pain and darkness.

I felt like a dying man. Images formed in my head: faces. Father Zimmerman, his face contorted in death-agony. Brother Rickard, torn in half. Schtutt. My wife, Filomena, and my son Karl, smiling, the last morning I had ever seen them. And the half-face of a dead Norse girl whose name and story I would never know.

No. My job here was not finished. I had Morr's work to do.

Something poured a last burst of strength into my tired limbs. My arms found his, breaking his grip around my neck and pushing him off from me, so he rolled away across the whiteness of the burial site.

I rolled over to follow him. He was crouching, trying to get to his feet, one hand groping to pull the knife out. I kept rolling, crashing into him. I felt him fall sideways and slip, and then he grabbed my cloak and hung on. For a moment I couldn't understand why, then I felt his weight pulling at me and I knew the truth: we were at the edge of the cliff, and he was part-way over.

I didn't know if he was trying to pull himself back or wanting to take me down with him, but it didn't matter. I was sliding across the snow, being pulled over the edge of the cliff. I flung out my arms and legs, trying to get any kind of grip. All I found was soft snow. I slid further towards death.

My left hand found a small crevice in the rock, and I held onto it for dear life. I could see over the edge now. Below me, Gilbertus – the man I'd called Gilbertus – dangled. One of his hands was wrapped in my cloak, the other grasped desperately at the sheer stone of the cliff. The wind caught his garments, whipping them around him. Below us, an infinity of snow whirled and blew, obscuring everything else.

Gilbertus raised his head and stared into my eyes. His were pools of glistening darkness, like gazing into an ancient well. Even at this moment I could read nothing there. His face was as white as ice. Below, blood still spurted from his wound, spiralling away to the blizzard below.

'Pull me up,' he said. There was weakness in his voice.

'No,' I said. I wanted to batter away at his hands, to make him let go, but I was afraid that the slightest movement would make me slip further over the edge.

'Pull me up,' he said again, 'and I will take you to your wife and child.'

'You're lying,' I said, and at that moment there was a tearing, rending sound as my cloak ripped across. The necromancer swung sideways across the cliff face, held suspended in the air for a moment by the thicker fabric of the hem, and then it also parted and he dropped.

His body plunged down, fading, blown away among the blizzard, and disappeared into the whiteness. There was no scream or sound of impact. Possibly it was muffled by the snow.

I lay there for a while. Blood hammered in my temples, and my hands reflexively gripped onto whatever they could find. The snow and the rock were cold against my face. It reminded me I was alive.

EVENTUALLY I pushed myself back a yard, slowly, and stood up. Blood stained the area, but flurries of snow were already covering the pools and strands of crimson, and the footprints and marks of the recent scuffle.

My ribs ached. I looked around. The area was still deserted. No signs, no evidence, no witnesses, no complications. I whispered thanks to Morr.

For an instant I saw Gilbertus's face again, felt the weight of him suspended from his fist in my cloak, and heard his last words. He hadn't known anything. He couldn't have known anything. He would have said anything to save himself. No. He had been lying. He must have been.

His spirit had gone to Morr now. Even necromancers had to make their peace with the god of death eventually. It occurred to me that although I still thought of him as Gilbertus, I didn't know his real name.

I turned away, to walk back to the temple. Now Gilbertus was dead his spell should be broken and I should be able to lay the dead girl's soul to rest. I'd say a blessing for his spirit as well, and if anyone asked me what I had done today, I would say that I had given peace to two unquiet souls.

I wondered if I would ever do the same for my own.

Catch as Catch Can

THE INVISIBLE BOY had been in the city for a whole year now, and he was celebrating that triumph. He still had no job, nor any prospect of one, and his meagre supply of ready cash was reaching its limits again. But by nightfall he would have a good meal and a few glasses of beer inside him, never the less.

He had been called Wheezer, back when there were people who spoke to him or knew him, back before the city. Now he was nobody. But he was happy.

The smell of the city had burned at his nostrils and throat for a while when he had first arrived, and the stench had made him feel ill, but gradually he had come to ignore it. He was especially happy because he hadn't sneezed or wheezed once during the entire time he had lived in the city.

Back in the old good country air, he had suffered all year round from a nose that ran constantly. Through the spring and summer, he never stopped sneezing and his eyes never stopped streaming. And during harvest, he wheezed. That was how he'd come by his name. He was Wheezer.

Now he saw the funny side of all those years spent breathing good, pure country air. Bless the city's filthy, smoggy atmosphere, where, summer or winter, he felt better and better! His

49

old nickname was now a kind of private joke. If he ever found anyone to ask him his name of course. It had been a year and no one had spoken to him. No one noticed him. No one even seemed to see him.

THE WEATHER WAS cold, wet, dark and miserable. Never mind winter, the change to spring was by far the worst part of the year.

Kruza sneezed heavily into a beautiful linen handkerchief that he had, only minutes before, lifted out of the pocket of some local gentleman. He wouldn't be able to sell it now, but he needed a good nose-wipe at this time of the year, and with all his other work the loss of the fence's price of one handkerchief was a trifle.

Kruza didn't feel much like work. He begrudged going out in this awful slanting drizzle, and the wind was the kind that went through you instead of round you. But it was his day tomorrow and he still had the small matter of his quota to fill. He would have finished days ago if it hadn't been for the fact that he'd found a new and very accommodating fence, and had decided to sell one or two of his better items on the outside. Just so long as the master didn't get wind of it.

'Wind, damnable wind,' Kruza muttered to himself as he passed out of the Altquartier and made his way down the steps to the Great Park. Even on a day like today there would be people trading there, which meant there would be other people with full purses. And aside from sitting in a nice little tavern somewhere drinking a long glass of ale, or better yet a hot toddy, the market gave the best shelter of anywhere in Middenheim. The stalls' awnings almost touched in places, shielding the people as well as the produce from the worst of the wind and rain.

Kruza mooched around for a while, strolling between the stalls, taking his time to pick out a likely victim. A little care spent choosing his mark now cut down on the number of targets he needed, and in the long run would give him more time in that tavern later in the day.

WHEEZER FOLLOWED the old cut-purse into the market in the big park. He loved the market. Mostly he stole what he needed, and of course that included money, but he took great delight in robbing the market stalls to fill his larder and make the derelict hovel he called home as pleasant as possible.

During his first year in the city, he had successfully filched enough cooking utensils, bed linens and other household items to furnish a warm and friendly nest, albeit one he enjoyed entirely alone. He'd stolen his entire wardrobe, and he'd even managed to pinch a series of small mirrors, including one in a gilt frame. He loved the mirrors and stood or hung them indiscriminately around the single room he lived in.

Today though, Wheezer needed cash. He had to eat and while his own larder (the outside sill of his single high window at this time of year) was all but full, he was celebrating his first anniversary in the city tonight and had decided to eat in style at one of the better taverns. He might even find himself a girl, he thought, and that would certainly mean hard cash.

Wheezer had his mark in sight. He usually chose the older cut-purses, although he knew, to his cost, of one or two who were still as quick of eye and fleet of foot as he was. This old coot with his one patched eye looked safe enough, though. Wheezer kept close to the old thief, feeling no need to slink or skulk about. He watched as the old man made his move.

Wheezer stood by as the old man lifted a tiny gold sundial from the pocket of an equally aged butler out doing the daily provisioning.

No good, thought Wheezer. *Who needs another timepiece? Next time.*

He followed the man on a little further, up a short cobbled slope, and round the side of a tiny handcart selling illicit liquor. Wheezer pocketed a bottle as he sidled past, just for good measure. After all, he was supposed to be celebrating today.

The old cut-purse's next target was a fat, bossy middle-aged woman. She had stopped to reprimand the man with her, surely her scolded and erstwhile cuckolded husband. Wheezer was mesmerised for a moment, the woman might well be as big as a barge and well past the prime of her life, but she was also very feminine.

Yes, a wench tonight, I think, Wheezer said to himself as he passed the woman and the cut-purse, doffing his cap to one or other of them, or perhaps to both. Neither one of them saw him, and he didn't expect them to. Putting his cap back on his head at an angle, Wheezer watched the old cut-purse snatch the little bag of money from the fat woman's waist. It was done in a moment, without anyone noticing, and the purse looked satisfyingly heavy to Wheezer. He loitered for a moment at a stall, picking up a couple of bars of rough soap and casually pocketing them while the owner's back was turned, before following the old thief onward.

KRUZA STOOD BY a stall, fingering a woman's silk shawl, when he saw Strauss. The old cut-purse had been the best in his time, and had earned himself the right to work solo in Middenheim. After twenty years of toiling for the likes of his Low King, not to mention training three generations of cut-purses, including Kruza, Strauss was in his retirement. He visited the market once a fortnight or so, just to keep his hand in, and always liked the dullest days and the oldest marks.

Kruza was not surprised to see him today and greeted him with as much cheer as he could muster, given the cold and his reddening nose.

'Well met, master,' he called as the near-blind old thief drew level with him.

'Is that you, Kruza, my boy?' the man returned, beaming his toothless grin from ear to ear. 'How goes it with you?'

'It's too cold and too damp and I have a quota to meet,' answered Kruza, trying to make it all sound like a joke and failing.

'You young pups of today,' Strauss remonstrated, 'never happy in your work. Still giving the master his pound of flesh then, are we? Only another fifteen years and a couple of hundred recruits and perhaps he'll let you off his hook.' He laughed.

'Only if he or I live that long,' Kruza said.

WHEEZER WATCHED as the old man, with his pocket full of another woman's money, stopped to speak with the tall, broad-shouldered fellow, who was apparently examining women's clothing. An odd occupation for such a strong, confident-looking man.

Now's your chance, Wheezer, old son, he thought to himself. He cleared his mind and moved in a little closer.

What is the old man blathering on about, he wondered as he slid two long, slender fingers into the side pocket of the old coat that hung from the blind old man's shoulders. He was walking away slowly and very calmly when he heard the words 'Stop! Thief!' begin to ring out – and then stop short very suddenly.

KRUZA, ASTONISHED at the brazen outrage, wanted to cry out to stop the young chancer robbing his old friend. But since the purse had originally belonged to someone else, he realised it would do no good, and the words 'Stop! Thief!' came out strangled and barely loud enough to be heard by the old man standing next to him.

'I'll get him!' he said firmly, but very quietly to Strauss, and walked away purposefully toward the young man in the cap. He wondered why he couldn't remember what the boy looked like, except for the vaguest impression of a teenage kid with fair hair. Kruza prided himself that he never forgot a face, not the face of a mark, not the face of a fellow cut-purse and especially not the face of an enemy. There was something odd about this one. He realised at once that he would have to stay close to the boy; if he let him out of his sight, he would not know him again.

WHEEZER LEFT THE park by the north-east gate and worked his way up the winding steps and slopes towards the north part of the Altquartier. He had made his home in a derelict building in the far north of the quarter where life was rough, but not so bad as it was further south in the heart of the district. He had stumbled upon the place, back then little more than tile-patched rafters open to the sky with rotting attic boards, late one night only a few days after he had arrived in the city. It had been cold and wet then, as it was now, and he had needed to find shelter fast.

It had taken Wheezer only a matter of days in the city to get the lay of the land, even though some of Middenheim's native citizens knew only the streets and byways of their own local quarters despite a lifetime of city dwelling. It had taken him a little longer to find a permanent place to sleep, but not too long.

Wheezer's room was the only occupied part of the ramshackle old building and was towards the top, on the third floor. His one window looked down into a narrow courtyard and the windowless backs of other buildings, so no one overlooked him. The front of the building was barred and boarded, but there was a cellar window at the side that served as a convenient front door where Wheezer could not be seen entering. The room was as solitary and isolated as he was himself, but it suited him well, and he had no desire to spread himself out among the other rooms that must exist in the building, but which Wheezer had never explored.

THERE WAS HONOUR among thieves, even in Middenheim, and so if it took Kruza all afternoon to track down the brazen knave who had robbed venerable Strauss he would do it.

Discreetly Kruza followed the cocky young cut-purse out of the Great Park and watched him as he climbed in through the cellar window of the tall, narrow, crumbling building. Two minutes later, as the clatter of shod feet on old wooden stairs died away, Kruza slid his body, shoulder first, through the cellar window and looked around to get his bearings. In no time, he had found new scuff marks on the dusty floor and followed the ragged footprints up three flights of rickety, creaking stairs. He took his time, moving silently, as he didn't want to warn the young thug of his arrival.

Five minutes later, Kruza was leaning nonchalantly in the doorframe of a cluttered, low-lit room, watching the scrawny kid take off his cap and coat, utterly oblivious to the fact Kruza was there. Kruza gently ran his thumb down the length of his short-sword, reassuring himself of its cutting edge.

He looked on as the small, slender boy took soap and liquor from where he had secreted them in his pockets along with the heavy purse that Strauss had lifted. Then Kruza began to take in the room properly for the first time. It was extraordinary. The floor was thick with rugs and carpets, and there was a low couch covered in a colourful array of fabrics and cushions. Clean clothes and spare shoes were neatly arranged in one corner, half shielded from the room by an elegant, foreign-looking screen of pale wood. There was a deep bowl and ornate pitcher of eastern design gracing a low oval table and a large sheet of thick coarse material hung on a hook nearby. Then there were the mirrors. Kruza didn't believe he had ever encountered so many mirrors in one room, nor so much opulence in the room of a petty scoundrel. Yet despite the mirrors, the young thief was obviously used to being alone, since he had still not noticed his intruder.

Kruza had planned to surprise him. He had wanted the young thief to turn and catch him standing in the doorway, preferably running his thumb along the blade of his short-sword. But the boy just hadn't noticed him, though Kruza had held the relaxed menacing pose and repeated the gesture several times. Kruza began to feel rather silly repeating the theatrical threat.

Eventually, bored with looking into the remarkable room, Kruza was beginning to want to take a seat on that inviting couch. Then the tickle started and he knew that introductions were imminent. He had no choice in the matter, so he raised his short-sword in an aggressive stance. The sneeze came in a torrent of wet snot and doubled Kruza over with its force, his sword hand still pointing the gleaming weapon at the thief's back.

The young man, standing in the middle of the room with his back to the door, clutched his chest suddenly and fell to his knees.

Kruza thought for a moment that he'd killed his foe without even waving his sword, and cautiously entered the room to assess the situation. The lad was white, dark circles of fright ringing his wide grey eyes. Kruza realised that the thief was little more than a child and he almost felt sorry for him. Kruza didn't want to kill him like this; he didn't want the lad to die without knowing what he'd done. He tucked his sword in the back of his belt for easy access and knelt on one knee beside Wheezer, pulling him up.

'Don't faint on me, you little runt,' Kruza said. 'I don't plan to have to carry you over to that couch. I'd sooner kill you right here.'

'You already scared me half to death,' replied the pale-faced, quivering youth.

'It was just a sneeze,' Kruza said. 'Be thankful. At least it saved you from a full frontal short-sword attack.'

Wheezer flopped down on the couch. Kruza stood over him, his hands on his hips, leaning in so that he was looking down directly into Wheezer's face.

'Now listen to me,' he began, putting one hand squarely on the pommel of his sword, ready to draw it at any moment. 'What do you mean by stealing from old Strauss? There's honour amongst thieves in this city! Has your boss never told you the rules?'

'Strauss? Boss? I have no idea what you're talking about!'

'Strauss,' Kruza explained impatiently, 'is the name of the man you robbed this afternoon in the market.'

'But he was a thief,' Wheezer said, matter of fact. His voice had an unusual inflection, almost as if he was not used to talking. 'You can't steal from a thief, when what you're taking doesn't belong to him.'

'What about the stall holders on the market? You stole from them.'

'Hardly,' Wheezer said, 'When one man has more soap or liquor than he can use or sell, that's not stealing either. I never take from an empty stall or a busy one.'

Kruza looked down at him quizzically. 'Did your boss teach you nothing?'

'What boss?' Wheezer asked innocently.

'Ulric take me! You know,' Kruza was becoming impatient. 'The man you work for. The man you sell merchandise to.'

'I don't have a boss,' Wheezer answered.

'Then who do you sell your stolen goods to? Who's your fence?'

Wheezer shook his head, as if the street thief was suddenly speaking Bretonnian. 'Do you want a drink?' he asked suddenly.

'I– what?'

'A drink. I'm celebrating today. And you know, you're the first visitor I've had here, so it's only right.'

Kruza blinked. Had he missed something? The kid was... strange.

'Look, who do you sell your merchandise to?' he repeated, slowly and carefully.

'No one,' Wheezer said, beginning to catch on. 'I don't sell anything. I just take what I need or sometimes what I want. Why would I want to sell anything to anyone?'

Kruza didn't know whether to pity or laugh at this lost, lonely boy with such strange, innocent ways. There seemed to be nothing immoral about him, nothing memorable about him, almost nothing real about him at all. He did what he did and that was an end of it.

But then how, wondered Kruza, had he become so good at the stealth-craft, without a teacher. The kid must have the gift. The kid must be a natural. Kruza smiled suddenly. A thought had occurred to him.

'Perhaps I will have a drink with you after all,' he said at last, taking his hand off his sword hilt and sitting down again.

'Good, because as I said: I'm celebrating!' Wheezer announced, selecting two rather elegant, if mismatched, goblets and the bottle of pear brandy he had liberated that afternoon.

WHEEZER WAS SO excited to finally have an audience that he talked non-stop for a very long time. But Kruza didn't mind. He needed to put the lad at ease. Besides, the liquor was warming and the room was extremely comfortable. Wheezer got up, still talking, and lit a fire in the small grate just before dark. It burned gently, bringing warmth and light to the room, making it seem even more exotic than it had when Kruza had first beheld it.

'I arrived here a year ago to the day,' Wheezer was saying, 'come to collect my inheritance, or rather to be recognised by my illustrious parent.

'I turned twenty and left the forest for the city, my real home. You see, my mother lived here when I was born. She was the most beautiful artiste of her era, treading the boards of all the great theatres in all the great cities. She came to Middenheim once a year to perform, and it was on her last visit here that she met and fell in love with my father. He was young, of course, and impetuous and fell for my mother at first sight! Back then, who wouldn't have? Now, his great and noble family weren't too impressed with him, and had the gall to try and buy my mother off with cheap trinkets and idle promises, not to mention a great deal of money.

'Naturally, she declined and stayed in the city to have me, so that my father would have to recognise me. Great plan, but of course things never work out the way we expect and she died. A horrible death really. She died three days after I was born. She bled to death.

'So, off I went. Actually, I didn't go away, I was taken away by an old wet-nurse who worked for my grandfather. She was paid to take me into the forest and well, you know, kill me. She didn't have the heart to do it, of course. Instead she stayed with me and then her sister came to live with us too. Wonderful women, we never wanted for anything. They're both dead now and I wonder if they were witches, 'cause though we never went without, neither of them did anything practical. We didn't raise pigs or keep a garden, but there was always meat and greens and good bread…'

Kruza let the story wash over him as it rattled on. He was beginning to feel that the story and the kid were just part of some elaborate fever-dream brought on by his infernal ague.

'So I became a man, and before she died, my "aunt", who must have been over seventy before she took to her deathbed, told me everything. After I buried her and her sister – they died right there in the same bed on the same day – I set out to the city from the forest that had been my home my whole life. And that's it, well most of it. I can't mention my father's name, of course, not before he recognises me, officially, so to speak, but I can tell you he runs a great city, lives in a great palace and doesn't live a million miles from here. In fact, on a clear night I can see the top of his palace roofs from my little window.'

Kruza's head was floating about the room with all the good strong liquor he had drunk, but he knew when he was listening to an outrageous fairytale, or several woven together. Still, it was no business of his. He wanted the boy to relax and trust him.

KRUZA LEFT LATE. Remembering he still had a quota to fill, he secreted a little gilt mirror as he left, sliding it beneath his jacket.

'It's all right,' Wheezer said, having noticed. 'You have it. I took it from a thief. It doesn't belong to anyone now, so take it by all means.'

Kruza felt guilty for the first time since he was a child. 'Look, what's your name?' he asked.

'Oh, I don't have one,' the lad replied cheerily, 'being a bastard and everything. And my mother didn't live long enough to give me a name. When I was big enough to need a name my aunts called me "Wheezer". You can call me that.'

'Okay,' said Kruza. 'My name's Kruza.'

'Funny,' said Wheezer, 'I thought your name must be "Sneezer",' and he laughed at his joke. 'Did you hear that?' he asked rhetorically, 'Wheezer and Sneezer!'

Kruza blinked again, forced a grin. 'I'll see you around,' he said, and left.

A NATURAL, that's what the boy was. The gift in his fingers, his tread, in his sheer anonymity. It was rare. There were a lot of good thieves in Middenheim, Kruza amongst them, but there was only a handful of true naturals. If the boy proved to be what Kruza thought he was, then Kruza was duty bound to begin recruiting him for his Low King.

Or keeping him for myself, Kruza wondered. The thought kept coming back to him. How easy would it be to fill his quota then, to get the Low King off his back, to finally start getting ahead, getting somewhere on his own?

But recruiting the boy wasn't going to be that easy either way. Wheezer had all sorts of crazy rules about whom he would steal from and what he would take. He saw no reason to steal for the sake of selling goods on at less than their value. He stole only to live.

But he was so good at it, and Kruza hated to see such raw talent wasted.

He left it two days, and then the next morning shadowed the sleepy alley where Wheezer lived until he saw the boy emerge from his ruin. Kruza strode from the shadows, as if he was just passing, a chance encounter.

'Oh. You again,' he said.

The boy's face lit up. *He is so unaccustomed to being spoke to, Kruza thought with a touch of pity.* Just a touch; there wasn't room for much except business in Kruza's heart.

'Where are you going?'

'To work,' Kruza said, sniffing. It was another cold and wet day.

'Can I come?' Wheezer asked.

And that was how the games began. That simple.

The two of them strolled down to the Great Park, Kruza hunched over with the cold and sticking close under the awnings that would keep the wind and rain off. Wheezer almost strutted through the park, throwing out his puny chest and taking deep breaths of the freezing, damp air. He appeared to be in his element. Kruza led him to a stall crammed with all manner of household goods and they watched as a local gentlewoman, escorted by her houseman, fondled bolts of cloth on a stall nearby. Kruza almost gasped as Wheezer picked up a package of spills and half a dozen tallow candles from the stall, tucking them into his jacket. But no one else seemed to notice.

A natural, by Ulric. Kruza smiled. He nodded to his brazen companion. 'Bet you can't lift madam's money pouch,'

'Where?' Wheezer asked, looking about him.

'There,' Kruza answered, 'with the snooty-looking houseman in the short grey cloak.'

'No problem,' Wheezer said, a cock-eyed smile across his face. He walked off past the affluent woman with the heavy pouch at her waist and nipped it off without even touching her. Kruza watched, only feet away, amazed at the speed and skill with which Wheezer performed the dare. He had been ready to step in and cause a little confusion to cover Wheezer when he got caught, which had seemed inevitable with the houseman standing guard.

But it never happened. Wheezer walked around the next stall and came back behind Kruza.

'Good, good…' Kruza murmured as they walked on together. 'Where is it then?'

'Where's what?' Wheezer asked innocently.

'The pouch, you dolt,' Kruza replied. 'How much was in it?'

'No idea,' Wheezer said, 'but it was heavy enough. You can check it if you like. It's in your jerkin pocket.'

Kruza looked wide-eyed at Wheezer and slid two fingers into the pocket, drawing out the full pouch. His bottom jaw dropped so far, so fast, he almost dislocated it. He hadn't felt a thing and he was one of the best. The kid was amazing. Invisible.

Wheezer seemed to like the game, and would take any dare. As the day went on, Kruza became more and more intrigued by what the young, untrained cut-purse could do. Kruza didn't need to recruit Wheezer. The kid would give him anything and do anything for him so long as it was prefixed with 'I bet you can't…' Kruza was looking at a meal ticket.

Wheezer stole lunch for them from a stall-holder while having a conversation with him at the same time. They sat and ate the fresh sausage, a small earthenware jar of pickles and two small loaves of good bread, sitting on an empty, covered handcart behind one of the clothing stalls. Kruza's tall, athletic frame perched next to Wheezer's small compact one. Kruza was a grown man of twenty-four. Only a few years older than the other. But sitting next to him, Wheezer looked like a child from the slums.

Kruza's mood had improved dramatically. It was worth coming out in the cold and wet to watch Wheezer at work, especially when Wheezer was working for him.

During the afternoon the lad lifted two time-pieces from the inside pockets of gentlemen whose outerwear looked completely impenetrable, and completed the hat-trick by removing a barely visible necklace from a middle-aged gentlewoman whose cloak was buttoned high to her throat. Together, the conspirators then liberated a total of seven items from one young dandy who they tripped and then 'saved' from an undignified fall down a steeply stepped lane. While dusting the man down, Wheezer managed to empty three of his outer pockets and two that were concealed beneath. He had also taken the short dagger that the dandy kept in the top of one of his long boots. He was a marvel.

As EVENING FELL, Kruza and Wheezer retired to the Drowned Rat in the Ostwald district. Kruza opened the door from the grubby street with its lengthening shadows, and they all but fell into the tavern. Pockets full, a good day's work done, and coins to spend on beer and a good supper.

Several of Kruza's friends and colleagues were crowded into the small bar, and introductions were made all round, but no

one could remember Wheezer's name and very soon they forgot he was there at all. Wheezer thought them all fine fellows,
apart from that chap with the flat hair, Arkady, who seemed a
little churlish. Idly he found himself wondering if he had been
Kruza's last best friend.

Soon the drink was flowing and the food forgotten as Kruza
exchanged stories and information with his colleagues. They
talked constantly of the 'Boss', although sometimes they called
him 'The Man' or 'The King', complaining about him, cursing
him and generally displaying their hatred for him.

Some time later a fight started. Good-natured at first, just a
few fists flying to prove a point, then someone pulled a dagger
and chaos broke out. Wheezer had no idea what they were
fighting over, and slid down off his stool and sheltered
between the barrels that held up either end of the bar. He
stayed there with his arms wrapped round his knees, watching
the mayhem.

Kruza threw himself with gusto into the melee. There was
nothing like a good brawl to end a good evening. Eventually,
the fight broke up when the landlord began arbitrarily swinging a club around his bar, screaming that enough damage had
been done and he would call the guard. Four men had sus-
tained gashes and one had had his earlobe bitten off. The
others had slashed clothes, and bruises were rising up on their
faces and bodies from the blows of fists and hilt-pommels
jabbed hard against flesh during the closer, hand-to-hand bouts
where there was no room to use a blade.

Wheezer was astounded to see them all on good terms when
they were kicked out of the tavern, united now in cursing the
pot-man, as they had been in cursing the Low King.

A WEEK LATER Kruza and Wheezer were meandering back to
Wheezer's room. The place was more comfortable and private
than Kruza's, and he had begun to adopt it as his own. Wheezer
could not have been more happy. He had company at last.

They turned east, and cut across the Wynd and up into the
south side of the Altquartier. From there they turned north
toward the crumbling old building where they now both lived.
It had been a goodly walk and Kruza decided there was time for
one more drink. The single pale light outside the Cocky Dame
shone to him like a beacon and he was about to enter the sleazy
one-room tavern with its cabbage smell when Wheezer stopped
him by grasping his forearm.

'I've seen that before,' Wheezer began, pointing out a covered handcart steered down the sloping street by a sombre man in a long cloth cape. 'What is it?'

'The dead,' Kruza said plainly. 'No one's concern but the priests of Morr.'

'They carry them off the streets?' Wheezer asked, 'Where do they take them?'

'That one'll no doubt end up turning over and over in the air until it lands at the bottom of the Cliff of Sighs, more broken than it is already.'

'The old priest who tended people back in the forest always came to their homes. Bodies weren't moved and if a homeless body was found in a field then that was where it was buried. Don't the people here bury their own people on their own land?' Wheezer asked.

'Huh!' Kruza snorted, raising his hands and turning his body in a gesture that encompassed the entire city. 'What land? The wealthy find a resting-place in Morrspark, but even they are buried one above the other, five or six deep. The rest tumble over the cliff. The priests seal the bodies and bless them and for all but the most destitute there are mourners. But this city has little sentiment. It goes about its business, and leaves the priests to go about their's.'

'What of their belongings?' Wheezer was full of questions tonight and Kruza was still only three parts full of good ale.

'They are priests – they have few belongings…'

Wheezer interrupted. 'Not the priests!' he exclaimed. 'The dead!'

Kruza pushed through the tavern door, dragging Wheezer behind him. 'You're far too ghoulish for my liking. Come and have a drink with me and let's have an end to this talk of corpses.'

But the talk of corpses did not end. It began again later that night, when Kruza was settled on the couch in Wheezer's room, and Wheezer himself was lying on a pile of cushions on the floor. Kruza was now full of ale and more tolerant of Wheezer's questions – up to a point.

'The dead people,' began Wheezer, 'where do their possessions go?'

'I don't know,' Kruza said. 'Some are robbed before they're cold. Those who die quietly among their families are relieved of their possessions by their loved ones.'

'And the rest?' the other asked, innocently.

'The rest?' Kruza replied. 'I suppose the priests of Morr collect their belongings and return them to their mourners. Perhaps if there is no one to pass the possessions on to then they go into the coffers of the Temple, or perhaps to the Graf himself.'

'Or should I say your "illustrious parent"?' he added, and laughed so much he had to stagger off his couch and take a leak out of the room's single window. When he returned to the couch, he was asleep and snoring a ragged drunken snore before Wheezer could form his next question.

In the morning, however, Kruza remembered enough of the previous night's conversation to give Wheezer a word of warning.

'If you are thinking of robbing the dead, think again!' he said firmly. 'The dead are respected by all but the lowest of the low-scum in this city, which has its share of grave-robbers. Friendless, perverted men.'

'Sure,' Wheezer said.

'Friendless, Wheezer,' Kruza reiterated. 'If I get wind that you have robbed a corpse, I shall cut you off and I'm sure you don't want that!'

Wheezer looked at his feet. 'It's just that a corpse can't own any–' he began, but was interrupted with a glare.

'Friendless, Wheezer!' Kruza said between gritted teeth, holding the much shorter man by the front of his jerkin and lifting him to his toe tips. 'Friendless!'

KRUZA CONTINUED his work, and his manipulation of Wheezer's talents continued to make him prosper. It had been a very good month. Two or three days out of every week the two would pair up and visit the markets and crowded areas of the city. By night they would eat and drink in various seedy taverns. One night Kruza took Wheezer to the Baiting Pit, but the youth didn't like it much and they left.

'I saw bears in the forest, where I lived with my aunts,' Wheezer explained. 'They were beasts of the wild and harmless enough if you respected them.'

Kruza shook his head. The kid was from another world.

WHEEZER HAD promised Kruza that he would not rob the dead, even though he didn't understand how it could be called stealing at all, let alone the lowest of low crimes.

He wasn't going to rob the corpses, of that he was convinced but he had become fascinated by the biers and carts that were wheeled around the streets with their dead cargo. Sometimes he would see an important-looking man in temple robes, calming the bereaved or asking questions or leaning over biers. Often the biers were steered through the streets wheeled by one man, or sometimes two, in long drab cloaks. Other times he saw corpses being tossed onto any available vehicle and being driven off by one of the city watch, and once he saw a body being removed by a White Wolf Templar, splendid in his plate armour.

Wheezer became quite fond of a good funeral, witnessing grand burials in Morrspark and simple ones at the Cliff of Sighs. No one seemed to mind him being there. In fact, no one ever noticed that he was there – except for one time.

He had climbed up to the Cliff about a fortnight after his conversation with Kruza and watched a lone priest performing a ceremony. The priest had stood over a rough plank coffin going through the necessary rituals and chanting the prayers that were almost familiar to Wheezer by now. Wheezer expected nothing, and was ready to turn away and make his way back into the city, when the strangest thing happened.

The priest stopped and spoke to him. Just briefly, pitying his loss, saying something about the corpse being at peace.

Wheezer didn't hear the actual words. This was only the second person to speak to him voluntarily since his arrival in the city more than a year before. Kruza had been the first.

'THE DEAD OF Middenheim,' Wheezer began out of nowhere, one night as they made their way to a tavern. 'They're not all taken away by priests, are they?'

'No, not all,' Kruza said. 'Since the Temple of Morr burnt down there aren't really enough of them to do all the burial work, without having to go out to collect every single body in the city.'

'I saw they were working on the temple,' Wheezer said. 'So, can anyone take a body away?'

'There are the men in long grey cloaks,' Kruza answered, 'I don't know who they are, but the priests use them a lot to carry bodies. They also ask the City Watch or anyone else who is considered more or less trustworthy.'

'Like the White Wolf I saw?' Wheezer asked rhetorically. 'You said before that the bodies were taken to the temple, Morrspark and the Cliff of Sighs, but what about the other place?'

'What other place?' Kruza asked. 'Where else would they take them?' He was becoming impatient now, Wheezer could tell,

and he didn't want to make his mentor angry, so he said no
more. But there was another place.

HUNGOVER AND groaning on the couch the next morning, Kruza
didn't notice Wheezer sneaking out, or if he did, he didn't care.
Wheezer rose early and went into the city to watch for carts. He
was almost obsessed by the bodies and their resting places now,
and if Kruza couldn't tell him what the 'other place' was then
he would find out for himself.

Wheezer quickly spotted his first body of the day, some old
man who had died in the night – perhaps violently, since this
was the Altquartier – but maybe just quietly in his bed. His
body was carried the short distance between where he had died
and the nearest place the vehicle could get to the corpse: across
a courtyard and down a short alley. Then it was heaved onto
one of the narrow handcarts and wheeled away by a guard who
had recently been relieved from his night watch. The middle-
aged, thickset man was disgruntled at having been given the
task when he was due home for his breakfast, and he manhan-
dled the body as though it were a sack of grain. Wheezer
followed the guard and his cargo until he realised they were
heading toward the Temple and not that 'other place'. He let
them go and began to look around for the next body.

Leaving the Altquartier and following the Garten Ring round
the eastern side of the park, Wheezer detected a commotion on
the other side of the wall. A cut-purse had been careless and was
being attacked by his mark. The cut-purse, a man who
reminded Wheezer of Kruza, what with his height and square
shoulders and casual style of dress, won the fight shortly after
producing a dagger from his boot. And a woman was now
lamenting the loss of the bold, stout man in his thirties who
that day had decided not to be a victim of robbery and was now
lying on the mossy slope, a victim of murder.

Wheezer stayed close as first the City Watch and then the
priest of Morr appeared. It was half an hour before a pair of
constables was dispatched with the body and it was soon
apparent to Wheezer that they, too, were heading for the
Temple of Morr.

It was almost noon and Wheezer was prepared to give up his
corpse-chasing for the day when a tall man in a long, drab cloak
crossed in front of him, hauling a long body-shaped barrow
with two large wheels at its centre. A second man, similarly
dressed, brought up the rear of the vehicle, clutching a pair of

handles on the back of the makeshift bier and following his colleague. Wheezer decided he would try one last time to follow a corpse to the 'other place'.

Wheezer followed the cart without much expectation of success. He had already failed twice today. He was delighted when the cart's course turned west and then north. Wheezer had been in this part of the city before, with its wide streets and grand houses. He had dressed carefully that morning in clean, anonymous clothes so that he could walk about unmolested by the city watch, who seemed never happier than when they were ousting some wretch or urchin from the better parts of the city. Wheezer had thrown a tatty old cloak over his neat ensemble for his walk through the poorer regions but discarded it now, as the cloaked men with their cart turned left at the Temple of Shallya. Wheezer could hear the orphans inside chanting prayers by rote, accompanied by the sporadic coughs and pained cries of the patients in the infirmary next door. He had gone there once himself when he had torn his hand open, fortunate to have the money to pay for his treatment. The physician who had attended him there had neither looked at nor spoken to Wheezer while he cleaned and dressed the wound.

Now Wheezer was in the Nordgarten district, amongst the homes of merchants and gentlemen. He did not hide in the shadows or skulk in doorways. He thrust his shoulders back and marched down wide, cobbled streets within sight of his quarry. He passed errand boys and visiting shopkeepers in the street, but it was a damp day, and cold, and the local residents were happy enough to stay in the warmth and comfort of their opulent homes.

Wheezer began to get excited. He would find out something that Kruza did not know, perhaps something new about the dead and their belongings. The 'other place'.

Wheezer saw the house ahead. It was taller and narrower than those around, giving it an imposing air. He did not know what it might once have been, but it didn't look much like the other houses in the area. Perhaps it had been a minor temple once. It was a tall, slender tower with narrow windows and a strangely curvaceous spire, which rose up in soft waves to a tiny dome at its crown. Under the base of the spire was a deep gallery of arrow slits. A second circular tower was fixed to the side of the main building, the breadth of perhaps two men passing, but with its own tiny dome and more of the unusual slits for windows.

Wheezer drew level with the makeshift bier as the two men worked it between the pair of narrow doors on the alley side of the building. It was darker in the alley, and these doors could not be seen from the street. Standing to one side of the double doors, slightly in view of the cloaked men, if they had cared to see him, Wheezer casually slid a hand out and lifted the rough, ragged-edged tarpaulin that covered the wagon. He lifted it a little higher as the two men continued to struggle with the bier, which was almost as wide as the doors.

His first glimpse suggested to Wheezer that this was no body, and his second, longer look confirmed it. On the wagon were all manner of objects, most of which Wheezer did not recognise at all, although he suspected that some of the odd-shaped glass vessels had come from an alchemist's shop. There were other things which he did recognise and, since there was no corpse to be robbed, he thrust his hand at the nearest shiny, metallic object under the tarpaulin. He pulled it out and tucked it into his jerkin. Then he stepped out entirely from behind the door-post, doffed his cap at the cloaked men, who still did not seem to see him, and walked out of the alleyway and back towards the Temple of Shallya where he had left his cloak.

Having retrieved it, Wheezer wanted to get back and confront the sceptical, dismissive Kruza with his findings. But there was something else he needed to do first.

Wheezer crossed back into the Great Park by its south-west gate and headed toward the herbalist and apothecary stands that huddled together in their own tiny enclave, shielded on one side by a bank and on the other by the east wall of the park itself. Trade in this part of the market was thin, but Wheezer had no problem picking up the bits and pieces he wanted and he was soon on his way home. In his pockets he now carried a small, scented beeswax candle; two bundles of herbs; and a couple of rough crystals hewn from different types of rock. He wasn't quite sure what all the things under the tarpaulin had been, but it couldn't hurt to take a few simple precautions.

'KRUZA!' HE CALLED, almost before he had reached the third flight of stairs, and ran up them stretching his legs to make them climb two stairs at a time. 'Kruza?'

He found the cut-purse sitting on the edge of the couch in only his shirt, which spilled to his knees. His head was in his hands and almost between his knees as he leant forward, the weight of his head almost unbearable with its attendant hangover.

'Shhh!' exclaimed Kruza and winced.

Wheezer wanted to laugh, but instead he crossed to the small, segmented wooden box that sat in a corner, where the gilt mirror had once lived. He lifted the lid and drew out a clutch of dried herbs. He took the ever-simmering kettle from its frame high over the fire, lest it dry up, and made a tea from the twigs and dry leaves. He handed it to Kruza, who balked at the smell of it, but downed it when pressed.

Wheezer let Kruza alone for half an hour, but the older cut-purse felt better surprisingly quickly and no sooner felt ravenously hungry than Wheezer had provided him with a plate of cold meat, pickles and bread.

'Now that you feel better,' Wheezer said, excited, 'I have something for you.' He lifted the object that he had stolen from under the tarpaulin, taking it out of his jerkin at the collar button and holding it out at arm's length in front of him. It swung in small circles before their eyes.

The thing Wheezer had stolen was quite beautiful and both of them gazed at it with equal hypnotic wonder. It was a chain made up of large, flat, square sections joined by fat gold links at the corners. Every square section was engraved like an elaborate belt buckle, each bearing a different motif or scene. In the centre of the chain, which was long enough to hang around a broad man's shoulders, was a larger ornament.

'Like the chain of office the Graf wears on feast-days,' murmured Kruza in a husky undertone.

'It's trying to eat itself,' Wheezer said, mesmerised.

The ornament consisted of a great dragon or snake forming an eternal circle by feasting on its own tail. Every scale of its armour-plated body was etched into the solid gold from which it was crafted. Its eyes were domed orbs of sightless ivory.

'It's beautiful!' breathed Kruza.

'Take it, then,' Wheezer said, thrusting it at arm's length, closer to Kruza's face. 'And when you get tired of it, perhaps it can help with your quota.'

'The quota!' Kruza cried, leaping off the couch as if a fire, lit long ago under the offending piece of furniture, had finally penetrated its solid base and was now biting at Kruza's backside.

'It's my day and I haven't filled my quota! Sigmar's blood!' He snatched up the heavy trinket and thrust it into his shirt. Then he pulled on breeches and boots and his short leather coat and hurried out of the room, snatching up the cloth sack holding his other acquisitions before slamming the door behind him without another word to the youth.

'CURSED THING!' Kruza yelled, storming back into the room with no regard for disturbing Wheezer. He threw the trinket onto the couch. 'He wanted nothing to do with it. The Man, who will sell anything and deal in anything, wouldn't touch it… and so my quota was lacking.'

'Oh.'

'Do you know what my penalty is for being short of my quota?' Kruza yelled, his voice still hoarse from the previous night's revelries. 'Take your trinket and may it bring you good fortune!'

Wheezer thought Kruza would leave, but instead of turning for the door, the cut-purse slumped down on the couch. Wheezer had failed, as the month had gone on, to realise that Kruza needed him more and more with every day that passed. While the cut-purse used the skills of the young, invisible thief, his own stealth-craft had become dull with lack of use and too much good living. He slouched on the couch, fingering the flat square plates of the unacceptable ornament, trying to read the story etched and carved there.

'Where did you get this, anyway? It must be tainted or horribly important for the master to turn it down flat with such an odd expression on his face. Come to think of it, I don't think my quota was doubled for any reason other than the insult of offering him this particular piece of merchandise.'

'I got it from the "other place",' Wheezer said, disinterested now, trying to work out how he could repay Kruza for his faux pas.

'What other place?' Kruza asked. And then recognition dawned. 'Ulric damn you if you stole this from a corpse!'

'No! No!' Wheezer exclaimed, backing away. He didn't care to feel the tip of that short-sword at his throat again. 'That's just the point! There was no body on the bier that went to the other place.'

'Don't talk in riddles, boy,' Kruza returned. His mood was dark and furious, and he felt like lashing out.

'I followed a corpse barrow… well, more of a covered hand-cart really. Anyway, I followed it to the "other place", the place I told you about. The place where the cloaked men take the bodies when they don't take them to the Temple of Morr. Only they don't take bodies at all. I lifted the cover on the wagon.

There were so many things there. I snatched that thing off it,' he said, pointing to the chain. 'But I swear I wasn't robbing a body. There was no body!'

'Smugglers,' Kruza said to himself.

'What?' Wheezer asked.

'It has to be smugglers. They dress like servants of the priests of Morr, so that they can move merchandise around Middenheim. The only people never stopped by citizens or the Watch in this city are the dead. And bearers of the dead.'

Realising at last what his companion had said, Kruza leapt off the couch and grabbed Wheezer by the arm.

'Take me there!' he said. 'Now!'

WHEEZER MANAGED to persuade Kruza to wash and shave and tidy up his dress before taking him into the Nordgarten, a district that Kruza seldom visited. The pickings might be rich, but the risks were high. The Watch would be on him quicker than Altquartier rats on a dog's corpse if they suspected the smallest misdemeanour.

Kruza had little confidence walking the broad, curving streets of the better districts of Middenheim, and he unconsciously copied Wheezer's upright stance and confident gait as they passed the Temple of Shallya. The orphans were still chanting.

Wheezer walked straight up to the strange tower-building and around into the adjoining alley. He was ready to enter, without a qualm, but Kruza was more cautious.

'Let's take a lookabout first,' he suggested. 'There may be people. The cloaked smugglers you saw before.'

But inside himself, Kruza was itching to get on. He could smell riches in there. Riches that his Low King would accept. One swift robbery, with his silent partner in tow, could shorten his working week by several days and lengthen his leisure time by the same.

They exited the alley, back out onto the main street, and followed the building round to the tall, slender, curved tower on its other side. The tower was sheathed in gloom and shadow and Kruza began to feel rather more at home. There was no effort involved in finding the squat door in the side of the tower below a line of glassless, slit windows. It was low and black and smelled oddly of pitch.

Wheezer opened the door and Kruza took a deep breath before ducking his head and shoulders to follow the lad in. They stood together on the small square landing that signalled the ground floor level and looked up and then down at the winding, spiral staircase. Looking directly up through the shaft of the stairs, they could see shafts of light coming in through the west-facing windows. Looking directly down, they could see nothing.

'Down,' hissed Kruza, turning from the lit upper floors. Unlike Wheezer, he was only invisible in the dark. Wheezer trotted happily down the stairs, looking back to his comrade, who took every step slowly and carefully so as to make as little noise as possible. He realised for the first time that Wheezer could be as soundless as he was invisible. Kruza's own careful steps made a sloppy 'tak' sound, while Wheezer's footfalls were like a whisper.

'Keep looking down,' hissed Kruza, anxious that Wheezer might walk into something and have them both killed before they had even seen a foe. They continued down the stairs, one flight and then, just for good measure, a second. Wheezer looked to where they were going and the slow and nervous Kruza looked to where they had been.

At the second floor below ground, Wheezer stepped out onto a wider, arched landing that led to only two or three shallow, curved steps and then, as far as he could see, nothing. He had reached the bottom. Thirty seconds later Kruza joined him, almost knocking him down the last few steps as he continued to keep watch behind them.

There was still no light. There was a slight smell of spoiled milk, which Kruza didn't notice, but which Wheezer thought odd in a room two storeys below ground level. The air was very still and slightly chill and while the steps down had been damp, the floor of the cellar room was perfectly dry, even dusty underfoot.

Wheezer steadied Kruza, whose widening eyes shone out stark and white in the gloom. Then he reached into his pocket and took out the beeswax candle, which he lit, filling the air with the pungent scent of spices, casting a pool of light around himself and Kruza and making shadows in the underground place.

The cellar was a kind of circular lobby and Wheezer walked around it from one vaulted arch to the next. He stopped at each, examining the posts either side that made the doorways and then moved on, completing the circle and not crossing the centre of the floor. Kruza had stayed resolutely where he was, looking back up the steps every few seconds as if he had a nervous tick.

'This is just an entrance hall,' Wheezer said, 'but there are more rooms beyond those arches.'

He undid the top two buttons of his jerkin and pulled out a large pouch, tied around his neck with a cord. He took something from it that Kruza couldn't see.

'What are you doing?' Kruza asked, before jerking his gaze anxiously back up the stairwell.

'It's all right,' Wheezer answered, beginning to work his way back around the circle of arches, slowly. 'Someone's scrawled glyphs all over the doorways. But a little country magic will soon cancel them out.'

'Glyphs!' Kruza exclaimed as loudly as he dared, his voice still little more than a hoarse whisper. 'Magic! Right, this is all starting to spook me out! Bodies! Jewels that even a filthy fence won't buy – and now glyphs!'

What had seemed like such a good idea now was rapidly turning sour.

'What are you doing? What do you mean by "country magic"?' he hissed as Wheezer began to brush an arch support with a bundle of dry old leaves and twigs, holding his candle up to each glyph in turn and murmuring what sounded like old rhymes.

'You know the kind of thing: herbs, spider webs, rabbit droppings, all good fodder for simple country magic, just as good as your fancy town stuff any time. And these glyphs are pretty basic,' Wheezer said, moving to the next arch support.

Is there no end to this kid's weirdness, thought Kruza, *or was he really raised by witches?* Down here, the half-remembered details of that nonsense story seemed so much more believable.

It began to get lighter as Wheezer entered each side-room for just long enough to light a lamp and then on to the next.

Somehow it didn't seem quite so cold to Kruza now, or so menacing, so when Wheezer reached the fourth archway, Kruza crossed the floor to watch him weave his little bit of country magic, kicking up dust as he went.

Wheezer heard him and turned, seeing what Kruza had not.

The tall, athletic cut-purse ordinarily had a long stride, but now he was creeping and cautious. Any other time Kruza would have stepped over the thing on the floor. Now he shuffled through it.

'DDDDOOOOO...!' Wheezer started to scream out, but it was too late.

Kruza looked up at the scream, standing squarely in the confusion of sandy dust around his feet. He saw Wheezer's mouth, wide, in full scream and he felt the tension in the kid's body.

Ulric damn me, he thought very quietly to himself.

Wheezer's candle went out and the soft glow the oil lamps were giving out turned to a hard white light. More white light filled all the rooms around the lobby and for a moment Kruza thought he saw the glyphs on the arch supports whirling and dancing. Kruza could not move or speak and Wheezer's frozen face with its half-finished warning cry was locked in its strange and terrified expression. The moment seemed to last forever.

Don't let it end, Kruza thought, knowing that it must.

'OOON'T!' Wheezer's cry finished as eight tall, grey-cloaked figures emerged from the eight archways. The man in the fourth arch from the left, standing right behind Wheezer, was lifting his arms. Kruza could see bone-pale, wasted forearms and gnarled, taloned hands emerging from the cloak. He could see nothing of the face beneath the hood. Wheezer stepped neatly to one side and stood against one of the tall columns that separated the arches, but the man kept coming. Straight for Kruza.

Kruza wanted to run. He wanted to run very badly. He could not.

He looked at Wheezer. The lad seemed to be shrugging.

He looked at his feet.

For the first time Kruza saw what he had stepped in to: the remains of an elaborate sand painting, criss-crossed with lines of black ash and swirls of cobalt and purple crystalline sand that Kruza did not recognise. He recognised only that this was a trap and he was caught in it.

Why are they taking so long? Kruza wondered, looking again at Wheezer. There was something flying through the air between them.

Kruza caught and snatched open the pouch Wheezer had thrown to him. Seeing what it was he dropped it onto the sand in disgust. An unlit scented beeswax candle, and a bunch of dried twigs and leaves, fell out of the pouch.

Kruza laid his right hand on the pommel of the short-sword which stuck out of his belt, under the back of his jacket. He took hold of the hilt and pulled it free, high over his head. His left hand came to join his right and he stood with his feet shoulder-width apart, knees slightly bent, four-square in front of the cloaked man who was still walking towards him.

I have all the time in the world, he thought as he bent his arms, bringing the short-sword up, at an angle, to shoulder height. Attack, his mind told him. He waited just a moment.

Kruza brought his sword down at the very moment the cloaked figure reached his hands out as if to strangle Kruza. The sound the sword made as it sliced into the side of the cloaked figure's neck was one of a blunt knife through a sheaf of dry paper. Never-the-less, there was blood. It gouted out of the wound in short, thick spurts, bright red in the white light, almost purple against the grey cloak.

Stunned, Kruza lifted his sword to strike again. Adjusting his stance, he realised that he had taken a step outside the sand trap. He was free of it. The bleeding man stood, his arms still in front of him, apparently unaware of the deep wide slash that had taken his head half off his body and ripped partway down into his torso. Then he sank slowly to his knees and his hands came down toward the sand.

'KKKRRRUUUZZZAAA!' Wheezer screamed.

Kruza looked up at the lad, who was pointing to the single foot that remained inside the edge of the sand painting. Kruza skipped to one side as the bleeding figure's taloned hands landed in the sand and it began to whirl with colour, coming to rest in its original pattern. The body of the cloaked figure was gone. So was the pouch and its spilled contents.

Seven remained.

The remaining cloaked men began to emerge from their archways in a kind of staggered formation. None of them saw Wheezer. They all saw Kruza.

He stepped forward again, looked once at Wheezer who remained pressed against the pillar, and once at his short-sword. The blood was gone, but the blade gleamed a promise to Kruza. The cut-purse didn't know if time had really slowed or whether it was the strange vitality in his body; whichever it was, it seemed to be working in his favour for the moment.

With the next two swings, one high and sloping, the second low and slicing, he took out two more of the grey men. He heard the paper sound again, but this time the blood remained on his sword. There was a path now between the men emerging from the right and left. Wheezer was standing right in front of him, flanked by two empty archways. Kruza looked once behind him, but the circle of men was too complete. They could not get out the way they had come. Facing front, he made a break for it, catching hold of Wheezer's arm as he went and spinning him into one of the antechambers.

Bathed for a moment in bright white light, the pair were confused. Then Wheezer saw another archway and they ran off through a series of underground chambers, which must have covered a large area beneath this part of the city.

'We need to get out of here!' Kruza managed to speak with confidence and at full volume for the first time since entering the cellar. 'We need to get back to the steps.' But Wheezer had already sprinted on, down a long, wide corridor with a high vaulted ceiling. It could almost have been a room if it wasn't for the fact that every few yards a wide archway or sometimes a door, led in to other places that dwarfed the connecting corridor.

Wheezer stopped, eyes wide, looking into a great, circular room, isolated on one side of the corridor. There were no other doorways and no windows in the large open space, but there was much more. A series of small carts and stretcher-wagons littered the room, some covered in tarpaulins, some brimming over with their contents spilling and scattering randomly across the room. There was also a large pile of clothes, some ragged and worn, but others quite respectable and even elegant. If these people were smugglers they were smuggling a very strange array and variety of goods.

Kruza had not thought for a long time that they might be smugglers. Something much bigger was going on here. Kruza did not know what it was and Wheezer seemed completely oblivious.

The youth was working his way over the piles, picking out the things he could carry easily, mostly jewellery, of which there was a great deal, and smaller household items that he could tuck into various pockets in his clothes. Wheezer began to pull the tarpaulins off the carts, first one at a time and then, in a great flurry of activity, he went round the whole lot, tearing covers dramatically from carts to reveal all manner of riches beneath. Kruza stood and stared, impressed that the kid could be so single-minded, so confident or perhaps just terminally oblivious to his situation. Then Kruza remembered the cellar lobby and the cloaked men that had attacked him there and realised the fact that essentially Wheezer was invisible and that, consequently Wheezer was safe. He, on the other hand, was not.

'Wheezer! Come on! We have to get out of here!'

'Look at all this stuff!' The other exclaimed eagerly. 'There's weeks' worth of quota here and we may not get the chance to come back!'

Kruza thought he would never come back even if he ever did get the chance. This had turned into a dangerous fool's errand and one he swore he would never repeat.

'Come on, Kruza! It's there to be taken!'

Wheezer turned and lifted the last tarpaulin from the last pile of goods. The biggest pile, wider and higher than a man, closest to the doorway on the opposite side. Kruza, who only stood in the doorway and watched, could not see this corner. The tarpaulin slid off in a fluid motion like silk on highly polished wood. It had no right to do that. The tarpaulin almost rippled as it fell to the floor with a whisper. It had no right, Kruza thought afterwards.

Wheezer stood back from the smugglers' great pile of goods, so that Kruza could see the look on his face. It had never looked whiter. His eyes were great grey, vacant orbs. Kruza strode across, grasping Wheezer by the elbow for fear the lad would faint, and looked to the corner where the tarpaulin lay. On the floor was a pile of bodies, strewn into a corner, stacked as a farmer might stack hay with a pitchfork. To begin with Kruza did not know what he was looking at. Then he began to make out arms and legs and torsos and one or two swollen heads. The bodies had no natural angles; they were so broken that they had no form. The pile might have been old clothes filled with sawdust that had spilled out. No one was left in these bodies. No life. They were like scarecrows. But they had been alive once. Wheezer saw it, but Kruza felt it.

Some little thing caught Kruza's eye and he moved gingerly toward the mountain of human debris. Grasped in the hand of a dead arm that appeared not to be attached to any other dead thing in the heap, was a long, broad chain made up of flat sections joined together with links at the corners. Hanging from the chain, which was big enough to go around a broad man's shoulders, was a talisman. A great scaled snake or dragon, eating its own tail.

Kruza could not bear to look at it. He turned the mesmerised Wheezer around by the arm and began to march him away from this place. He would rather walk back the way they had come and confront the grey cloaked figures than stay for a moment longer in this place.

They strode back up the arterial tunnel, both taking firm steps, feigning the confidence that Kruza knew he for one, did not feel. If he felt his fear now he was dead for sure. He could not feel it and he could not show it.

There was nothing to hear, but the cool slightly damp air of below ground had given way to the spoiled milk smell that wafted freely from chamber to chamber, becoming stronger as they neared the entrance.

Kruza felt sure they must come upon some of the grey cloaked men, but they did not. They walked solemnly, half scared, back to the place where they had come in. Wheezer's sense of direction was unerring, just as it was when he was above ground in the city. They were soon back in the white-lit chamber that they had run from. Kruza had been waiting all the time for the grey cloaked figures to follow them, but they had not. Wheezer stepped out into the archway, which led back into the entrance cellar, Kruza close behind him.

Before them they saw eight grey cloaked figures all standing with their backs to the central sand-painting that was whirling and coalescing. The sand was spinning like a small typhoon, rising up in spirals of cobalt, purple and black among the yellowish grey of the dust. All eight figures had their hands raised in a similar gesture to that of the first grey man that Kruza had killed. They could see eight pairs of withered arms and gnarled hands, taloned but old and lifeless. These were not smugglers. Kruza believed now that these were not even men. He had thrust his short-sword into them, three of them, and killed one. One had disappeared before his eyes. All three had now been replaced. Wheezer began to walk around the circle as the sand began to swirl more slowly, and losing height, but not shape, the whirlwind laid itself out in another intricate pattern on the floor.

As Kruza followed Wheezer, his mind whirling with panic and unanswerable questions, he saw the weapons. Each grey man was now armed with a pair of blades: a long, elegant sword with a narrow edge and heavily caged hilt and a shorter, slender dagger with a viciously curved hilt that would do serious damage to any blade it might encounter. Kruza's hand flew to the pommel of his own short-sword. He was never afraid of a brawl, but fighting off eight unknown entities with a total of sixteen blades was nothing short of madness. He would pull his own weapon only if attacked, otherwise he did not wish to provoke – only to leave.

Wheezer tried to shield Kruza from the cloaked men. He had become confident in his ability to remain so anonymous that he was virtually invisible. But Kruza was nervous, his adrenaline was pumping and he smelled of fear. Wheezer didn't know how long he could protect his friend and mentor, but he had got him into this.

The circle that was formed by the grey men began to change formation, always facing outward. The circle divided at the furthest point from Wheezer and Kruza and the figures at the two ends swung around, forming an arc that threatened to cut them off from their escape route.

Wheezer stood very still. Beads of sweat formed on Kruza's forehead, despite the chill that had fallen over the room, and he could feel his hair pasted to his head in sweat. It trickled down his back and dripped down his sides and the insides of his thighs. Kruza knew he had to wait for the attack, but felt panic rising with the gorge in his throat.

White light from the surrounding rooms glowed more strongly and the pattern at the centre of the room appeared to be giving off its own multi-coloured light, like a rainbow, rising straight and vertical from the floor.

The grey men had completed their arc. They lifted their arms away from their sides, straight out, parallel to the floor. When their blade tips touched they took a small step backward, widening the arc. Then all sixteen blades came forward together, pointing straight at Kruza.

He knew they could not all attack at once, not without killing each other, although perhaps that did not matter to them. The room was silent except for the sound of Kruza's breathing and the cold swish of blades in the air. He did not know whether his own body smell was worse, more acrid, than the smell of old, spoiled milk that was so intense now that it burned in his nostrils. His senses were heightened. He could feel every dink and dent in the pommel of his old short-sword. He moved his hand down and felt the cold hilt of the weapon. It was rough and beginning to flake, but it fit his hand now like nothing else could.

Wheezer stepped forward. They did not see him. He was not armed.

Kruza took one small sideways step, his back firmly against the wall. A grey-cloaked figure took a step toward him. Kruza had unsheathed his sword and swung it round, sending sparks from the wall behind him as the tip of the blade came into contact with stone. The sparks held in the air, vermilion for a moment, and then died. Swung hard, the short-sword disarmed the first assailant of his longer blade, leaving only the dagger. The grey cloaked figure chopped at the air, hoping to catch the blade of the short-sword and twist it, break it off.

Kruza thought he had never moved so fast. The short-sword came swinging low, below the line of the dagger. Its superior reach sliced, superficially, across his bizarre attacker's midriff, baring the flesh under the cloak, which stood out pale and unreal against the blood which oozed from it. Startled, the grey man looked down as Kruza swept his blade up through the figure from navel to sternum and beyond. The dagger dropped and the figure crawled away, his place taken instantly by another.

Kruza killed three of the men in grey. They were like automata, cold-blooded, thoughtless of the risk, and they fought with one style. Kruza began to catch the rhythm of their attack and was more confident, dispatching the third villain with a single, shoulder-high side-swipe. It was the only blow in the bout and it was deadly. Kruza heard the torn-paper sound and turned to rebut a new onslaught.

Wheezer watched the battle, unarmed and unregarded. Kruza forgot he was there.

The next three grey men, seeing their colleagues fall at the hand of the intruder, attacked together. Six blades moved close, weaving between each other, thrusting, parrying and rallying to attack again. Kruza fought hard and fast, his short-sword in three places at once, but he knew he was defeated. First came the long slash down his arm, his blood pouring down his sleeve and onto his free hand. He held the arm across his body, lest it become a weak point, and thrust with renewed vigour. Then came the slash to his head, curving down in an arc over his face, missing his eye, which was soon filling with blood from the long gash.

Wheezer looked on. No longer silent, he was shouting instructions and warnings to his friend and stamping in the sand.

Kruza was blind on one side and still he hadn't harmed any of his current assailants. He thrashed harder and stronger, turning to his blind side and fighting on, but the grey men were advancing and were close to ending the fray. The blow came soon and was almost welcome. He was struck in the shoulder. A long blade, thrust high and straight, made its way into his body through his leather jerkin – and out again through the back. There was little blood. The sword was steaming hot and cauterised the wound as it was withdrawn.

Kruza fell to his knees, his short-sword still gripped in his hand. His grasp had locked around it when his shoulder was opened and he could not let it go. He dropped his head, waiting for the fatal blow.

Wheezer stamped and screamed, but the five remaining figures did not flinch or turn. The youth let out a huge roar, ready to launch himself at the nearest grey man. But something made him look round. They took no notice of Wheezer. They didn't see him. But there was something they would take notice of.

Wheezer took half a dozen fast strides, almost running, to the centre of the cellar. Then he slid down onto his knees through the multi-coloured dust ornament that adorned the floor and which, until Kruza had dropped to the ground had, been giving off its eerie light.

Dust and sand flew everywhere and Wheezer found himself in the middle of the sand-painting on both knees, unable to move. He held his hands together, high in front of him, like he was praying, and, filling his lungs, he let out a blood curdling cry the like of which Kruza had never heard and hoped never to hear again.

'KKKKKRRRRUUUUZZAAAA!'

The scream hung in the room, echoing in circles around the vaulted ceiling, as though it would never escape.

The grey figures were turning away from him as Kruza heard the second cry.

'RRRRRRRUUUUUUNNNNNN!'

He did not think. He should have been dead and he had no idea if he could even stand, but he had no choice. Wheezer's screams compelled him.

Kruza stood, his arms crossed over his body. He staggered slightly. The sword still in his grasp made him look like some iconic statue of a great warrior-thief. He looked once at the backs of the grey men as they descended on the sand-painting. He did not see Wheezer. He turned and ran.

He ran up the stairs, out through the pitch-covered door and into the alley beyond. He ran out of the Nordgarten and didn't stop running until he reached the tall derelict house in the north of the Altquartier. All the time he ran he believed that Wheezer was right behind him. The lad had played bait, given himself the job of decoy so that Kruza could escape.

But the lad was invisible and he would escape, more easily than I, Kruza thought. *Wouldn't he?*

KRUZA WAITED for Wheezer. He slumped onto the couch in the attic room, and waited. When he awoke it was fully daylight and Wheezer had not come.

When he awoke the second time it was dark. The blood of his open wounds had dried and was flaking off onto the couch below him and Wheezer had still not come.

When he awoke a third time he found the energy to wash in the cold water on the washstand. He ate from Wheezer's windowsill larder. The bread was stale. The youth had not come.

Kruza did not know how long he had been in that room, but his wounds were scabbed and the food on the windowsill was gone or spoiled. Wheezer had still not come.

When it came light again, Kruza pulled himself off the couch and straightened the cushions. He emptied the cold, bloody water out of the wash bowl.

After an hour or so, Kruza left Wheezer's room, closing the door firmly behind him. On the stairs down he noticed that there were no footsteps showing in the thick layer of fresh dust. He slid out of the window, wounded shoulder first and closed it firmly behind him.

Kruza walked away. He knew, as surely as he had known the lad was a natural thief, that Wheezer wasn't coming back.

Mitterfruhl

A Wolf in the Fold

IT WAS THE milk-girl who saw them first.

On a late spring evening, one month past Mitterfruhl, the sky was a dark marble blue and the stars were out. Thousands of them, polished and glinting in the heavens.

The Ganmark family had ruled the border town of Linz, a cattle-market hub at the edge of the Drakwald, for sixteen generations. Two hundred years before, the serving Margrave had established the manor at the edge of the long lake, three miles from the town. The manor house itself was a fine dwelling, with farmlands adjoining, a park and splendid prospects across to the dark stands of the Drakwald to the east.

Lenya, the milk-girl, liked working there. The work was as hard as it had been on her father's little farm, but to work at the manor house, to live in the manor house, it was almost like living at the Graf's palace in far Middenheim. It felt like she was advancing herself. Her father had always said it would be one of her many older brothers who made something of himself but here she was, the last child, the only daughter, working at the Margrave's hall, thank you very much.

She had a straw bed in the servants' wing, and the food was always plentiful. She was only seventeen, but they were good to her – cook, the chamberlain, all the senior staff. Even the Margrave had smiled at her once. Her duties were simple: in the morning, collect the eggs, at night, perform the evening milking. In the meantime, polish, clean, scrub, peel or chop anything you were told to.

She liked the evening milking, especially at this time of year. The spring sky was so clear, and the stars were, well, perfect. Her mother had always told her to count the stars when you had the chance. To make sure they were all there. If an old star went out, bad luck was sure to follow.

As she crossed the stable yard to the dairy, she noticed there seemed to be more stars out that night than usual. Like the speckles on an egg, or the twinkling bubbles on the lip of the milk pail. So many. And that beautiful blue one down by the horizon…

New stars. A good sign, surely?

Then she saw the other new stars, stars in the tree-line above the manor house. Burning, hot stars, like eyes, like–

Lenya dropped the pail.

She realised they were torches, flaming torches held aloft in the black, armoured fists of three dozen sinister horseback warriors.

Even as she realised this, the raiders broke into a charge, thundering down on the manor house. They seemed to move like part of the darkness, as if the night was blurring, as if they were made of smoke. There was a strong scent in the night air, sweet but dusty-dry.

She cried out a little, in surprise and confusion.

Then she saw the other, smaller stars… the fires that were burning behind the matt-black visors and in the sockets of the flaring, infernal horses.

Lenya Dunst cried out again. Fiercely, lustily, she cried out for her life.

'IN THE NAME of Ulric, now we'll see some fine sport!' Morgenstern announced, bellowing a laugh. Around him, in the stable block of the Temple compound, his fellow knights of White Company joined his laugh, and playful comments flew back and forth. Thirteen powerful steeds were saddled and near readiness for action. There was power in the straw-floored stone chamber, the bridled power of great horses and potent fighting men.

'Ten shillings, I'll wager you,' Anspach said with a chuckle, 'I'll have badged my armour with the blood of the enemy by the first night! Yes, I will!' he roared at the hearty gainsayers all around.

'I'll take that,' Gruber said quietly.

There was a stunned silence. Gruber was the oldest and most worthy of the company, and everyone knew how he disapproved of rakish Anspach's wagering habits. But there had been a new spring in his step, a new fire in his eyes, since their great victory in the Drakwald before Mitterfruhl. Jurgen, their dear, lost leader, had been avenged, and honour had been returned to them. Of them all, Gruber most personified the reanimation of their spirits.

'Well?' Gruber asked the dumbstruck Anspach, a wry grin on his old, lined face.

Anspach roared and stuck out a mailed fist. 'Done!' he cried.

'And done!' Gruber agreed with a more mirthful laugh.

'Now that's the spirit of the company I like to see!' howled the huge warrior Morgenstern and clapped his hands together.

Off to his right, the company's young standard bearer, Aric, smiled and made a final check of his mount's saddle. Straightening up amidst the hubbub, he caught the eye of youthful Drakken. Drakken was barely twenty, just a wolf cub really, transferred into their company to replace one of the brave souls they had lost in the Drakwald raid. He was a short, yet powerful, stocky young man, and Aric had seen his skill with the horse and hammer in practice, but he was completely inexperienced, and was certainly overawed by the boisterous, oathing company.

Aric crossed to him.

'All ready?' he asked, good-naturedly. Drakken quickly set to his saddle again, trying to look efficient.

'Relax,' said Aric. 'It was only yesterday I was like you: a virgin to war, and to the company of Wolves like these. Go with it, and you'll find your place.'

Drakken gave him a nervous grin. 'Thanks. I just feel like an outsider in this... this family.'

Aric smirked and nodded. 'Yes, this is a family. A family who lives and dies together. Trust us, and we'll trust you back.'

He cast a glance round the room, and picked out a few of the rowdy company for Drakken's benefit. Each of the warriors wore the gold-edged grey plate armour and white wolf pelt of the Temple. 'Morgenstern there. He's a prize-winning ox, and he'll drink you under any table anywhere. But he's got a good heart and heavy hammer. Gruber... stick close by him;

no one has the experience or sheer courage of that man. Anspach… never trust his judgement or take his wagers, but trust his right arm. A fury on the field. Kaspen, the red-headed fellow there – he's our surgeon too. He'll see to any wounds you collect. Einholt and Schell, why they're the best trackers we have. Schiffer, Bruckner, Dorff – great horsemen all.'

He paused.

'And remember you're not alone in being new. Lowenhertz also transferred in, same time as you.'

Their eyes wandered across to the last knight, who was alone in the stable corner, checking his horse's shoeing.

Lowenhertz was a tall, regal-looking man, handsome and aquiline. It was said he had noble blood, though Morgenstern had sworn this was a bastard heritage. He was quiet and aloof, almost as quiet and reserved as Einholt, if that was possible. Ten years he'd served in the White Wolves, first in Red Company, then Grey. It seemed he had never found a place to suit him, or one that wanted him perhaps. No one knew why he had come to them, though Anspach wagered it was because he was biding his time until a command came up. Gruber thought so too, and that was enough for all of them.

'Lowenhertz?' murmured Drakken. 'He's not new blood like me. He's had time in the companies, and he… he has an air to him. He frightens me.'

Aric thought about this and nodded. 'Me too.'

Their conversation was shut off by the slamming open of the stable door. Ganz, the young company commander, resplendent in full plate and wolfskin, strode in.

'This is it…' Kaspen murmured.

'Moment of truth,' Schell agreed, his whipcord face tense with anticipation.

Dorff broke off from a wavering, tuneless whistle.

'Well, sir?' Anspach asked.

Ganz faced them. 'We ride for Linz at once–'

He had to wave down their cheering. 'Enough! Enough! Lads, it's not the glory we were hungry for. I've just had our orders conveyed by the High Priest himself.'

'And? What does the old fart have to say?' Morgenstern asked raucously.

'Respect, please, Morgenstern!' Gruber yelled.

'My apologies, old friend! I should have said what does *his highness* the old fart have to say?'

Ganz looked sad and tired. He sighed. 'Three companies of Knights Panther have been sent out to Linz to hunt down these raiders and make sure no harm befalls the town itself. We must go to provide… escort.'

'Escort?' Gruber said.

The silence which followed was total.

'The Margrave, his family and many of his household staff escaped the raid that burned his manor. As you know, Linz owes fealty to the Graf here in Middenheim, and his excellency the Graf is most concerned for his cousin the Margrave's safety. A long story cut short, we are to escort the Margrave's entourage back here to the city to keep him and his safe.'

There was an audible, collective groan.

'So the Panthers get the glory?' Anspach mused. 'They get to hunt down and battle these raiding jackals while we get nurse maid duty?'

Ganz could do nothing but shrug. 'Technically, it's an honour…' he began.

Morgenstern said something both uncomplimentary and physically challenging about 'honour'.

'All right, old friend,' Ganz said, unamused. 'Let's just do the job we've been asked to. Mount up. White Company rides with me.'

It was two days' hard ride to Linz. Late spring rain, brisk and horizontal, washed across the meadows and trackways as they rode. Then the pale sun came out again.

They could see the ruins of the Ganmark manor from several miles away, and smell it even before that. Dark, almost oily smoke hung in the air like a sinuous raincloud against the spring afternoon and there was a curious smell, like sweetmeats and spices mixed with the ash from a funeral urn.

Riding beside Ganz, Gruber wrinkled his nose. The young commander looked over at him.

'Gruber? What is it?'

Gruber cleared his throat and spat sideways as if to rid his mouth of the smell on the breeze. 'No idea. Like nothing I've ever smelt.'

'Not in this part of the land,' said a voice from beside them. Ganz and Gruber looked over to see the chiselled profile of Lowenhertz. The tall knight rode in beside them, skilled and coolly measured.

'What do you mean, brother?' asked Gruber.

Lowenhertz smiled a not entirely friendly smile. 'My great grandfather was a Knight Panther. Went on two crusades into those hellish distant lands of heat and dust. When I was a child, he used to tell stories of the ancient tombs and mausoleums, the dry, deathless things that haunted the nights. He told me stories. I remember them clearly, stood in his old solar, where he kept his books and mementoes, the old armour, the banners and gonfalons. There was always a smell in that old room – mortuary dust, dry bones, and the sweet pungent stench of the grave spices. He always told me it was the smell of death from the far-off tombs of Araby.'

He shrugged. 'I can smell it once more. And so much stronger than I did in my great grandfather's solar in childhood.'

Ganz was silent as their horses jogged on through the open meadow. Small, green butterflies, early risers in the fresh spring, whirled in formation across their path. Ganz looked ahead, down the sweep of the valley, to the blackened timber skeleton which was all that remained of Ganmark manor. Smoke still curled up, like dark fingers clawing the air.

'I'd take it as a personal favour, Lowenhertz, if you didn't share such observations with the rest of the men.'

Lowenhertz nodded curtly. 'Of course, commander.' With that he spurred his mount forward and rode ahead of them down the winding track.

AT THE GATES of Linz, an honour-guard squadron of Panther Knights rode out to meet them, haughty and resplendent in their decorative, high-crested helms and armour. Their captain saluted Ganz stiffly and the White Wolf returned the greeting. There was little love lost between the Templars of Ulric and the regal warriors of the Graf's household bodyguard.

'Sigmar bring you safe! Captain von Volk, Knights Panther, Graf's First Royal Household.'

'Ulric look to you! Ganz, Commander, White Company.'

'Welcome to Linz, Commander, I stand relieved.'

The Panther captain fell in beside Ganz and his men rode around in a precision display until they were perfectly flanking the Wolf formation as an escort. The Panthers were in precise line, and even the light hoofbeats of their graceful steeds was in perfect time, compared to the powerful, tired syncopation of the straggled and dusty Wolves. Ganz felt someone was showing off.

'Glad you're finally here, Commander Ganz,' von Volk said curtly. 'We've been chafing to get off after these creatures, but of

course we couldn't leave the Margrave and his entourage unde-
fended.'

Ganz nodded. 'You've sent scouting parties out?'

'Of course. Four field groups. They've had no success, but I
feel confident that once I field my entire force I'll have these
raiding scum good and proper.'

From behind them, Gruber snorted with quiet derision.

Von Volk turned in his saddle. He was a tall, thin, fierce man
with bright, flitting eyes. They lustred behind the golden grille
of his ceremonial visor. 'What's that, soldier? Oh, I'm sorry, old
man... were you just talking in your sleep?'

Gruber did not rise to it. 'Nothing, sir. Just clearing my
throat.'

Von Volk turned away without a care. The silk draperies of his
helmet's crest fluttered out behind him. 'Commander Ganz, the
Margrave awaits you in the Guild Hall. I'd like you to have him
and his party away by dusk.'

'And travel at night?' Ganz was all reason and charm. 'We'll
leave at dawn, captain. Even a raw recruit knows that is the best
time to embark on an escort drill.'

Von Volk scowled.

'Mobilise your men and get on your way,' Ganz added. 'We'll
take it from here. Good hunting.'

'MY DEAR, DEAR fellow!' the Margrave of Linz said, pumping
Ganz's hand. 'My dear, dear fellow! How we've waited for you!'

'Sir,' Ganz managed. The vast panelled chamber of the Guild
Hall was full of baggage crates and rolled carpets. Around it
hung the twenty or so servants and staff who had escaped the
raid on the manor.

And presumably carried this stuff to safety, Ganz mused. *How in
the name of Ulric do you roll a carpet during an attack?*

The Margrave, a portly, pale aristocrat in his late thirties, had
put on his best robes to greet the Wolves, but sticking-out tufts
of hair and an overwhelming scent of clove oil told that he had-
n't seen decent sanitation since the attack.

'I asked for Wolves, most particularly,' said the Margrave. 'In
my letter to my dearest cousin, the Graf, I requested Wolves
above all, a company of Wolves. Oh, let the gaudy Panthers do
the hunting work, but give me Wolves to see me and my family
home.'

'The Panthers are fine warriors. They'll find your attackers,'
Ganz said smoothly, not believing it for a moment. 'But,

assuredly, we'll get you home. Now how many are you?'

The Margrave ushered him around. 'We fill three coaches and four baggage carts. Sixteen servants, the luggage, plus myself and my children, and their nurse…'

He pointed to a pair of ghastly, knickerbockered five year olds who were thumping each other ferociously on a pile of rugs. An elderly and emaciated black-robed nurse watched over them.

'Hanz and Hartz!' sighed the Margrave, clasping his palms together. 'Aren't they adorable?'

'Unbearably,' Ganz said.

'And then, of course, there's my wife…' the Margrave added.

Ganz looked round as indicated. Her ladyship was pouring drinks for the thirsty Wolves herself, from pitchers her servants carried.

She was tall, shapely and hypnotically beautiful. Her dark, ringletted, luxuriant hair ran all the way down to the extraordinary curve her hips made in her sheer silk gown. Her skin was pale, her eyes dark and deep like pools. Her lips were full and red and–

Ganz turned back to look at the ugly children very quickly.

'They're not hers, of course,' the Margrave continued. 'Their dear, dear mother died in childbirth. Gudrun and I married last year.'

Gudrun, thought Ganz. *Ulric! Heaven has a name!*

'WINE FOR YOU, brave knight?' she asked softly.

Gruber took the beaker and gazed at the vision before him. 'Thank you, lady,' he said. She was amazing. Quite the most beautiful woman he had ever seen; dark, exotic, mysterious… yet here she was serving all these dirty, stinking warriors wine. Serving them by hand herself.

'You are our salvation, sir,' she said to him, perhaps noticing his puzzled look. 'After our nights of terror and pain, this is the least I can do.'

'She's amazing…' Anspach breathed, clutching his untouched goblet as she moved on.

'If I was thirty years younger and a hundredweight lighter…' Morgenstern began.

'You'd still be a fat old wastrel with no chance!' Einholt finished.

'Lord Ulric above us,' Drakken murmured to Aric. 'She's quite lovely…'

Aric couldn't take his eyes off the Margrave's wife, and he nodded before realising Drakken wasn't looking at her at all.

'Drakken?'

'Her, Aric.' Drakken smiled and pointed to a young girl huddled amid the servants. She was barely eighteen by Aric's guess, short and trim, but dirty and soiled from the adventures that had overtaken her, and dressed in a milk-maid's smock. She was… pretty, he had to admit.

'Drakken!' Aric hissed. 'First rule of Wolfhood… if a goddess gives you wine, you don't drool after her cherubs.'

'What goddess?' asked Drakken, staring at the milk-girl.

Aric smiled and shook his head.

THEY LEFT LINZ at dawn. The carts and coaches rolled out in line, flanked by the thirteen Wolf Knights, into the rich dawn mist.

At the head of the column, Ganz called Gruber, Anspach and Lowenhertz to him.

'Ride ahead. Scout the woods,' he told them. They spurred away.

Aric, the standard of the company held aloft, moved up beside Ganz.

'Drakken needs some purpose to settle his nerve, sir,' Aric said.

Ganz thought for a moment. 'You're right,' he said at last and called back for the youngest knight. Drakken rode forward eagerly.

'Join the scouts,' Ganz said. 'They could use an extra hand.'

Smiling fit to split his face, Drakken charged forward at a gallop off into the smoky woodland.

ANSPACH REINED up sharply. For a moment, he had almost lost his bearings in the mist. The sun was up, but there was barely any light amidst the swirling vapour and dark trees.

'What was that?' he said to Gruber, just a few yards away.

'Probably Lowenhertz,' said Gruber. 'He went off to the left.'

'No!' said Anspach sharply, heeling down his prick-spurs deep to turn his horse hard. 'With me, Gruber! Now!'

The two warriors plunged through the woodland, kicking up dirt and wafting the mist. They caught a sweet and dry smell of ash. Anspach freed his hammer from its clasp.

They found Drakken in a clearing. His horse was dead, and so was one of the black knights who had ambushed him. Drakken's grey plate armour was ripped open and his shoulder

was gashed, but still he screamed fiercely, swirling his warhammer to crack another head as he had the skull of the man who
brought him down.

He was surrounded.

There were four more dark warriors, each clad in strangely
angular black plate armour with spike-pointed, almost bulbous
helmets. They swung dark blue, serrated swords that hooked
into fang-like curves, and a fine mesh of chainmails rattled
around their waists. Their horses were huge and black, and, like
the knights themselves, their eyes glowed with an internal fire.
There was something almost insubstantial about the edges of
them, about the hem of their swirling cloaks, as if they were
solidifying out of the mist and darkness itself. The smell of
sweet spice and ash was intense.

Drakken ducked a swing that severed a young tree behind
him. Anspach and Gruber leapt their horses forward to avoid
the crashing timbers and branches.

Gruber swung his hammer round and came about. The nearest of these almost ghostly raiders filled Gruber's nose with the
dry, dead stink and swung forward with his sword.

Anspach and his horse exploded into the gap between them
and he crushed the enemy's head with a downward blow of his
warhammer. The matt-black spiked helmet shattered and dark
fumes billowed out as the glowing eyes went dark.

Gruber found another two on him hard, slashing with their
venomous hookswords, relentless.

'Ulric curse you!' he spat, battling for a break.

Lowenhertz blasted out of the mist and undergrowth, his
horse at full leap.

His whizzing hammer smashed the first warrior out of his
saddle, and then with a skilled and powerful reverse turn,
Lowenhertz broke the chest of Gruber's second attacker.

The remaining dark warrior spurred forward with a raucous,
unintelligible curse, his red eyes blazing from behind his visor
slit, his vile horse wretched and stinking.

Anspach swung his hammer round sideways over his shoulder and destroyed the last warrior outright.

For a moment, the impact resounded around the deadened
clearing.

Anspach leapt down and helped the shaken Drakken up.

'Well done, youth! You're a Wolf now, no mistake.'

Gruber turned to Lowenhertz.

'Thanks go to you. You saved my life,' he said.

'Think nothing of it,' said Lowenhertz. He gazed down at the bodies of the foes. Inside the rent-open armour of the nearest, nothing but powdery bones could be seen, flaking away like ash in the breeze.

There was a long, chill silence.

'In the name of Ulric!' Gruber hissed, fear clawing deep. 'Let's get back to the convoy!'

'THE DEAD DON'T lie still,' Gruber murmured to Ganz as they rejoined the halted train. Anspach was helping the injured Drakken to a cart, and Kaspen had dismounted to tend the young man's injury. Lowenhertz rode in silently, a way behind Gruber. A hush had fallen when the four warriors had returned, the bloody Drakken sharing Anspach's horse, all of them flecked with dark smudges of blood. Ganz was dreadfully aware of the way the Margrave's people stared at his men in fixed horror and silent alarm.

'Don't riddle, report!' he hissed.

Gruber shook his head, fear still shaking him, easing off his mailed gauntlets. 'We met a bevy of dark... things – Ulric save our souls! They were not... mortal! No doubt the very same abominations who took down the Ganmark Manor. Caught Drakken but by Ulric's teeth he gave them what for. We did the rest, Lowenhertz, the lion's share. But they're out there. Ulric help us, commander! These things are spectres!'

'You mean ghosts?' asked Ganz, in a tight whisper.

'I do not know what I mean! I have never met their like before!'

Ganz cursed. 'Hundreds of miles of forest and farmland, Knights Panther hunting for them, and they stumble on us! What are the chances?'

'What are the chances?' cut in Lowenhertz quietly but significantly. He seemed to appreciate the commander's urge to keep the talk out of civilian earshot. 'They raid the manor, then they find us...' He trailed off.

'What do you mean?' Aric asked, easing his grip on the lofty standard.

'I mean: maybe they're after something. Something that was in the manor, something that's here with us now!'

There was a long silence. Horses whinnied and shook off flies.

Ganz wiped his fist across his mouth. 'You seem to be remarkably well-informed, Master Lowenhertz,' he said finally.

'What do you mean?' answered the knight, his eyes hooded.

'You seem to know much of the ways of darkness,' said Ganz frankly.

Lowenhertz laughed out loud. There was little humour in it, but it shook the clearing and made everyone look.

'It is merely logic, commander... these creatures have wit. They are not brute beastfolk, not savage greenskins from the rockslopes. They move with a purpose; they have a meaning and a task to all they do. This is not a random chance.'

'Then we'll be careful,' said Ganz, simply.

'We should try to discern the nature of their purpose, sir. Perhaps by–'

Ganz cut Lowenhertz short. 'We will be careful,' he repeated more firmly. 'Aric go check and see Drakken is comfortable and ready to move. We will ride on.'

He looked down as the Margrave hurried up on foot from his carriage. He was attended by two servants who scrambled after him and his face was not happy.

'Are we in danger, sir knight?' he asked breathlessly.

'You are in the company of Wolves, noble sir,' Ganz said gracefully. 'You requested us, I seem to recall, and knew we would see you safe...'

'Aye, indeed! I don't mean to doubt... But still... Are they still out there?'

'On my honour, Margrave, on the honour of my men and the in the name of Ulric who guides us, we will be safe.'

By his side, Gruber sat back in the saddle. He was still shaking from the combat, his pulse thundering. *Too much, too hard for an old man*, he thought. His eyes scanned the carriage train as they made ready to move out.

In the door window of the Margrave's wagon, he caught sight of the nobleman's wife. She gazed out from the shadows, a wicked smile on her lips.

Gruber looked away. He wished to dear heaven he had not seen her look.

Aric rode back to the cart where Drakken was being minded. It carried several of the kitchen staff and the elderly nurse of the noble children. Drakken did not seem to notice. The milk-maid, Lenya, was vigorously helping Kaspen dress his wounds.

'Keep them clean and dry, and watch for infection,' Kaspen told her.

'I know what to do, Red-hair,' she nodded curtly, obediently.

Lenya stared aggressively down into Drakken's eyes as Kaspen got down off the wagon and balled up a cloth from the bowl of water to wring it out.

'I'll look after you, Wolf. Don't worry. I've tended to my brothers' wounds and scrapes often enough, many worse than this,' she said.

'I… I thank you,' said Drakken, a foolish smile on his face.

Aric watched them, chuckled and rode back to Ganz.

'Drakken's as happy as a cub,' he told the commander.

'Then we ride. Move on!' cried Ganz. 'Move on!'

AT NIGHTFALL, they camped on a rocky slope overlooking a bend in a nameless stream. The Wolves built watch-fires all around the perimeter and stood in guard shifts all through the night.

At midnight, Ganz did his round of the duty. He passed a few moments with Einholt and the hulking Bruckner at their posts as the rest of the party settled down for sleep.

Crossing to check on Aric, Ganz saw a dark shape out beyond the edge of the firelight.

He stiffened and crept out into the darkness, his hand sliding his hunting knife from its sheath.

'Lowenhertz!' he hissed.

The knight turned in surprise, lowering a beautiful brass astrolabe through which he had been sighting the heavens.

'Commander?'

'What in the name of the Wolf are you doing out here?'

'It is difficult to take accurate readings close to the firelight,' Lowenhertz began.

'Readings?'

'Of the stars, commander. To see if any strange patterns or manifestations could be discerned. My great-grandfather taught me that celestial signs and augurs accompanied the machinations of the deathless ones…'

Ganz cut him off, angry and snarling. 'I now see why you have never made command yourself! They don't trust you, do they? Our Temple elders don't trust you with the lives of men because you are too far gone, too close to the darkness itself!'

Lowenhertz paused and frowned. 'Oh!' he said at last. 'I see. Commander, you think it's me, don't you? You think I'm a part of this danger?'

'I–' began Ganz, wrong-footed.

Lowenhertz laughed as if at a truly rich joke. 'Forgive me, sir. I am just what I seem to be: a loyal servant of Ulric whose mind sometimes asks too many questions! My father was a Knight Panther. He died at Antler Hill, torn open by the hounds of Chaos. I have always sought to be one step ahead, to know more of my foe than they know of me, to serve the Temple as best as my body – and mind – are able. I would not have you distrust me! But if I can serve you and you can trust me…'

There was a long silence. Ganz extended his hand for the astrolabe. 'So have you found anything?' he said quietly.

DRAKKEN CURLED UP in the rolls of carpet behind the wagon and relaxed in the firelight. A shadow fell over him and he blinked up out of his half slumber. Lenya was there, her smile luminous in the shadows.

'Are you thirsty, knight?' she asked.

'My name is Drakken,' he said. 'Krieg Drakken. I wish you would call me that.'

'I will, Krieg. On two conditions. One, if you tell me you're thirsty and two if you call me Lenya.'

'I am thirsty, Lenya,' he said softly.

She snorted and turned away to fetch a drink.

Drakken settled back and closed his eyes. His shoulder ached, but all in all this was turning out to be a fine debut as a White Wolf.

A shadow fell across him again.

'I hope the water is cool…' he began, then tailed off when he realised it wasn't the returning Lenya. The old nurse crouched down by him.

'Calm now, my little pet,' she said warmly. 'Oh, but I know I'm not so handsome as yon milk-maid, but I care as much for the well-being of my guardians. And you have had a long day.'

Drakken relaxed and smiled. Her tone was so reassuring and calm. No wonder she made her life as the custodian of children.

'I only stopped by to bless you, my lamb,' she said and reached into the neck of her smock. 'I have a lucky charm, given me by my mother years ago. I would have you take it in your hand to speed you to health.'

The nurse held out a glittering amulet attached to a long cord around her neck. Its mount was pewter, but the thing itself was a curve of glass, shaped like a claw, a fragment perhaps of something else, something very old.

'Always brought me luck and health,' she said.

He smiled and took it in his hand. It felt warm.

'Now blessing be on you, my poor wounded knight. The blessing of all the gods.'

'Thank you, lady,' Drakken said. He felt warmer, safer, more whole.

'Now Lenya returns with a cup of water,' said the nurse, taking back the charm and getting up. 'You'll have no more time with an old fool like me. Be safe, knight.'

'Again, thank you,' said Drakken.

Then Lenya was at his side again, offering the cup to his lips.

'Old Maris fussing over you again?' she said with a grin. 'She's so kind. The children dote on her. The Margrave was lucky to find her last year when he needed a wet-nurse.'

'She's a fine old lady, and very caring,' said Drakken between sips. 'But I know who I would wish to have care for me...'

'DO YOU MAKE a habit of spying on women?' asked the Margrave's wife with a delicious curl to her lips.

Gruber stopped in his tracks and fumbled for the right words. 'I was patrolling the camp, my lady.'

'And that brought you back behind my carriage as I was dressing for bed?' she returned.

Gruber turned away, too conscious of the fact he was in the company of a woman who wore little more than a satin shroud. 'I apologise, lady. I–'

'Oh hush, knight!' she said with a chiming laugh. 'I'm flattered a man as worthy and distinguished as you would blush in my company. I appreciate your efforts. We are all in your care.'

Gruber shifted awkwardly and then turned to go.

'What is your name, knight?'

'Wilhelm Gruber,' he said, turning back. He felt suddenly bold. 'Who are you, lady?'

'The wife of the Margrave of Linz, unless that had passed you by,' she replied, laughing again.

'Is that all?' he asked sharply.

She said nothing in return. There was a long silence.

'You'd best return to your patrol, Gruber,' she said at last. 'I don't know what you think I am, but I'm not happy at the implications.'

'Neither am I, lady,' Gruber said as he strode away. 'We'll see.'

GANZ WATCHED THE stars through the polished lenses of Lowenhertz's astrolabe. He was about to ask the name of another constellation when Lowenhertz gripped his arm hard.

'What?'

'Quiet!' hissed Lowenhertz. 'You smell that?'

Ganz inhaled. The sweet, ashy flavour of death as unmistakable.

They ducked low, and saw the glowing eye slits of warriors moving down in the vale by the stream.

'I have nothing but my knife!' whispered Ganz.

Lowenhertz tossed him his warhammer and pulled a long war-axe from his saddlebag.

'Give the word, commander. They've come back for us.'

IT WAS A dark blur of night and firelight. Ganz thought he counted fifteen of the foe as they charged the camp from the east on foot. They were silent, the shades of the dead.

Ganz was not silent. He bellowed his warning as loud as his lungs could bear, and he and Lowenhertz leapt across the stream-side rocks to meet the silent charge.

The camp came to life. Hallowing answers came from the sentries, and roars from the sleeping men as they roused. Screams and cries rose from the terrified civilians.

Einholt met the first of the attackers, blocking and whirling his warhammer as he bayed out a call to his wolf brothers. In five seconds, Bruckner and Aric, the other two sentries on duty, were by his side, blocking the passage between the crackling watch fires against the red-eyed ghouls that swept out of the night.

Ganz and Lowenhertz were with them a few seconds later.

There were at least twenty of the attackers now, Ganz was certain, but it was so hard to disentangle their dank shapes from the night, or their flashing eyes from the blazing fires. It was as if they were made out of the night itself.

A gleaming jet blade whistled past his head and Ganz swung back to guard himself. In doing so, his feet slipped on the earth and he half stumbled. The dark one rose up over him, blade poised. Morgenstern, only half-armoured and bedraggled from slumber, burst through the darkness and laid the creature low with a two-handed hammerblow of huge force. Ganz leapt up and called his thanks to the man-mountain, who was already driving on into the press.

He saw Aric fall, gashed in the shoulder. Einholt and Lowenhertz leapt to block him, standing their ground as he pulled himself up again. Lowenhertz's axe whistled in the cold air.

With wolf-fire in his blood, Ganz spun his borrowed hammer, used the haft to block a hard sword swing, and then slew his attacker with a sideways smash of the hammerhead.

'For the Temple! For Ulric! White Company!' he bellowed.

ACROSS IN THE camp: pandemonium. Hammer held tight, Gruber tried to marshal the chaos.

'Kaspen! Anspach! Get the Margrave and his people into cover by the wagons! The rest of you forward to fight!'

Screaming servants and crying children ran in every direction. Cook pots and fire hearths were upset and kicked over.

'Damn it!' Gruber cursed.

He saw Drakken limping into the centre of the camp as fast as he could manage. 'My weapon! Any weapon!' cried the young man hoarsely.

'You're more use to me here!' Gruber shouted. 'Get the children in a wagon. Keep their heads down!'

There was another scream, more piercing than before. Gruber wheeled and saw two dark warriors had burst into the encampment from the opposite direction to the main attack, a sneak pincer to get round the cordon. They charged in towards the wagons.

It was the Margrave's wife who had screamed. She was in the open, trying to catch hold of her two terrified children. The nurse was by her side, trying to scoop the boys into her arms. The warriors bore down on them, swords raised.

Gruber raced forward, lashing out a one-handed hammer swing that shattered armour and knocked one of them to the earth. The other he met and blocked, glancing his hammer haft against the slashing blade once, twice, three times to ward off the deadly swings. By then, the first dark warrior was back on his feet.

Gruber dented the helm of the second one and sent him sprawling in time to meet the renewed attack of the first. He stared into the red-lit slits and met the furious assault, swinging a blow that smashed its shield. Then he stabbed hard with the butt of the haft, connecting with jaw. The foe went down and this time a well-placed blow ensured it would not rise again.

The second one was upright again now, intent on the Margrave's wife once more.

With a roar, Gruber hurled his hammer. The great, spinning weapon swooshed across the clearing in flickering circles and broke the creature's back.

Gruber crossed to the Margrave's wife and helped her up. The nurse gathered up the children.

'Get to the wagons!' he hissed.

'Th-thank you…' she stammered.

'They were hell-bent on getting to you,' Gruber snarled, fixing her eyes with his. 'What is it about you? Are you the jinx who brings this darkness down?'

'No!' she implored, horrified, 'No!'

There was no time for debate. Gruber recovered his hammer and rejoined the fight.

'THEY'RE RETREATING!' Anspach announced at last.

'Thank the Wolf!' murmured Ganz. The fight had been intense, and too close for comfort. Several of his men were wounded, and there were seven dark warriors twisted, skeletal and dead on the ground. The others, like the wraiths of fairy tales, melted away into the trees.

'Regroup!' Ganz told his men, 'Let's get inside the camp and build up the firewall. There's a long time till dawn.'

'Commander!' Gruber was calling.

Ganz joined him. The warrior whose back Gruber had snapped was still alive, twitching and hissing like a reptile on the ground. The civilians stood round in a wide, fascinated horrified circle.

'Clear these people aside!' Ganz snapped to Dorff and Schiffer. He turned to Gruber. 'I'm beginning to think Lowenhertz is right. We have something or someone these creatures want – that's why they took the manor and now hound us.'

'I agree. This was not a raid, this was a mission to retrieve. They were too direct, putting themselves at risk to get into the camp rather than harry us from a distance.' Gruber took a deep breath. 'I believe it's part of the Margrave's household, and I think I know what…'

'You think it's me,' said a voice from behind them. It was the Margrave's wife, clutching one of the sobbing children. 'I don't know what I've done to earn your mistrust, Sir Gruber. I can only imagine that you are threatened by me. All my life, my dark looks and lively manner have made men imagine me some she-devil, some brazen thing to be feared. Can I help my looks, or my appetite for life? Can I help the way I was made? I am no daemon. On my life – on the lives of my children, sirs! – I am not the root of this!'

Ganz looked over at his second-in-command. The older, white-haired man dropped his gaze to the earth.

'Seems both of us have jumped to conclusions today, old man. Both of us wrong.'

'You too?' Gruber asked.

Ganz nodded. 'Milady, take the children to cover in the wagons. We will finish this. Lowenhertz!'

The noble knight arrived. His chest plate and shoulder armour had been badly damaged in the fight and so he was stripped to his woollen pourpoint now.

'Commander?'

'You have learning, Lowenhertz… or so you like to tell me. How do we get information from our guest here?'

Lowenhertz looked down at the crippled dark one and sank to his haunches. He listened for a moment and shuddered. 'I can make little out from its rasping… the language… perhaps it is the tongue of far Araby. There is one word it repeats…' Lowenhertz thickly repeated the word back to the creature with distaste. It stirred and hissed and yelped. The White Wolf then muttered the low, guttural word again.

Ganz turned. 'We're getting nowhere…'

Lowenhertz tried the sentence again until the creature replied at last with a guttural response of his own.

'I don't understand him. The words are too strange.' Lowenhertz tried harder, repeating the word. It was no good.

Then the creature reached out and with a bony hand drew a curved symbol in the dust.

'What is that?' asked Ganz.

'I wish I knew,' said Lowenhertz. 'I cannot understand him. That picture makes no sense. What is that? A harvest moon? A crescent?'

'It's a claw,' said Drakken suddenly, from behind them. 'And I know where it is.'

THE OLD NURSE, Maris, backed away against the wagon, terror in her eyes and her hands clutched tight to the throat of her dress.

'No!' she said. 'No! You shan't have it!'

Ganz looked round at Drakken and Lowenhertz at his side.

'She's just the wet-nurse,' he said.

'She has the amulet, shaped like a claw. She blessed me with it,' Drakken said.

'If it is what these creatures of darkness seek, lady, you must give it up for all our sakes,' Lowenhertz firmly said.

'This trinket my old dam gave me?' stammered the old woman. 'It's always brought me luck.'

Gruber joined them. 'This makes sense of it. Those warriors I fought... I thought they were after the Lady and her children, but they were after the nurse.'

The Margrave and his wife approached.

'Please, sir!' the old woman cried. 'Make them stop this nonsense.'

'Dear Maris,' the lady pleaded, 'you have always been kind to my children, so I will defend you from harm, but this is too important. Let us prove this. Give me the charm.'

Wizened hands shaking, the old woman produced the claw talisman and handed it to the Margrave's wife. She turned and marched across to the stricken foe. Ganz made to stop her, but Gruber held him back.

'She knows what she's doing, that one,' he told his commander.

'Lenya told me the nurse had only been with them for a while. Her predecessor had fallen ill and she was brought in from far away,' said Drakken.

Lowenhertz nodded. 'If this malign charm has been in her family for some time they may have known nothing of its power. But it has brought them after her every step of the way. They have caught her scent – or the scent of the thing she owns.'

'But what is it?' asked Aric.

'The talon of some dark daemon they worship? The shed nail of a god?' Lowenhertz shrugged. 'Who knows? Who wants to know?'

'A man of learning like you?' Ganz asked.

Lowenhertz shook his head. 'There are some things better left un-known, commander.'

The Margrave's wife showed the charm to the broken creature and then jumped back as it reared up, snarling and mewling, clawing at her.

Gruber slew it with a quick, deft blow.

'There's our proof,' he stated.

Everyone froze as a keening sounded through the forest around them. The grave-smell of spice and dry bone wafted around them again.

'They have the scent again, fresher than ever,' said Lowenhertz. 'They're coming back.'

'To arms!' Gruber cried, rallying the men.

Ganz held up his hand. 'We'd never take them. They have superior numbers and the night on their side. We barely drove them back before. There is only one way.'

The White Company and their civilian charges drew into a huddle at the centre of the firelight. Beyond the ring of flame, they saw the dark riders approach and heard their hooves. Dozens of red eyes glowed against the blackness, like infernal stars.

Ganz counted the dark shapes out beyond the fire. Once again, there were twenty, despite the number the Wolves had killed. He swore softly. 'They will always return at full strength,' he whispered to Gruber. 'We will never wear them down. We cannot fight because they will overwhelm us. We cannot run because they will outstrip us. They are driven beings of the dark who will not stop until they have what they want.'

The foe stood beyond the flames, a ring of evil forms that circled the camp entirely. The sweet ashen smell was wretched.

'Then what do we do? Fight to the last? Die in the name of Ulric?' Gruber whispered.

'That… or deny them,' said Ganz. 'Perhaps this is the only chance for survival we have…'

He took the charm and stepped forward so that the dark riders could surely see him. Then, before they could react, he set it on a rock, and swung Lowenhertz's warhammer up and round in a powerful over-shoulder swing.

The riders screamed in horror with a single voice. The hammerhead crushed the talisman. There was a burst of light and a flash of green, eldritch flame. The blast knocked Ganz backwards and vaporised the head of the hammer.

The talisman was gone.

Red lightning, like electric blood, speared around the clearing horizontally, and there was a fierce hot wind. The wraith-like creatures shrieked as one, twisting, swirling in the air like flapping black rags until they were at last whisked up into the darkness of the night and were gone.

FOUR DAYS' GRUELLING drive brought them back to Middenheim. White Company escorted the Margrave's party right to the Graf's palace where they were to be cared for and tended. There were many partings now. As the Margrave effusively thanked Ganz time and again, Ganz found his eyes wandering the courtyard. He saw Drakken, sheepish and clumsy, kiss the feisty servant girl, Lenya, goodbye. Not for the last time, Ganz was sure. He saw Morgenstern and Anspach horseplaying with the children, and Aric consoling the frightened old woman Maris. And Gruber stood with the Lady Margrave.

'Forgive me, lady,' Gruber was saying softly. 'I mistrusted you, and that is my shame.'

'You saved my life, Sir Gruber. I'd say we're even.' She smiled and his heart winced again.

'If only you were younger and I was free,' she murmured, saying what he was thinking. Their eyes met, fierce for a second, then they both laughed aloud and said farewell.

IN THE GREAT darkness of the Temple, the Wolf Choirs were singing low, heartfelt hymns of thanks. The voices hung in the still, cool air.

Lowenhertz was knelt in prayer in front of the main altar. He looked up as he heard the footsteps come up behind him.

Ganz looked down at him. In his hands, he held an object wrapped in an old wolf pelt.

'The Panthers will be most aggrieved we stole their thunder,' Lowenhertz said as he rose.

Ganz nodded. 'They'll live. And to think we thought we were going to miss the action.'

There was a long pause. Ganz fixed him with a gaze. 'I suppose you'll be transferring again now.'

Lowenhertz shrugged. 'Not if you'll let me stay, commander. I have looked for my place for a long time. Perhaps it is here in this company of Wolves.'

'Then welcome to White Company, warrior,' Ganz said. 'I will be proud to have you in my command.'

'I must see the priest-armourers,' Lowenhertz said. 'I need a new hammer consecrated.'

Ganz held out the pelt bundle. 'No need. Ar-Ulric himself allowed me to take this from the Temple reliquary.'

The old warhammer in the pelt was magnificent and covered in a patina of age and use. 'It belonged to a Wolf called von Glick. One of the bravest, a fellow and a friend, sorely missed. It would please him for his hammer to be carried by a Wolf again, rather than tarnish in an old relic chest.'

Lowenhertz took the venerable weapon and tested its weight and balance. 'It will be an honour,' he said.

Around them, the song of the Wolf Choir rose up and soared, out of the great temple and beyond into the skies above Middenheim like smoke.

The Bretonnian Connection

IT WAS ONE of the workmen who told us, running over from the charred shell of the Temple of Morr where he had been working. The news must have been all over Middenheim by the time we heard it, retold from marketplace to coffee house, from inn to slum, shouted from window to window high above the twisted streets and steep alleys. It would be on everyone's lips by now. We stopped digging, rested on our spades and pickaxes, and stood in the half-finished grave as we contemplated what we had learned. It was the start of a spring day in the City of the White Wolf, and death was in the air.

Spring comes late to Middenheim. The ground in Morrspark stays frozen for months. Digging graves is hard and we welcomed the rest, although there would be more work soon. Countess Sophia of Altdorf, courtier and Imperial Plenipotentiate to the Graf of Middenheim, former wife of the Dauphin of Bretonnia, beauty, socialite, diplomat, patroness of orphans and the diseased, had been murdered in her bed. We felt more than sorrow at the death. We were priests of Morr, God of Death. This would be a busy week for us.

We looked at each other, placed our tools on the ground and walked through the gravestones towards the Temple of Morr where it stood at the centre of the park, swathed in scaffolding as if wrapped in bandages and splints. There were people crossing the park, hundreds of them in ones and twos, heading towards it as well. Some of them were crying.

THE RECENT FIRE had burned the temple almost to the ground, but the underground Factorum and the catacombs, where the wealthy dead rested, were intact and in use. All of Morr's priests in Middenheim – four of us, plus one from the Temple of Shallya assisting while the priests who had died in the fire were replaced – gathered in the darkness of the Factorum, the ritual room where the dead are prepared for burial, cremation or the long drop off the Cliff of Sighs to the rocks far below. Corpses lay on two of the granite slabs and the doorway to the burial vaults stood, black and forbidding, like the mouth of the underworld. The room was filled with the smells of death, embalming oils and tension.

Father Ralf came slowly down the steps into the Factorum, clearing his throat noisily. The High Priest's chain of office hung heavily around his neck, and he fingered it as he looked at us. Approaching sixty and with bad arthritis, he had never expected to rise as high as this job and didn't particularly welcome it, but there had been nobody else. All the other priests were too young, too inexperienced, or me. He didn't like me. That was fine: nobody liked me. Many days, I didn't like myself either.

'I'll keep this short,' he started. 'I'm sure we're all shocked by the death of Countess Sophia. But the job of the Temple is to provide moral and spiritual reassurance at a time like this. We must be strong, and be seen to be strong.' He broke off for a fit of coughing, then resumed: 'I myself will see to the late Countess's funeral arrangements. Pieter, Wolmar and Olaf, you stay in the temple. There will be many mourners, and they will need your presence and counsel. The rest of you will attend to normal business.'

'The rest of us,' I said, 'is two of us.' I gestured at myself and Brother Jakob. 'And the Countess's murder won't stop ordinary people from dying.'

Father Ralf glowered at me with his rheumy eyes. 'These are exceptional times, brother. If you had not burned down the temple, then perhaps your workload would be lighter.'

I thought about reminding him that I'd burnt it down partly to save his life, but it wasn't a good idea. Not today, not with this mood in the air. Ralf might be inexperienced at running things, but he was keen to make his authority felt, and prone to over-react. Best to let it go. 'So,' I asked, 'should Brother Jakob and I return to grave-digging, or is there more pressing business for us?'

'Jakob will finish the grave. As for you, a flophouse in the Altquartier, Sargant's, has sent word that a drunk beggar has died there. You seem to have a fondness for such people: deal with the body. And brother, don't make a mountain out of it. We have more important things to worry about.'

I waited while the others left, filing up the stairs into the day-light and the crowd of mourners outside. Jakob hung back as well. I felt sorry for him. He'd only been at the temple a few months, and the upheavals which had followed the death of Father Zimmerman had unnerved him. Now there was some-thing really big happening, and instead of being allowed to help he had been sent to dig graves.

'Why us?' he asked, and there was bitterness in his voice.

'Because you're young and I'm not liked, and neither of us would do a good job of comforting the mourners,' I said. 'You'd best get on with that grave while the sun's thawing the ground.'

He looked at me with curiosity in his eyes. 'What did Father Ralf mean when he said you had a fondness for beggars?'

'Go and dig,' I said.

I THOUGHT about Jakob's question as I walked through the ancient city's winding streets to the Altquartier. Was it beggars I cared about? No. But anyone who died alone and unmourned, whose death nobody cared about: those were my people. Somebody should care for them, and if no one was willing to do it before they died, then I would do it afterwards. People often showed their best side in death, losing their unappealing habits, becoming calm and serene. It was much easier not to hate them in that state; and besides, it was my job. If that job sometimes brought me unexplained deaths, then I regarded it as my duty to find out what I could about them. Besides, as I told my few friends, it passed the time.

The town was awash with news and gossip about the death of the Countess. People saw my robes and stopped me in the street to pour out their grief, and it seemed that everyone had something to say: some testament to her goodness, some anec-dote about her legendary love-affairs, or just sobs and moans. I noticed that it was only the humans who seemed to be so carried away. The elves, dwarfs and halflings seemed to be more reserved, but they have always been few in Middenheim. The marketplaces were still busy but the street-entertainers were absent: no jugglers, no dwarf wrestlers, no illusionists making bursts of pretty lights with their petty magics. The city was more alive than at any time since the last carnival, but its life was strangely subdued.

All the talk on the streets was of the killing: was it murder or assassination – and if the latter, who was to blame? Most of the people with theories seemed to believe the Bretonnians were behind it somehow. The Countess's death would not only allow the Dauphin to re-marry, but she was still well-loved in her own country. Tensions had been high between the Empire and Bretonnia for the last few months, and there are few better ways to spur an invading army than the murder of a national treasure, particularly one in a foreign country who might be embarrassing if left alive. Other theories blamed beastmen, probably remembering a few months back to when the Templar's Arms was attacked by mutants, or mythical skaven creeping up from the long-abandoned tunnels under the city. I heard all these ideas and more, and I let them wash over me like spring rain over the city's granite walls. It was just a death, no more important to me than any other.

The twisting streets narrowed and became darker, lost in shadows from the high buildings, as I entered the Altquartier. Buildings come and go here but its slum-like feel never changes. Sargant's flophouse was a new name to me but looking at its exterior, a former merchant's warehouse off a typically steep Middenheim alley, I knew what it would be like inside: infested with lice, fleas and vermin, with straw mattresses on the bare floors of long dormitories, and the smell of boiled cabbage, dirt and desperation. Like every other flophouse in the city, it stank of wretchedness. Shapeless men in rags, some with crutches or terrible scars, stood outside and passed a skin of cheap wine between them. As I approached the door they moved aside, respectful of the robes of a Morr worshipper. Even those with nothing to live for are still afraid of death.

A big, bald man, muscle gone mostly to fat, was waiting just inside. His clothes were mock-opulent, cheap copies of the latest fashions, and he wore a short, business-like knife on his belt. I didn't expect him to be worried by my appearance, and I was right.

'You're Sargant,' I said.

He didn't move, but stared at me for a long moment.

'Didn't you used to be Dieter Brossmann?' he said, an edge to his voice. I met his gaze.

'That was my name a long time ago,' I said slowly. 'For eight years I have been a humble priest of Morr. Now, the body.'

'Aye. Follow me then.'

I accompanied him down dark corridors, hoping he would ask no further questions about the man I had once been, and waited as he unlocked a thin pine door. The room beyond was small and windowless, and Sargant didn't follow me in. I saw a bed with a body on it, and one chair nearby. A small oil lamp stood on it, illuminating the face of the corpse.

It was Reinhold. Morr take me, but it was Reinhold! He looked old and worn and tired and dirty, but he hadn't changed so much from ten years ago, when I ran the largest family firm in Middenheim and he was my eyes and ears. Little Reinhold, who knew every watchman and warehouse guard in the city, who could pick any lock in half a minute, and who even knew at least a part of the ancient dwarf tunnels under the city. Reinhold, who had taught me so much. What had brought him to this end, I wondered, and then thought, I did. Partly, at least, when I closed down the firm and became a priest.

But there would be time for such thoughts later. I had a job to do. Grateful that Sargant had left me alone, and guessing that he couldn't have known the link between Reinhold and my former self, I placed my fingers on the body's forehead – the skin felt greasy and cold – and began to chant the Blessing of Protection, to seal it against the influence of the dark forces that prey on corpses. Reinhold's soul was already with Morr and beyond my help. I'd light a candle for him when I returned to the Temple.

In the candlelight, Reinhold's face looked old and solid, as if carved from the pine-wood of the Drakwald. I moved my fingers slowly over his face and downwards as I intoned the ancient words of the prayer. I reached his throat – and stopped. There was a mark, an indentation about the size of a gold crown, pressed deep into the flesh around his Adam's apple.

I'd heard of this trick. You wrap a coin or a stone in a piece of cloth. Then you loop it around your victim's throat and pull hard. The coin cuts off the windpipe – or the main vein, I was never sure which – and death comes a little quieter and less obvious. Reinhold had been murdered.

His pockets. Sargant would almost certainly have been through them, but there might still be something there that could tell me a little. Reinhold's clothes had the hard, clammy feel of grease, dirt and sweat that comes from being worn day after day for months, and with a smell to match, and I felt unclean handling them. More than that, it felt like I was invading my dead friend's privacy. But that didn't stop me.

A handkerchief, filthy. A grubby copy of a small Sigmarite prayer-book. Five bent strands of wire, which I recognised as improvised lock-picks. Bits of gravel. No money. The right pocket was even clammier than the left one, and contained only a small clasp-knife, very blunt and rusty. I pulled out the blade, and was not too surprised to see it had reasonably fresh blood on it. That was the Reinhold I'd known.

I sat in the semi-darkness and thought for a moment, then resumed the Blessing of Protection. There was little I could do for Reinhold now. Part of me knew that Reinhold's last journey was destined to be the long drop off the Cliff of Sighs, the pauper's exit from life and the city, but that was inevitable. He had no family vault under the Temple, nor the money to pay for a grave-site in Morrspark where the more wealthy dead already lay four, sometimes five deep. The best I could do for him was to find out why he had died. I wasn't looking for revenge: that's not what being a priest of Morr is about. It would be enough to find out the reason.

As I finished the blessing the door opened and Sargant came in. 'Done?' he asked.

'Almost.' I stood up and moved to the door, heading back towards the street. No point in letting him know what I knew. 'I'll send a cart for the body. Did he die in that room?'

'Aye. Most nights he was in the dormitory wi' others, but last night he came up late with money and asked for a room for himself. He smelled of drink and he had sausage and a skin of wine for his friend. They drank past eleven bells, then he went asleep. This morning, there he was, stiff as a board. "Eat, drink an' be merry," he said t'me yestiddy, "for tomorrer we die." An' he were right.'

I stared at him. Did Reinhold know he was going to die – that someone was planning to kill him? And if so, why did he go quietly to it instead of fighting? Had life on the street really ground him down so far that he wouldn't even defend himself against assassination? Or was there another reason? I needed to know more about Reinhold's recent life, and I knew I wouldn't get the information from Sargant.

'This friend of Reinhold's,' I asked. 'Can you give me a name?'

'Louise,' he said. 'Little Bretonnian rat, she is. Here most evenings. They were courtin'. Wanted to spend last night together, but I won't be havin' that kind o' behaviour, not in my house.'

No, of course not. You'd take money from people with nothing for a night's shelter in this squalor, but you'll forbid them anything that might give them a moment's comfort, even something as little as the warmth of another person's care. I knew too many men like Sargant: Middenheim was full of them. We were almost back at the flophouse's front door when I noticed something that surprised me. 'You're wearing a black armband,' I said. 'Are you in mourning?'

The big man looked down at his arm, as if momentarily surprised. 'Aye,' he said.

'For Reinhold?' I asked.

He stared back at me. 'Not that old drunk,' he sneered. 'The Countess.'

He turned and was gone, back into the sordid darkness of his domain. I watched him go, then looked over at the group of beggars who still stood around the door. One of them glanced up at me and I caught his eye. He twitched like a mouse trapped by an owl. 'Don't run away,' I said. 'I'm looking for Louise.'

IT TOOK A couple of coins and two hours of being guided through the city's many back-alleys to cheap inns and beggars' hideaways in old cisterns and abandoned cellars, but eventually we found her: a bag of rags and bones huddled near a brazier down near the watch-post beside the ruins of the South Gate. She looked up as we approached, recognising my guide. Her face was bloody and bruised. I crouched down in front of her.

'Who did this to you?' I asked.

'Men.' The word sounded thick and blurred, although whether it was from her Bretonnian accent or her torn lip was hard to say. I realised I had no idea how old she was – twenty, thirty, fifty even. Street people age fast, and rain, frost and cheap wine hadn't been kind to her.

'What men?'

'Men who hear my voice, who say I am spy, I kill the Countess. Stupid men, Lady take them!' she said. 'Who are you to ask such things?'

She gazed at me with grey eyes, and I remembered another woman. But she had been blonde, and her face had been filled with life and joy. Filomena had been her name and I had loved her… and not seen her for eight years. There was a silence. I remembered Louise had asked me a question.

'I was a friend of Reinhold,' I said and she turned away, her shoulders hunched. I didn't move to comfort her: she had so little left in her life, I felt I should let her keep her grief. At least I didn't have to tell her the news. After a long minute she turned back to me, tears streaking the filth on her face.

'You are priest, you bury him, yes?' she said.

'I will attend to him in death.' The reply seemed to satisfy her. 'Louise… was there anyone who hated Reinhold?'

'Hated?' She looked blank. I tried another tack.

'What did Reinhold do yesterday? Was he working?'

Louise wiped her face on a filthy sleeve. 'Didn't get work. He went looking but didn't get.'

'So what did he do?'

'Morning, Wendenbahn for begging.' I nodded: the street was popular with merchants, who gave charity to beggars for luck. 'Came back at two bells, scared.'

'Scared?'

'Saw a man. Reiner said man looked for him. No friend. Then he take his… he go out again and he…. He come back late,' she finished lamely. No, that wasn't it. She was hiding something from me, something important, because she was nervous of me. I knew how to deal with that: move to a safe subject, build up her confidence, and come back to the secret later.

'Louise,' I asked, 'do you know who this man was? Did Reinhold tell you anything about him?'

A long pause as she tried to remember. 'From the west. From Marienburg. From past days, Reiner said. Called him "Grubworm".'

Grubworm: Claus Grubheimer. I remembered. Strange, however much we try to escape our pasts, it's always there, waiting behind us to tap our shoulder or slip a blade into our back. Ten or eleven years ago, a fresh-faced merchant with an Empire name and a Bretonnian accent had arrived in Middenheim, bringing big ideas and a permit to trade herbs from Loren. While I shook his hand and talked to him of partnership and assistance, Reinhold had picked his locks, copied his paperwork and stolen his samples. Then we planted some Black Lotus on him and tipped off the Watch what he was trading. I'd had a five-crown bet with Reinhold that they'd have his head on a pole before he could flee the city. Reinhold had won, and that was the last time either of us had seen Grubheimer. Until yesterday.

But had Grubheimer killed Reinhold? And if he had, was he looking for me? And what about Yan the Norse and Three-Fingered Kaspar, who'd also worked for me then? I hadn't seen them in years. Perhaps they were dead too. Fingers of cold panic gripped my shoulders. Be calm, I told myself, be calm. And yet my old instincts, long buried under my life as a priest, were screaming that if Grubheimer was in town, it was for one reason: revenge. I needed time to think, but if Reinhold was already dead then time was the one thing I didn't have.

'I have to go back to the Temple,' I said and stood. Louise's eyes followed me.

'Money?' she asked, in her voice the only sound of hope I'd heard from her. I looked down at her pitiful form.

'Reinhold gave you nothing at all?' I asked. She said nothing, but her eyes broke away from mine. There was something she didn't want to tell me: that hidden detail again. It could wait. I turned away, to begin the walk back through the maze of cold streets filled with sorrowful people. Something in me was crystallising, hard and sharp. I knew I'd find out what it was in a moment.

'Wait! The Countess–' she said behind me.

'No. Don't talk to me about the Countess,' I said, and walked away.

The hard thing inside me was steely-cold with fear, and something else. I knew that if Grubheimer was back in the city, he was here to kill me: he might be a citizen of Marienburg but his blood was Bretonnian, and they were not a people to forgive their enemies. I had forgiven mine eight years ago, when I became a priest and tried to forget all of the many bad things I had done. I regretted none of those things, but when I joined the Temple of Morr I knew I would never do anything like that again. Now, eight years later, a priest would be an easy target for Grubheimer to kill.

Ever since my wife and child had disappeared, a part of me had wanted to die but it was a very small part, and as I passed through the narrow streets I could feel the hardness in me building, to fight against it. Grubheimer was a desperate man, a man who would garrotte a beggar in his bed for a ten year-old revenge. If the priest I now was was to survive this, then I would need to be hard. I would need to become once more the man I had left behind: to think about life in a way I had tried to forget for eight years. It was not an appealing prospect.

But even as I wondered about it, I felt the coldness in me swell and grow, filling me with dead emotions, covering the mind of the priest of Morr and replacing them with old thoughts, old behaviours. Was the life I had led for eight years really so easily overcome? Had the past I had fought so hard to bury really risen so close to the surface? And having let the wolf out from the cage, could I ever get it back in there again?

Part of me felt panicked and sick, but I looked down at my right hand. My fist was clenched; not in anger, I realised, but in resolution. And then I looked up at an alley I was passing, and I knew what needed to be done. I walked into the gloom I used to know well, knocked hard on the door of the Black Horse tavern, and entered.

Its decor had not improved. The noontime drinkers were fewer and more subdued than I remembered, and I didn't recognise the young man in the apron who moved towards me as I crossed the threshold. He opened his mouth.

'Stop,' I said. 'Is Grizzly Bruno here?'

He chewed his lip, which is what you'd do if you're new in your job and a priest comes into a hole like the Black Horse and asks for a man with a reputation like Grizzly Bruno's. But his eyes flicked to the ceiling. I thought they would; I'd been watching for it.

'He's upstairs,' I said.

'He's asleep.'

'No I'm not,' came a heavy voice and there was Bruno, as huge and bear-like as ever. We stood awkwardly, unsure of how to greet each other. Finally he said, 'Father,' and I, grateful to escape one of his hugs, said, 'Bruno.'

'Been a long time,' he said.

'It has.'

'I take it this isn't social.'

'It isn't.'

'Well, father,' and he put weight on the word. 'What business can I help you with on a day like today?'

'Bruno, do you remember a Bretonnian herb trader called Grubheimer? About ten years ago? Got himself chased out of town for smuggling Black Lotus?'

'Can't say I do, father. It's been a long time.' But he looked interested.

'Some associates of mine,' I said carefully, 'were not unacquainted with the bag of weed that the Watch found on him.

Now he's back in town, and from what I hear he's not happy. *Very* not happy.'

'I thought you'd put things like that behind you. When your wife and boy went missing.'

There was a pause. It came from me. 'I did,' I said, 'but it looks like he didn't. And I do not care to be reminded of it.'

'So – what? You want him warned away? Out of the city? Dealt with?'

'I need to know where he's staying. That'll suffice for the time.'

'A shame,' Bruno said, 'but I'll get someone on it. Can I offer you a glass of brandy and the warmth of my hearth? I'd appreciate your advice on a piece of tricky business.'

'I'm sorry, Bruno,' I said. 'I don't do that any more.'

'But you still ask for favours from old friends. I understand.' I started to say something but he held up one slab-like hand. 'No. Today I forgive you. With such a big death in the city, Morr's people must have much to do.'

'All deaths are the same size,' I said. 'It's only the living who think different.'

He looked at me for a moment, then shrugged. 'Whatever you say. You're the priest. I'll send a messenger to the Temple if I hear of your Grubheimer.'

'Thanks, Bruno,' I said. 'And any time you or your boys need advice on death, you know where to find me.'

He chuckled. 'Maybe I'll do that. But when it comes to death we have more experience than you, I think.'

A recent memory filled my head: a man plunging down into blizzard-whipped snow from the Cliff of Sighs, his blood still warm on my hands. 'Oh,' I said, 'you might be surprised.'

THERE WAS NO need to bring Reinhold's body back to the Temple. A pauper's body should be flung from the Cliff of Sighs with the briefest of blessings. But however he might have died, Reinhold had lived as more than a pauper. Besides, with Father Ralf and the others occupied with the death of the Countess, nobody was going to notice, and preparing the body would give me time to think.

On my way back to the Temple, crossing from the hubbub of the streets into the relative solitude of the frozen Morrspark, I heard the sound of a spade ringing against the unyielding ground. Brother Jakob was still digging. He was standing in the grave, and the sight of him there sent an unexplained shiver down my back. I walked over, and he looked up, his face pale with cold.

'I don't suppose you're here to help,' he said bitterly.

'No, brother,' I said. 'I have other business.'

He put down the spade, rubbed his hands to get the blood back into them, and looked at me.

'You told me you're not liked around here, brother?' he asked.

'It's true enough,' I said.

'So why do you stay?'

I looked down at him. 'Why? Don't assume that "being hated" is the same as "hating", brother. I have devoted my life to Morr. I work in his temple, and I tolerate the pettiness of those whose dedication is less than my own.' I paused to stamp my feet; they were going numb. My words sounded hollow, even to me. 'But that's not what you meant to ask. You want to know why you should stay.'

He stared at me as if I had just told him his innermost secret. He paused. 'I hate it here.'

'I know.'

'I want to run away.'

'What do you want to do?'

'I want to be a knight, fight for the Empire, live and die a hero. But without my father's help I'd never get a rank or a command.'

Ah, his father, some minor noble with three sons in the army and the youngest sent into the priesthood to pray for them. 'Run away. Join a band of mercenaries,' I suggested.

He looked at me with disdain. 'There's no honour in that,' he said. 'And mostly they're Tilean too.' He spat on the cold earth.

'But it would be better than being a priest, eh?' I said. 'Life's what you make of it. If you do not make your own way, a way will be made for you. You must choose, brother, you must choose.'

He didn't reply. As I walked away I heard the ring of the shovel against the earth, striking out like a slowly tolling bell.

THE HALF-REBUILT Temple was crowded with mourners, its normally quiet spaces filled with noise and jostling. Father Ralf's coffers would be doing well and he would be revelling in the attention which was being paid to him. The throng of people, normally obedient to one wearing the robes of Morr, seemed not to notice me and I had to shove my way between them as I made my way towards the entrance to the priests' quarters in the far wall, and my cell which lay beyond.

I didn't get there. A wailing woman tugged at my robe, begging for a blessing, and then a man in rich clothes wanted to know what the Countess's death augured for the spring rains, and I was trapped by the crowd, speaking words of comfort and saying short prayers for someone I didn't care for to people I hated. Then Father Ralf stood beside me, at my shoulder.

'Is the soul of our departed brother flying to Morr?' he asked, using the Temple's code to ask if I'd tipped the corpse from the Cliff of Sighs. I shook my head.

'Sadly, his passing was swift but not welcomed,' I said, meaning he was killed. Father Ralf looked exasperated.

'I sorrow. I must learn more of this. Be in the Factorum in five minutes.' He turned away to minister to the needs of some well-dressed goodwife. I left: I'd been heading to the Factorum anyway. The Watch would be bringing Reinhold's body there soon.

The Factorum was cold and smelled of death. I sat on one of the scrubbed marble slabs, thinking, waiting for the corpse, and trying to piece together what I knew. Reinhold had failed to find work yesterday, but he had come back with money all the same: money, and the news that Grubheimer was back in town. He returned late, got drunk, took a room alone, and there he was killed. Killed by an assassin, killed almost as if expecting it, almost as if he offered no resistance. Almost as if he felt he should die. That's a rare thought for Middenheimers, who cling as tenaciously to life as their ancient city clings to its rocky mountaintop.

Yet the more I thought about the way Reinhold had looked, the more I believed he had been prepared to die. He hadn't put up a fight. People reach that state for many reasons but desperation is not one of them: it may be a reason to take one's own life, but not to lie back quietly and let it be taken. Drugs, perhaps his wine was drugged? No; if they wanted Reinhold dead, they could have poisoned the wine. There was something more here. I'd seen it before: the sense of something completed, finished, over. A man who was determined to leave on a high note, so when people looked at his life they'd say, 'What did he accomplish? He accomplished this.'

But Reinhold had been a down-and-out, unable to find a day's work to pay for a night's lodging. The thought of imminent death can drive one to incredible ends, but only to escape it – not to welcome it. What had happened to him?

I knew I didn't have the secret of this yet but, looking at the facts, I thought I knew where it had to be hidden. I needed to find where Reinhold had got the money, and I needed to know whether he had got it before or after he saw Grubheimer in Wendenbahn. This wasn't some penny-pamphlet tale of intrigue: I was already certain that my friend had been killed by Grubheimer or someone hired by him. And I knew that meant Grubheimer would come after me. Possibly he wanted to kill my old associates first, working his way through what was left of my organisation, knowing that I'd know he was coming for me. That was good. It might give me some time.

There was a sharp knock at the door and Father Ralf entered without waiting for permission. He glared at me. I stood up, my knee-joints cracking.

'I told you to deal with this matter quickly,' he said, 'and you start a murder enquiry out of a flop-house stabbing.'

'It was more than that,' I said. 'I sense it. The dead man was a friend of mine.' My voice sounded false to me. It was my old self, Dieter, playing the role of a priest of Morr. It made me uneasy.

Father Ralf glared at me in exasperation. 'Friendship has no place in the life of a priest of Morr, brother. Besides, I did not think you cultivated friends.'

'He was a friend in my former life.'

No answer. Even Father Ralf knew of my past and my old reputation, and therefore what sort of man the deceased must have been. There was a long pause. Our breaths formed white mist, swirling in the cold lamp-lit air.

'Well,' he said, then stopped a moment. 'And another thing. I've learned you spent the afternoon walking around the city with beggars, refusing to listen to mourners who tried to speak to you. This is not behaviour becoming of a priest of our order, brother. It makes us look haughty at a time when we must be at our most open and approachable. Ar-Ulric himself mentioned the matter to me.'

I said nothing. I didn't remember ignoring anyone on the street but that didn't mean it hadn't happened. But I doubted that Ar-Ulric, the highest priest of Ulric in the whole Empire, had taken any interest in the matter. Father Ralf was trying to intimidate me and make himself look important at the same time. It might have worked if I cared about either him or Ar-Ulric. But I didn't.

'At six bells we are holding the mass ritual of mourning and remembrance for the Countess,' he continued, 'to be led by myself and Ar-Ulric. You will take part prominently because it is important that you are seen there. And you will be seen to weep for the Countess. Am I clear?'

'Yes, father,' I said plainly. Disagreeing would only have started an argument, and I needed to get rid of him so I could think. He seemed to want an argument anyway, but we were interrupted by another knock at the door. I opened it, and in a blast of cold air there was Schtutt.

'Help me get this dead bugger inside, father,' he said, gesturing to a lump lying on a cart behind him 'I'd have brought one of the lads but everyone is over at the Nordgarten, minding the mourners at Countess Sophia's townhouse.' Then he noticed Father Ralf behind me and dropped into an embarrassed silence.

Ralf made for the door, turning back to me as he reached it. 'Six bells, brother. Do not be late,' he said, and left.

Together Schtutt and I lifted the body – the rigor mortis was wearing off and Reinhold felt like a sack of logs – and carried it down the steps, dumping it on one of the marble slabs. Schtutt was panting.

'I'm not as fit as I used to be in the old days, eh?' He wiped his brow. 'But none of us are. He certainly isn't.' He gestured at the body. He seemed to be in a mood to chat but I, aware of the passing of time and the presence of Grubheimer somewhere in the city, wasn't. Still, a thought pricked me.

'Schtutt, do you remember a Marienburger named Grubheimer? Tall, greasy black hair, Bretonnian accent, got run out of the city for smuggling Black Lotus? About ten years back?'

'Can't say I do. But if he sounds Bretonnian he wants to watch out. The city's too hot for them at the moment, with the rumours about them killing the Countess and all. There've been two stabbed in brawls already, and another one fell from a high window and broke his neck.'

'Unfortunate,' I said nervously, feeling panicky and distracted. The notion struck me that if Grubheimer had learned which flop-house Reinhold was staying in, he must know by now that I had become a priest, and if I stayed around the Temple I would be an easy victim. I needed to move. 'But I should–'

'Though,' Schtutt said, warming to his theme, 'I've heard from the best authority that the Countess was not assassinated.'

'No?' I feigned interest.

'No. More like a robbery, they reckon. There's an old dwarf tunnel as comes out in the Countess's cellar. Nobody knew it was there, but the murderer got in that way. And a stack of her jewels was missing, including the Dauphin of Bretonnia's engagement ring. Money gone too. She must have come across the robber, and–'

So the dwarfs were likely to pick up the blame for the killing. They didn't do well in Middenheim. 'A tragedy, truly,' I said. 'We are all the poorer for her loss. Now, there is much I must do.'

'Aye. I'll be off.' He looked discomforted at having his chat cut short, but left anyway.

I sat on the cold slab next to Reinhold and stared down at the body of my friend. How did his death piece together? And why were my instincts telling me that it was important to work out why Reinhold had lain down to die, when there was a man in the city trying to kill me? When I had allowed myself to think like my old self once more, I had expected a surge of ruthlessness, of sudden thought and decisive action, but there had been none of that. Perhaps the thing I had feared, the part of me I had buried eight years ago when I joined Morr's temple, had lost its edge in time, as I had hoped. Perhaps I had succeeded in destroying my dark half. Perhaps that success would lead to my own destruction.

I still needed to know where Reinhold had got his money. If I was honest, other than running and hiding, I could think of nothing better to do. The old Dieter had never run or hidden, and I wasn't going to start now. I needed to talk to Louise again.

THE SUN HAD set by the time I left the Factorum and the wind had picked up. Down by South Gate it chilled my marrow and blew the embers of the guards' brazier into fierce redness. I gazed out over the long, twisting bridge, lit by torches, as it curved down from the cliff's edge to the ground hundreds of feet below. Workmen were still busy with ladders and ropes, lanterns and stone and mortar, toiling to repair the huge breach in the viaduct that the magics of the traitor-wizard Karl-Heinz Wasmeier had caused, as he fled from the city after the last carnival. It would take weeks more to finish the job.

Behind me, in the glow of the brazier, Louise finished the pie I had bought her with the appetite of a woman who has not eaten all day. Now she would be more inclined to talk. She knew I had been Reinhold's friend, but I would still be asking hard questions. Better to start with softer ones, to make it sound as if I cared.

'How did you come to Middenheim?' I asked. She glanced at me in that way that horses do if they're nervous and about to shy. I smiled at her, my face feeling odd at the unaccustomed gesture.

She said, 'Back home, in Bretonnia, I worked for a woman. She was with a noble, brought me here when that was... when she left him. She was wild, fierce, but much money. I serve for six years. Then she throw me in the street with nothing. For no reason.' She stopped. I had expected anger or rage, but she must have told this story so many times that its emotion had all drained away. Yet I could tell there was still deep, black pain, far below. But was there resentment? Hatred? I didn't know.

I looked at her for a moment while I groped for the right thing to say. Then it came to me, all of it, in a sudden rush like a spring flood, and I said, 'You're talking about the Countess! You said her name this afternoon. You were trying to tell me something.'

Louise didn't speak but her eyes said I was right.

'Louise, what are you afraid of?'

She said nothing.

'Did Reinhold give you something last night?'

She nodded, despite herself. Tears were beginning to streak her cheeks. With frightening speed, skeins of logic were weaving themselves together in my mind.

'Reinhold knew how much you hated the Countess, didn't he? And you're afraid that he had something to do with her death. You're scared, because you realise now that you don't really want her dead, and because you don't want to believe Reinhold could do something like that... and because if he did kill her, then people might think you're involved too.'

She shook her head. For a moment I was confused.

'Louise, do you mean that's not what you believe, or,' and the realisation hit me hard and sudden, 'or because it's what you know?'

She nodded, a little nod, her silent weeping unabated.

'Did he give you some jewellery last night?'

A tiny nod.

'And you recognised it.'

Another, tinier.

'Because it was the Countess's.'

She didn't need to nod. I already knew I had the truth. I took a deep breath. This wasn't going to be easy.

'Louise, you have to trust me. The jewellery was the Countess's, but Reinhold didn't get it from her. He stole it from the man who killed her – that Bretonnian he saw earlier that day.'

'The Grubworm,' she said in a small voice.

'Yes, Grubworm. And then Grubworm went to the flop-house and killed Reinhold to get it back, but he'd already given it to you.' I paused. She said nothing. I had no idea if she believed me. 'Louise, it is my duty as a priest of Morr to understand death. We commune with Death, we speak to it. We live our lives surrounded by it, and we comprehend things about it that most people could never understand. We know who killed the Countess. He will be arrested soon. Reinhold had nothing to do with it.'

I paused to let my words sink in. She still said nothing, her head buried in her hands. The cold wind blew between us, the thin flames of the brazier warming nothing at all.

'But you must give me the jewellery,' I said.

At last she looked up and met my eye. A long moment passed, and then she scrabbled amongst her dirty rags, and I knew I had won. She held out a balled fist, and I reached out to receive what lay within. As I did, she grabbed my arm with her other hand, and held hard.

'I have your word for the truth?' she hissed.

'You have my solemn word as a priest of Morr,' I lied.

A jewelled ring fell into my hand: heavy, with the soft warmth that only solid gold has. I cradled it, thinking. I didn't know what I was going to do with it, but I knew that at least I now had the truth of yesterday evening in my grasp.

Because Reinhold *had* killed the Countess. He knew the old dwarf tunnels under the city better than anyone except a dwarf. He could pick the locks, there had been blood on his pocket-knife, and he'd given Louise that ring. More importantly, I'd known Reinhold for long enough to understand what he was capable of doing. He believed that the ends justified the means, and his means were ruthless. I'd never asked him to kill anyone, but he had killed while working for me, more than once.

So he'd seen Grubheimer in town. Maybe Grubheimer had spied him and threatened him. Or maybe Reinhold had simply heard that the man was back and asking dangerous questions. Anyway, he'd realised his days were numbered, and so he looked for a grand gesture, a last stab at posthumous fame, on which to die. And given that his lover had reason to hate her, what better than the murder of the beloved Countess Sophia?

He'd stolen some of her jewellery to make it look like a burglary, fenced most of it cheaply before the murder was discovered, drunk or gave away most of the money and used the rest to buy a squalid room for the night. He gave his girlfriend her ex-employer's famed engagement ring. Then he died. Maybe he died happy. I hoped there had been a tiny shred of contentment in his mind as Grubheimer's garrotte had throttled the life from him.

But Reinhold wasn't stupid. He knew – he must have known – that the jewellery he had stolen, fenced or given to Louise would be traced back to him, and his name would resound around the city: Reinhold the Knife, the man who killed Countess Sophia. A black legend, but for some people infamy is better than anonymity. Particularly if you're dead. I guessed – no, knew – that he had wanted that to be his epitaph.

Louise coughed, a long, racking cough, and I remembered where I was. There was still the business with Grubheimer to be concluded. The ring in my hand could come in useful, though at that moment I didn't know how.

'I must go,' I said, and turned away. Louise grabbed my arm again.

'One thing more,' she said. 'You say you Reinhold's friend, but he never mentioned priest. What friend were you, to let him live like this?'

I turned back slowly. 'When Reinhold knew me,' I said quietly, 'my name was Dieter Brossmann.'

Louise dropped my arm, staring wildly. She made a strange sound, half gasp, half scream.

'You!' she spat. 'You betrayed him! You let him sink in life, to the dregs! You – you are no friend! He should have killed you! You should die! You are evil! Evil! Give me my ring!' She made a lunge for me. '*Give me my ring!*'

Two Watchmen began to hurry towards us. A Bretonnian beggar-woman screaming at a priest – they would know who to arrest. I turned away, leaving them to it, and walked swiftly back up the steep streets towards Morrspark and the Temple.

HALF THE CITY must have been crowded into the park. It was full: nobles, knights and rich merchants jostled by shoemakers, peddlers and servants. They were all packed into the cold, dark expanse, lit by occasional torches on high poles. People were even standing on the graves to get a better view of the ceremony on the Temple's steps. And yet there was no sound from any of them. As I pushed my way through the silent masses I could hear Ar-Ulric's great voice booming out over the park, interspersed with the higher, weaker tones of Father Ralf. I didn't bother to listen to what they were saying. All that mattered was that I had missed the start. There would be trouble later. If I lived that long.

I shouldered my way between the gathered ranks, heading for the Temple and the small door at its rear. I needed to be alone, and to hide the Countess's ring, and my cell would be the best place for both. As Father Ralf and Ar-Ulric were on the steps at the front of the temple, the press was less great at the back and as I approached the door I could see it was ajar.

As I put my hand on the ornate handle, a voice behind me said, 'Dieter.'

I whirled around. There, a few paces away, was a figure I knew: medium height, greased hair greying at the temples, and a nose that spoke of aristocracy and brawling. He was larger these days, fatter or more heavily muscled. I didn't want to find out which. Instead I leapt through the door and slammed it behind me.

Grubheimer! Grubheimer was here. He had spoken to me. He had wanted me to see him. He hadn't tried to kill me. Which meant… which meant… he must have set a trap for me. And I had almost certainly jumped into it.

He had called me Dieter, and I had answered to that name for the first time in eight years. I did feel more like my old self now: calmer, more confident, more ruthless. And part of me, the priest, felt appalled and scared by that, but I ignored it. For now I had to be Dieter, or die.

I ran to my cell. It was pitifully obvious that someone had moved the thin mattress since I had been here. I lifted it, and underneath lay a small leather pouch. I pulled it open and stared at the fine grey dust inside. I didn't have to smell it to recognise it: Black Lotus powder. A foul substance. Fatal to its owners, in more ways than one. Grubheimer had put this here. He was framing me the way I'd framed him ten years ago.

Then I heard footsteps, fast and light, in the corridor. They stopped outside. I tucked the pouch in my robes, grabbed a chair as a weapon, and yanked the door open. In the corridor stood Brother Jakob.

'I saw you come in,' he said. 'Father Ralf is furious. I thought I'd better tell you.'

If he'd thought that might worry me, he was wrong. I moved forward, into the corridor, grasping him by the arm. 'There are bigger things in the air tonight. Come with me.' The implications of the Black Lotus were still flooding through my mind. Grubheimer must have known I'd find the drug. He must want me to be caught with it in person, and that meant he'd act as soon as he could. I had to dispose of the powder immediately. One hiding place came to mind and I acted without thinking of the consequences. Like Dieter.

'Take this for safekeeping,' I said, thrusting the pouch into Jakob's hands before he could protest.

'What is it?'

'Something many men would kill for. If you see trouble, stick close to me.'

I unbolted the door and we stepped outside. The massed mourners were singing the last verse of a funeral hymn, filling the world with the music of sorrow and regret. At any other time I would have been deeply moved by it, but right now it was a distraction. Almost dragging Jakob by the arm, I made my way around to the front of the Temple.

We didn't get far. A knot of Watch uniforms was moving roughly through the crowd towards us, carrying flaming torches to light their path. At their centre was Grubheimer. He pointed to me. 'This is the man,' he said. 'He is the one who offered to sell me Black Lotus this afternoon.'

'Officer, this man lies,' I said, not to Grubheimer but to the Watch Captain with him, a man I didn't know. 'I am nothing but a priest of Morr.' My voice sounded loud: the hymn had ended and from the front of the Temple Father Ralf was proclaiming a prayer. I knew its words well. The crowd around us were silent, their attention on us.

'Search him,' Grubheimer said, his voice gruff, his accent strong. 'A brown leather pouch.'

Jakob stared at me, suddenly trying to pull free of my grasp. I didn't let him go. And with a lurch I realised that I still had the Countess's ring in my closed hand. If they searched me, Grubheimer would have been more triumphant than he could possibly have dreamed.

'I have no such pouch,' I said. Jakob pulled harder. From the temple steps, I could hear Father Ralf nearing the end of the prayer to Morr.

'Maybe his catamite has it,' Grubheimer said. I drew myself up, aware of the aura my priestly robes would give me, and knowing how little they matched my terrified thoughts. And suddenly I remembered a cool, calm voice – not mine, not Dieter's, but Reinhold's – and I knew what to do.

'You accuse me of this crime,' I said slowly and with emphasis, 'because I know who you killed last night.' Grubheimer's face showed surprise, but not worry. I took a quick step forward. Before he could react I had dipped my hand into Grubheimer's waistcoat pocket and a moment later held up a heavy gold ring to the Watchmen's eyes. A simple sleight-of-hand. Reinhold had taught his friend Dieter how to do it, too many years ago.

'The Countess's engagement ring,' I said, measuring my voice carefully against the last words of Father Ralf's prayer. 'This is the assassin who killed her.'

The prayer ended. Silence spread across the park.

'This Bretonnian,' I proclaimed with a voice like the wrath of the gods, 'is the man who killed the Countess!'

Scared realisation broke across Grubheimer's face like a crack of thunder. There was a murmuring of voices. Hundreds of people had turned to look at us. How must it seem to them? Two priests, members of the Watch, and one accused man. Grubheimer knew he was caught: I saw it in his face. I grasped Brother Jakob's arm more tightly and watched as Grubheimer did what I'd expected: he panicked. But not the way I'd hoped. He didn't run. He pulled a knife and lunged at me.

Without thinking, I spun away, dragging Brother Jakob around in front of me as I went. His feet slipped on the cold, hard ground, and he screamed as he began to fall. Grubheimer's knife met his chest, slicing through the thin black robes. Blood sprayed across the crowd. I lost my balance and fell.

Someone shouted, 'Murderer!' and people began to run.

I hit the earth hard, smashing my nose against the frozen ground and knocking the wind out of myself. Grubheimer stood fixedly above me, staring down, knife in hand. He looked so startled. Something had emerged from his breast. It was six inches of sword-blade. Over the Bretonnian's shoulder, I could see the man who had stabbed him: tall, bearded, scarred. He seemed familiar. In an instant he had pulled out his sword and disappeared into the milling crowd. Grubheimer crumpled slowly to the ground like a puppet, and died there. He didn't take his eyes off me for a moment.

There was movement: people were milling about, and there were cries of terror and sorrow. A rush of noise, of whispered words, swept across the park. The solemnity of the service was broken and lost.

Beside me on the ground lay Jakob. With one hand he was trying to staunch the bleeding from the slash across his stomach, but he wasn't succeeding. The light in his eyes was fading but he stared at me as if to say: You did this.

I reached over to him and placed my hand on his breast, over his heart, and tried to think of some farewell that would make sense, to either of us. I felt his heartbeat flutter and cease, and I realised there was only one thing I could say. I knelt beside him, placed my other hand on his forehead, and began the Ritual of Final Parting, willing his soul into the arms of Morr.

That was the last touch. It was done. I was safe. Overwhelming relief and tiredness swept through me and I slumped, lying beside Jakob, my face level with his dead eyes. You, I thought: a life among the dead was no place for a man like you. You said you wanted to die a hero's death. Well, you did. The man who gave his life to stop the Countess's assassin from escaping. And perhaps you died happy.

I doubted it, but it didn't matter. What mattered was that I would be the person who attended to his corpse, and that would let me dispose of the Black Lotus.

I would need a story to explain how I had discovered Grubheimer's guilt and the ring, but that could wait. The people of Middenheim had their assassin. With the murderer revealed as a Bretonnian, the diplomatic crisis would get worse and there might even be a war, but if that happened it would be far away. Father Ralf would be furious I had spoiled his service of remembrance, but I would live with the consequences of that tomorrow.

And what of Louise? She had lost the man who made her grubby life worth living. And Reinhold: I had stolen his triumph, his posthumous glory, the infamy that would have kept his name alive long after his body had been devoured by worms, and I had given it to the man who killed him. But I had saved Louise from the knowledge that her lover had killed her mistress. Maybe that was a good thing. I didn't know, and I wasn't sure if I cared.

But it had worked. It had all come together. I had survived. Only one innocent had died. Reinhold was avenged. It felt good. I almost grinned.

A voice I recognised said, 'Father.' Above me, Grizzly Bruno offered me his hand, and I took it and climbed to my feet. Somehow I knew that his presence was no accident. People had gathered around us, pushing and shoving, trying to get a glimpse of the two bodies, and the Watch were attempting to keep order. The mood of mourning had been shattered; everyone was talking excitedly about the assassin. I could just hear Ar-Ulric's strident voice battling against the noise, but nobody was listening any more.

I turned to the man who had helped me. 'Thank you, Bruno.'

'More thanks than you know, father,' he said in a low voice. 'The man who stuck your Bretonnian? One of mine.'

'You had me followed?'

'And with good reason,' he smiled. 'You didn't notice?'

'No.' I forced a smile. 'The priestly life slows the instincts.'

'Not too much I hope, father. You owe me a favour, and I'd still appreciate your advice on that business I mentioned this afternoon. Right up your old street, it is.'

'My old street,' I repeated, a strange thoughtfulness in my voice. This afternoon I had wondered if I would be able to cage the wolf of my old memories and instincts once I had dealt with Grubworm. I had forgotten to ask myself if I would want to. I had forgotten how good victory tasted. I had forgotten so many things.

Bruno looked at me. 'How about it, father?'

I smiled and reached out to shake his hand.

'Call me Dieter,' I said.

My Brother's Keeper

THEY COULD SMELL the city long before they could see it.

As that last day of their journey wore to a close, a pungent scent began to reach the caravan, carried on the cold, wet, spring air. A smell of industry: tanneries, blacksmithies, breweries, wood-fires, charcoal burners. A cloying combination of metal tang, ash, chimney-soot, and the sweetness of malting hops.

In the jolting confines of the staff carriage, Franckl oathed his distaste and emptied his insulted nostrils noisily into a lace kerchief. Curled in a corner seat, surrounded by piled strong boxes and chests that threatened to topple onto her, Lenya Dunst looked away in mild revulsion. Franckl was the Margrave's houseman, a fussy, prissy pustular wretch in his late forties, too in love with cross-gartered breeches and stiffly-laced doublets to realise they made him look like a bloated spatchcock ready for the griddle.

'That awful reek,' he moaned, wiping his pendulous nose on a corner of lace. 'What manner of place are these Wolves taking us to? Is this salvation? I think not!'

The other members of the Ganmark household crammed into the lurching carriage had no answer for him. The undercook was asleep and snoring wetly, the two chambermaids were pale and dumb with fear and fatigue, and the pot-boy had received too many claps to the back of his head from Franckl in his life to start conversing with him now. Maris, the old wet-nurse, was lost in her own dreams. Or nightmares, perhaps. Since Commander Ganz had destroyed her trinket and saved them all, she had been distant and listless.

Lenya caught Franckl's eye.

'I thought a man as... worldly as you would have visited Middenheim before, Master Franckl,' she said sweetly.

Franckl harrumphed, and then realised that the lowly milk-maid was his only audience. He dabbed his nose. After all, she was a pretty little thing, almost comely in a wildcat sort of way.

'Oh, long ago, my pet, long ago... As a younger man, I journeyed far and wide, visiting many of the great cities in the Empire. Ah yes, the adventures I've had... Hmm. It's just that the sweet woodland airs of Linz had quite stolen the stench of Middenheim from my memories.'

'Indeed,' Lenya smiled.

Franckl leaned forward conspiratorially and smiled loath-somely into Lenya's face. He put a hand on her knee. It was still clutching the snorted-on kerchief.

'My dear young pet, I was quite forgetting that such a place would be new to one such as you, a lithe, healthy damsel reared in the free pastures of the country. Hmmm. It must be an overwhelming prospect.'

'I'm looking forward to it,' she said through a gritted smile.

'So young, so brave!'

So eager to get there! thought Lenya. Despite all she had been through, this was an opportunity she relished. To go to the city! To Middenheim! To move in high circles, to advance herself! As it was, she relished the stink Franckl made such a show of loathing. To Lenya, it smelled of nothing more wonderful than the future.

Franckl squeezed her knee.

'Now, you mustn't be afraid, my pet. Middenheim will be frightening to you. So many people, such a great wealth of experiences and... and odours. You must always remember, when it gets too much for you, that you have a stout and true friend to turn to. Are you afraid, Leanna?'

'That's Lenya, actually. No, I'm not.' She tensed her leg under his hand, so he could feel the tight, lean thigh muscles bulge and twist. 'Are you?'

He took his hand away sharply and looked for something else to do. He slapped the pot boy's head for a start.

Lenya leaned over and pulled back the window drapes on the carriage to peer out. Rain fell outside. The distant perfume of Middenheim was stronger. The escorted caravan was just now clattering onto metalled cobbles from a dirt track. Lenya started back as a White Wolf cantered up alongside her carriage and glanced in at her. His smiling eyes found hers.

'Everything all right, milady?' the darkly handsome Wolf asked, majestic in his gold-edged plate mail and white pelt.

Lenya nodded. What was the Wolf's name? She hunted her memory. Anspach, that was it, Anspach.

'Everything is fine. Where are we?'

Anspach gestured ahead. 'We're just reaching the western viaduct into the city. Another half hour, and we'll be home.'

Lenya leaned out and looked down the cobbled pavement ahead. The long slow slope of the viaduct which led to Middenheim seemed to go on forever. The city itself was invisible in the drizzle.

The household carriage was one of the last in the now bedraggled caravan. The two smarter carriages ahead carried the Margrave and his family, followed by a series of four or five farm carts. A flatbed, carrying household essentials and covered in oilcloths, brought up the rear.

Franckl suddenly pushed past Lenya and stuck his head out to speak to the Wolf. Through the drizzle, he got his first glimpse of the city of Middenheim.

'By Sigmar!' he exclaimed as he caught sight of the vast rock for the first time. 'Look at it!' he cried. 'It's like a monster rising out of the ground!' Lenya and one of the chambermaids struggled to get a look too.

Lenya gasped despite herself. It was true. Middenheim was a huge, black monster. One she was dying to meet.

ON A CLEAR DAY, Middenheim could be seen from miles away, a great black monolith penetrating the sky. Now, in the thick wet of spring, they came upon it almost by surprise. The smell of the city grew stronger. The industrial odours mixed with those of people going about their business, thousands of people. Smells of food and clothes, house-dust and bodies came together in the air and drifted into every crevice of the wagon where Lenya sat with the houseman, the nurse and the rest of the staff.

As they advanced up the titanic western viaduct, the gloom melted away. With the clouds parting and a huge orange sun setting behind it, the Fauschlag stood stark and craggy against the gauzy sky. The jutting rock was indivisible from the great city that grew around its slopes and rose above it in a series of hard spikes and steeples.

As the convoy neared the city, traffic on the viaduct grew denser and the low rumble of the noisy city began to separate into a rich weave of individual voices. The caravan's progress was impeded by all manner of vehicles: hay-wains, wagons, trains of oxen, noble carriages, straggles of pilgrims, peddlers with handcarts, outrider messengers with miles to go, surly details of city militia. Motley clad people were leaving the city for their homes on the outskirts or entering it to ply their trade.

'Keep the caravan tight,' Ganz called to his men and they all moved a little closer in formation. He could see the increasing mass of people ahead. Some were no doubt trying to sneak in or out of the city, past the guards, for reasons of their own, and Ganz didn't want any trouble now. They edged round a milliner's heavily-laden wagon with a broken axle that was impeding the flow. Morgenstern and Aric rode smartly ahead to hold back the oncoming traffic so that the noble convoy could pass. Morgenstern cursed at a Sigmarite devotee who tried to interest him in a lead pilgrim's keepsake of his god. They pressed on, up the slow curve of the viaduct towards the snarling city above.

Lenya sat by the window of her carriage and gazed out in awe, breathing it all in. Even when they were forced to run close to the low wall of the viaduct to pass the broken cart, she did not flinch from the yawning drop below, the travertine supports of the ancient viaduct which reached away into the depths of the misty chasm. Franckl glimpsed the drop and fell back into his seat, looking green.

Lenya leaned out further to look ahead. Heavily-laden carts and oxen-rigs made slow progress cheek by jowl with grand vehicles and gilt landaus, urchins banging the wheels with sticks and running away, giggling at their own audacity.

The caravan managed to stay together as dusk fell and a heavy purple sky settled over Middenheim. There were no clouds, and the stars and the rising pair of moons made the forty foot high wood and stone keeps, either side of the city southgate, appear even grander than they would have by daylight.

'Well, we've arrived at last,' Franckl said. As he pointedly pulled closed the window curtain for the last time before entering the city, Lenya saw walls the height of four tall men and three times as thick as a guardsman's torso growing proudly out of the seamless rock face below. The rock had been hewn into a great city wall by hundreds of dwarf masons, but they had done more than tame the rock; they had given it hard lines and a form that only appeared to add strength and longevity to the stones.

Passing through the south gate, there was light once more, the light of thousands of braziers and lamps burning for the folk of Middenheim. A soft yellow glow to light their way and to keep them safe from the city's human parasites, who stalked the unwary to rob them of their possessions or their lives.

Lenya pulled the window drapes open again and pegged them up to let in the light. It let in noise too: the noise of thousands of people hawking their wares, screaming at each other or calling out at them from street corners. And all the smells that had collected and built during the last stage of the journey now came together in a wave that took Lenya's breath away and apparently scorched the hairs in the houseman's nostrils.

'Sigmar save me!' Franckl gasped. 'Too much, too, too much!'

Nothing like enough, thought Lenya.

She looked across at Maris. The wetnurse had almost stopped breathing altogether as she sat huddled in the corner of the wagon.

'I don't think I can bear the noise a minute longer,' she moaned.

'Or the stink,' Franckl added. 'Haven't these heathens heard of latrines?'

'You can't crap in a field when you live on a rock, so you'd better get used to it,' Lenya said, coarse and unsympathetic as she drank in the sights inside the city walls. The caravan was crawling now, thanks to the press of people around them. Lenya was stunned by the relentless grey stone of a myriad disparate buildings. 'This is what they've brought us to and there's no getting out of it now. But it must be nothing new to a travelled man like you, Master Franckl.'

Franckl fell glumly silent.

Others in the Ganmark convoy looked out in wonder. Most of White Company's charges were new to Middenheim. Some had never seen any city before, much less one so large or so grand. While the Wolves marched them steadily onwards and upwards past the Square of Martials and then the Konigsgarten on their way to the Middenplatz, the eyes of amazed passengers took in the awesome uniformity of barrack buildings and the Parade Square. This was the only truly flat land on the rock, used by the militia for drilling and military parades, but now it was empty, save for the central fountain spitting silvery water up from its heart.

Franckl was the first to catch sight of the Graf's palace itself, their destination.

'By all that's holy!' he exclaimed. 'Did you ever see such a place?'

'I thought you said you had?' Lenya snapped, pushing him aside to get a look.

Maris the wet-nurse huddled tighter into her corner. Her hands over her abused ears and a wide kerchief folded and tied around the lower half of her face, she looked like a frightened bandit.

Lenya leaned out of her window to see a series of great stone buildings surrounded by tall, iron railings ending in spear tips, as much for security as for decoration. Beyond the railings, the private quarters were faced with beautiful carvings which softened their lines and bulk, while adding exquisite ornamentation. The tall, scrolled marble pillars made the Graf's home unique among the buildings of Middenheim. No dwarf hand had wrought such decoration. The pillars and facade of the inner palace were the work of legendary artisans, brought in from Tilea and Bretonnia, and sent away again richly rewarded for their efforts.

They passed in through the Great Gate and down the flags of the entrance drive into the yard of the Inner Palace. The caravan came to a halt. Lenya heard Ganz shouting out orders to dismount and stand attendance. She pushed open the carriage door and was down before the houseman could move. The palace yard was wide and cold. She gazed up at the buildings, quite the most beautiful structures she had ever seen, even in her dreams. Franckl almost fell out of the carriage behind her, slapping at the pot-boy's head and sending him after their luggage.

The undercook woke at last and climbed down. The chambermaids cowered together beside the horses. Maris took a long time to emerge.

Lenya saw the Wolf commander with the Margrave, shaking hands, her master effusive and excited. Nearby she saw handsome Anspach and the huge Wolf, Morgenstern, chasing the royal children in play around the yard, whooping and laughing. She saw the old warrior Gruber in quiet conversation with her lady. The tall young knight named Aric appeared behind her, taking Maris by the arm to look after her. Lenya turned again amid the activity, and found Drakken in front of her. He was smiling his sleepy, winning smile.

'I–' she began.

He kissed her.

'I'll look for you later, Krieg,' she finished.

He smiled again, then he was gone and the Wolves were departing under curt orders from their commander.

Pages and servants in pink silk livery were emerging from the palace to take in the Margrave's luggage. They were flanked by others who held torches and lamps. A tall, emaciated man in a regal, black, high-collared jacket and lace choker strode out to meet them all, pacing the ground with a silver-knobbed cane. He wore a white, ringletted and ribboned wig of the latest fashion and his skin was aristocratically powdered white.

'I am Breugal, chamberlain to the Graf,' he said in a strangled, haughty voice. 'Follow me and I will show you to your quarters.'

'Sir, I greet you!' Franckl started, striding forward, hand outstretched to take the chamberlain's. 'As one houseman to another, I rejoice in the welcome you–'

Breugal ignored the hand and turned aside. He jerked his silver-topped cane at his waiting pages. 'Get them inside! The night is chill and I have better things to do.'

The pages scurried forward, snatching up luggage. Franckl remained with his hand outstretched and untaken, amazed.

Lenya felt real sorrow for him then, sorrow and shame. Breugal strode away on clacking high heels, cane-end ticking rhythmically on the flags. Franckl and the undercook picked up their few personal belongings and followed a disdainful page into the palace.

'I shan't stay,' Lenya heard the wet-nurse muttering to the Templar, Aric, as he escorted her inside.

Lenya followed them into an inner courtyard. She lifted her eyes to look at the buildings around the small cobbled space. They were shockingly spare, dank and plain compared to the great courtyard, but some of the windows were lit and Lenya could hear people moving around inside, looking out, invisible to her. As she got used to the sounds, she began to pick out voices.

'By Ulric, that old nursemaid won't last five minutes,' she heard a half-broken voice laugh. 'And the old houseman ain't fit for overmuch either,' it continued.

Lenya realised she was alone and began to walk across the courtyard to the open door.

'Look at the poor, lost, little milkmaid,' the voice came again, joined in laughter by another youthful cackle. 'We can share that one if you like... but I get first go!' Lenya picked up her ragged skirts and, scared now, hurried toward the safety of the archway and her travelling companions.

This was Middenheim. Palace life. Not what she had dreamed of. Not at all.

THE FIRST WEEK at the palace was tough enough, but Lenya knew it would get tougher. It was a friendless place. She seldom saw the other servants she had arrived with, and the palace staff treated her like horse flop. Less than horse flop. She found herself craving the company of Franckl or the pot-boy. At least they knew who she was. The palace staff, the haughty ladies, Chamberlain Breugal, even the lowliest of the low, like the grate sweepers and the spit-boy, treated her with utter contempt. And there was a particular page, a rat-arse called Spitz. Spitz was the page that she had heard slurring her when she arrived. She despised him, but he was not her only problem. Endlessly, she found herself lost in the bowels of the palace. No matter what, she still couldn't find her way around. For all its fancy stonework, the palace was a dark labyrinth.

The Margrave and his entourage had been invited, albeit briefly, into the staterooms the evening they arrived. Lenya had been impressed by how grand they were, but soon realised she was unlikely to see them again. The Margrave received little more than political charity from the Graf, and his entire household were second-class citizens taking up space. Their given rooms were damp, and many of them were dark and windowless. They were oddly shaped and unaccommodating and Lenya, who could scout her way successfully across any heavy woodland, still could not find her way from one dingy room to another without becoming hopelessly lost.

At the end of the first miserable week, Maris left. The wetnurse, who had spent the entire time locked away, refusing to eat or drink and virtually unable to perform her natural functions, just upped and left. With the house at Linz completely gone, the nurse still preferred to live in a barn rather than endure the horrors of city life a day longer. She wandered away out of the north gate one nightfall, her bag in her hand.

With the nurse gone, Lenya became the constant companion of Gudrun, the beautiful Lady Margrave, who plunged herself into self-imposed isolation in the palace and dragged Lenya with her. The lowliest servants of the palace saw fit to scold, abuse and beat Lenya for a week or two. But it wasn't long before she was fighting back.

It was mid-afternoon, although Lenya could hardly tell time in the windowless recesses of the palace. She had been sent on an errand to the main kitchen. Returning, cross and spiteful after a particularly prolonged tirade from the larder man, she felt a hand land squarely on her behind, causing her to drop the jug of warm water that she had been sent to beg. Loud laughter behind her made Lenya turn.

'You'll have to beg for another, now!' screeched the barely grown voice of the adolescent page who stood behind her. It was Spitz. He was short and wiry with thin hair, pallid face and large teeth, and he'd been following Lenya around since he'd seen her standing alone in the courtyard on the night she had arrived. All he wanted from his wretched little life was to become the next Breugal. He was a loathsome creature, full of his own importance, and he took Lenya for an appealing, easy target. Most of the ladies of the house, even the serving women, were completely inaccessible to him, but this was one pretty girl who had no status and, better yet, no defences.

Leering at her, spittle spilling from the corners of his lips, Spitz pushed his hand hard against Lenya's thigh and squeezed.

'Take your filthy hand off me,' Lenya growled. 'Or take the beating of your life!'

Spitz laughed again. 'Who's going to defend your honour then, my little milking cow?' His other hand came to meet the front of her dress, low on her belly.

Lenya's arms came up and under the page's hands, thrusting them off her body. Then she took his greasy head between her hands and held it firmly, as he looked at her in shocked wonder.

'You want me?' Lenya asked sweetly and then pushed his head down as hard as she could. She folded the page in half, cupping her forearm under his neck and lifting him into a tight stranglehold. Then she thrust his head between her skirt knees, squeezing until his face went a greyish puce and he passed out. She let go, dropping him to the floor. She made a wiping motion with her hands and began to walk away.

She turned to the slumped body as the page began to come round, clutching his head.

'That's the last time *any* of you touches me,' she said.

THOSE FIRST WEEKS that Lenya spent at the palace felt like months. No, like an eternity. Lenya was not given to sentiment; she only knew that life in the country had been better than this, but she suspected that the city could be better than anything. Unfortunately, the Lady Margrave had decided that Middenheim was far too dangerous a place for any of her servants to explore unescorted, and with no friends in the palace and enough enemies among the staff to last her a lifetime, Lenya's opportunities for recreation were limited

One afternoon, she stood with her elbows on the wall of a balcony, her hands under her chin, looking again at the view, as she remembered events of the last month and tried to put them behind her. From her vantage point Lenya could see clear across Middenheim. She could hear the buzz of a thousand voices, accented with the louder cries of a multitude of street traders. She could see down into the wider streets and avenues in the north of the city. South and east the streets became narrow in a tightly packed grey maze that she could never follow. In some places the roofs were so close together that all she could see was a narrow strip of darkness. She could only guess at what might happen in those dark, grimy, intimate places. She knew there were thieves and beggars and people of strange races, and she knew that her only hope of some kind of happiness was to escape into that city and become part of it.

Lenya had her back to the balcony door and did not hear the footsteps coming up behind her. She didn't know she had company until a pair of thick, solid hands came over her head to cover her eyes. With the shift in her light, Lenya swung round, one tight, hard fist jabbing into the silhouette of a face right behind her.

'Lenya! Ow!' Drakken cried. 'It's me.'

'Krieg! Gods, never surprise me!'

'Rest assured, I won't,' Drakken replied, wiping his bloodied nose against his sleeve. 'Jaws of Ulric, it was supposed to be a nice surprise.' He looked meekly down at the tiny, fearsome, tight little woman who sometimes cradled his heart and once or twice had bloodied his face.

'Call yourself a Wolf?' she snarled at him, watching his heart sink in his eyes. Then, hating herself for hurting him, she repented. 'I'm sorry, Krieg,' she said. 'It's just… I need to get out of here!'

'So let me take you for a walk in the Konigsgarten.'

The safety of the formal garden close to the palace was not quite what Lenya had in mind. She had taken numerous walks there with Drakken, He was a White Wolf, of course, and she had seen his bravery in battle. She wished he would be strong like that with her. Instead he was as strong as dishwater, as passionate as the well-laid, over-clipped, mossy pathways of the Konigsgarten. Oh yes, there were trees and grass and flowers, but they were forced to grow where few plants would choose to grow naturally. The rock yielded only lichens and tiny faded rock-plants. There was no soil. To Lenya, there was no nature in the garden, the plants were either forced or non-existent, and green was supplied by mosses rather than grass and twisted, stunted trees that could find nowhere to root and consequently grew only sparse dark leaves or brittle needles. There was as much spontaneity and liberty in those tight clumps of faded petals and blocks of spongy moss as there was in Lenya's life. And she hated it. She sighed.

'Not today,' she said. 'Go and wipe your nose – and stop being such a lap dog!'

Drakken turned away, hurt and puzzled.

Lenya listened to his footsteps retreating in the quiet. She looked out towards the uniform grey of the buildings of Middenheim, and then turned fast on her heels. Fearing he was gone, she called Drakken's name.

'Krieg? Krieg!' She could see him before she heard his footfall. 'You could take me out!' she said. The idea suddenly felt real to her and she smiled at him. 'Wolf Drakken,' she began again, 'would you do me the honour of escorting me into the city?'

Her smile made his heart tumble all over again. Nobody had ordered him not to take Lenya out of the palace and grounds, yet he knew that the Lady Margrave insisted Lenya be close at hand at all times.

'Lenya,' he began, hating himself for disappointing her. He could see it in her face now, a mixture of petulance and defiance and a kind of bravado. A face he could love, but feared he might never understand.

'Don't tell me,' she said. 'I know. The Lady Margrave *wouldn't approve.*' That last she said in a haughty, crabby voice that, to herself at least, exactly mimicked her ladyship. 'Then I shall go alone!' she insisted, spinning on her heels and folding her arms. Lenya had developed the skill of flouncing by practising on her father. He had sired a series of strong, lively boys before producing his only, cherished daughter. She wondered if perhaps she'd gone too far with Drakken, given him the chance to see through her little tantrum. Drakken could at least get her out of the palace.

'All right,' Drakken said, quietly. Then, realising the opportunity to escort and protect and be alone with this wonderful girl, he brightened. 'Lenya, I'd be proud to escort you into the great city of Middenheim,' he said and her broad, bewitching smile quenched any last doubts he had as to the wisdom of the venture.

Drakken and Lenya left the palace grounds without incident. Those Panther guards who recognised the young Wolf of White

Company acknowledged them with a nod; those who did not merely allowed the short, powerful man in uniform and his tiny companion to pass unmolested. Drakken was proud of Lenya and she of him, although their relationship caused constant comment amongst the staff at the palace and no small amount of envy in the unmarried women there.

Drakken decided he first wanted to show Lenya his spiritual home, the Temple of Ulric.

'I've had quite enough of grey rock buildings and cold, dead places,' Lenya complained. 'I want to see people! Life! Excitement! There must be somewhere in the city where people go for their leisure, away from the dark streets and grey houses. There must be life here somewhere.'

Drakken grabbed Lenya's hand in his great paw and hurried her away, south, down a steep avenue of grand houses. They were weaving in and out of the throngs of people that Lenya had been watching from above for the past month. This was more like it.

'So, where are you taking me?' Lenya asked.

'To the Black Pool, a famous landmark,' Drakken answered. 'And if we take this road, I can still show you the Temple.'

Lenya was not pleased. She did not want to see a temple at all and the Black Pool didn't sound very lively either, but Drakken had grasped her hand so tightly and seemed so excited that there was nothing left for her to say. As they hurried down the avenue, tripping up and down short flights of steps and around steep slopes, Lenya tried to look about her at the rich houses, and the merchants and gentlemen and women who were visiting them. For so long she had seen nothing of the city and now she was being whisked through it too fast for her to take any of it in.

They turned a corner. Ahead, she caught sight of a tall, slender building and wanted to ask what it was. Drakken said something she couldn't hear and bustled her onwards.

Enough, she thought. She picked up just enough speed to come level with Drakken and jabbed her foot in front of his, an old trick she'd developed for use on her brothers. The Wolf lunged forward, arms splaying, his feet feeling for the stone pavement. Two, three mid-air steps and he managed to level his head, which he felt sure would plunge into the slabs and knock him unconscious in an instant. He found his feet and straightened. Behind him, Lenya had her hand to her face, ready for horror or hilarity, depending on the outcome of her lover's trip. As he turned, red in the face, she giggled.

'Let's slow down before we have an accident, shall we?'

Grudgingly, Drakken began a slower guided tour. Lenya caught sight of a mass of people congregating behind the low wall across the street. She could hear snippets of conversation and the low buzz that signalled excitement.

'What's that?' she asked.

'The Great Park,' he replied.

'Can we get in there? I want to see.'

'There's no gate nearby. We'll follow the ring around.'

They went on, but Lenya glanced at the activity over the park wall at regular intervals. There were people here; maybe some of them would be her kind of people. She might even begin her search, the secret purpose she had kept from everyone. At the very least she could be herself. At the palace she was invisible to the gentry and despised by the servants.

Drakken led Lenya around the Garten Ring, towards the nearest park gate. He was happy enough to do this because the route naturally took them past the Temple of Ulric, his place of worship, and also, since it housed the barracks of the White Wolves, his home. He looked at the massive structure with proud eyes.

'What do you think?' he asked. She didn't answer. He looked round to find her striding on without him for an entrance to the park.

Drakken cursed. He was about to run after her when a voice called out from the Temple atrium. It was Ganz, his commander. Drakken was torn. He couldn't ignore his commander's summons, but Lenya was almost lost in the crowds of the Garten Ring already.

'Wait there!' he yelled to Lenya. 'I'll only be a moment! Wait!' He wasn't sure if she'd heard him. Ganz called him again.

LENYA WAS SO taken with the hubbub of the street-life, she didn't really concern herself with Drakken's absence He'd catch up, she thought. She hunted for an entrance to the park.

Following the Garten Ring, south, down more steep and winding paths, Lenya quickly found the west gate into the Great Park. The gate, swung open on its posts, was made of that same dark timber used everywhere in Middenheim, and the walls were cut from the same grey rock, but what beckoned from within seemed more alive than anything she'd ever seen.

Lenya raised her head slightly as she passed a soldier from the City Watch at the gate. Dressed, as she was, in borrowed finery, the lady-in-waiting's cast-offs that her mistress had insisted she wear, she had some vestige of confidence. But the country girl within her made Lenya certain she would have to endure some quizzing at the hands of this authority figure and she wanted to make herself look as important as possible. She had nothing to fear. The Watchman merely nodded a slight bow in her direction, before going about his business.

The Great Park wasn't a park at all. It was a labyrinth of paths which wound between a ragged collection of stalls; open carts with burners selling hot snacks, which smelled of rancid grease, and tall, narrow stands with racks of food stuffs, old clothes and household goods. Loud men waved their arms, demonstrating wares that they sold suspiciously cheaply and in huge numbers.

Lenya was mesmerised. There were people everywhere: buyers, sellers, browsers, barterers, families, couples, household staff from noble homes on provisioning errands, urchins dashed between adult legs causing their own particular brand of chaos. Lenya forgot that she was alone and began to walk around, listening to snippets of conversation, examining the goods for sale and taking it all in. She had never seen so many people in one place, clad in so many styles of dress, nor heard so many different dialects. Ahead of her a noisy crowd was gathering around a narrow handcart. She could just see the top of the tousled straw-coloured head which belonged to the man standing on the cart.

'Miladies and gentlemen!' bawled the voice, sing-song. 'Don't just stand there gawping – put your hands in your pockets for this once-in-a-lifetime purchasing opportunity!' A pair of long arms flailed above the tousled head and Lenya saw a huge showman's grimace. The crowd laughed, heckled and some began to move away. Lenya smiled to herself, pushing in to get a better look.

She felt a movement behind her rather than heard it and was only mildly surprised when she felt the brush of a hand against the side of her waist. She'd been expecting lightfooted

Drakken to catch up with her sooner or later, though she'd warned him not to surprise her. His mistake. She didn't think twice: she rammed her elbow hard behind her, following it with a straight forearm and balled fist. It wouldn't hurt Drakken, not a big tough Wolf in armour like him. But instead of connecting with the broad solid torso of the White Wolf, Lenya's elbow and then her fist connected with a soft, bony, unfamiliar target.

'Whhooff!' a small voice choked from behind her. Lenya heard a slight body fall heavily. The crowd around her fell silent and began to turn in the direction of the sound. Lenya felt a dozen pairs of eyes on her as she turned to look at what or whom she'd hit.

Sitting on the ground behind her, clutching at his stomach, legs splayed out to either side, was a gangly young man, tidily dressed with flat black hair and a wounded expression. He was all arms and legs and Lenya had to step over one protruding knee to take a good look at him.

'By all that's wise!' she exclaimed. 'What have I done?'

The crowd returned their gaze to the salesman, who'd begun his banter again, dismissing the sort of scene they saw every day in the city. The man on the ground looked quizzically at Lenya and then let out a huge, bellowing laugh.

'I'm terribly sorry, sir!' breathed a stunned Lenya, grasping the youth by the elbow and trying to help him to his feet. He laughed again.

'Don't worry,' he answered. 'Truth is, I was due a rousting anytime about now. Just caught me unawares that's all.' He clutched his stomach again as he tried to laugh through the ache that Lenya had planted there with her tight fist. His humour was infectious and Lenya began to laugh with him, not knowing what he was laughing at, but enjoying the freedom. She hadn't laughed properly out loud in weeks.

Back on his feet, the young man gently took Lenya's arm and led her to a narrow set of winding steps with tall walls either side. She felt no apprehension. When they were alone, he began to talk to her.

'So, what's a country girl like you doing walking around in city finery?'

'And what's a city boy like you doing grabbing at young ladies in public?'

'Touché,' the youth answered, bellowing his startling laugh once more.

The pair sat on the stone steps, aware only of each other and the hum of the crowd that spilled over the walls surrounding them. For the second time, an opportunistic young man had seen Lenya as an easy target. This time the man had been after her purse.

The gangly youth with the flat hair introduced himself as Arkady, petty villain, pick-pocket and general scammer. He had no reason not to be honest. He might not be quite what he seemed, but then neither was this milkmaid dressed in all the finery of court. He'd expected the rich purse of a dolt who wouldn't even notice it was missing until she tried to pay for something, and when she found her money gone would probably have a swooning fit. Instead he had got an elbow in the stomach and a fist in the solar plexus and serve him right.

Lenya found herself telling him about the farm near Linz where she'd been raised, about her brothers – and how she'd come to Middenheim. She spoke of the revolting page and the dark damp rooms she was forced to live in. She talked of the palace, but not how she had come to be at liberty in the Great Park. She was talking to a criminal after all and didn't want to confuse things by telling him about her White Wolf. She had another thing to talk about. Her secret.

'My brother came here,' she said, finally. 'It must have been a year ago now. Came to make his fortune. I never thought I'd reach Middenheim, but now I'm here, I want to find him.'

'In a city this size?' Arkady laughed again – then stopped abruptly, realising this wasn't funny to the naïve but feisty country girl. 'Look, if he came from the country,' he began, 'he's probably back in the country by now.'

'And if not?' Lenya asked.

Arkady looked at his scuffed shoes. He didn't want to hurt the girl, but she had to know the facts of life. 'If he's still here, he's probably joined one of the less… recognised guilds. One of the local lords of the underworld may have recruited him to "run errands".'

Lenya looked dismayed. 'He's honest! He'd find honest work first!'

Arkady snorted. 'There's no honest work in Middenheim for outsiders. The roads aren't paved with gold and the guilds have business tied up tighter than a houseman's codpiece. It's all nepotism and dead men's shoes. Why else do you think there's so much "free enterprise" in Middenheim? Yon market trader on his handcart – the mouthy sod with the straw hair – shunts carts in and out of the city every week. Most of them are hijacked somewhere on the other side of the wall...' Arkady's story tailed off.

'So my brother's a criminal?' asked an indignant Lenya.

Or dead, Arkady thought, but instead said, 'He's probably back in the country by now.'

Lenya thought for a moment, then took a deep breath. 'If he's here, I still want to find him,' she said, determined. 'Where do I find one of these "lords" to talk to? Someone has to know where he is.'

Arkady was doubtful. This girl hadn't been anywhere except the palace and this was her first visit to the streets. She knew nothing yet of the filth, squalor, and poverty, not to mention the ruthlessness of the people who populated the poorer quarters of the city. On the other hand, she had taken him out single-handed with her elbow and one puny fist when she shouldn't even have heard him.

'You're going to take me to one of these knowledgeable gentlemen!' she told him fiercely, seeing the reluctance in his open face.

'Whoa! No way! Look, there are better methods. I know someone, a rogue, but with a good heart. I'm small beans, girl... I don't have contact with any of the "Low Kings". Too dangerous for a sprat like me. But he does. He carries a little more weight. And you'll be safe with him. He'll look after you and he just might be able to find something out about that long-lost brother of yours.'

Arkady got ready to leave. 'Meet me here, day after tomorrow. Can you find this place again?'

'I think so,' Lenya answered. 'But can't you take me now?'

Arkady looked over the wall. The sky was darkening to its familiar purple hue and the Great Park was becoming quieter. He was safe enough, but Lenya wouldn't be safe for long in this place at this hour of the day.

'It's late. You might be missed. Go home, girl, straight home. Come and find me the day after tomorrow.' And with that he started to jog down the steps two at a time. In half a dozen steps he had turned a corner. Lenya watched the top of his head bobbing up and down above the height of the wall and in a few more seconds he was gone. She stood and looked around her. It was getting dark, but she could find her way back. Then she remembered Drakken.

'Sigmar! Krieg!' she exclaimed under her breath and hurried up the steps and around the wall. She'd just have to find her way back to his beloved temple and hope he was still there.

NIGHT FELL FAST in Middenheim and by the time Lenya retraced her way to the great Temple of Ulric, it was dusk and the yellow evening lamps of the city were being lit. Cross at herself and at Drakken, she paced about outside the Temple for a few minutes and was ready to find her own way back to the palace when she realised just how difficult that might be.

Lenya was not known at the palace, not by anyone outside the Margrave's entourage or the domestic staff. If she tried to enter the palace grounds at any time, let alone at nightfall, she would receive short shrift from the guard. Her day's adventure was fast wearing thin. Now she realised she had to find Drakken if she was to return to the palace at all tonight. She had no very strong desire to go back to the foetid rooms she was required to call home, at least for now, but she also had no choice. Arkady had gone and she was alone in a city that, while it enthralled her, began to look sinister in the low meagre light. Silhouettes of buildings around her loomed black, hard and spiky against the sky. Pools of yellow light gave the grey stones a sickly colour. The stones seemed to absorb light, sucking it into their surfaces and draining it to small, murky pools. Shadows were long and forbidding and seemed to bear no relations to their owners. Darkness masked the uneven ground beneath Lenya's feet, making steps and slopes even more treacherous than they were by day.

Don't panic! Lenya told herself. *This is Drakken's home, he must be here. And if he isn't someone will be.*

Lenya was ready to knock on the great door of the Temple and even open it if needs be. She threw back her shoulders and lifted her fist. Putting what she hoped was a confident smile on her lips, she knocked on the door. There was no answer.

Lenya squared up to the door again and then jumped wholesale out of her skin when she heard the voice behind her.

'Can I help you, my lady?' asked the voice. A voice full of confidence and ease mixed with authority and power. Lenya turned slowly and stared at the man behind her, seeing only as high as his slender, powerful chest. She didn't need to answer.

'What are you doing out of the palace precinct?' Gruber asked as he recognised the brave farm girl from the Margrave's entourage. 'This won't do. I'll escort you back. If young Drakken knew you were missing, he'd be sending out a search party.'

Lenya lifted her eyes slowly to meet the concerned look of the veteran soldier. Drakken did know she was missing. He'd never take her out again. She wanted to cry with anger and frustration. She'd be locked up in the palace for good now.

BACK IN THE comparative safety of the palace, Lenya spent a day and night working out what to do. She thought about her next meeting with Arkady as she bathed in cold water from the dish on her bed-stand that grew mould overnight. She thought about it as she tended her pale, frightened mistress in the sloping, windowless room that she never left; and she thought about it as she ate the cold leftovers, congealed on grubby plates, that had become the chief part of her diet.

She was grateful that Drakken had decided to keep away. He wouldn't take her out again and she didn't want to hear about how worried he was and how concerned he had been for her safety. She could rely on herself and she wouldn't have anyone suggesting otherwise.

Gruber had treated her well and kindly. Returning her to the palace via one of the more discreet side-gates, he had stopped and spoken to men from the City Watch on duty there. He introduced her to them as a girl under the direct protection of the Temple. The sentries nodded solemnly. None of them wished to get on the wrong side of the White Wolves. Now there were several of the gate guards who would recognise her if she needed them to. If any of these men were on duty, she could get in or out of the palace grounds without any trouble. If not it was a short walk to the Temple and she guessed that if Gruber had recognised her so easily then others would too. She would never be short of a trusty escort back to the palace.

Two days later therefore, Lenya left the Graf's palace, walked south towards the Great Park and found again the entrance she

had used before. It was around the same time of day and the
place was thronged with people again. The rocky paths were
slick with the light rain and when clumps of people diverted
her path onto the mossy terraces, the dark, spongy surface was
almost greasy underfoot. She kept her eye on the milling people, but they all had business of their own to attend to and
ignored her. She was also wary of the rougher looking element
and even crossed one path and joined another to avoid a
bawdily drunken clutch of youths ready to leer at anything in a
skirt.

It took her two or three attempts to find the flight of narrow
steps where she had sat with Arkady only days before, and
when she did find them she stumbled upon them by accident.
She sat three or four steps down from the top, out of sight.
After half an hour or so, Lenya began to wonder if they were the
right steps after all. Then, suddenly, she looked up sharply,
without knowing why. She hadn't heard anything new above
the hum of the crowd, but as she fixed her gaze she caught sight
of a head with flat black hair and stood, sighing with relief, to
greet Arkady.

He came within a few steps of her, keeping low so as not to
be seen over the wall, and beckoned her to follow him. As the
steps led downward, turning sharply left and right as they went,
Lenya realised why they had not encountered anyone else on
the staircase. As they dropped steeper and narrower, the walls
rose higher around them, becoming a low arch that dripped
slightly with the thick black liquid of rotting vegetation. The
steps went from being damp to being dark and wet and covered
in old, slippery moss. The hem of Lenya's dress became heavy
with brackish water and her tall boots began to leak.

She stopped. 'Where are we going?' she asked, apprehensive
for the first time. She was with a complete stranger. Trusting
him with her life in a strange city and he seemed to be leading
her underground into silence and darkness.

He caught the tone in her voice. 'Trust me,' he said, and
laughed. 'Honestly, it's all right. See, no one uses the old stairs
much anymore, but they're safe and they'll get us to where we
want to be.'

She looked at him in the gloom. 'Soon,' he said. 'I promise.'

Within a matter of minutes, the steps came to an abrupt end
and Lenya followed Arkady across a tiny closed courtyard

where facing roofs almost touched overhead. From there, she entered the back room of what she thought must be a private home, but was, in fact, one of the many one-room drinking holes that littered the alleys of the south-east corner of Middenheim.

'Now!' Arkady exclaimed. 'What in all the gods' names are we going to do about that awful garb?'

Lenya looked down at her dress. She'd never liked it and she already knew she couldn't wear it and walk safely through this district of the city. She needed no more than her instincts to tell her that.

'Can you get me a pair of breeches and a knife?' she asked Arkady, tugging at her dress sleeves. He looked at her, puzzled, then handed her the short knife he kept in the back of his own breeches. She had not noticed it before.

'I'll be back with the other in a moment,' he said, turning and leaving the way they had come.

Lenya took the knife and cut the sleeves off her dress at the armhole, showing the plain sleeves of her shift underneath. Then she cut the bottom four inches from her skirt; they were sodden now and smelled of standing water. Tossing the cloth into the fire, along with her petticoats, Lenya had another idea. She poked the dwindling black log on the grate until it flared and spat ashes through the grill. She spread the ashes with a twisted shovel from the hearth and rubbed them into her hands. Then she massaged the soot into the bodice of her dress and began on the panels of her skirt. When Arkady returned she was well on her way to looking like a common woman. He held out the breeches to her.

Lenya turned her back and cut right through the front of her skirt, from a little below the waist right down to the hem. Then she cut several inches from the bottom of the breeches and put them on. She turned to Arkady and held her hands up in a dramatic gesture, waiting for his approval. He smiled and reached out to her hair, which he tousled mercilessly until it sat in a lopsided mass on her head, dripping down onto her brow and neck. He stepped back and bellowed his great laugh.

'Almost there,' he said. 'See, those milkmaid arms are a dead give away, but I think I've got just the thing.' Ducking out again, Arkady returned a moment later with a short, battered leather jerkin. It belonged to the pot-boy and Arkady had whipped it

off the hook behind the door. He held it open for Lenya to
shrug into. It fit well enough, and completed her reinvention.
Lenya could pass anonymously through the darker streets of
the city now, could pass for anyone or no one. She was ready
to meet this rogue that Arkady was so proud of knowing.

KRUZA SAT HUNCHED over a pot of ale in the single public room
of the seedy establishment that incongruously called itself a
tavern. He was partial to a pot of ale, but this weak, rancid mixture was turning his stomach and he belched loudly as Arkady
and Lenya entered through the pot-door behind the plank-and-
barrel structure which served for a bar. Arkady laughed his
trademark laugh and Kruza lifted his head without any movement in his sloping shoulders.

Seeing the small, comely girl in clothes that were coming
apart along several promising seams, Kruza straightened up.
He smartened the front of his jerkin self-consciously and
smiled.

'I thought you were bringing some rough and tumble farm
girl!' he murmured to Arkady. 'This creature doesn't look like
she belongs anywhere near a cow.'

'Wait till she opens her mouth,' Arkady grinned and Lenya,
gritting her teeth, kicked him hard in the shin. 'I guess I'll leave
you to it then,' he said, winking at the girl before retreating out
of the door behind him.

Lenya sat next to Kruza, searching his green eyes for anything
that might help her understand why she felt so drawn to him.
Something there made her a little afraid and then he smiled
again and her body relaxed.

'Arkady tells me you're looking for someone,' Kruza began.

'My brother, Stefan. Older than me by two years. A little
taller. Fair-haired. Eyes like mine. He left Linz for Middenheim
a year ago. Arkady said he was probably working as an errand
boy for one of the... what did he call them? Low Kings?'

'More likely dead,' said Kruza, looking down into the fuzzy
ale that he was never going to drink. 'And if he isn't, there must
be a thousand men in Middenheim who fit his description.'

'But there's only one Stefan!' Lenya exclaimed. 'If you won't
help, then I'll find these Low Kings for myself.'

Kruza looked again at the girl. Arkady had told him how she
had fought him off in the market, but she didn't look nearly as

tough as she talked. And he was sure she didn't have the money to pay him for his services. He sighed.

'Very well,' he said, 'I'll help you. But we're not going to the Low Kings. The last thing you want to do is tangle with men like Bleyden. We begin with the priest.'

Lenya was ready to protest. What use was a priest to her? But Kruza had already taken her hand and before she knew where she was, they had left the tavern and begun to walk along the narrow, dim and filthy street. This, she guessed, was the Altquartier, the roughest, poorest, most depraved part of the city. Lenya had only seen it at a distance, from her balcony in the palace. The narrow, winding thoroughfares were full of bustling, dirty people. Women shrieked at barefoot urchins and threw their waste indiscriminately onto the streets. There was almost no light: the sky was a series of thin, grey, jagged stripes above her, largely blocked out by the low roofs of leaning buildings. Ragged dogs growled and barked and slunk away when kicked by the indolent men who sat on narrow steps on the street. There was no order here, only bad smells, bad light and too much noise. Lenya stayed close to Kruza, as they became invisible among the ragged people of the slums.

Lenya soon realised she couldn't remember where she had come from. Her sense of direction was utterly blind down here. This was the steepest part of Middenheim, with more twists and turns and more slopes and steps. Alleys seemed to end in front of her and then would shift in a new, unseen direction at the last minute. She felt like she was in a maze with no clear way out, yet she knew the palace lay only a few minutes' walk away.

They hurried through the rat-runs of the Old Quarter for several minutes before Kruza began to slow down. Then he came to a stop, leaning against a wall and putting his fingers to his lips, suggesting to Lenya that she follow suit, although she felt that this would only draw attention to them. The alleys and byways of this part of Middenheim were by no means deserted. Several seconds later and Lenya began to feel bored and fidgety, until she realised that there was something going on and began to listen to the voices beyond the wall.

'Hans, oh my poor Hans!' a woman wailed, obviously deeply distressed. A low voice, indistinct, some snuffles. Then, 'Don't touch him! Don't touch him!' The wail turned to a shriek.

The calm, low voice answered, seeming to cajole the fretful woman, but concentrate as she did, Lenya could not hear his words, only his soothing, monotone.

Kruza turned and beamed at Lenya. 'That's our man,' he said, satisfied, and Lenya began to peel her back off the mossy damp wall. But Kruza made no move, so she settled back impatiently against the wall. She watched for a sign from her guide. For the second time in one day, she was putting herself in the hands of a complete stranger.

Waiting, she looked about her, but the alleyway had drained of people. She watched fascinated as a rat worked its way through a miserable and spreading pile of detritus. Pickings were slim in these parts. They smashed bones for the marrow and then crushed the bones to thicken their soups. Here, people ate the whole fruit – pips, cores, skins and all – and the same with vegetables. And when people in this quarter ate meat, they ate the whole animal, saving blood for sausages and chewing the gristles and sinews until they were soft enough to swallow. The only waste here was human waste. The people here were ragged-looking creatures with missing hair and teeth. The scrawny, balding rat with only half its share of fangs reminded Lenya of the people. Feeling something between pathos and horror, she realised just how low the inhabitants of the Altquartier had been brought. Rats prospered everywhere – but here even the rats struggled to survive.

When the voices from the other side of the wall began to subside and people began to trickle back into the alleyway, Kruza made his move. Taking two steps he turned to look at Lenya and watched her for a moment watching the rat. Then he took her by the wrist and led her out into the tiny courtyard beyond the wall. A narrow handcart with an awkward wheel was being pulled out of the courtyard by two men dressed in drab, full-length cloth capes. A third man stood for a moment, as if in contemplation and then followed. As the handcart swung hard round a corner Lenya saw its cargo roll and sway before a hand fell from beneath the old weatherproof skin that covered it. She tugged at Kruza's sleeve.

'There's a body on that cart!' she exclaimed in horror and surprise.

'We had to wait for it to leave,' Kruza explained 'before we could speak to the priest. He has work to do and a little respect for the dead is always welcome.' Lenya wanted to ask more questions. She did not understand what was going on and she didn't like it.

Kruza and Lenya followed the men for two or three more streets, by which time the cart with its gruesome cargo had pulled away from the man that Lenya had supposed to be the third member of the party. She was relieved to see the handcart disappear out of sight as Kruza stepped up to speak to the fellow.

The man turned, a benign, almost vacant look on his face. She didn't know what she had expected, but it was not the elderly, haggard gentleman that she now beheld.

'A word, sir, if we may,' Kruza started. 'My companion is looking for a relation in the city… We hope you won't be able to help us, but…'

'I hope so too,' the man answered in his calm tones. 'Come, we will sit and talk. If the news is bad it should not be given in the street.'

Lenya and Kruza followed the man, Lenya pulling Kruza a few steps behind.

'Who is he?' hissed Lenya. 'What bad news?'

'He is a priest of Morr,' Kruza answered. 'He deals with the dead of Middenheim and sometimes uncovers their secrets.'

'And if Stefan is not dead?' Lenya asked in a panicked whisper.

'If Stefan is not dead then the priest of Morr will not know him.' With that Kruza quickened his step to catch up with the priest as he entered a hostelry a few streets north of the courtyard where the man Hans had died.

Kruza had missed his afternoon pot of ale and gladly furnished himself and his companions with a rather better class of beverage than had been available so far that day.

'And what is your brother's name?' the priest asked as Kruza returned from the barrel.

'Stefan Dunst. He left the country over a year ago. I haven't heard of him since,' Lenya replied.

'I have attended no one of that name,' the priest answered. 'Describe him to me.'

'He was small for a man,' Lenya said, her voice shaking slightly. She cleared her throat. 'Short and slender, but strong. His skin and hair were very fair, his eyes were pale grey and large, like mine.'

'And perhaps they still are,' said the priest. 'I have not attended any soul of that description whose name I did not know.'

Lenya relaxed with relief. 'Are you sure?' she asked.

'Quite sure,' the priest said as he stood, and left without another word. His glass of ale stood untouched on the table.

'Well, that's that!' Kruza exclaimed, draining his glass of ale and smacking his lips. But Lenya was not going to be put off.

'Not quite,' she said. 'He's alive. Now all we have to do is find him. And I think you know what that means.'

Kruza knew exactly what it meant and he didn't like it. He was just like a great many petty thieves and con-men in the city, perhaps a little more successful than most, but really just the same. Kruza worked for someone. He took fewer orders than the bulk of the low-grade parasites that worked in the city, he wasn't quite the errand boy that most of them were. And he commanded at least some respect; after all, he was useful. But the bottom line was that Kruza had a boss. It went with the territory.

And that territory was his and not a safe place for a girl like Lenya.

'There's nothing more we can do today,' Kruza said as he looked at Lenya. 'It will be getting dark soon and you should get back to the palace.'

'But you said you'd help me!' Lenya yelped.

'I can help you again another day,' Kruza said, trying hard to put the girl off.

'No!' Lenya said, her tone urgent. 'Today!'

'Besides,' she changed her tack, 'I can't go back to the palace until I can find something decent to wear. You don't think I arrived in the Altquartier dressed like this, do you?'

Lenya found herself caught in a cleft stick again. The last time she had ventured into the city she had almost got herself locked out of the palace and this time the change in her appearance would exclude her for certain. Or, at the very least, someone would want to know why she looked so dreadful. What had happened to her? Who had attacked her? Questions that she was not ready to face today, or any other day for that matter. Ruining her clothes had seemed like a good idea at the time, the only sensible thing to do. Now Lenya was horrified at the prospect of returning to the palace in such a sorry state of dress.

'I'm perfectly attired for street life in this city, especially after dark,' she said. 'What better opportunity will I have to find my brother?'

Kruza wanted to laugh, partly because she was right, but more because she was standing with her feet apart and her hands on her hips, looking for all the world like a cross between a common tart and a female streetbrawler. Her tone was as demanding and petulant as a dissatisfied new bride's. Taken all in all, this particular picture of Lenya was too persuasive to deny. Kruza decided he would simply have to look after her.

'All right,' he said, 'we'll try. But, I make no promises and I know a fine seamstress, who will provide you with a new suit of clothes before the night is out. And when she does, you will return to the palace.'

Lenya grinned. 'Good!' she said. 'Let's get started.'

'Not yet,' Kruza said holding her arm and gently drawing her back into her seat. 'First we must eat and there are things you need to know about the people we will be meeting tonight.' Kruza waved at the woman who sat on a stool beside the barrel, smoking a clay pipe with a long stem. Lenya felt like she was being fobbed off, but she didn't mind. She suddenly realised how hungry she was.

The sullen woman, the pipe still hanging between her lips, brought them a meal of fatty, meatless chops, black bread and preserved cabbage. While they ate, Kruza talked about the Low Kings and, in particular, his own boss, although for now he remained nameless.

'The Low Kings are aptly named. The monarchs of the underworld, the absolute rulers of the streets. Some are the lowest of the low: users, parasites, loan sharks. They run all the organised crime in this city and almost all cut-purses, scammers and petty thieves owe some allegiance to the lords of the dark. And only a handful of these Low Kings run the city of Middenheim. The Graf thinks he runs the city, so do the guilds. But the men who run the real city, the men who control the streets, run the whores, traffic drugs, fund the gaming houses, are very few. They hide behind their thugs and streetwalkers, and use bumpkins and out of city runaways as cannon-fodder. They never get caught and anyone who works for them in any capacity is dispensable. Do you understand?'

Kruza looked at Lenya, noting her expression. *She's scared*, he thought. *Good!*

The Altquartier didn't look quite so awful in the semi-darkness that awaited Lenya and Kruza as they left the tavern. The pale yellow-grey light was incapable of picking up the worst details of street-life and the small braziers which stood on innumerable street corners dissipated some of the smells that gathered in the damp warmth of the daylight hours. The narrow alleys were still full of people, but they seemed less harried in the gloom. Or perhaps Lenya was simply getting used to the environment.

The two of them walked together, without hurry, down a series of streets and alleys, turning this way and that. Then Kruza stopped and turned to her.

'Do you know where you are?' he asked Lenya.

'No,' she said. 'This place is a worse labyrinth than the palace.'

Good, thought Kruza again. He didn't want her to be able to find her own way here if she should be dissatisfied with his efforts at finding her brother.

The dark was almost complete when Kruza led Lenya into the West Weg. Crowds of people were collecting and she could hear the beating of drums and raucous pipe music pounding through the air. Turning a corner, the crowds now gathering in force and laughing and screeching with anticipated pleasure, Lenya looked up for the first time, her mouth falling open in wonder.

The building in front of her stood out like a squat stone drum, squeezed between lopsided buildings, its belly spilling out into the street as though it were pushing outward from its jostling companions. Large braziers outside the building sent long, flickering shadows and tall bright flames up the sides of the building, giving the impression that it was throbbing. Above the cries of the crowds pushing to get into the building, Lenya could hear other sounds, like animals in cages being poked and tormented. Faint roars of frustration and fear rose to her ears.

Kruza was impatient to move on and drew Lenya away from the crowd as more people came up, pressing behind them.

'What is this place?' she asked, having to shout above the fast increasing volume of the crowds.

'This is the Baiting Pit,' Kruza said with a tone that sounded a little like disdain or maybe resignation.

'Why are we here?' Lenya asked.

'You wanted access to one of the Low Kings of Middenheim. The man who runs this place, and others like it, knows more about the criminal workings of Middenheim than any other man I know or have heard of. He should do: he's the greatest, most successful, perhaps I should say lowest of the Low Kings.'

The quality of Kruza's voice made Lenya anxious. She had been so sure that she wanted to meet this man, so sure that he could help her find Stefan. But Kruza was obviously afraid of him, and looked and sounded like he would rather be anywhere than here.

'I couldn't bring you here by daylight,' Kruza said carefully, 'Too dangerous with only the boss and his henchmen around. We're safer now with the crowds and noise. If anything happens to upset or disturb you, anything at all, get in among the crowd, sit out the show and then leave with them. And when you leave, find someone safe to stay near. A city guard even, if you have to.'

'If we have to go in there, why aren't we going in with the crowd?' Lenya asked.

'There's another way in. Bleyden runs this place, I know my way around.'

'Bleyden?' Lenya asked. 'How do you know him?

'I work for him,' Kruza answered, something like shame in his voice.

'The gods save us, Kruza, surely you couldn't work for such a man? You talk as if you despise him.'

'All who work for him despise him. All who owe him money despise him. He is a man with a great deal of money and power and no friends.'

Lenya saw the narrowest of alleys between the Baiting Pit and its neighbour, closed off with a tall ironwork gate. Kruza looked around him and then, opening the gate a bare few inches he sidled in, taking Lenya with him. She almost tripped on a top step that she could not see in the gloom. She steadied herself by grabbing at the gate behind her, making it clang shut heavily. Kruza's head whipped round, his green eyes glaring at her through the dusty darkness, but no one seemed to have heard them.

'Come on!' he hissed.

* * *

TWO NIGHTS BEFORE, on the day of his walk into Middenheim with Lenya, Drakken had returned to his barrack dormitory very late. Morgenstern had laughed about the boy having a heavy date with his pretty country girlfriend.

'He's lost his virginity on the battlefield. Perhaps tonight's the night he'll lose it in a bed!' the veteran Wolf laughed, his voice thick with drink.

'Or against the wall of a palace courtyard,' Anspach cut in and they all laughed. Gruber sat on his cot, thinking about Lenya safely back in the castle and wondering just where young Drakken might actually be, when the man burst into the dormitory hot and cross.

Drakken threw off his pelt and the pieces of his armour, sat on his bed and put his head in his hands. Gruber crossed over to him, waving a discreet hand at the others to get on with their own business and leave Drakken alone.

As Gruber sat down next to Drakken the thickset young man dropped his hands to his lap and looked up.

'I lost her,' he said quietly. 'I lost Lenya in the city. I – I couldn't find her again. Ulric's teeth, Gruber; what will become of her alone in the city at night?'

'Don't take on, lad,' Gruber smiled a reassuring smile. 'I found her outside the temple hours ago, safe and sound. I took her back to the palace. She's probably been sleeping for hours by now.'

For one awful moment Gruber thought Drakken was going to hug him, the poor boy looked so relieved. But Drakken simply stood up and then abruptly sat again, anger and frustration showing clearly in his broad face.

After a good night's sleep, Drakken's anger had subsided and all he wanted was to make sure that Lenya was safe. He had almost decided to go to her, but he could already hear her telling him nothing was wrong and chiding him for wanting to control her. So he didn't visit his sweetheart.

Instead he watched her. Drakken spent the whole of that day monitoring Lenya's movements. To his relief, she didn't leave the palace at all. Perhaps she'd been frightened by her day in Middenheim and decided the palace was a much safer bet. Drakken doubted it.

On the afternoon of the next day, he followed Lenya when she slipped out into the city. He watched as she made her way around the Garten Ring and into the Great Park, and he stood back as she wove her way through the crowds there. He saw her disappear down the steps where she had arranged to meet Arkady for the second time.

Drakken was deeply puzzled that she should know about the steps – and very worried that she had used them. He didn't know that she had merely taken a seat and was waiting. Drakken hurried out of the Great Park. He would have to move fast if he was to get to the bottom of the steps and keep up with Lenya. They led directly to the Altquartier and his own route, on foot, was much more circuitous. Less than ten minutes later, Drakken was hiding, panting, in the shadows of a tiny court-yard at the bottom of the Great Park steps. He was sure he had missed Lenya, but he didn't know what else to do except wait.

Half an hour later, Drakken was trying to formulate a new plan when he heard footfalls on the steps and plunged himself silently back into the shadows. A stab of jealousy lurched through him as he saw Lenya with Arkady, crossing the court-yard in front of him. What was his girl doing with this young cut-purse?

Drakken was there too when Lenya met the priest of Morr. He spoke to the priest himself after he had left Lenya and a sec-ond unknown cut-purse in the tavern. Drakken couldn't fathom what was going on. There had been two strange men, the priest of Morr and, to top it all, Lenya had done something awful to her dress. What the priest of Morr told the young Wolf made no sense to him either. Lenya had never mentioned any lost brother.

Now Drakken stood outside the Baiting Pit of the West Weg, wondering why anyone would bring Lenya to such a place, when he heard the clang of the side gate closing. He watched, only feet away, as Lenya and the unknown man descended the steps into the bowels of the Pit. Drakken had a terrible feeling of foreboding. He knew at once that he would have to save Lenya. He just wasn't sure from what.

'YOU CAN'T COME in here!' a blunt voice came out of the shad-ows and noise as Lenya and Kruza crossed the threshold at the bottom of the steps. 'We're closed!'

Lenya didn't like the sound of the voice that seemed to force itself out past a mouthful of food. She didn't like the smell of frightened animals and adrenaline-choked sweat which filled the air.

'Kled?' Kruza called out as the dwarf appeared. Lenya had never seen his like before. He was as broad as he was tall and heavy, hard muscle stood out on his thick torso and short neck. He was naked above the waist and hairless. His short, solid hand made a fist around something that he was tearing lumps from with his sparse and irregular teeth.

'Kruza!' Kled the dwarf exclaimed. 'We're closed! It's not your day.' Then the short man, who oddly reminded Lenya of a cruel parody of Drakken, looked past Kruza and grinned broadly, showing the contents of his mouth.

'Been recruiting, Kruza? Give her one yourself, have you?' Kled leered shamelessly, walking round Lenya in a tight little circle, leaving a ring around her where he had disturbed the newly raked sawdust of the Baiting Pit.

'No!' The single word that Kruza uttered sounded like a threat. Kled laughed, throwing back his head before filling his mouth once more.

'I want some information,' Kruza continued. 'Information about a young man, a country boy.'

'Probably dead,' Kled said.

Lenya had had enough of this beast. He didn't scare her! At least, she told herself he didn't. Lenya stepped past Kruza.

'The priest of Morr says not,' she said and swallowed the hard lump in her throat that was making her voice sound cracked. 'Take me to Bleyden. I need to talk with him.'

'Take you to Bleyden?' repeated the dwarf, his face pressed so close to hers that Lenya wanted to step back. 'Speak not so freely of my master, trollop, or you will regret it.'

'I have to find Stefan Dunst,' Lenya said, barely able to hold her ground. 'Your master may know where he is.'

'And the price he will ask may be too great,' Kled said, his voice all threat.

Kruza stood behind Lenya in consternation. He'd promised himself he'd look after her, but she wasn't helping.

'Kled,' he began, 'I don't see any reason to disturb Master Bleyden. Perhaps you could find out if Stefan Dunst has worked for him?'

'Not a chance,' said Kled. Behind him some invisible beast lurched against the grille of its cage, roaring a hysterical sound and making the pit echo with the clang of a huge weight throwing itself against metal bars. Kled spun around, picking up a club and moving to scold the animal.

Lenya saw her opportunity. Taking Kruza's hand, she moved away from Kled toward a low door in the wall opposite. She could see light spilling from around the door's poor seal and guessed it might lead her to the Low King they called Bleyden.

FROM HIS VANTAGE point, crouched at the top of the narrow stairwell, Drakken listened intently. He was hunched sideways on the steps, unable to sit squarely in the space that was somewhat narrower than his body. Listening and concentrating hard, he managed to hear every word of Kled's welcome. He waited, hoping that would be the end of the encounter. But when the animal roared and tried to tear its cage apart, the White Wolf heard only danger and careered down the flight of steps, as fast, but as noiselessly as he could.

LENYA PULLED AT the door handle, but it wouldn't open. Behind her, Kruza, beginning to sweat, moved her aside. He saw that there was no going back from this now. He took hold of the door handle and pulled. Then, in his frustration and near panic, he pushed, putting the weight of his shoulder against the door.

It flew open and Kruza fell heavily inwards, taking Lenya with him. As the door opened the sound of hundreds of excited, expectant voices rose to greet the pair. This was followed by a sudden lull, which was broken by a slow, solitary handclap of dissatisfaction. Lenya pulled herself up and began to brush sawdust from her skirt. Kruza, still on the floor on his hands and knees, raised his head, looking for all the world like a dog sniffing the air. He was not ready for what he beheld.

KLED BEAT THE cage of the frightened creature with his club and turned back to oust Kruza and his feisty tart once and for all. But they were gone, and the pit door stood open. Kled heaved it shut before animals could get loose into the undercrofts.

Something was wrong. The audience above had gone quiet and then began to clap out a slow, strange rhythm that the dwarf had never heard in all his years at the Baiting Pit. Kled dropped his club, took his jacket from its hook and was shrugging his great shoulders into it as he raced up the winding staircase that would take him to the trainers' viewing stand.

DRAKKEN STOOD AT the bottom of the stairs, looking into the cellar beyond. He saw nothing, but heard the beating of a cage and the low murmur of the audience. Then clapping. And then a huge cheer.

KNEELING IN THE sawdust, Kruza looked into the snarling muzzle of a stocky, barrel-chested dog with a square head and tiny, glinting eyes. The spittle on the bull terrier's gleaming fangs dripped and the wound on its side leaked a yellowish liquid. In less time than it took to take one shallow, frightened breath, Kruza was on his feet, jumping over the dog. A huge cheer rose from the astounded audience.

As Kruza rose and leapt, Lenya got her first view of her surroundings. Behind Kruza, a tall thick pole stood in the centre of the packed arena. Chained to it was a massive, howling, dirty brown beast. From the huge, studded collar around its neck hung several feet of heavy link chain. The great paws that stamped the sawdust floor were manacled together, restricting its movement.

Around the massive rearing bear several more bull terriers lurched and snapped, their crazed eyes desperate for a piece of the action. Lenya turned to run. But the door they had come through was closed.

STANDING AT THE edge of the trainer's platform, Kled put his fingers in his mouth and whistled a high pitched sound that cut across the raucous noise of the arena and made the bull terriers turn their heads for an instant. But only an instant.

Kled waved a curt message at the four brawny men who had risen from their seats in the frenzied crowd at the sound of the whistle, and were making their way down the tight tiers of seats that made up the auditorium. Planting their feet firmly on the bench seats, they worked their way effortlessly through the crowd. Soon four huge bodies, clad in leather armour and pulling on horned helmets, made their way to the tall wall which surrounded the arena stage and vaulted down.

'Get them out of there!' Kled yelled at them. 'Get them out!'

There was already chaos. The crowd were running mad with excitement. Kled's men moved in.

One of the four dropped down right behind Lenya and tried to lift her up. He hadn't reckoned on the small woman being quite so fast. She ducked under his arm and slid between his legs. As he turned to see where she had gone he felt a hot, sharp pain in his calf. The dog that Kruza had come face to face with had lost his first target and now homed in on the thug's leg as his next good meal.

The remaining thugs armed themselves with the spears that stood around the arena walls, in case of emergencies, and began to stab at the dogs. Their job was to control the situation and get the intruders out of the arena as fast as possible, before the whole show turned into a farce. Kled watched anxiously from his vantage point.

Kruza landed within feet of the bear. Crouching down on his haunches, he held out a calming hand to the frantic animal. It raged, great jaws frothing, pulling at its chains, desperate to get at its tormentors after months of repeated abuse. Dogs snarled and circled around it. In another moment, one of the thugs was closing in on Kruza, jabbing dogs ahead of him with his spear. He was a huge man with dark tattoos showing on the parts of him that were not covered in shiny, black leather armour. His nicked steel helmet with its horn ornaments and low forehead was imposing enough, but the massive, square jaw and wide red mouth with its gruesome hare-lip were positively terrifying.

Still looking up, Kruza lowered his hand to the floor and then lunged forward with his shoulders, grabbing the fearsome gladiator around his impressive calves. Black leather hit the sawdust amidst a spray of dust. Kruza sat on his torso and started tearing at his helmet, one hand grasping each of the bone horns and swinging from side to side, half-throttling the man inside with the tautly-twisted chin strap.

There was a roar of laughter from the crowd. Prize fights were one thing, but this comic-tragic battle was something else. They'd certainly got their money's worth.

Kled put his head in his hands. Things were going from bad to worse. He would be out of a job tomorrow for sure. He looked up as he heard the rabble rising to their feet, stamping and cheering and clapping their hands above their heads. He looked out into the arena.

* * *

IN THE ENTRANCE to the arena, in front of the bait door, stood a figure. Kled looked again. A huge, masked man filled the doorway. He was naked to the waist and already slick with sweat. He carried a huge mallet in one hand, with a long haft and a heavy iron head. In the other he carried a crude wooden cudgel, tipped with a series of sturdy iron spikes. Not weapons, but tools, the tools of Kled's trade, taken from the cellar by this awesome gladiator. The man stood for what seemed like an age, long enough for Kled and the audience to take in his leather breeches and knee boots, the bands wrapped tight around his wrists and his glistening torso. The man was shorter than average, but what he lacked in height he surely made up for in breadth. Over his head the man wore a crude mask, a small sack with holes cut for his eyes.

An instant later, the mallet was being swung above his head as the gladiator worked his hand down its haft. He had seen something that everyone else had missed. They had been watching him – but he had been watching the bear.

The noise of the crowd and the unfamiliarity of the number of human bodies cavorting around the arena had brought the bear to a point beyond panic. It threw itself against the post with all its weight and then lunged away from it, falling to all fours. The top of the post had splintered with the force and the chain came away. The bear was loose.

The dogs around it were too slow to react. It savaged one, mauling it with teeth and claws, and then ripped another up into the air, its back snapped, howling. The remaining dogs scurried back, fearful at this change in the odds. The bear, berserk now, sprayed dog-blood from its muzzle as it shook it and lumbered forward at the human targets around. The crowd were howling.

Standing his ground, the masked gladiator swung his mallet hard, the end of the haft now clasped firmly in his grip. He let go. Swinging high into the air, the mallet turned twice, echoing the spin that the gladiator had used, and landed with a crashing thud against the side of the bear's skull. It moaned once and collapsed to the floor, burying two of the terriers, whining, beneath its immense bulk.

The crowd roared again, and Kruza leapt off the torso of his half-choked opponent, looking to avoid the next confrontation when it came.

Lenya turned, distracted, to look at the gladiator, and some-one picked her up from behind. She looked around: it was the thug with the chewed leg. He was bleeding, but still strong and upright. Lenya struggled and kicked and the audience laughed.

Their laughter ended in another great roar of approval as the mysterious gladiator swung his cudgel, two-handed, into the thug's armoured back, making him drop Lenya and stagger back. The man turned, pulling a long knife from his belt. A thrust, another slicing attempt to sink the blade into the masked gladiator's chest. The gladiator replied with a second swing of the cudgel, which left the thug lying face down on the floor, blood and gore mixing with sawdust to form a thick, dark stain.

Kled looked on in awe. Two of his best men had been taken out by Kruza the cut-purse and this mysterious fighter. Not to mention the bear, his trusted ally and performer for more than two years now, and not easily replaced. Then Kled heard the chant from the auditorium of Masked Man! Masked Man! He smiled to himself. Perhaps he had stumbled upon something after all. Perhaps this masked man could use a job.

The gladiator picked up Lenya and the crowd booed. She looked over at Kruza as he tried to drag her away and she protested, kicking and screaming and shouting.

'Kruza!' she called.

'This is no place for you, lady!' the gladiator said.

Beating the masked man's chest, she hurled abuse. 'You bas-tard! Let me go! I have to help Kruza!'

To her surprise, he let her go.

The remaining dogs in the arena had turned away from the action when they realised that the bear was down and a meal awaited. The last two thugs, who had been trying to keep the dogs under control with their long spears, now turned on Kruza. The audience waited with bated breath as the leather-clad fighting machines circled the cut-purse, their spears low to the ground and threatening.

Someone in the audience shouted 'Kill!' Other voices joined in until the whole auditorium was filled with the rhythm of hundreds of slowly stamping feet, measuring out each rising call of the word. 'Kill!' 'Kill!' 'Kill!' 'Kill!'

Kruza shuffled his feet in the sawdust of the arena floor, preparing himself. The first spear came in to tangle his legs, but

Kruza leapt at just the right moment and it missed him. The second spear tip came in higher, shoulder height, and as soon as his leap was over, Kruza was forced into a low squat, letting the spear blade whistle close over the top of his head. The jabbing spears came in thick and fast, but Kruza was quick on his feet. The audience were almost silent, watching the three men go through this curious dance.

Lenya threw herself on the back of the thug nearest to her, the way she'd fearlessly tackle her brothers in pretend fights back home. She'd had to jump just to get her hands over his shoulders and haul herself up; Kruza's assailant was taller than Lenya by almost two heads. She put her arm around his neck, so that her elbow nestled against his throat. Then she locked her wrists together with opposite hands and threw the entire weight of her body back and down. Her feet dangled in mid-air for a moment, but she could feel him going. She lifted her knees into the small of his back and kicked out again, throwing herself clear as she brought him down on his back, retching and coughing from her choke-hold.

THE MASKED gladiator sidled around the fight, one eye on the feeding dogs, and picked his mallet up from the floor. Then he went for the remaining thug. His first swing matched exactly with the low forward lunge of the leather-clad fighter. Both missed, but the masked man's balance never wavered, and he brought the mallet round in another long arc. This time it connected. The double horned helmet flew off the thug's head and sailed way up into the auditorium, grasping hands rising up to catch the souvenir. Long before his helmet was caught, the thug was lying on the ground, his legs twisted in an awkward direction with the momentum of the blow, his head bloody and gaping.

Kled stood stolidly in the stand, counting his losses. Two useful armed fighters, at least a couple of dogs (and the rest would be useless for at least a fortnight after their vast meal), and his favourite baiting bear. And his gains? Well the masked man would counter any losses if he could be persuaded to fight again.

The thugs Kruza and Lenya had disabled were getting back to their feet, but neither looked like they wanted a rematch. The crowd were making a noise fit to raise the dead.

The masked gladiator turned to Lenya and Kruza. 'We're leaving. Now,' he told them, shouting over the din.

'The bait door's closed – ' Lenya began.

The gladiator raised his mallet. 'Not for long.'

KLED SCRAMBLED back down the winding stairs to the cellar, desperate to catch up with his new find before he disappeared into the night. Wild applause still rang in his ears, soon to be followed by cries of 'More!' and 'Masked Man! Masked Man!'

ON THEIR WAY out of the cellar, the gladiator, the sackcloth mask still firmly over his head, lifted a bundle over his shoulder and led the dishevelled pair away from their unexpected adventure. Lenya noticed that the bundle appeared to be wrapped in some kind of skin or fur.

THE STRANGE TRIO hurried away from the deserted exterior of the Baiting Pit and down a series of empty alleys. They stopped in a tiny square between the backs of tall buildings. There was barely room for the three of them, but there were no windows and they could not be overlooked. The masked man knelt down to his furry bundle and began to untie it. Then, impatiently, the masked fighter tore off his sackcloth hood, leaving his hair glued firmly down with sweat to his glistening forehead.

'Krieg!' Lenya exclaimed in a tight, breathy squeak. 'Krieg… But how….? What…?' She was so surprised she couldn't catch her breath and her fingers began to tingle. She thought she was going to throw up.

'You know him?' Kruza asked. Then the cut-purse saw what the half-naked man was taking from his bundle. He thought for a moment about running, but there was a look in the other's eyes that told him not to chance it.

Once dressed again in his pelt and breastplate the White Wolf, Krieg Drakken, led Lenya and Kruza to a nearby hostelry. Kruza did not know what to say, so busied himself at the barrel, furnishing all three with tall pots of good ale. He didn't like mixing with such a powerful authority figure, not one bit. But he didn't feel like leaving Lenya after what they'd been through.

'I could have helped you find your brother,' Drakken was saying in a stern tone. 'Why didn't you trust me? I nearly brought disgrace to my Temple, having to go into the pit to rescue you! If any had recognised me…'

'I'm sorry,' she said. She wondered why she had not confided in him. Was it simply that she owed him so much already? She didn't want to think about it.

'No one's going to find him now!' she murmured in a hollow voice. 'After all this…'

Lenya had never felt such hopeless futility. All the leads had been false, all the trails cold, all the risks not worth the taking. She had fought against it as valiantly as she could, but at last the great bulk of Middenheim had overwhelmed her will and her strength

'Oh Stefan!' she exclaimed. 'Why did you have to come to this place! Brave little Wheezer, out to make his fortune!' Her hands came to her face and tears began to fall.

'What did you say?' Kruza asked sharply. 'You said his name was Stefan.'

'Yes,' she sniffed, 'but when we were children his nickname was Wheezer…'

'Wheezer…' Kruza repeated, barely audible over Lenya's sobs. 'Ulric damn me!' he exclaimed. He stood up in alarm, his chair crashing down behind him.

'Your brother was Wheezer?'

Mittherbst

Wolf's Bane

THE NIGHT WAS old and dry. The lemon-rinded moons of high summer hung sullenly in a sky of soft purple. Moths beat against lit windows and masked lanterns. In the dim precincts of the Great Temple of Ulric, a warm silence filled the long hallways and cloisters. It was past midnight, and still the heat of the day had not subsided. Cooler than the streets in daylight, the great stones of the Temple building now radiated the heat they had absorbed, sweating warmth out of the walls and pillars.

Aric, the White Company's standard bearer, crossed the shadowy atrium of the mighty shrine, by the light of two hundred smoking candles. Sweat beaded his broad, young brow. Custom and observance forced him to wear the grey-gold plate mail and white wolf pelt of the Templar uniform, but he dearly wished he could strip it all off.

Guard duty. White Company had the vigilia watch, patrolling the palace of Ulric until first light and the chime of matins. Aric longed for the fresh chill and mist which he hoped the predawn would bring to signal the end of their duty.

By the arched door of a side chapel dedicated to fallen sons of Ar-Ulric, Aric saw Lowenhertz. The tall Wolf had leant his warhammer against the jamb, and was standing, peering out across the city from an unglazed lancet. At the sound of Aric's approach, he spun like lightning and raised the hammer.

'Stand down, brother,' Aric said with a smile.

'Aric...' Lowenhertz muttered, lowering his hammer.

'How goes the night?'

'Stifling. Smell the air.'

They stood together on the narrow parapet under the arch and breathed in. Sweat; woodsmoke; corrupting sanitation.

'Ah, Middenheim,' Aric murmured.

'Middenheim in high summer,' Lowenhertz returned. 'Damn its rocky heart.'

Somewhere down below in Altmarkt, hand bells were chiming furiously and there was a distant fuzz of orange. Another fire in the tinder-dry streets. There had been a dozen or more that week alone. And beyond the city, brush-blazes, sparked by summer lightning, had regularly lit portions of the forest at night. Wells were drying up, latrines were stinking, brawls were flaring, disease was rife, and clove oil sales were booming. A hot, smoky summer by any standards and for Middenheim an exceptional season.

'Hottest summer in eighty years,' said Lowenhertz, who knew such things.

'Hottest I've ever known,' Aric answered. He paused, significantly.

'What?' Lowenhertz asked, looking round.

Aric shrugged. 'I... Nothing.'

'What?'

'I half expected you to tell me why. With your learning and all. I half expected you to tell me that a summer season as stifling as this was a sure sign of some disaster.'

Lowenhertz looked faintly angry, as if mocked.

'I'm sorry,' Aric said. 'I should continue with my rounds.'

As he walked away, Lowenhertz called out. 'Brother Aric?'

'Lowenhertz?'

'You're right, you know. A summer like this... not from any learning of mine, or signs, or portents. But heat like this gets to men's minds. Bakes them, twists them. Before autumn, there will be trouble.'

Aric nodded solemnly and walked away. He liked Lowenhertz, but there was nothing the man couldn't see the bad side of.

* * *

'THEN TAKE IT OFF!' Morgenstern snapped. The sweltering night had done nothing for his demeanour and his huge bulk was rank with sweat. He had shed his wolf-pelt and his armour, and was sitting by the font in the main chapel, dressed in his under-shirt, pressing his face and neck against the cool stone of the water-filled basin. Above him, the great statue of Ulric rose into the gloom, silent, immense.

And probably sweating too, Morgenstern decided.

'It's against the rules!' protested Drakken, the youngest of the Wolves and the newest recruit, who had drawn this duty to share with the great, ox-like veteran.

'Ulric eat the rules!' Morgenstern spat, with a sideways nod of respect to the vast statue. 'If you're as hot as me you'll ditch that armour and sweat it out! Name of the Wolf, you're hot blooded enough to be courting that fiery maid from the Margrave's court! You must be curdling in there!'

Drakken shook his head wearily and pulled his pelt around his powerful, stocky form as if to defy the heat.

Short, surly, thick-set, stubborn, Morgenstern thought. *Our boy Drakken undoubtedly has dwarf blood in his ancestry. His bastard forefathers surely dug this city out of the rock itself.*

He got to his feet, aware that Drakken was trying not to watch him. Morgenstern reached into the font.

'What are you doing?' Drakken hissed.

The old veteran pulled a corked bottle of ale out of the holy water. 'Cooling down,' he said. He unpopped the flask and poured the chilled liquid down his throat. He could almost hear Drakken choking on his own saliva and envy.

Drakken spun round and strode across to the big man. 'For Ulric's sake, give me some of that!'

'*Some of what?*'

Aric advanced down the centre file of the great chamber, the thousands of candle flames rippling at the sudden breeze of his billowing pelt.

Drakken froze. There was a fluid plop as the bottle dropped out of sight into the font from Morgenstern's chubby fingers.

'Morgenstern?'

The huge Wolf turned soberly and dipped his cupped hands into the font water, raising them to baptise his face in a cascad-ing splash of dancing silver.

'Holy water, Brother Aric,' Morgenstern said, shaking out his sodden locks like a hound. He saw how Aric stared at his unar-moured bulk. 'At late hours like this, I like to chasten myself with the watery blessing of Ulric, so that I may be fresh for duty.'

'Is that so?'

'Oh yes,' said Morgenstern, splashing his face and torso again. 'Why, I'm surprised an earnest young devotee of the Wolf like you doesn't know the ritual. Why else would I have stripped off my armour? I'm absolving my sins, you see? Before Ulric. Absolving, oh yes. It's chastening. Very chastening.'

'Very chastening,' agreed Drakken.

Morgenstern knew the young Templar was a heartbeat away from laughing. He grabbed Drakken by the neck and plunged him face down into the water of the font.

'See? Young Drakken is willing! He thirsts for chastening! Can I oblige you with a nocturnal baptism too?'

Aric shook his head. 'Forgive me for intruding upon your observances, Brother Morgenstern. I had no idea you were so... devout.'

'I am a Brother of Wolves, Aric. It wounds me to think you would believe me to be tardy in such details. A lesson to you. You imagine us veterans to be a slack lot, more interested in wine and song and womanly comfort.' Morgenstern held Drakken's struggling head under. 'The likes of me shame you younger Wolves! Why, I have half a mind to go outside right now and beat my naked back with bitter withy twigs to scourge my soul for Ulric's sake! When was the last time you did that?'

'I forget. Again, forgive me,' Aric said, turning away to continue with his rounds. 'I stand humbled before your strict devotion.'

'Don't mention it.'

'You might want to let Drakken up before he drowns, though,' Aric added as he walked away, smirking.

'What? Oh, yes...'

'You bastard! I nearly drowned!' Drakken said as he came up. Or that's what he would have said, had he not been trying to vomit up a lung. He lay gasping and retching on the tiles by the font for a good two minutes after Aric had gone.

Morgenstern kicked him playfully in the ribs. 'See the trouble you'd get me into, boy?' Morgenstern asked. He dipped into the font and pulled a second cooled bottle out.

A MOTH KNOCKED repeatedly against the lamp. Anspach thought to swat it, but it was a good bet a warhammer didn't make for an effective moth-swatter. He was just considering what odds he'd take to swat a moth with a warhammer when Aric appeared.

'How goes the night, Brother Anspach?'

'Hot and lousy, Brother Aric.'

They stood together at the foot of the steps under the corbel-vaulted ceiling of the entrance to the regimental trophy chapel. Beyond the cage door, on the wall, bas-reliefs and frescoes showed Wulcan, the smiting of Blitzbeil, the commemoration of the Fauschlag Rock and a score of other images from the long history of Middenheim.

'The patrol?' Anspach asked, obviously bored.

'Nothing. Lowenhertz watches the Chapel of the Fallen. Drakken and Morgenstern are clowning in the main hall. Kaspen and Einholt are falling asleep in the weaponarium annexe. Gruber paces the high turret solemnly. A quiet night.'

Anspach nodded, and pulled out a flask from under his pelt. 'Something to cool you down?' he suggested.

Aric hesitated and then accepted the offering. 'Tastes good,' he began appreciatively.

He handed the flask back and turned away. His toe kicked against something on the flags, something that skittered away. Searching for it, Aric picked it up.

A padlock.

'How long has this been lying there?'

Anspach shrugged, coming over. 'I have no idea…'

They both turned to look at the portico of the trophy chapel. The iron cage door was ajar.

'Oh no! Oh, curse me, Ulric!' Anspach spat leaping forward. Aric was beside him. They shoved the loose cage door open and thundered inside. Aric held up a lamp, and moths battered and wove around him.

The plinth in the corner of the shrine, under the great wolf-skin, was empty. The Jaws of Ulric, a silver inlaid relic made from the fangs of a great forest wolf in olden times, the greatest of their treasures, was missing.

Aric and Anspach backed away in horror.

'I'm in trouble,' Anspach breathed.

'You're in trouble? Anspach, we're all in trouble.'

MATINS. DAWN CAME, hot, branding, intense. In a private annexe deep inside the oven heat of the Temple, Ganz listened attentively to Ar-Ulric, the High Priest. Every now and then he murmured 'Yes, High Priest,' or 'No, High Priest' or 'Obviously, High Priest'.

'The Teeth of Ulric,' the High Priest was saying, his breath exhausting itself in the hot air. 'Of all relics, our most prized!'

'Yes, High Priest,' Ganz said, obligingly.

'It must be returned.'

'Obviously, High Priest.'

Flies and beetles pattered against the window grills.

'If we were to admit we had lost the relic, Middenheim itself would lose heart. The city folk would round on us, and despair. An ill omen. The worst.'

'Yes, High Priest.'

'I can give you two days' grace.'

'Sir?'

'Two days to find and recover the relic before I have to go public and bring shame and torment on us all – especially the White Company who were on guard duty when it was stolen.'

'I see, High Priest.'

'Two days, Ganz. Do not fail the Temple.'

HE WOULD NOT. Not. *Not.*

But for the life of him, he didn't know where to begin. Stalking back from the High Priest's chambers, through chapter gardens where feeble mists baked off the beds, Ganz cursed himself over and again. He had no choice. He had to... to... enlist them all to his trust...

Even Morgenstern – and Anspach.

'Well, sir,' Anspach said, looking suitably solemn. 'I think our best bet–'

'Silence!' Ganz barked. The room held the silence for a second and then sound thundered again as Ganz slammed the door on his way out. The remaining members of the Wolf Company looked at each other. Aric sighed. Dorff began to whistle, nervously and tunelessly. Morgenstern slowly and belatedly lowered his legs from the table he had been resting them on. Gruber skulked darkly at the back of the room. The others shuffled.

'I only said–' Anspach began.

'Oh, shut up,' Aric muttered. 'We've disgraced him. Disgraced our order. Our Temple, our city.'

'Is it really that bad?' Drakken asked quietly and suddenly wished he hadn't.

'The Teeth of Ulric were cut from the muzzle of the great White Wolf of Holzbeck by Artur himself, bless his fine spirit. They are holy of all holies. And on our watch, we let them be stolen.' Lowenhertz moved into the centre of the room as he spoke, his voice low, like the intonation of a funeral bell in the Temple of Morr. 'Disgrace barely covers it.'

Anspach rose to his feet. 'I know what you're all thinking. It was me. I was watching the reliquary. I was the one who failed.'

'I was with you when we found the broken lock–' began Aric.

Anspach shushed him back. 'After the event, I'm sure. It was me, Aric. And you all think I must have been drunk or stupid or distracted…'

'Were you?' asked Gruber, a stiletto voice from the back of the room.

Anspach shook his head. 'No, Gruber, not that anyone would believe me. Fact is, I thought I was performing my duties with particular vigilance.'

'I was drunk,' Morgenstern said suddenly. They all looked at him. 'On the way, at least,' he qualified. 'Drakken was in no state to stand a good watch either, thanks to me. I'm as much to blame…'

'I was covering the vigilia watch. For Ganz. It was my duty,' Aric said quietly. 'I saw Morgenstern's clowning. I saw Anspach ready at the gate. I saw Einholt and Kaspen dozing in the weapon hall.'

Einholt and Kaspen looked down.

'I saw us all! Neglecting our duties or performing them, one and the same. It was a quiet night and nothing was wrong. I should have charged you all with the spirit of Ulric so that none shirked. I did not. This is down to me.'

'Well,' Gruber said, walking into the light and igniting his pipe with a soft kiss of flame from the spindle. 'Aric may be right. Maybe it is his fault…'

'I was drunk!' Morgenstern exclaimed.

'Sleeping!' cut across Einholt.

'Distracted!' Lowenhertz snapped.

'Unwary!' Anspach cried.

'Enough! Enough!' Gruber cried, holding up his hand. 'All of us to blame… None of us? That's the whole thing, isn't it? The company failed, not any individual. And let's think about this carefully. I've seen Morgenstern drunk as a lord and still notice a goblin sneak by. Anspach may gamble his life away, but still his nose is sharper than any in the company. He would not have missed a theft like that. Lowenhertz, the sternest of us all; he would not have passed over some clue or hint that treachery was in progress. Einholt, not he, not even sleeping, Kaspen likewise. Drakken, with his eager eyes and sense of duty... Do you not see?'

'See what?' asked Aric.

'Magic, Aric! Magic stole the Jaws of Ulric! Despite our failings, only magic could have snuck in and robbed us of the prize. If we'd all been sober and studious and alert... still it would be gone! Go and fetch Ganz back. We have work to do.'

IT FELT STRANGE... wrong, somehow, to be out in the streets of Middenheim without the familiar weight of the armour and wolf pelt. Aric scratched inside the chafing collar of a light linen cape that he hadn't worn since he had first been admitted into the Company as a petitioner.

But this was how Morgenstern and Anspach had said it should go, and for all their manifold failings, they knew such things. If White Company was going to scour the city of Middenheim for the Teeth of Ulric, shake down every tavern, question every fence, prise up and examine the underside of every cobble, they could not do so as Wolf Templars.

So here they were, as the sun rose to mid-morning above the raked roofs, here they were scrubbed and shaved and heavy-headed after the long night, wearing ill-assorted tunics, capes and robes, most of which had festered in long-boxes and chests in the cellars of the chapter house for months and years. Morgenstern, in fact, had been forced to send Drakken out for new clothes. Since he had last worn his civilian garb, he had added many pounds and many more inches. Morgenstern had also appropriated a large-brimmed hat which he imagined gave him a dashing, mysterious air. It in fact made him look like a bulbous forest toadstool on the wilt, but Aric said nothing.

They all looked so odd, so unlike themselves. Gruber in a faintly genteel, faded robe and tunic that seemed a decade or two old-fashioned; Schell in a surprisingly rich velvet cape that smelled of pomanders; Lowenhertz in rough breeches and a leather tunic, like a woodsman. Even the ones who looked normal seemed odd. Aric wasn't used to seeing any of them like this.

Except Anspach, in his tailored coat, polished boots and suavely draped cloak. Though they all spent off-duty hours in the city's stews and taverns, only Anspach habitually dressed out of armour or company colours. Where Morgenstern could carouse until dawn in full armour in the Man o'War, the gaming halls, arenas and dice parlours that were Anspach's particular vice demanded a more refined mode of dress.

They assembled in the street, new men to each other, not speaking for several minutes in the warming glare of the strengthening Mittherbst sun. The air was yet clear and cool, the sky porcelain blue.

Finally Ganz joined them, almost unrecognisable in a serge doublet and hooded woollen over-robe. He said nothing, for there was no need for words, not many at least. Gruber, Anspach and Morgenstern had convinced Ganz of the correct course of action left open to them, and the labour ahead of them had been divided. Now as Ganz came out, he gave a nod acknowledged by all his men, and the party broke into smaller groups, heading away from each other into different quarters of the ancient town.

'LET ME DO the talking,' Anspach told Ganz and Aric as they approached the south doors of the Baiting Pit off West Weg. At night, on those times he'd passed it, this squat stone drum of a theatre had seemed to Aric like a mouth of hell, with its flaming braziers, hooting pipe music, drums, the pounding and cheering and roaring. The roaring of men and animals.

In daylight, in the unforgiving brightness of the summer light, it was a miserable, flaking place: worn, soiled and stained by all manner of unwholesome deposits. Hand-bills fluttered and shredded along the travertine walls between the daubings of less than sober or less than literate citizens. The blackened metal braziers were extinguished and dead. Two men were sweeping the gateway, pushing all manner of trampled trash out of the steps into the gutter trench. Another was pumping water from the street spigot into a row of buckets. All looked sour and half awake.

'It would have been better if we'd come tonight,' hissed Anspach, 'when the place is open. There would be activity to cover our–'

'There's no time,' returned Ganz. 'Now, if you so want to do the talking, do it to someone other than me!'

They entered, passing through the suddenly freezing shadow of the gateway into the tall-sided, circular pit, where tiers of wooden galleries overlooked a deep stone well, at the bottom of which was dirty sand and a few deep-set posts with manacle points. Caged grills in the pit wall at arena level led off into the place's dingy undercrofts. Down in the pit, another man was scattering sand on dark brown stains. The air smelled of mingled sweat and smoke, an overwhelming odour.

'We're closed,' said a blunt voice from their left. The trio swung around. A hefty dwarf, stripped to the waist and hugely muscled, tipped forward and got up off the stool where he had been sitting, chewing on bread and sausage.

'Where's Bleyden?' Anspach asked.

'We're. Closed,' repeated the dwarf. He took an unfeasibly large bite off the sausage and chewed, staring at them.

'Kled,' said Anspach with a soothing cock of his head and a shrug. 'Kled, you know me.'

'I know nothing.'

'You know you're closed,' Anspach corrected.

The dwarf frowned. He put the sausage to his mouth to bite again, then the bread, and then the sausage, undecided. His eyes never left Anspach.

'What do you want?' he asked, adding, 'we're closed,' again in case any had missed it, and to show that by enquiring what was wanted, he was making a huge exception.

'You know I've had a run of... ill fortune. Bleyden's been good enough to extend me a line of credit, but he insisted on me making some interim repayments as soon as possible. Well, here I am!' Anspach beamed.

The dwarf, Kled, thought for a moment more, his cheeks and lips bulging unpleasantly as his tongue chased lumps of meat out of the sides of his gums. Then he beckoned with the gnawed end of his sausage.

Anspach nodded to Ganz and Aric to follow smartly. Ganz was glowering, his face as dark as Mondstille.

'I hope you both have money,' Anspach said in a hushed voice.

'If this is some con to get me to settle your gambling debts–' began Ganz, choking on the words.

They were passing into a sequence of smelly, stuffy wooden rooms under the seating. Boxes of junk lined the walls, rows of empty bottles, buckets, the occasional dirty billhook. The dwarf stomped ahead, passing neatly under every low doorway where each of the Templars had to duck.

'Bleyden owns this place, and four like it,' Anspach said. 'He runs all the girls in Altmarkt, and has a lot of other business... dealings. He knows a lot about the fate of, shall we say "purloined" goods? But he won't talk to us unless he's got a good reason. And my outstanding ninety crowns is a very good reason.'

'*Ninety?*' Ganz barked, the word almost becoming a squeak as they ducked under another low beam.

'My dear Anspach,' a soft voice said from the smoky gloom ahead of them. 'What a *delightful surprise*.'

'LOOK THERE,' Morgenstern whispered from under his preposterous floppy brim. 'Ah! Ah! Ah! Not so obviously, boy!'

Drakken adjusted his stare to look at something on the ground by Einholt's feet.

'You see them? By the fountain, pretending they're not watching?' continued Morgenstern, looking studiously the other way.

'No–' Drakken began.

'I do,' Einholt said. Jagbald Einholt was the quiet man of the company, tall and broad and bald with a jagged beard and a long scar across his eye, cheek and throat. With his milky eye, it was often hard to tell which way he was looking. Now, with a furtive measure as practised as Morgenstern, he was assessing the watchers by the fountain while apparently regarding the weather cock on the Merchant Chandlers.

'Big bruisers. Four of them. Been with us since the Cocky Dame.' Morgenstern stretched as if he hadn't a care in the world.

Drakken dropped to his knees to adjust the strapping of his boot and got a good look from behind the cover of Morgenstern's voluminous cape.

'You were asking a lot of questions,' he said, straightening up and whispering to Morgenstern. 'Five taverns we've been in now, and in each one you've bent the ear of the barman with vague questions about something lost.'

'We've got someone's interest and no mistake,' Einholt mused.

'Let them make the move,' Morgenstern said, heading off. 'We'll try the Tardy Ass next. It's past midday. We can take an ale there too.'

'This isn't an excuse for a tavern crawl,' Drakken began.

Morgenstern looked hurt. 'My boy, I'm taking this all too seriously. What other morning would I have gone through five taverns before noon and still not had a jar?'

They moved west down the rolling cobbles of Scrivener's Passage, dodging between the pack carts coming up from the markets. A hundred yards behind, the four men left the fountain and followed.

* * *

THE GUILDHALL of the Apothecaries on Ostwald Hill had a noxious, yellow pallor to it. It was a rotting, half-timbered building of great age and veneration that sagged as if poison was in the wood and stones. Gruber and Lowenhertz entered into the close air of the audience hall through an unattended archway, and gazed around at the stained glass fronts of the many workshops and apothecums.

'You know this place?' Gruber asked, wrinkling his nose. The air was dry, with an oxidised reek.

'I come here from time to time,' replied Lowenhertz, as if such visits were as natural for a soldier like him as a trip to the armour smiths. The response made Gruber smile, a thin grin cracking his old, lined face. The tall and darkly handsome Lowenhertz had been an enigma since he transferred to White Company in the spring. It had taken a while for them to trust him past his overbearing intellect and strange, wide learning. But he had proved himself, proved himself loyal, proved himself in the field of combat. Now they looked at his odd, educated ways with gentle good humour, and none in the company denied he was an asset. A man with the learning to think his way around a thousand subjects and still fight like a pack-sire wolf when the blood was up.

'Stay here a moment,' Lowenhertz said, moving away into the dimmer reaches of the Guildhall, under a stained and alarmingly singed Guild banner. Gruber loosened his cloak, checked the dagger in his waistband and leant against a wall. He thought of the others, in twos and threes, scouting the city just now. Aric and their commander, Ganz, following Anspach's lucky-charm ways into the gaming places and the wager-pits; Schell, Kaspen and Schiffer in the markets; Bruckner and Dorff checking with their drinking friends in the Watch and the Militia; Morgenstern, Drakken and Einholt doing the rounds of the taverns. He didn't know what alarmed him most – that Anspach's cavalier attitude might provoke untold trouble from the criminal underclass, that Bruckner or Dorff might say too much to their cronies, that Schell and his party might get inveigled into the clutches of the merchant class, or that Morgenstern was visiting taverns. No, that was it. Morgenstern was visiting taverns. Gruber sighed. He prayed to Ulric that between them, steady old Einholt and earnest young Drakken would have the strength to keep Morgenstern's thirst reined in.

As for them: it had fallen for Gruber to go with Lowenhertz to pursue the latter's lead. Lowenhertz had suggested that the

Teeth of Ulric might have been taken for some mystical purpose, and in these alchemical workplaces that answer might be
found. It had been Gruber's suggestion, after all, that magic had
played a part in the theft.

He felt uneasy. Science didn't agree with him, and he was disarmed by the notion of men who spent their days mixing vials
and philtres and potions. It was a short step from that to sinister black what-not in Gruber's book.

Lowenhertz reappeared under the Guild awning and beckoned. Gruber went over.

'Ebn Al-Azir will see us.'

'Who?'

Lowenhertz frowned at him. 'The chief alchemist. I've known
him for years. He is from foreign parts, far away, but his work is
excellent. Be appropriately humble.'

'Very well,' Gruber said, 'but it may kill me.' Gruber had precious little time for the outland types with their strange skins,
odd scents and bewildering ways.

'Remove your boots,' Lowenhertz said, stopping him on the
threshold of a narrow doorway.

'My what?'

'A mark of respect. Do it.' Gruber saw that Lowenhertz's feet
were now bare. He cursed quietly as he yanked off his kid-skin
riders.

The narrow door let onto a narrower staircase that circled up
into the gloomy reaches of the Guildhall. Above, they ducked
through a lancet archway and into a long, high attic room. The
air seemed golden here. Sunlight streamed down thickly, like
honey, through angled skylights of pumice glass, and was caught
and suspended in rich hangings of silk and net. The room was
carpeted in a rug of elaborate design, the hues and weaving
astonishing and vibrant. Intricately wrought lamps and jewelled
censers of gold filigree smoked around the room illuminating,
in addition to the slow sunlight, a cluttered space of books and
scrolls, chests and wall-hangings, charts and articulated skele-
tons – birds, beasts, and things akin to men. Stove fires cooked
blue-hot under sculptural glass vessels in which liquids of vivid
colours hissed and steamed and gave off oily vapours. A bell was
chiming. The air smelled of rich, cloying sweetnesses. Gruber
tried to breathe, but the air was too close. Perfume clogged his
senses for a moment, perfume and incense.

On a rounded foot-table nearby, on the ivory inlaid top, lay
a puppet, a glaring man in clown's pantaloons with jewelled

joints and a belled cap. The puppet lay discarded, strings loose, in a rictus of death, like so many figures Gruber had seen on the field of war. That's how we all look when our strings go slack, he thought. The snarling stare of the puppet glared up at him out of a white porcelain face. Gruber looked away. He laughed humourlessly to himself. A sixty year-old veteran like him, afraid of a puppet a foot high!

A figure rose in the gloom, parted hanging nets and stepped out to meet them. He was small, dressed in a high-throated blue gown with embroidery at the neck and wide cuffs. His face was waxy and sallow, and there was a look of great age in his hollow eyes. Age, or perhaps…

'My old friend Heart-of-a-Lion!' he said. His accent was melodious and heavy.

Lowenhertz bowed his head, 'Master Al-Azir! How go your stars?'

The little man put his hands together. Long-nailed and dark, they emerged from his cuffs like the recessed blades from some mechanical weapon. Gruber had never seen so many rings: spirals, signets, loops, circles.

'My stars travel with me and I follow them. For now, my house is benign and it smiles on me the gift of heaven.'

'For that I am happy,' Lowenhertz said. He glanced a look at Gruber.

'Huh? Oh… as am I, sir.'

'Your friend?' asked Al-Azir with a flash of white teeth, inclining his head and circling a hand towards Gruber.

He moves like a puppet, thought Gruber, like a damn puppet on strings, all grace and motion lent by the hand of a trained puppeteer.

'This is my worthy comrade, Gruber,' said Lowenhertz. 'What trust you give to me must also go to him. We are brothers of the Wolf.'

Al-Azir nodded. 'Refreshment?' he asked.

No, it wasn't a question. It was an obligation, Gruber decided. Al-Azir made a brief hissing sound through his teeth and a huge man came out from behind the nets; bald, monumentally muscled and naked except for a breech-clout. His eyes were shadowed and unforthcoming, and he carried an ornate tray on which sat three tiny silver cups, a silver spouted pot and a bowl of jagged brown crystals with a pair of clawed tongs resting in them.

The vast servant set the tray down on the foot-table and retreated, taking the puppet with him. Al-Azir ushered them to sit on bolsters and satin cushions around the foot-table. He poured steaming oil-black fluid from the pot into the three cups with attentive care, each move slow and graceful.

Gruber watched Lowenhertz for a cue. Lowenhertz lifted the cup nearest him – it looked like a silver thimble in his hands –and dropped a cluster of the crystals into it with the tongs, which he then used to stir the thick fluid. He muttered something and nodded before sipping.

Lowenhertz didn't die choking and frothing, which Gruber took to be a good sign. He mimicked the process, lifting the cup and stirring the crystals in with the clawed tongs. Then he murmured, 'Ulric preserve me' and nodded. But there was no way he was going to sip.

He suddenly became aware of Lowenhertz glaring at him fiercely.

Gruber took a sip, licked his lips and smiled. Keeping that sip down was the hardest battle he had ever fought. It tasted like tar; smoked tar; smoked, boiled tar. With a bitter taste of mildew and a syrupy flavour of corruption.

'Very good,' he said finally, when at last he was certain opening his mouth wouldn't result in the reproduction of his last meal.

'Something troubles you,' said Al-Azir.

'No, it's quite nice really–' began Gruber, and then shut up.

'Something is lost,' went on Al-Azir, melodious and soft. 'Something precious. Eh! Precious.'

'You know this, master?'

'The stars tell me, Heart-of-a-Lion. There is pain in the ruling house of Xerxes, and both Tiamut and Darios, Sons of the Morning, draw hooked blades against each other. Eh! It is seen and written in water.'

'Your learning astounds me as ever, master. The heavens convolute and you read the signs. Tell me what you know.'

'I know nothing and everything,' replied Al-Azir, sipping slowly, head bowed.

Then cut to the latter, Gruber cursed inwardly. *Enough with this stars stuff!*

'What has been taken, Heart-of-a-Lion?' asked Al-Azir gently.

Lowenhertz was about to speak when Gruber cut in.

'Why don't–' He saw Lowenhertz's angry snarl and held up a hand for calm.

'Forgive my bluntness, Master Al-Azir,' Gruber corrected himself, 'but this is a matter of delicacy. We would appreciate knowing what you know before we unburden ourselves fully.'

He glanced at Lowenhertz, who nodded cautious approval, his lips pursed.

'For such help,' Gruber went on, 'my Lord Ulric may surely shine his thanks upon you. I am sure his light lurks somewhere in your firmament.'

'I'm sure it does,' Al-Azir replied with an ivory-white smile. 'Somewhere.'

'My friend is in earnest, Master Al-Azir,' Lowenhertz said. 'Can you tell us what you know?'

Al-Azir set his cup down and folded his hands so they each disappeared up the opposite sleeve. He stared down at the intricate inlay of the tabletop. 'The Jaws of the Wolf, so the stars say.'

Gruber felt his guts clench. He leaned forward to catch every soft, curling word.

'Jaws of the Wolf, precious jaws, bone bright. They are precious and they have been taken.'

'By who? For what purpose?' Lowenhertz asked.

'By darkness, Heart-of-a-Lion. Foul darkness. They cannot be recovered. Eh! I have seen woe on this rock-city! Pain! Pestilence! Eh! I have seen misery and weeping and lamentation!'

'Cannot be recovered?' Lowenhertz's voice seemed suddenly frail. 'Why not, master? What is the darkness you speak of?'

'Night. But not a night of the stars to read and learn from. A night without stars. That is when the Jaws of the Wolf will bite the living heart from Middenheim rock-city. Eh!'

Gruber looked up. Lowenhertz seemed on the point of leaving, as if he'd heard enough.

'What can we do?' Gruber asked directly.

'That's it,' said Lowenhertz. 'Master Al-Azir has said his piece. We must go now!'

'I'm not going anywhere!' snapped Gruber, shaking off Lowenhertz's hand. 'Master Al-Azir, if you know this much, you must know more! I beg you, tell us! What can we do?'

'Enough, Gruber!'

'No! Sit down, Lowenhertz! Now!'

Al-Azir made gentle shushing motions with his hands and Lowenhertz sat again. 'It is as I said. They cannot be recovered. They are lost to you forever.'

Gruber leant across the table to face Al-Azir. 'Your pardon, sir. I am a White Wolf, of White Company, beloved of Ulric. I know when a battle is lost and when it is won, but I will still stay the course. The Jaws of Ulric may be gone from us and beyond recovery, but I will fight on… fight on, I say! A Wolf fights to the death even when the battle is lost! So tell me this at least: who is the enemy I am losing to? What are his signs?'

The huge servant emerged from behind the nets, flanking his master. His sword was splayed and curved and almost as tall as Gruber.

Gruber didn't back off. He had a hand on the pommel of the blade in his waistband and his nose right in the face of the tiny, old alchemist. 'Tell me! It may not do me any good in your eyes, but tell me anyway!'

Al-Azir waved a hand and the servant and his sword departed. 'Gruber of the Wolf, I pity you. But I admire your courage. Eh! Even though you will lose what is dear to you. Look for the Black Door. Look for the north of seven bells. Look for the lost smoke.'

Gruber sat back on his bolster. He felt stunned. 'Look for–'

'You heard him,' Lowenhertz said from the doorway.

Gruber looked up into the eyes of Al-Azir, which fixed upon him for the first time. Gruber was amazed at the clarity and humour of the brown eyes in those sallow hoods.

Without thinking, he took up his cup and drained it. Then he reached his hand forward and clasped Al-Azir's as it was extended. 'If you've helped me, my thanks,' he said.

Al-Azir smiled. A genuine smile. 'You cannot win, Gruber. But make a good job of losing. Eh! It has been interesting talking with you.'

Out in the courtyard, Gruber was smiling as he pulled on his boots. Lowenhertz growled, 'What do you think you were doing in there? There are ways, customs, protocols!'

'Aw, shut up. He liked me… Heart-of-a-Lion.'

'I thought you were going to attack him.'

'So did I,' Gruber said cheerfully, leading the way to the exit gate. 'But you know what? I think he liked me better than you. You've been round there so long with your yes master, no master, and here I am, an ignorant Wolf, and he tells me what's what.'

'Maybe… but what have we got?'

'A lead, Lowenhertz – or weren't you listening? We've got a lead.'

'But he said we'd lose any–'

'Who cares? Come on!'

BLEYDEN WAS A small, slight man, little taller than the dwarf Kled, but rake thin. He wore an immaculate silk doublet and curious

gloves of black hide. He perched in an upholstered throne chair
that was set up on boxes to give him commanding height. Aric
thought it just drew attention to his diminutive stature. He
couldn't help smiling at the way Bleyden's clerical desk was
similarly raised on boxes so he could reach it from the chair.

The little man took the bag of coins that Ganz handed him.
Aric saw ice in Ganz's look as he handed over the bag. *He may
kill Anspach for this,* Aric decided.

Bleyden opened the draw-string of the bag and peeked inside
like a child with a bag of sweets. A delighted look flashed across
his small, drawn features. *He must be eighty, judging from his thin
silver hair and tight waxy skin,* thought Aric, *and no bigger than a
stable lad from the Wolf Barrack. And this man is the Low King who
rules the crime syndicates of the eastern city?*

Bleyden began to count off coins from the bag onto his desk
top. His nimble, gloved fingers made neat, ten-coin piles in a
row, each pile meticulously straightened and flushed. It took all
of three minutes, three silent minutes where the only sound
was Kled chewing the last of the sausage and scribing marks in
the old doorframe with a large, rusty knife he had suddenly
produced.

'Forty-seven crowns,' beamed Bleyden, looking up from the
neat stacks and handing the folded purse back to Ganz. The
commander took it wordlessly.

'A down-payment on my debt. Satisfactory, I trust?' Anspach
said.

'Quite satisfactory,' the tiny man replied. He slid a red-bound
ledger from a shelf under the desk, opened it carefully and
made a deliberate mark in ink with his quill. He looked up. 'I
am impressed with the fraternal loyalty of the Knight Templars,'
he said, his voice oozing like treacle. 'To stand payment for a
colleague.'

'We Wolves stand together,' Ganz replied without a trace of
irony. Or emotion.

We'll stand together all right, Aric thought, *and watch as Ganz
beats Anspach to death in the stable block tonight.* There was a
smile that was battling to get out and stretch on Aric's face. He
bit his cheek hard.

'Was there anything else?' Bleyden asked. 'I am busy. And we
are closed, as I'm quite sure Kled informed you.'

'Information,' Ganz said. The word was hard and solid, like a
splinter of the Fauschlag Rock. 'Anspach tells me you know
things. About the circulation of... goods in the city.'

Bleyden raised his eyebrows at Anspach. 'Does he? I'm surprised at you, Anspach. You know what loose tongues do.'

'Fall out,' Kled said ominously from behind them.

Bleyden chuckled. 'What is your name, friend of Anspach?'

'Ganz.'

'Commander of White Company! Well, I'm honoured!' Bleyden chuckled again. 'I had no idea I was in the presence of such greatness. Commander Ganz... well, well, well. A stranger to my establishments. Why is that?'

'Unlike Anspach, I find no need to take risks or see death when I'm off-duty. My working life is amply full of such activities.'

'And the fact that you are standing before me alive implies that the death you speak of is the kind you deal out. My, my, Commander Ganz. That's about as close to a threat as anything I've heard in years.'

'You should get out more,' Ganz said.

Great Ulric, but he's pushing him! thought Aric. He suddenly wondered where the dwarf and his rusty knife were. Behind them still. Should he risk settling a hand on the haft of the dagger in his belt, or was that going to give Kled all the excuse he needed? Aric swallowed. *Careful, commander,* he willed.

Bleyden was still smiling. 'Information comes at a price, Commander Ganz. All you've done is diminish Anspach's tally. I've seen nothing today that suggests to me I should volunteer information.'

'What would?' Ganz asked.

'Settling Anspach's debt might make me reconsider. Settling it with interest.'

'But I've given you all my–'

Bleyden pursed his lips and shook his little head. 'Coins are coins. If you're out of them, there are other ways to pay. A favour, perhaps? I would value greatly the idea that I could call upon a commander of a Templar Company when I needed it. Consider it a down-payment of trust.'

Aric could see how Ganz's shoulders tightened. Anspach looked worried. Aric knew the last thing he had intended was for their commander to pollute his hands by making an honour-promise to a beast like Bleyden. This was not going well.

But there was the honour of the Temple too, of the Wolves as a whole. Aric suddenly realised in his heart that Ganz would be prepared to take the offer, to corrupt himself and leave himself honour-bound to this scum if that was what it took.

Ganz was about to speak when Aric pushed forward and dropped his own purse on the desk. Bleyden looked at it as if it was a bird-dropping.

'My own coins. Fifty-eight crowns. Count it. That, with my commander, pays Anspach's dues... with interest.'

Bleyden sucked at his teeth.

'As I said, I am impressed with the fraternal loyalty of the Knight Templars. Ask away.'

Anspach cleared his throat. 'Has anything of... singular value passed into the secret trade this morning? Something that might fetch an impossible price?'

Bleyden tapped his teeth with his gloved finger tips. 'Have you Wolves lost something?'

'Answer!' Ganz hissed.

'No. Nothing. On my honour, however you value it.'

There was a long silence. For all that effort, nothing! Aric felt like striking the grinning child-man. He certainly knew how to string along his dopes for extra revenue.

'Let me out of here!' Ganz barked and turned to go. Kled stood aside from the door and made an 'after you' gesture that any chamberlain in the Graf's palace would have been proud of.

'Don't go away angry, Commander Ganz,' Bleyden said suddenly. 'I am a vicious and conniving businessman, but I am still a businessman. I understand the mechanisms of trade and I know when a customer should feel he's got his money's worth. Listen to me now...'

Ganz turned back.

'I don't know what you've lost, Wolf, and I don't care. If it comes into my hands, I'll get the best price for it and you'll get first refusal. All I can offer now is this... you're not the only ones.'

'What do you mean?'

'Last night, many noble bodies in this city were deprived of valuable things. You're not the first to come here today asking questions. Not the last either, I'll warrant. Everyone knows of Bleyden's skill in disposal of valuables. There is a word on the street too.'

'And?' said Anspach.

'Your money's worth, if it will help. Last night, the Merchants' Guild was robbed of the stamped gold scales that stand in their Guildhall, the symbol of their trade. Last night, something of great symbolic worth was taken from the chapter house of the Knights Panther. Last night, the ceremonial pledging cup of the

City Militia went missing. Last night, the Alembic of Crucifal was taken from its locked cabinet in the chancel of the Alchemists' Guildhall. Last night, the Temple of Shallya was robbed of the Unimpeachable Veil. Is this picture clear to you? Is it worth your down-payment? Those are all I know of, but you can wager there are others. Last night, someone systematically robbed all the great institutions of this town of their most hallowed icons.'

Ganz breathed a long sigh. It was worse than he had feared.

'I don't know what's going on in Middenheim,' Bleyden said. 'This isn't a crime spree. This is a conspiracy.'

Ganz motioned the others to follow him. He paused at the door. And turned. 'My thanks, Bleyden. However you value it.'

'Immeasurably, Commander Ganz. And I ask you a favour.'

Ganz paused. 'What?'

'When you find out what's going on, tell *me*. Frankly, it's all rather worrying.'

THEY LEFT THE Tardy Ass by the back door and stood in a shadowed alley while Morgenstern relieved himself against a wall.

'One ale, you said,' Drakken remarked.

'We kept him to three; be thankful,' Einholt said wearily.

'And yet something!' said Morgenstern triumphantly, rearranging his clothes. 'I told you nothing happens in this city without the innkeepers knowing it first!'

Drakken frowned and shot a look at Einholt. Had he been in a different tavern, listening to a different conversation?

'What something?' asked Einholt.

'Didn't you see how dreary and dull it was in there? Didn't you see what was missing?'

'I'm not quite the expert you are in the details of Middenheim's hostelries,' Einholt said sourly.

'Pretend we didn't notice and tell us before we die of old age,' Drakken added.

'The Cup of Cheer! *The Cup of Cheer*! It was obvious!'

They shot him wounding looks of incomprehension.

As if he was explaining it patiently to babies, Morgenstern began. 'The Cup of Cheer is the mascot icon of the Guild of Vittalers. Every year they compete for it and the winning tavern sets it in pride of place above the bar, the stamp that marks them as the best ale-house in town. The Tardy Ass won it last Mitterfruhl and where was it? Aha! Under the cloth draped over the alcove above the bar? I think not! It's gone too!'

'Let me get this straight,' Einholt said. 'You're suggesting we compare the loss of the Teeth of Ulric to the theft of some battered chalice that innkeepers hold dear?'

'We each have our own treasures,' Morgenstern said. He was probably going to explain further when the four long shadows passed across them.

The four men from the fountain. They approached down the alley, two from either end, faces fixed and grim.

'Time for some fun,' Morgenstern remarked. And charged them.

His huge bulk felled the pair advancing from the western end, smashing one aside into a stagnant pool of horse urine and slamming the other against the wall. The other two were on Drakken and Einholt in a second.

Drakken dropped and swung low, punching the ribs of his attacker and then throwing him over his head, propelled by his own charge. Einholt was locked with his man, grappling and thrashing, overturning crates of empty bottles and refuse.

Morgenstern was busy slamming the head of his assailant back into the mouldy alley wall. He seemed intent on finding a space between the bricks that it would fit. His other attacker was now back on his feet. A glimmer of steel lit in his hands.

Drakken cried out. Ducking the renewed assault of the man he had sent flying, he dodged two, three, four punches before planting one of his own, which laid the man out on the cobbles, his jaw lolling. Einholt broke his man's grip with a knee to his softer parts and smacked him to the ground with an open hand. The man's flailing legs came round and ripped Einholt's feet out from under him. They went down into the muck and sewage, clawing and biting.

Drakken sprang down the alley past Morgenstern and his sagging victim, and tackled the man with the knife. He looped his hand in low, catching the wrist, and threw the man against the wall. A slam of the wrist, then another, and at last the knife flew loose.

Down the alley, Einholt finally got the better of his opponent and left him stewing unconscious in the drain ditch.

Drakken was locked in fury with the last one, hands around his throat. Morgenstern suddenly leaned over them, holding the fallen knife by the blade.

'Drakken! Boy! See the hilt? See the markings? These men are Knights Panther. I think we should talk to them, don't you?'

* * *

A HOT, DULL caul of evening hung around the city, and surly strands of twilight filtered into the window spaces and archways of the Templars' barracks. In the long, suffocatingly hot Temple eating hall, ranged around in the fluttered candlelight, sat White Company in their motley garb, and four others – the rather battered individuals encountered by Morgenstern's party. Ganz leaned down into the face of their leader, who was dabbing a bloody lip with a fold of cloth.

'When you're ready, von Volk of the Panthers.'

'I'm ready, Ganz of the Wolves.' The man looked up at him. The last time they had exchanged such grim looks, they had been on horseback at the gates of Linz in the spring.

Von Volk patted his swollen lip again and cast an angry look across at Morgenstern, who smiled broadly. 'Last night, at the chime of compline, the regimental shrine of the Knights Panther at the palace was robbed.'

'What was taken?' Ganz asked.

'Does it matter? We were out to retrieve our loss when we came upon a group of rascals asking questions and seeking information. It… it seemed to us that they knew something about our loss, so we tracked them and intercepted them.'

'Oh, that's what it was! Interception!' Morgenstern chuckled. 'And I thought it was a sound trouncing!'

Two of the Panthers sprang to their feet, eyes blazing and fists clenched, but Ganz shouted them into place.

He looked at von Volk a minute more and then sank onto the bench beside him, their eyes fixed. 'Panther, we too were robbed. And, as far as we can be certain, so was every other great institution of the city.'

Von Volk seemed surprised at Ganz's candour. He turned away, thoughtful. 'A conspiracy, then?' he murmured.

'And one we have a lead on,' Gruber said, stepping forward.

Ganz and von Volk looked at him.

'Ah, not a good one,' Gruber was forced to admit, grilled by the stern looks of the company commanders. 'But a lead nonetheless…'

AS VESPERS STRUCK and twilight dropped across Middenheim like a damask curtain in a theatre pit, they spread out again. Wolves and Panthers together, splitting into parties to search the city even more thoroughly than before. Von Volk had summoned ten more Panthers from the Royal Barracks and they had arrived, clad in plain clothing, to be apportioned off into the working groups.

Aric was with the third group: Lowenhertz, Gruber, Einholt, von Volk himself and two arrogant, silent Panther knights named by their commander as Machan and Hadrick. They passed out into the streets, under the gently swinging lamps. Sultry evening swaddled around them. Now they were all shrouded in heavy capes to disguise their weapons and partial armour.

Gruber paused to look up at the sullen sky with its haze of ruddy, cloudy light. 'A night without stars…' he murmured.

'The stars are there!' Lowenhertz snapped. 'It's early yet, and the twilight haze and cook-smoke of the city are obscuring the heavens. But it will be a clear night. Not a night without stars.'

'Maybe,' Gruber returned, unconvinced.

They were on Tannery Hill, pacing the steep cobbles up to the crest of the city. To either side of them, taverns shook with laughter, music and carousing.

Eight o'clock struck. The bells of the city chimed irregularly, and mis-matched. Aric listened to them. Bells, he thought. Just as Gruber had spoken of in his cryptic clues. The first, a delicate plink-plinking note down in Altmarkt. The second a dull bong from Temple Square. The third a triple chime, emptied by distance and the wind, from Ostmark. Then the fourth, a tinny strike from the small church in Sudgarten.

A pause, then the fifth, sixth and seventh came together, overlapping. The last peals drifted away from the College Chapels on the upper slope of the Palast District.

Then a long break, and afterwards the slender tower of the Milliner's struck eight. To the north of them, by several hundred yards.

'Is it just me…?' Aric began. He looked round to see both Gruber and Lowenhertz, transfixed by the staggered sounds and positions of the chimes.

Gruber stroked his lean chin and glanced at Lowenhertz.

'Well, Heart-of-a-Lion?'

'Just… just a coincidence. What are the chances? We happen to be standing where we can hear seven peals to the south and then one to the north. Al-Azir couldn't have–'

Gruber turned to face Lowenhertz fully. His face was expressionless, but Aric could hear real anger in his tone. The Panther Knights and Einholt looked on, uneasy.

'You bemuse me, Lowenhertz,' Gruber hissed. 'You seem to know more about the mystical and esoteric world than all of us, you bother to chase leads from strange foreigners who would bewilder us with their customs, you urge us to look for secrets in the fabric of the earth… and you deny this? Why? Ulric take me, I'm a blind old heathen next to you, but even I can imagine that your Al-Azir, if he has the skills and knowledge you reckon of him, would have given us a portent-clue, particular to us!'

Lowenhertz sighed. 'You're right, old man. You don't understand the delicate ways of enlightened souls such as Al-Azir. Ulric! I don't even pretend to! There was more to his meaning than this! His intellect and understanding is refined far beyond our capacity! He–'

'Would have given us a clue we could understand if we were sharp enough?' cut in Aric smartly. 'How would you explain the complex tactics of a cavalry formation to one untutored in the arts of horse-war? Simply? In words a simpleton could understand? I think so!'

'Aric's right,' growled Einholt. 'I respect you as a battlebrother, Lowenhertz, and respect your learning, but I think you're thinking too hard.'

Gruber smiled. 'Well put, Jagbald, old friend. Lowenhertz, you know your foreign friend was trying to help me, not you. I was the one that asked – a dumb soldier, not a man of learning like you. Wouldn't he have couched his meaning in a way I could understand? And do you not doubt his powers, to know ahead of time we – I – would be in the right place to understand that meaning?'

Lowenhertz was a silent shadow in the gathering dark.

'North of seven bells, he said,' Gruber went on. 'Could it hurt to test that? Could it hurt to believe he has a vision beyond ours? Wasn't that why you took me to him in the first place? And made me take off my damn boots and drink that foul tar?'

Lowenhertz sighed and nodded. He turned and strode uphill, north towards the thin spike of the Milliner's clock tower.

They checked the streets and alleyways around the Milliner's Hall for the best part of an hour. As the clocks chimed again, true dark was settling over the Fauschlag. The hot clouds of sunset had wilted away. The dark bowl of heaven was black-purple and starless.

Von Volk took Aric's sleeve suddenly and gestured upwards. 'Look for lost smoke, Wolf. Wasn't that the damn riddle?'

Aric nodded. He looked where the Panthers' commander was indicating. The night air above the street was hazed by chimney smoke from the homes and taverns around them. The smoke was almost invisible, but it dimpled and blurred the cold solidity of the darkness.

'Then where's that coming from?' asked von Volk.

Aric looked, and realised the Panther's eyes were keen. One column of faint haze seemed to have no source, no obvious flue or chimney to emit it. It simply vented from a space between stacked roof-slopes, ghostly and slow.

'Ar-Ulric seal my lips!' Aric began. He turned and looked at von Volk fiercely.

'Lost smoke?' the Panther asked with a predatory grin.

Aric called the others in to join them and together, the seven men prowled down Chute Lane towards the complex clump of ancient dwellings that the smoke was exuding from.

'Gods!' Einholt spat. 'Where's its source?'

'Nowhere...' murmured the Panther Machan dangerously, his hand inside his cloak, clutching the hilt of his sword.

Gruber stopped them all with a wave of his hand. They were edging into a dark alley, having to stoop low because of the way the buildings on either side leaned in, making a tunnel of relaxed, sooty brick. The alley was full of refuse, mire and a trickle of water. Rats chittered and darted around their feet. Einholt, Hadrick and von Volk filled hand-lamps with oil from a flask and lit them from the same taper, holding the pottery dishes up above their stooped heads as they led the way in.

Fifteen yards down the gently turning alley, probing deeper than anyone but rats or fleeing cut-purses had been in years, they saw it.

'Ulric damn me!' Gruber said, almost voicelessly.

A door. Lower than a man, more of a hatch, built into the brick wall of the alleyway tunnel. Timber-built and strong. And black with pitch.

'Look for the black door,' Gruber said.

'The lost smoke, the north of seven bells...' added Aric.

'On a night without stars,' Lowenhertz finished.

Lowenhertz pulled out his warhammer from under his cape and smashed the black door in off its hinges.

Darkness beckoned them.

WITHIN, A narrow stairway led down below street level. They had to stoop and hunch, knocking scalps and elbows against the confines.

'Dwarf-made?' Aric wondered.

'As old as the Fauschlag itself,' agreed Einholt, ominously.

From what little they could see around them, by the flickering lamp-flames, the steps were hewn from the rock and turned gently to the right. The walls were travertine brick for as long as the old foundations of the buildings over the alley descended, and then became smooth, tooled stone. They'd gone down at least thirty feet. Leading the way by his lamp, von Volk touched the rock wall and his fingers came away with sticky blackness on their tips.

'Caulked with pitch, like the door. Like a boat's keel.'

'And fresh too,' Lowenhertz muttered, also touching the walls. 'This place is well-tended and maintained.'

'But why the pitch?' Machan asked. 'To keep the damp out?'

'Or to keep something in,' Lowenhertz finished.

The steps levelled out and they found themselves in an underground tunnel tall enough for them to stand up in, but so narrow they could only move in single file.

'Which way?' Hadrick asked.

'North,' Gruber replied with great and awful certainty.

They moved north. After a hundred yards, they came upon another flight of steps down and they descended. The air began to smell of damp antiquity, the sweat of the old rock that now surrounded them and on which Middenheim was raised.

Von Volk's lamp sputtered out and Einholt refilled it from his oil-flask. Once the lamp was reignited, Einholt tossed the empty flask away. 'That's almost it for light,' he told them all. 'I have a little more oil left,' Aric said. 'But maybe we won't need it,' he added, sliding past von Volk, scraping his back on the tarry rock wall. He edged ahead, his feet silent on the smooth, cold, damp of the stone. 'Look. Am I imagining that?'

He wasn't. Light. Cold, fretful light, ahead and below them. With Aric in the lead, they followed it, extinguishing their lamps to save oil as the light grew.

After another hundred yards and another descending stairway, they came out into a wide tunnel of rough rock, like a mine. Threads of tiny silver lamps were looped on wire along each wall as far as they could see in each direction. The rough rock wall was rich with scintillating shards that caught the light and made it seem as if they were walking amongst stars.

'Glass specks... crystal...' murmured Gruber, stroking the rough wall with his fingers.

'Or gems, precious gems,' returned von Volk, looking more closely at the shards. 'This is the spur of an old dwarf mine, or I'm a Bretonnian! An old place, dug long before the city was raised.'

'I fear you're right,' Lowenhertz said. 'This is an ancient, for-gotten place.'

'Not forgotten, Heart-of-a-Lion,' Gruber said quietly. 'Who lit the lamps?'

Aric and Einholt both paused to inspect the silver lamps. They were intricate metal trinkets with compact glass chimneys. Their wicks burned with an intense white light, sucking fuel from the reservoirs beneath them.

'They're not burning oil,' Einholt said.

'Indeed not. I've never seen anything like this!' Aric muttered, amazed. Lowenhertz joined him to look. He sucked in a short, startled breath as he studied the lamp.

'Alchemy!' he said, turning to the others. 'These lamps are fired by an alchemical mix, a contact reaction… Gods! The best I know, Al-Azir included, could perhaps have wrought one such lamp in a month of industry!'

'And there are hundreds of them… ranged as far as we can see.' Gruber's voice seemed deflated of strength at the wonder of it.

They paced on down the lit tunnel, two abreast now, gazing about themselves. Gruber and von Volk took the lead, with Hadrick and Einholt behind them, then Aric and Machen, and Lowenhertz bringing up the rear. By now, all had drawn weapons: warhammers in the hands of the Wolves, swords in the hands of the Panthers. Hadrick also carried a crossbow, which he had wound to tension and let swing around his shoulder on a leather strap.

A crossway now, as the mine tunnel they traced intersected with another. The one they followed was lit with lamps and the other dark. There seemed no doubt as to the route they should take. Aric felt beads of perspiration gather on his scalp, despite the musty chill of the rock around him. He had lost all sense of time since they had come down here.

The passage widened and let out into a long, low cavern sim-ilarly draped with alchemical lamps. The walls seemed to be made of solid quartz and glowed like ice in the lamp-light. They advanced across the uneven floor.

'I'd be careful, if I were you,' said a voice from nowhere.

The Panthers and Wolves froze, looking about themselves, mystified.

Three figures approached from a side chamber none had seen was there. The Wolves and Panthers swung their weapons up ready. 'Make yourselves known!' cried von Volk.

The three figures stepped into the light of the lamps: a tall man in a long green cloak flanked by two Tilean mercenaries in leather hauberks and quilted leggings, their longswords drawn and their faces dark and stern behind the grilles of basket-helms. The green-cloaked man, whose face was long and clean-shaven, smiled a chilling smile which creased his pale, smooth skin. His eyes were hooded and deeply shadowed by dark skin.

'I am Master Shorack. My full title is longer and more burdensome, so you may know me as that. This pair are Guldo and Lorcha. They have no longer or more burdensome titles than that. They are, however, experienced and terrifying killers. So let's know you without delay.'

Von Volk and Gruber were about to move forward aggressively, but Lowenhertz stayed them both and pushed between them to face the cloaked man. Instantly, the two Tileans swung the tips of their long, gleaming blades to the point at his throat.

'Master Shorack, well met,' Lowenhertz said calmly, as if the swords weren't there.

'Is that you, Lowenhertz of the Wolves?' the cloaked man asked, squinting into the light. He made a subtle gesture and the Tileans smartly withdrew their blades, falling back behind him. He stepped forward. 'My, my, Lowenhertz. Who is this with you?'

'A mixed pack of Wolves and Panthers, master. Seeking the same as you, if I'm any judge.'

'Really? I'm very impressed. Everyone in the city running hither and yon to find their lost treasures, and you… Wolves and Panthers… get as close as me.'

'Who in Ulric's name is this, Lowenhertz?' Gruber spat indignantly.

'Master Shorack, Master Magician Shorack, of the Magicians' Conclave,' Aric said from behind. He'd never met the man, but he recognised the name.

'In person,' smiled Shorack. 'Humour me, Temple-Knights… what led you here?'

'A hunch,' Aric said.

'Determination…' von Volk said.

'Lowenhertz,' said Gruber, stepping forward. 'Or rather, me. From devious clues left by another of your stripe, Ebn Al-Azir.'

Shorack scoffed loudly. 'That charlatan? My dear sir, he's an alchemist, a tinkerer with the world's elements, a child in the realms of creation! I, sir, am a magician. A master of my art! There is no comparison!'

'I happened to like old Al-Azir, as a matter of fact,' Gruber said reflectively, realising he was voicing his thoughts. He paused, then continued anyway, turning to look into Shorack's dark eyes. 'Which is rare for me. Ordinarily, I'd have no truck with such people. In my experience, there are men who walk bravely in the light of goodness, and there are creatures who haunt the darkness and play with magic. There… is no comparison.'

Shorack cleared his throat, looking at Gruber intently. 'Was that some kind of threat, old warrior? An insult?'

'Just a statement of fact.'

'Assuming we're here for the same purpose,' Aric said softly from behind Gruber, 'maybe we should skip the insults entirely and work together.'

'Unless Master Shorack here is behind the injustice we seek to rectify,' von Volk said coldly.

Gruber grunted in agreement. He had been the first to ascribe the thefts to magic, and nothing he had seen so far had disabused him of the notion. Now an actual magician crossed their path, damn his hide…

'Sir! If I was your enemy, you would not be alive to conduct this charming bar-room spat!' Shorack's teeth gleamed in the light. 'Indeed, did I not first cry out a warning?'

'Warning?' Lowenhertz asked, clearly uncomfortable at the confrontation.

'Take it as a gesture of good faith. The hallway you were about to venture down is warded.' The Wolves and Panthers turned to look down the rough-hewn, glowing quartz chamber.

'Magic awaits the unwary and the unprepared here. Guarding magic. Simple stuff, so very much beneath my powers, but it would surely have caught you had you advanced.'

'And done what?' von Volk asked the magician.

Shorack smiled. 'Have you ever been drunk, soldier?'

Von Volk shrugged. 'On occasions. At feast days. What of it?'

Shorack laughed gently. 'Think how it feels to be drunk – if you are a tankard of ale.'

He turned and strode down the uneven floor, raising his hands wide, muttering a few high-pitched words that made Aric think for a moment of fingernails on glass. The sound made him catch his breath slightly. There was a smell too, a distant odour of decomposition, like a drain had been cracked open somewhere nearby.

'It is safe now,' Shorack said, turning back. 'The ward of guarding has been dispelled. We may all continue safely.'

'I stand in awe of your work, Master Shorack,' Gruber said, apparently with great humility. 'You speak baby-talk, break wind and tell us your invisible magic has saved us from a sorcerous trap we couldn't see.'

Shorack paced right up to Gruber till they were face to face. The magician was smiling again. 'Your scorn delights me. It is so refreshing to be disrespected. What is your name?'

'Gruber, of the Wolves.'

Shorack leaned forward until he was nose to nose with the old Wolf. His smile disappeared and was replaced by an expression as cold and hard and threatening as a drawn dagger. Gruber didn't even blink. 'Be thankful, Gruber of the Wolves, that you do not see. Be thankful that the magical world is invisible to your dull eyes, or you would claw out those eyes and die screaming in terror.'

'I'll remember to mention you to Ulric in my prayers,' Gruber replied tonelessly.

'Enough!' barked Aric, losing patience. 'If we're going on together, let's go on! Why don't you tell us what you're here for, Master Shorack?'

'You know already,' Shorack said, turning courteously to Aric. 'We know the Magician's Conclave must have lost something precious, as we have, a treasure as you put it. What?'

'It cannot be named. A charm. Priceless. To describe its properties and purpose would rob you of sanity.'

They all turned as Einholt chuckled. 'Invisible this, unspeakable that! Gruber's right – isn't it funny that we've only got this fellow's word for everything, and that he keeps sparing our sensitive ears from the actual truth. You should work the theatres, Master Shorack! You're a fine melodramatist!'

Shorack looked at him. Aric saw a strange look cloud the magician's face. It seemed like recognition… and pity.

'Einholt,' Shorack said flatly, at last.

'You know me, sir?' Einholt asked.

'Your name just came to me. The invisible world you mock spoke it to me. Einholt. You are a brave man. Stay out of the shadows.'

'Stay – what?'

Shorack had looked away, as if he found the sight of Einholt's face uncomfortable. *No*, thought Aric, *not uncomfortable. Unendurable. As if it… terrified him.*

'Shall we continue, Wolves and Panthers?' asked the magician brightly. Too brightly, in Aric's opinion. Shorack led the party down the quartz hall, his bodyguards at his heels.

'What did he mean?' Einholt hissed at Lowenhertz. 'What was that about?'

Lowenhertz shrugged. 'I don't know, Brother Wolf. But I know this: do as he says. Stay out of the shadows.'

MORE STEPS, a lamp-lit stairwell descending from the rear end of the quartz hall. As far as Gruber could judge, the steps brought them another hundred feet down into the rock, along a wide, sweeping staircase. Three times, Shorack had them stop so he could perform more pantomime and save them from invisible traps.

Enough theatrics! Gruber heard himself think. But there was no denying the cold chill of the nonsense words Shorack used for those pantomimes. Gruber caught Aric watching carefully and with concern. He saw, too, the black worry on Einholt's tense face.

Gruber edged down the steps until he was descending beside Shorack.

'You're a man of esoteric learning, Master Shorack. Have you any explanation for the troubles we find ourselves in? Why the thefts? Why something from each of the city's great institutions?'

'Do you know how to place a charm on a person, Gruber? A love charm, a luck-knot, a curse?' Shorack answered.

'No. I'm a soldier, as you know.'

'Any charm, from the simplest to the most abstract, requires a signifier. Something belonging to the individual you wish to charm. For a love-potion, a hank of hair; for luck, some coins from his purse or a favourite ring; for a curse... well, a drop of blood is the most efficacious. The signifier becomes the basis for the charm, the heart of the ritual that sets it.'

The stairs turned to the left and descended again steeply. The air was getting colder, damper, and now there was a taste of smoke.

'Imagine now you wished to place a charm upon something larger than a man – a city, let's say. A hank of hair won't do. You need signifiers of a different kind.' Shorack glanced at Gruber, one eyebrow raised to enquire if he was making sense.

'The items we've lost, those are the signifiers?'

'Indeed. Oh, I cannot be sure. We may be on the trail of some deranged trophy collector. But I doubt it. I believe someone is setting out to place a conjuration upon the entire city of Middenheim.'

Gruber sucked in his breath. In fairness, he had already begun to imagine such a thing, before he'd even conversed with the prim magician. From the battlefields of his career, he had seen the way the unholy enemy treasured marks of their foe for their mystical potency. They would go to great lengths to take standards, weapons, scalps, skulls. Gruber said nothing more, and led them down the steps.

The stairs brought them out, at last, into a huge chamber that Aric would think of ever afterwards as the cellar. Paved with violet tiles, it was as vast as the drill field of the Wolves' Temple barracks, but broken into sections by rows of pillars that flared upwards into corbel vaults. Aric imagined that once this place had been a huge larder, a wine-storehouse, a provisionary, crammed with racked flasks of dwarf brew, shelves of jarred root vegetables, muslin-wrapped cheeses and pickled fruit, and hung with salted meats. Now it was empty, the walls and pillars pitched black, strung with white lights. A stronger light source emanated from the far end, two hundred feet away, the glow criss-crossed by the back-lit shadows of the pillars. There was a low, sucking, rasping sound, as if the stones around them were taking long, slow breaths. And there was a smell of spoiled milk.

And another sound: a chanting. A murmur of priestly voices intoning something very far away. The sound came from the direction of the distant glow, and was given its rhythm by the beat of a bass tambour. The party spread out low, silently, hugging the pillars for cover. Gruber edged left with Einholt, Machan and von Volk. Aric took the right, with Hadrick and the Tilean, Guldo. Centrally, Lowenhertz advanced with Shorack and the other mercenary, Lorcha. They fluttered from pillar cover to pillar cover, darting between shadows, weapons drawn, moving towards the glow.

Lowenhertz settled into hiding behind a pillar. That sound – not the chanting, the seismic panting – filled his mind with fear. Shorack scurried up next to him, dabbing at the edges of his mouth with a silk handkerchief. There was blood on the cloth.

'Master Shorack?' whispered Lowenhertz.

'Nothing, my old friend,' the magician coughed back. Lowenhertz could smell the metallic stink of blood on his breath. 'Nothing. There are spirits loose in the air here – dead, vile things. The scent of them burns my throat.'

From his position in cover, Aric looked over at the source of the light. A wood fire, kindled in the stone basin of an ancient stone salting bath. The flames licked up, blazing the bundles of fragrant wood spindles incandescently, spilling off the sour stench. The smoke rose, as if pulled, up and out through a flue in the cellar's roof. *Now, at last, the source of the lost smoke becomes clear*, he thought.

Around the fire, stone blocks had been set like shoeing anvils or stools. They had been ranged around the central furnace in a peculiar, apparently random manner. On each one sat a priceless trophy: a glittering pledging cup, a crystal bottle, a gauzy fold of linen, a gold chalice, a beaded and pearled bracelet of panther claws, a mayoral badge, a sceptre, a silver timepiece, a furled dagger, a small silken bag... other items he couldn't make out. And one final one he could: the Jaws of Ulric, gaping, glittering in the firelight.

Aric could also see the twenty hooded figures kneeling amongst the blocks, facing the fire. They were the source of the chanting. One of them struck upon a drum.

At the heart of it all, his back to the fire so he faced the worshippers, stood a thin figure. Emaciated, wrapped in dark wadding, the figure seemed to jerk and move stiffly, like a puppet. It twitched in time to the beat. Aric could not see any detail, but he knew it was the most loathsome thing he had ever seen. He wished to be anywhere else now; fighting beast-packs in the Drakwald would be a holiday next to this horror.

Crouched behind the pillar next to Shorack, Lowenhertz realised how pale and perspiring the man had become.

'Shorack?' Lowenhertz whispered in concern.

Shorack settled his back to the pillar for a moment, trying to slow his breathing. His face was damp and pasty. 'This is... bad, Lowenhertz,' he murmured. 'Crown of Stars! I spend my life flexing my powers in the invisible world, and the gods know sometimes I tinker with the darker excesses. Their lure is great. But this... this is ritual magic so dark, so foul I – I have never seen or felt its like. Lowenhertz, I never even dreamed such abomination existed! This place is Death's place now!'

Lowenhertz looked at the magician in the dim light. The sense of him as a haughty, capable figure was all gone now, all his confidence and theatrical airs wasted away. Lowenhertz knew Shorack was powerful for an urban magician, among the best of his kind in the city. His skills had been enough to get them this far. But he was just a man now; a frightened man, way out of his depth. Lowenhertz felt immeasurable pity for the magician. And immeasurable fear for them all. If the great Shorack was scared…

From his vantage point, Gruber laid low on his belly and took in the scene. There were the lost treasures, and he had no doubt that they were being used, as Shorack had described, as signifiers in some great charm. *No*, he reconsidered, *curse is probably a far more appropriate word*. His flesh crawled. That panting, breathing sound around them, as if the walls were sighing. That beat, that chanting. And worst of all, that jerking puppet shape by the fire. Gruber wished Ulric had been merciful and spared him from ever having to see such a thing.

Von Volk was beside him. Fear made von Volk's eyes black, unblinking pits. 'What do we do, Wolf?' he whispered.

'Is there a choice, Panther?' Gruber mouthed. 'A great and stifling darkness is being born here that will overwhelm the city we guard with our lives. We must do what we were trained to do and pray it is enough.'

Von Volk nodded, took a deep breath, readied his blade and then looked across the cellar to Aric's group on the far side. The Panther commander caught Hadrick's eye and made a curt, chopping motion with his fist. Hadrick raised his crossbow.

The beat slapped. The chanting continued. The stones panted around them, sucking for breath. The fire cracked. The reek of death and decay choked the air. The puppet figure twitched.

Hadrick fired.

The crossbow bolt hit the twitching puppet in the chest and smashed it backwards into the fire. It shrieked – a ghastly, not-human noise – and clawed at the barb impaling it, floundering in the flames that licked into its filthy swaddling.

The hooded worshippers stopped mid-chant, jumped up and began to turn. A second later, the Wolves, Panthers, and Shorack's mercenaries were on them.

Aric charged the firelight, hammer whirling in his hand. It all became a blur. Lorcha was beside him, his longsword hissing through the air.

The puppet thing, ablaze like a torch, was still shrieking and trying to pull itself out of the fire.

The hooded chanters spun to meet them, throwing aside black velvet capes to reveal fierce men in mail-armour, brandishing swords and war-axes. Their screaming faces and their armour were plastered with blood and daubed markings.

Aric's whirring hammer smashed through the face of the first enemy he came upon. The hammerhead tore out the lower jaw, sending the pink, glistening hunk away like a blood-tailed comet, winking with exposed white bone. The next one was on him, and he blocked with his hammer-haft, stopping the axe-blow. Kicking low and hard, Aric dropped the attacker and then rolled in to crush his head flat between hammer and violet tiles.

Gruber waded in, breaking a neck out of true with his hammer, then spinning to face the next sword that came at him. Einholt was beside him, cleaving a ribcage with a sidewards strike. Von Volk broke his sword on its first clash with an enemy blade, and then savagely ripped the life out of his aggressor with the broken length, before throwing him aside and snatching up his axe. In von Volk's practised hands, it dug deep into the skull of the next foe within arm-reach.

Lowenhertz smashed a chanter backwards off his feet with a deft underswing that splintered a snarling face.

Machan struck at them, his sword whispering. Blood sprayed from the wounds he cut. Then he was scissored by two enemy blades. He dropped, screaming, in two, blood-venting pieces.

Hadrick had, by then, enough time to reload, and he slammed his bolt into the forehead of one of Machan's killers. A second later, he was carried back, shrieking, and pinned to a pillar by a foe whose lance had impaled him. Guldo decapitated the foe and pulled the lance out, allowing Hadrick to fall. But he was already dead.

Aric was nearly at the sacred jaws, but then he took a rip across the shoulder and went down on one knee. Gruber and Lowenhertz were hemmed in by fierce hand-to-hand on all sides. The top of Guldo's head was axed off and he fell, stone dead. Von Volk swung his axe up between the legs of a foe-man and split him to the sternum. But his captured axe was wedged and he tried in vain to pull it free.

Shorack raised his hand and with a gesture, at once slight yet full of unknowable power, wilted one of the chanters into fatty, smoking residue. The sounds and stinks of burning metal and flesh choked the air. The sorcerer shook slightly and took one step back as if to steady himself. Then he spun and destroyed the cultist closing on Gruber with nothing more than the clenching of his hand in the air. For a moment, Lowenhertz noted through the ferocious melee, the old Shorack was back with them, imposing, confident, capable, chilling.

Aric broke an opponent's hip and a ribcage. He turned. He saw. The burning, shrieking thing in the fire was getting up again, blackened and smouldering and tarry.

It looked at them through cindered eye-slits. It fixed its gaze on Shorack. It spoke through a mouth thick with fat blisters and crackling flesh.

'Die,' it said, its voice that of a dead thing.

Shorack screamed as if his insides were boiling. Gruber reached for him, but the magician was wrenched into the air by things none of them could see but all could feel. Cold forces of air, eddies of icy wind. Einholt smashed an axe-man aside and reached out to grab Shorack's trailing cloak. He realised with fear that he was seeing the effects of Shorack's invisible world for real now.

The magician spun up, away, out of his reach, thrashing and bedevilled by the harsh grip of unseen things. His green cloak, his clothes, one boot, all shredded off him and fluttered away. Weals and bloody rips scourged his flesh. Almost stripped bare, drenched in blood, half-butchered, Shorack slammed up into the vaulted roof. Bones snapped. It looked as if he had fallen upwards and hit the ceiling as if it was the ground. An immense, invisible force pressed him there, spread-eagled on his back. Blood pooled across the roof around him instead of pouring to the actual floor.

His ruined face, a mask of blood, glared down at Gruber and Einholt looking up from below. It was all the other Wolves, the Panthers and the remaining Tilean, Lorcha, could do to keep their attentions and eyes on the battle at hand. There was something mesmerising about Shorack's gruesome, inexorable demise.

Shorack looked down into the frantic face of Gruber. A moment before his eyes burst and his skull collapsed against the roof, he spoke. Eight words, forced out of a blood-filled mouth, the last act of his life, a monumental act of will power.

'Break. The. Charm. Without. The. Signifiers. It. Cannot.'

Eight words. A ninth, maybe a tenth, would have completed the whole, but the meaning was enough for Gruber.

An invisible force exploded Shorack's carcass across the roof in a shower of blood and meat. It coated the ceiling for a moment and then rained down on them all, leaving a pungent mist of blood vapour in the air.

Gruber was already moving, his hammer raised. Coated in Shorack's blood, he found two of the enemy turning to block him, axes raised. Gruber swung the warhammer round in a complete, whickering circle, both hands gripping the leather loop at the end of the haft, twisting his bodyweight to counterbalance the swing. Two skulls broke like earthenware before the swing was done.

Then he was clear, amongst the stone blocks set around the fireplace, each one bearing its precious icon. He knew he was within the weave of a great dark sorcery now, something invisible that laced itself between the signifiers. His skin prickled with static, his hair stood on end, and there was a smell that clawed at his sinuses. A smell of sweet corruption, like a week-old corpse. Magic, he knew, and would never forget. Black magic. *Death magic.*

He thought of Ganz, on the dangerous ride back from Linz, how he had driven the wraith-things back by destroying their precious talon. He knew he had to do the same... again... now... here. A signifier must be destroyed to break the charm. And he knew, clearly and coldly at last, what Al-Azir had really meant.

They cannot be recovered. They are lost to you for ever. Gruber of the Wolf, I pity you. But I admire your courage. Eh! Even though you will lose what is dear to you.

There was no choice. It was set, Gruber was sure, in the intricate and unchangeable workings of the stars. He had time for one blow and he knew, as a Wolf of the Temple of Ulric, where, in fairness, that blow should fall.

The Jaws of the Wolf, so holy, so precious, cut by Artur himself, glittered on the block before him.

He raised his hammer.

Something ripped into his back and agony lanced through him. Gruber screamed. Talons raked down his back from shoulders to waist, shredding off cloak, hauberk and undershirt and slicing deep cuts in his flesh. He stumbled to his knees. The blackened puppet-thing rose up behind him, its curled, skeletal fingers like hooks, red with his blood. It twitched, deathless eyes glittering, and smashed Gruber to the floor with a side-swipe. Blood poured down the side of Gruber's head where the swipe had struck. For the rest of his life, his left ear would be a rag of flesh, like a flower with the petals torn off.

Gasping, Gruber looked up at the monster that lurched and jiggled over him. Its long, angular limbs twitched and spasmed like a badly-worked marionette. *Or no*, thought Gruber, his pain lending his mind frightening clarity. *Like something half-finished. Like a mockery of a man, a skeleton that remembers how to move but hasn't the flesh or the sinew or the practice to do it well.* Backlit by the firelight, that was all it seemed to be: a large human skeleton, clad in shreds of tomb-dry skin and scraps of burnt bandage, twitching and jerking as it tried to behave like a man again. Tried to be a man again.

Only the eyes were whole: coral-pink fires of livid fury. It gazed down at him. Its bare, sooty teeth clacked open, tearing the dry, blistered flesh of its long-withered mouth.

'Die,' it said.

'Die yourself!' snarled Einholt, storming in from the side and smashing the dreadful thing into the air with an expert swing of his hammer. Twisting, the puppet-thing tumbled away into the darkness beyond the fire.

Einholt glanced down at Gruber once, but he didn't hesitate. It seemed the veteran Wolf had wit enough to arrive at the same conclusions as Gruber. Einholt swung around, hammer lifted over the block, resembling for all who saw, the great god who first wrought the Fauschlag. Then the Jaws of the Wolf, the precious icon of the Wolf Order, disintegrated into a million flying fragments under his hammerhead.

And then... nothing.

There was no great explosion, no fiery flash, no sound, no fury. The cellar just went cold. The walls stopped breathing. The reek of magic vanished and the static charge in the air dissolved. The fire went out.

Blackness. Cold. Damp. The smell of blood, and of death.

Flints scraped together and a small light pierced the gloom. A lamp was lit. Carrying it, Lorcha moved into the circle of blocks, retrieved the small velvet pouch and put it in his jerkin.

'It is made right,' he said to the others in the darkness around him, his accent thick with Tilean vowels. 'I will inform the Conclave.'

A moment later, and he and his lamp were gone.

Aric lit a taper from his pack and raised its small yellow light aloft. Lowenhertz did the same, lighting the last of the lamp-oil he carried. Faint light filtered into the gore-soaked chamber. Urgently, they took kindling from a stack behind the fireplace and made torches. Einholt helped Gruber from the floor.

'Ulric love you, Brother Einholt,' Gruber said, embracing him.

'May Ulric forgive me too,' Einholt replied.

By the kindling light, they gathered the trophies into sacks, Aric reverently handing the panther claw bracelet to von Volk.

The Panther took it and nodded to Aric. 'Ulric watch over you for what you have done here. Your sacrifice will be known to all of my order.'

'And perhaps our orders may not be such rivals from this time,' Gruber suggested as he limped over. 'Panther blood has been spilled to achieve this too.'

He and von Volk clasped hands silently.

'We have everything,' Einholt said. He and Aric carried sacking full of the most precious things in the city. 'I suggest it's time to get out of here. Our light won't last long and there are citizens of Middenheim who will be relieved to get these trinkets back.'

Lowenhertz loomed behind them, a torch raised. His face was pale and determined in the half-light. 'There's... there's no sign of it. The thing Einholt struck. It's destroyed or–'

'Escaped,' Gruber finished.

Confession

THE AIR ABOVE Middenheim was cold and still. Below, winds found their way in and out of every byway and alley, whining through gaps in the stones and sucking over damp cobbles. Autumn had come.

The street braziers were built higher, their flames licking against the stone walls, making their black surfaces matt with soot, their fires burning till dawn. Dusk came early now and for many the working day was foreshortened. Citizens were keeping shorter hours, preparing for the harshness of the winter to come, when many would die of the cold and the numerous winter ills and ailments that befell the towering city's population year in and year out.

But for some, the autumn season simply meant they began and ended their working days in darkness. One such was Kruza. He went about his work sleekly, picking his final mark of the day. The last of the merchants were leaving the city in torch-bearing gaggles, among them a rotund middle-aged man with a florid flare of red across his high, round cheeks and magnificent bulbous nose. His pockets looked heavy and, tucked half into the breast of a long, embroidered coat which would not fasten across the fatty mound of his chest, the strings and clasp of a pouch were clearly visible. Kruza spotted him coming out of one of the better alehouses at the edge of Freiburg and followed him into the north end of the Altquartier slums.

Kruza strode easily on past his mark, whose own rolling gait and small steps made slower progress down the steep cobbles. The cut-purse paused for a moment and then turned back the way he had come, checking the position of the purse in the merchant's coat as he passed him, very close. The mark took no heed.

Kruza had marked his target and was ready to make his move when he saw something ahead of him. He flicked his eyes up and away from his intended victim, just in time to see the hem of a long, grey cloak disappear into the doorway of a tavern on the opposite side of the narrow street.

Kruza paused, then took a few more hesitant steps. When he turned back to his mark, the man was disappearing down and round into a sloping side-way. Kruza began to follow the merchant again, trying to concentrate, reminding himself of his quota.

But he could feel the hunting eyes behind him now.

He turned sharply on his heels and this time the pair of cloaked figures, for there were two of them now, barely had time to duck out of sight.

In an instant, Kruza forgot his mark and ducked into the shadows himself. He held the cold palms of his hands flat together before his face, as if in prayer – to Ranald, maybe, the trickster thief-god. No, to any god who would listen. His hands were suddenly clammy with sweat. He felt a bead form on his forehead and find the groove of the long scar down the side of his face. It trickled down the scar to his jaw. It hung there for a moment, then it was joined by another droplet of sweat. The two fell as one from his chin.

He had watched for this moment for months, prepared for it over and over, but now it had finally come, he was not ready. He could never be ready for the return of the grey men who bore the gleaming tail-eating snake sigil. They had got Wheezer and now they would get him.

Kruza stepped out into the middle of the narrow street, looking about him, not for a place to hide, nor for support from others, but to get the lay of the land. He had a sick feeling that there was justice in them coming for him. They had taken Wheezer, and he had been an innocent. His soul wasn't soiled like Kruza's. Of course they would come for him, a hundred times as fierce.

There was only one way to deal with this. He had run before and Wheezer had paid the price. This time he would stand and fight. And if he died, then he would no longer have the boy's doom on his conscience. His hand on the pommel of his short-sword, Kruza stood with his feet braced on the cobble-ridges and his shoulders thrown back. He let out a huge shout – of challenge, of remorse, of warning. Those who heard it could not tell what it meant, only that they should stay away. Kruza heard doors bang and the shutters close on windows all around. Then silence.

The men in grey cloaks heard the cry too as they stood in the next alley, shielded from sight.

'A brave boy, this cut-purse of yours,' the taller, leaner figure said in a low, sardonic voice. 'He means to come to us!'

The shorter, heavily-built second figure turned lightly on his feet and stepped into the deserted street, pulling his companion after him. They stood, thirty paces from the braced figure of the cornered cut-purse, whose scream was still echoing around the close buildings and losing itself in the labyrinth of the Altquartier's streets and alleys.

The taller of the grey figures put a hand beneath his cloak, reaching for his weapon. His heavier companion raised his hands to the hood which cloaked his face in cloth and shadow, and opened his mouth to call out.

But Kruza flew across the thirty paces between himself and the grey men before any had a chance to speak. His short-sword was raised above him in a two-handed grip. He meant to bring it down hard, and fight to the death, even if it was his own. His bloodshot eyes, with their lids peeled well back, showed white all round the black holes of his massively dilated pupils. Another yell began to find its way past his gritted teeth.

Then came the impact.

Kruza barely held on to his short-sword as it bounced and twitched in his hands from the hammer blow which had swung from nowhere to knock it from his grasp.

He swung again in a crude, wobbling arc which was parried hard by a deft hammer-haft, sending tiny shards of steel and wood flying with the intensity of the blow.

Kruza's next swing came in low, but not deep enough. It tore a huge rent in the flowing grey of the taller figure's cloak.

The figure jerked away and threw his head back, freeing it from the shadowy cowl of the cloak's hood. Kruza saw a face with pink-flushed skin and dark eyes that gleamed back at him.

There was no sign of the papery skin and pallid thinness of the other grey men. This man was flesh and blood – and ready to fight for all he was worth.

A hammer came in again, swung by the shorter grey man. Kruza blocked it ferociously and sliced in with his sword. The shorter man dodged it. He, too, had removed his hood and had shrugged off half of the cloak. Around his body, Kruza could see the pelt.

He had seen that skin before. His mind raced as he swung his sword again at the fur-wrapped torso. As he cut deeply through the hide, missing the man beneath, Kruza thought of that other man. Weeks back, at the Baiting Pit! The man with his parcel of armour wrapped in a hide, just like this one. The masked gladiator!

Kruza looked into Drakken's face, confused. *The White Wolf. Lenya's White Wolf! Was he one of the grey men?*

Kruza's nostrils flared wide as he sucked in air to control his panic. Spittle coated his lips and his teeth were clenched, allowing no more sounds to escape his body. There were two hammers whooshing through the air around him in a show of Wolf Temple strength. Or was it the strength of the grey men? He did not know.

His short-sword found only air with its next strike. Then, turning and striking again, he felt flesh rip at the end of his sword. Before he could savour it, he was on the ground, doubled over, shocked and winded by a solid blow to the centre of his chest.

Why… why was he not dead? Why had the blow not killed him? Why had he been allowed to live when he was prepared to die?

Kruza let out a soft moan as he lay on the ground.

ANSPACH RUBBED a fist against the flesh wound to his shoulder, as Drakken knelt down by Kruza's sprawled form, tentatively reaching out a hand to grab the broken thief.

Anspach was thoroughly enjoying himself. Drakken had spoken to him of a cut-purse whom he needed to find – some personal feud, so it seemed, one he wanted to keep quiet. The young Templar had enlisted Anspach's help to do it. It wasn't so difficult for a man with Anspach's knowledge of the city's underbelly, and the little battle in the quiet street of the Altquartier was a positive bonus. Something to warm the cockles on this cold autumn night. Drakken had not told him the young thief had so much spirit, or such a strong sword arm. No harm done. A light flesh wound to the shoulder that would heal in no time, and the indignity, for Drakken, of having his pelt rent into two pieces, neither of which would be big enough to cover the huge young Wolf's torso now.

Explain that to Ganz, Anspach thought to himself. He smirked down at the strange picture of a bedraggled Wolf, offering his hand to a young street thug. He felt almost nostalgic.

ON THE NORTH side of Middenheim, a giant, blond Wolf Templar strode down the wide avenues just south of the Palace. Alongside him was a tiny woman, her feet skittering in a half-run, half-skip to keep up with him.

'But why did Krieg send you? And where are you taking me?' Lenya gasped, breathing hard and trying to hold her skirts and cloak up out of the rime that was beginning to glisten across the even cobbles.

Bruckner stopped in his tracks. Lenya almost overtook him, and then passed and leaned forward, holding her side.

'I have a stitch. Can't we go a little slower?' she asked.

'A little, perhaps,' Bruckner said, not really looking at her. 'Drakken asked me to escort you, for your own safety. He will tell you himself why he needs to see you.' He still did not look at his companion, possibly because he would have to stoop a long way to look her in the face – or perhaps simply because he had a job to do, a favour to perform for a colleague, one that held no interest for him.

Bruckner strode on southward, checking himself after a few of his long strides and slowing down just enough for Lenya to keep up with him. If she ran every other step.

DRAKKEN AND Anspach half frog-marched and half carried Kruza out of the street and into an adjoining alley, where he could recover for a moment away from the people who had heard the fight and were now coming out to see what had happened.

The cut-purse sat, his back to a mossy wall. He coughed and spat onto the dark, earthy ground between his jutting knees. He seemed meek enough now as Anspach stood facing him, leaning against the opposite wall. There was only just room for the two of them. Drakken stood to one side, waiting for the cut-purse to recover so that he could continue the business of the evening. He had expected Kruza to come quietly, expected him to be a coward, like all street scum. He felt grudging admiration for the bravery Kruza had shown in fighting them, however ill-conceived it might have been.

Kruza looked up briefly at Anspach. In a single flicker of his eye, he took in the stature of the man: the slight injury he had suffered; the position of his warhammer; his elegant, relaxed stance. Kruza had the eyes of a thief and he used them now. He marked every detail. Then he leaned forward in another loud, convulsing coughing fit. His head bent, his hand darted out, the elbow still resting against his knee.

Drakken did not know what was happening. Suddenly Kruza was on his feet, the point of a short dagger pressed into Drakken's neck, with Anspach crying out and stumbling back, caught, off-guard and unsuspecting for one fleeting moment. But only for a moment.

Anspach brought his hammer round low at little more than half-tilt and took Kruza out at the knees. The cut-purse fell on his rump, hard on the earth floor of the alley, and dropped the knife that he had taken out of Anspach's boot during his dramatic coughing fit. Kruza raised his hands, knowing, at last, that he was beaten.

'It's over. Use me, as you will. Or kill me,' he said. And Anspach smiled again. This was turning into quite an evening of entertainment. That young cut-purse had taken his knife without him feeling it! *Ulric, but he was good!*

Anspach gave his hand to Kruza. The cut-purse thought he saw the Templar grin as he pulled Kruza to his feet. But their gaze had met for only the briefest moment, and Drakken was pushing in to take charge of the situation again.

'Behave! There's someone I want you to talk to,' Drakken said. 'Follow me. Anspach, watch our backs.'

LENYA AND BRUCKNER continued south at a slightly more leisurely pace, but try as she might, the serving girl could not draw the Wolf into any kind of conversation.

'You must at least be able to tell me where we are going?' she asked.

'You'll see,' was his only answer.

'How far is it?' she tried again.

'Not far,' he said curtly.

Down another sloping street, along the north wall of the Great Park, and then south again. He said nothing more and Lenya did not know what else to ask. She watched her feet traverse the cobbles, first smooth and broad and flat, then, in the poorer quarters, ragged, chipped, uneven. Here, the stones were smaller and arranged in swirls and mosaics that bore no resemblance to the even brickwork to the north. So... at least she knew that they were heading toward the Altquartier.

KRUZA FOLLOWED Drakken, with his even stride, while listening to the relaxed, light tread of the one called Anspach behind him. They didn't have far to go. Turning north and west in the cold air, through almost empty lanes, they stopped outside the great double doors of the quarter's ostlers.

The ostler did a poor trade here. His stables were only full when the city was brimming with rich visitors. Sometimes the overspill from the more respectable handlers to the north would find its way here. But this establishment's richest customers were still only moderately comfortable merchants who left the city for their country dwellings by dusk and only needed somewhere to keep their horses during the hours of trade. It was not such a bad life for the ostler and his sons, and not a bad living. The stables were always empty at night, so the bedding straws were changed only with the turn of the moons, and the horses, who ate in their country stables at dawn and dusk, demanded little feed during daylight hours.

Drakken swung one of the doors open, just wide enough for the three to file in. There was the light of a single torch, resting in its rusty sconce against the courtyard wall. The yard opened into a series of narrow stalls, with stable half-doors. The place smelled of stale bedding-straw and age-old horse dung.

Kruza had never been near a horse. There were few in the Altquartier, and those he met with in other parts of the city he gave a wide berth to. But there was no noise here, no snort or trample, and the cut-purse relaxed slightly when he realised all the stalls were empty.

But he did not relax for long. Drakken rounded on him as soon as they were off the street, pushed him back against the coarse boarding of a stall panel. He stood with his face tilted up to meet Kruza's. Their noses were almost touching.

Drakken had a deep frown on his face and Kruza tensed all over again. His body felt like a series of taut cables and blocks of unyielding rock, like the pulleys and counterweights of the lifts that served the Fauschlag, yanking and stretching at themselves as they hoisted impossible burdens.

His chest felt so tight and hard he wondered how he would breathe. With Drakken right in his face, he wondered how much longer he would be allowed to breathe. Kruza looked slyly at Anspach, who stood guard by the great, black door, which hung on its hinges, just ajar. No ally there. Kruza knew the Wolves would stick together.

'She'll be here soon,' Drakken began.

She? thought Kruza and then realisation dawned. *Lenya! I must account to Lenya for Wheezer's death. That is why they have brought me here. And then this Drakken will kill me!*

'After the fight at the Baiting Pit, you took flight. I suppose I can't blame you. I scared you off, calling you a thief and a liar and a murderer. And mayhap that's what you are. But if you are, then Lenya deserves to hear it from your own mouth. She will not listen to me.'

'Lenya needs to know what happened to Wheezer. She sought him out. She talks of nothing but her brother, of the dead ends she followed. She talks of you knowing him. If you really know what happened to her brother, then you must tell it plainly and put her mind at ease once and for all. And if you killed him, then you will answer to the Watch,' Drakken finished grimly

What can I say to her? Kruza wondered. The moment when he could have told her everything was long gone. Gone with that last meeting, the night they were saved from the Baiting Pit by this same White Wolf. When he realised, with true shock, that her brother was the same boy he'd tried to forget. *I don't want to tell her any of it. I don't understand it. All these months I have tried not to think of it!*

But with this pair of White Wolves watching him, he knew that he would have to tell Lenya something. He decided in that moment that he would rather have paid with his life in the street where the three of them had done battle, than face Lenya with his story.

There was no more time for thought. Lenya was backing into the stable courtyard through the narrow door. She was talking to someone who must have been on the other side.

'Why would you bring me here? This can't be right!' she exclaimed and then, turning, saw them. Her eyes locked onto Kruza, who bowed his head and said nothing. Then she was running towards Drakken. She put her hands on his broad torso and he took her elbows gently, one in each hand.

'Lenya,' he said, 'I brought you here to talk to the cut-purse. Ask him what you like about your brother. He will answer your questions.' This last he said with his eyes locked on Kruza. It was a warning.

Lenya turned, Drakken still holding her gently,
'You knew Stefan?'

'No… I knew Wheezer…' Kruza realised they were repeating
the last words they had spoken that night after the fight in the
Baiting Pit.

'Leave us, Krieg,' she waved an arm at her Templar-lover, her
intent gaze not leaving Kruza's face.

'WHAT POWER the milk-maid has,' Anspach said wryly to
Drakken as they stood together in the street with Bruckner, outside the ostlers. Drakken looked at him.

'Power over the Wolf and the cut-purse both,' Anspach finished, amused. Drakken glanced down, a deep flush of anger
and embarrassment climbing up from his neck, over his face
and deep into his brow. It was followed by a frown that fur-
rowed into the flush on his crimson forehead, leaving purple
and white lines.

'I KNEW WHEEZER,' Kruza began by repeating himself. 'I knew
him by no other name. He said he had no name. The bastard
child of a nobleman and a mother who died in childbirth. I
couldn't know he was your brother.'

*I called him "brother", but I never even knew that for sure. No one
really knew him,* Lenya thought. *Mostly we barely noticed him. But
she said nothing.* Kruza was talking and she thought if she interrupted him, he would stop. She wanted to hear it, whatever it
was he had to say.

'He didn't look like you.'

He didn't look like anyone, she thought.

'You said he was honest, do you remember?' Kruza asked, but
he didn't wait for an answer. 'He was, in a strange way. I caught
him stealing from an old cut-purse, a teacher of mine. But he
only stole what didn't belong to anyone, or what was surplus or
excess. I was his first visitor. His first friend in Middenheim. I
hope I was his friend.'

If you were his friend, you were the only friend he ever had,
thought Lenya, and the memory pained her. *People were cruel to
him, if they saw him at all. In the end no one even seemed to see him.*

'I've never known anyone who could steal like he could.
Silently, without being seen. I… I used him.' He hung his head.
'I'm not proud of it, but at least I didn't recruit him and let
Bleyden get hold of him and use him worse. We were friends.'
It was as if he was talking solely to himself.

You couldn't use Wheezer. He had his own kind of freedom, his own ways, thought Lenya, but said nothing. She knew truth when she heard it.

There was a long pause, and she realised that they were still standing in the middle of the stable courtyard. It was open to the stars and the night was turning purple and cold. Grey and black clouds the colour of the Fauschlag Rock were scudding across the sky, obliterating the twin moons, and she felt the deepening chill. Kruza stood stock-still in front of her, as he had been standing when she first entered the courtyard. Lenya put her hand out to Kruza, who shrugged it off before it even met his sleeve.

'Don't! You won't like me after you've heard this. I used him... he stole to help me fill my quota. I would dare him. It was a game,' he said, not looking at Lenya.

Just don't try playing hide and seek with him, Lenya thought.

'He stole for me and I listened to his tales. He had the most extraordinary room, full of beautiful things. We drank together and I would fall asleep on his couch, half-listening to his stories. I knew I was using him, using his skills as a thief, but I meant him no real harm. He liked to play the game and then go back to talk about the witches that brought him up. Nonsense like that. No one else saw him, you see.'

Mother's little foundling, she thought, *and now I'll never know why she called him that, and why we all laughed, my father, my brothers, even my mother, sadness in her eyes. Maybe he didn't belong to us at all. Maybe he never belonged to anyone.*

'I think he died, Lenya. I'm sorry. I think he's dead.' Kruza had thought it for a long time, but he'd never said it before.

Dead! Before I could find him or understand him. Why did he have to die? The moan that was in her heart never found its way to her lips. She felt slightly faint.

'He was invisible, he should have been safe... but he didn't come out. He never came out.' Kruza's voice was low and he was surprised by how calm he sounded. He knew what to tell her now. 'I thought it was just a trick, or luck, that no one ever saw him. But it wasn't.'

'He stumbled on a smuggling scam, a big one.' Kruza paused, looking at Lenya for the first time. She looked pale. The girl shivered.

Lenya was cold and afraid. She turned about in confusion, looking for somewhere to go, somewhere to feel safe and warm. There were only the empty stables around them, but surely they would yield some heat. She turned her back on Kruza and walked toward the half-door on the nearest stall. She placed her hand on the old blackened latch. It was well-greased and moved easily under her hand. She turned again to Kruza. He realised she was waiting for him and walked toward her. She turned into the dark stable, which smelled much like the stables back in Linz. It reminded her of the horses she sometimes tended and the cows she often milked there. Kruza remained standing, slumped a little against the half-door. He was tired and heart-sore. Even though he had survived the ordeal with the Wolves, he felt the worst was yet to come.

'There were smugglers. Wheezer knew. He followed the bodies, told me the story,' he began again once Lenya was settled in a pile of old hay.

No one ever saw Wheezer. That's how he could disappear for days at a time. 'Off with his folk!' mother would say. Now, I don't think she was being fanciful. We never knew where he was or what he was doing, but I was always happy to see him return from the woods. I loved him and I loved his stories. Lenya took a breath when she remembered again that Stefan was dead, her memories of him tumbling over and over in her head.

Kruza went on, halting. 'Only they weren't bodies. And the grey men weren't from Morr's Temple. They were smugglers, bringing all manner of things into the city. Ah, I don't even know why I'm talking to you. Wheezer's gone.'

There was a part of Lenya that wanted to ask about the smugglers, who they were, where Wheezer had followed them to. But she knew if she asked, Kruza might not want to talk to her at all. She felt a chill that she hadn't expected in the warm, close air of the old stable.

Kruza made small circles in the hay dust on the floor with the point of one of his boots.

'Wheezer took me to the smugglers' place. I didn't want to go in there at first,' Kruza said, looking at Lenya in a way that prevented her asking the question he dreaded: Where did Wheezer die?

She sat still and Kruza continued to make the small circles with his foot. His head was bowed and she could barely hear him. 'Wheezer was excited. There was so much there, he said. "It's there to be taken," I remember his words. It seemed… it seemed like an easy job.' His voice dropped yet further.

Lenya leaned up onto her knees, closer to him, wanting to hear it all, whatever was left of his reminiscences. Kruza lurched back from her unhappily, as if he didn't want to be any closer.

'The smugglers were there, dozens of them. They saw us. I tried…' he blurted, unconsciously running his hand down the narrow scar on the side of his face, almost hidden by his hair. Lenya had not seen it before.

He got that scar trying to save Wheezer. He was Wheezer's friend, she thought. *Why does he doubt it?*

'I got out and I waited. I waited in his room. I don't know how long. I waited until there was fresh dust on the stairs, but Wheezer didn't come back.'

Kruza paused for a moment, then suddenly turned on his heels and left the stall. He crossed towards the door that led out onto the street, which was open just a crack. A moment later, it swung wider out on its hinges and Drakken stepped in out of the shadows.

'Well?' he asked.

Lenya, emerging after Kruza, was about to answer when she realised that Drakken was talking to the cut-purse. Kruza looked like he had seen a ghost. He had that same look he had when Lenya had first said the name Wheezer all those months ago.

'It's okay,' Lenya told Drakken, on Kruza's behalf. She took the lad's arm. 'Thank you,' she said, not knowing what else she could say. This man had tried to save Wheezer's life. He had a scar. There was nothing left. She had mourned Wheezer for too long already.

'Now do what you will with me,' Kruza said as Drakken stood before him. 'I will die peacefully, if die I must.'

'No!' Lenya cried, firm and unafraid. 'Let him go, Drakken. He has done no wrong. He was Wheezer's friend and he did him no harm.'

Lenya allowed Drakken to take her in his arms.

'And thank you, Krieg,' she said. 'I can let Stefan rest now.'

THEY PARTED. Kruza strode away from the place as fast as he could, trying to lose himself in the dark streets. He thought that he had put Lenya's mind at rest. Maybe…

He wondered if Wheezer was at rest. He wondered if his own mind would ever be at rest.

He had told the story. He had told what had happened to Wheezer. Well, so he had left some things out, things his mind had long sinced tried to blank. There were things in this city that you didn't speak of, that you forgot as quickly as you could. Like the grey-cloaked men and their hideous place.

Lenya knew quite enough. Now she could mourn and sleep easy. As for himself, he would forget. Forget it all. He would go to the Drowned Rat and wash it all out of his mind. Lenya, Wheezer, the damn Wolf... even the grey men.

Lone Wolf

THE MAGICIAN WAS *looking at him, intently, fiercely, as if he recognised him.*

'Einholt,' said Shorack flatly, at last.

'You know me, sir?' he asked, surprised.

'Your name just came to me. The invisible world you mock spoke it to me. Einholt. You are a brave man. Stay out of the shadows.'

Einholt sat up on his cot in the darkness. His mouth was dry and his skin was wet. The dream had changed. For the first time in twenty winters, the dream had changed, melted away, been replaced by another.

Perhaps he should be pleased, but he wasn't.

The dormitory around him was quiet and lit only by pre-dawn starlight shafting from the clerestory windows. His brothers in White Company snored or coughed under rumpled blankets on the rows of cots set against the white-lathe walls.

Naked except for his knee-length undershirt, Einholt swung out of his bed and put his bare feet flat on the cold stone floor. He murmured a hoarse daybreak prayer to Ulric, breathing deeply. Then he pulled his wolf-pelt around his shoulders and crept down the length of the dormitory, half-blind, his night vision still weak.

He pulled the heavy dormitory door closed behind him quietly and stepped out into the cloister yard. Hooded candles burned with pale light around the square, set on plinths next to the entrance of each of the Wolf Company dormitories. The sky was lightless yet, and the air was cold and grey with the dawn light. Not yet matins, Einholt thought. By the candle-plinth next to the entrance to White Company's sleeping hall, there was a jug of water and a pewter cup. Einholt took a long draft of the icy liquid, but his mouth remained dry.

'Your name just came to me. The invisible world you mock spoke it to me. Einholt. You are a brave man. Stay out of the shadows.'

He tried to shake the thought out of his head, but it was stuck as fast as a flint under a warsteed's shoe. Just theatrics, he chided himself. He'd said as much before, to the man's face, in fact. That haughty magician had been an actor, full of dramatic flourishes that meant nothing. He'd just been trying to scare him.

But Shorack had known his name. And there had been nothing theatrical about the way he'd died, crushed against that pitchy cellar roof.

Einholt paced his way through the sleeping precinct of the Temple, along cold halls and through vestries with rough matting floors.

Stay out of the shadows.

He murmured the prayer of protection they had all learned by rote on admission to the Order, over and over to himself. Torches that had burned through the night fluttered as they began to die in wall sconces. Dead smoke drifted through the cool air. Outside, far outside, early cockerels began to crow. Something rumbled. Distant, autumnal thunder, the cold sky rubbing icily against itself.

Einholt tried to remember his dream. Not the dream of the harsh night, not Master Shorack and his warnings. The original dream. The one that had lasted twenty winters. His scar twitched. Funny, it had been with him for so long, haunted him for so many years, and now it was hard to remember even a scrap of it. The new dream had usurped it completely.

Your name just came to me. The invisible world you mock spoke it to me.

He entered the Temple via the west porch, under the great barrel-vaults of the vestibule. Two Wolf Templars stood guard, warming their hands at a brazier set on a brass tripod. Fulgar and Voorms, of Grey Company.

'You rise early, Einholt of the White,' the latter said, with a smile, as he approached them.

'And dress informally,' Fulgar smirked.

'Ulric calls me, brothers,' Einholt said simply. 'Would you delay answering him by stopping to dress?'

'Ulric watch you,' they intoned reverently, almost as one voice, letting him pass.

The Temple opened to him. Ulric, a vast shadow in the dome, loomed over him.

Einholt knelt before the altar, the multitude of candles flickering around him. A long moment's contemplation, and he at last snagged the old dream, as one would catch the sleeve of an acquaintance passing on a busy street.

Hagen, twenty winters past. How could he have forgotten that? The Red, the Gold and the White Companies together, great Jurgen in over-all command of the field. The phalanxes of green-pigs down in the vale at the edge of the brook, raucous and whooping. Four hundred of them, more besides, shambling, heavy-set, shaking spears and axes into the winter noon.

'Now we'll see glory,' von Glick had said with a gleeful laugh that they all joined. Von Glick. Younger then, firm and thick with muscled middle age, hair dark and wild.

Gruber too, the great unswaying oak of the company, at Jurgen's right hand. Morgenstern, a trimmer man then, the company rogue, throwing witty jibes down the slope at the greenskin beasts. That was a time long before drink had coarsened and slackened his bulk, before Anspach had joined them and taken Morgenstern's crown as company joker, before he had become nothing but company drunkard.

Kaspen was there, of course, a red-headed youth, his first time on the field. Reicher as well, bless his arm. And long-mourned Vigor, Lutz and the boy, Drago, the young pup Einholt had been given to personally train, recently and heroically baptised in action and now hungry for more. Vigor would see another three seasons, Lutz another decade in the service of Ulric. Drago would not see another daybreak.

Jurgen rose in the saddle and beheld the foe. Grave behind his studded eye-patch, he turned to the Temple companies. He told them battle was drawn.

That's wrong, Einholt told himself. Dreams do that, they play with the facts. Jurgen lost his eye at Holtzdale, years later. But this was the great Jurgen as he remembered him best, branded

into his memory. And Reicher. Hadn't he fallen at Klostin, years
before the fight at Hagen?

Twenty long winters turning the events of that day over in his
sleep. No wonder the details weren't right anymore. Hadn't
there been one awful night, years back, just after the battle,
when he dreamed that he and only he, Jagbald Einholt, had sat
on the rise, facing the green-pig horde alone?

Kneeling before the altar, Einholt sighed. He leaned forward,
resting on his splayed hands now as well as his knees, as the
memories, both true and false, swirled up around him like
flames. As they had done, every night for twenty years. Until
tonight.

The massed charge down the slope. That was true. Jurgen's
booming order, the wailing cry of the Templars, the thunder of
hooves.

Dawn thunder rolled outside the Temple, outside his dream.
Hooves, he thought.

He could smell the mashed sap of the torn grasses, the roped
spittle of chargers, the stinking adrenaline sweat of the men
around him. He was moving, making his own thunder as he
came down the slope outside Hagen, horse and Wolf fused into
one fighting being.

They caught the enemy at the brook, riding them down
despite their superior numbers. More of the foe died from
trampling than hammer-blows that day.

His steed hit the water in a wall of spray, breaking two squealing pigs under its lashing hooves. Kaspen was next to him,
rejoicing in the glory of battle, his youthful fears forgotten.
How many times had Einholt seen that transformation since
then? Aric, on his first venture… Drakken at Linz… a wonder to
behold. A wonder in honour of the Temple. Wolf-cubs, thrown
into the fire and coming through unburned and jubilant. Like
Drago.

Had he ever been that young? Had he ever been baptised in
battle that way? Surely, but so very long ago.

For the glory of Ulric now, in the brook-bed, water thrown
up, blasting all around them, drenching them. Blood drenching
them. Scything hammers cutting the spray, shattering fanged
snouts. Broken, exploded green carcasses, floating in the water
around their steeds. On the far side, chasing down the strag-
glers, Wolves urging their mounts up into the bulrushes. Thick
stems snapping and whipping on either side. Screams from
behind. His hammerhaft slick in his hand.

Young Drago, galloping past, yelling out, 'With me, Einholt!' Drago turning to the left into a spinney of willows. Full of the wolf-spirit, over-confident.

Not that way. Not that way. He was bolting after Drago now, bending low under the slashing fronds of the weeping trees. Not that way.

Cut right, no, *left*! Where in Ulric's name was Drago?

Every time. Every night. The same fierce effort to change the facts.

Not that way. Not into the willow stand. Not this time...

Drago was screaming suddenly. A scream choked in blood. Too late! Always too late! Drago, down in the rushes, his dead steed on its back nearby, hooves curled up towards the weeping branches overhead. Blood-steam in the air from its ripped belly. Pig things, crowding round Drago, hacking down at him again and again and–

Einholt's curse was white hot. He ploughed into them, his hammer whirling. Bones snapped and things squealed. A greenskin reeled away, blood fountaining from its cloven skull. Drago! *Drago!*

Dismounting, running to him, blind to the danger.

You are a brave man. Stay out of the shadows.

Drago! There! Crumpled in the rushes, like a fledgling in a nest. Alive, praise Ulric please, alive! Struggling through the bulrushes to Drago, the shadows of the willows falling across him.

Stay out of the shadows.

Drago...

Dead. Unmistakably dead. Torn. Ruptured. Butchered. His splintered hammer still clutched in hacked-off fingers.

Rising, turning, raging.

You are a brave man.

A green thing right behind him. Foul breath. Snorting rage. A reek of animal sweat. An axe, flint-bladed, vast, already sweeping down.

Now, oh yes, now the point of the dream. The moment that always woke him, dry-mouthed and wet-skinned. Every night for twenty winters.

The impact.

Einholt swung back onto his haunches in front of the altar, realising he had cried out. His hand went to his face, an involuntary gesture, tracing the line of the livid scar with shaking fingers. From the brow, down through the eye, down the meat

of the cheek to the line of the jaw. Einholt closed his good eye
and let blackness wipe the world away.

'Ulric watch over me...' he murmured. A tear of pain trickled
from his good eye. His bad eye hadn't wept for twenty years.

'He is always there to watch over you, brother. Ulric does not
forget his chosen ones.'

Einholt switched round to see who had spoken. By the glow
of the candles, he saw a hooded priest of the Temple standing
behind him. He couldn't see the man's face under the fold of
the hood, but the priest radiated kindness and calm.

'Father,' Einholt breathed, recovering his scattered wits. 'I'm
sorry... a dream, a bad dream...'

'A waking dream, it looked to me.' The priest approached,
holding out thin, pale hands in a gesture of calming. He
seemed to limp, unsteady. *He is old*, Einholt thought. *One of the
frail, ancient masters of the Temple. This is an honour.*

'I have been troubled by my dreams for a... a long time. Now
I am troubled by the change in them.' Einholt breathed deeply
to clear his mind. What he'd just said already seemed stupid to
him.

The priest knelt beside him so they were both facing the high
altar. His movements were slow and shaky, as if old, rheumatic
bones might shatter if he moved too swiftly. The hooded cleric
made the sign of Ulric and uttered a small blessing. Then, without looking round at the Templar, he spoke again.

'The way of the Temple Knight is never peaceful. You are
raised and bred to take part in the bloodiest of wars. I have seen
enough Templars come through this place to know none are
ever untroubled. Violence perturbs the soul, even holy violence
in the name of our beloved god. I can't count the nights I've listened to the complaints and fears of Wolves who come to this
high altar for succour.'

'I have never shirked from battle, father. I know what it is. I
have seen a share of it.'

'I'm not doubting your courage. But I understand your pain.'
The priest shuffled his position, as if making his fragile old
form more comfortable.

'Your dream of twenty years. It scars you?'

Einholt managed a thin laugh. 'I was too late to save a good
friend's life, my pupil's life. And I paid the price. I wear my
scars, father.'

'So you do.' The priest seemed not to look at him, but Einholt
could not tell how the unseen head moved inside that cowl.

'This has troubled your dreams for years. I understand. But Ulric burns such things into our dreams for a purpose.'

'I know that, father.' Einholt wiped a hand across his sweat-drenched, bald scalp. 'The memory focuses my thoughts, reminds me of the duty and the dues we owe to the Great Wolf. I have never complained before. I have lived with it and it has lived with me. A badge of honour I wear when I sleep.'

The priest was silent for a moment. 'Yet tonight, for the first time in years, it brings you here, makes you cry out.'

'No,' said Einholt simply, then turned to look at the cowled shape beside him. 'I came because the dream has gone. For the first time, it didn't come to me.'

'And what did?'

'Another dream. The first new dream I've had since the Battle of Hagen.'

'And was it so terrible?'

'It was nothing. A memory.'

'Of something recent?'

'I was one of the brothers who destroyed the curse below the city just days ago. I smashed the Teeth of Ulric so that the magic would founder.'

The priest tried to rise, but faltered. Einholt reached out a brawny arm to support him, and felt how thin and skeletal the arms of the old man were beneath the robes. He helped the priest rise. Stiffly, unsteadily, the old priest nodded his thanks, the cowl barely moving, and shuffled round behind the kneeling Wolf.

'Einholt,' he said at last.

'You know me, sir?' Einholt asked, surprised. He felt a terrible sense of déjà vu. As if it was Shorack beneath the cowl, Shorack repeating the strange act of recognition he had made in the quartz tunnel under the Fauschlag.

'Ar-Ulric himself has praised your action,' the priest said. 'The commanders of the Knights Panther have sent letters of commendation. Other institutions in the city, on recovery of their trophies, have honoured your name. Of course I know you.'

'Will Ulric forgive me for my crime?'

'There was no crime.'

'I broke the Jaws of the Wolf of Holtzbeck. Our holiest of holies. With my Temple-blessed hammer, I smashed them apart.'

'And saved Middenheim, perhaps. You are a brave man.'

Stay out of the shadows.

'I–' Einholt began to rise.

'Ulric forgives you a thousandfold. You knew when to place valour above possession. When to put the city before the Temple. Your sacrifice makes you most beloved of Ulric. You have nothing to repent.'

'But the dream–'

'Your conscience belabours the act. It is understandable. You feel guilty for simply being part of such a momentous undertaking. But your soul is clean. Sleep well, Einholt. The memory will fade. The dreams will flicker and die.'

Einholt rose fully, turning to face the stick-thin figure in the cowled robe. 'That… that is not what I dream of, father. I know that breaking the Jaws was the right thing to do. If I hadn't done it, Gruber would have, Aric, Lowenhertz. We all knew it must be done. I do not repent the act. I would do it again, if events were repeated.'

'I'm glad to hear it.'

'Father… I dream of a magician. He was part of our fight. He died. The invisible world where Ulric dwells, that realm alien to me… tore him and broke him. Magic, father. I don't know anything about that.'

'Go on.'

'Just before we fought, he spoke to me. He knew none of the others, but he knew me. He said–'

'Einholt,'

'You know me, sir?'

'Your name just came to me. The invisible world you mock spoke it to me. Einholt. You are a brave man. Stay out of the shadows.'

Einholt realised he had paused.

'What did he say?' prompted the old man.

'He said the invisible world knew me too. It had told him my name. He warned me to… to stay out of the shadows.'

'Magicians are fools,' the priest said, jerking as he shuffled around to turn away. 'All my life, and believe me it's been a long one, I've mistrusted their words. He meant to scare you. Magicians do that. It's part of their power, to be theatrical and play upon honest men's fears.'

As I thought, Einholt realised, relieved.

'Einholt… brother… there are shadows all around you,' the old priest said, holding up a palsied, frail hand to gesture at the many sidelong shadows that were cast by the altar, the candles, the lancet windows in the gathering dawn, the statue of Ulric himself.

'You cannot stay out of shadows. Don't try. Middenheim is full of them. Ignore the magician's foolish prattle. You can do that, can't you? You're a brave man.'

'I am. Thank you, father. I take your words with gratitude.'

Outside, matins struck. Behind it, came a rumble of... hooves. No, Einholt reassured himself. Dawn thunder. An early winter storm chasing the edges of the Drakwald. That was it.

He turned back to speak to the Temple father again, but the old priest was gone.

HE HAD BEEN in the Temple balneary for almost an hour when Kaspen found him.

'Einholt?' Kaspen's call broke the steamy quiet. There had been nothing louder than the slosh of water and the sound of Temple servants pumping fresh water into the heating barrels in the adjacent furnace chamber since he had first come into the bath-house.

Einholt pulled himself up to a sitting position in one of the great stone tubs, wiping water from his goatee and looking across at his red-haired Wolf brother.

'Kas?'

Kaspen was dressed in his Temple workshirt, breeches and boots. His thick mane of fire-red hair was pulled back in a leather clasp behind his skull.

'Your cot was empty when we rose, and when you didn't join us to break your fast, Ganz sent me to find you. Some of Grey Company said they'd seen you in the Temple at dawn.'

'I'm all right,' Einholt replied, answering his friend's unspoken question, but he felt stupid. The pads of his fingers were wrinkled like dried fruit. The water in the stone basin around him was tepid. *Ulric, it didn't take a man an hour to wash night-sweat from his body!*

But some things took more effort to wash away.

Einholt pulled himself out of the water and Kaspen threw him a scrub-cloth and his undershirt. Einholt stood dripping on the flags beside the basin, rubbing water and dead skin off his body vigorously with the rough cloth.

'So... you're all right.' Kaspen turned and helped himself to oat-cakes and watered honey from the bench table by the door. Einholt knew that tone. He and Kaspen had been particular friends since the younger man had joined the company. That was... *twenty years since*. Einholt had been in his prime then, twenty-five years old, and the teenaged Kaspen had been one of the pups given to his charge to train. A red-haired youth, still clumsy and long-limbed, joining the other young cub already in his charge.

Drago.

Einholt pulled on his undershirt, wrapping the scrub-cloth round the back of his neck. 'What's on your mind, Kas?'

'What's on yours? Is it the dream again?'

Einholt flinched. Kaspen was the only other member of the company he had confided his troubled sleep to.

'Yes. No.'

'Riddles? Which?'

'I slept badly. I can't remember why.'

Kaspen looked hard at him, as if waiting for more. When no more came, he shrugged. 'Rested enough for weapons drill?' he asked.

THE HOURS between terce and sext were given to weapons drill each weekday for every Templar, no matter his level of experience. In the sparring yard, Gruber, Drakken, Lowenhertz and Bruckner were already at work, along with Wolves from Red Company. The other members of White Company were on a watch rotation at the Temple.

Einholt and Kaspen strode down the yard steps in full armour, pelts slung away from their hammer-arms ready for practice. The morning was damp and cool, though the dawn thunder had gone. The autumn light was glassy and sidelong, and threw long shadows off the canopies along the eastern side of the yard. Gruber and the other men of White were working at the row of pels in the shade, refining techniques against the wooden practice posts with double-weight weapons to develop their strength. The men of Red were wrestling on a straw mat, or putting stone shot to build their throwing power.

Einholt felt no inclination to join them. He stopped in the middle of the yard, in the clear light. Out of the shadows.

'Let's allow Ulric to guide us, Kas,' Einholt said, as he did from time to time in the yard.

Kaspen made no comment. He knew what that meant, had known it from the day Jagbald Einholt, his friend and one time mentor, first led him out into the practice square. He stopped beside him, facing the same way into the morning sun, placing himself carefully so that he was two hammer-and-arm lengths from his comrade.

Wordlessly, they began. Perfectly matched, perfectly synchro-nised, they raised their hammers and began to swing them. Round to the left, back to the right, high to the left, low to the right, two-handed holds, grips flexing expertly as they nursed the centrifugal pull of the heavy-headed hafts.

Then, smartly, full circles to the left ending in hard stops, hammers raised; a drop that allowed the hammer-heads to begin to fall before they used that descent to power into under-swings to the right.

Round again, the other way, hammers hissing in the air. Faster now, switching to a one-handed grip on the haft-loop; up right, figure-eight, switch hands. Down left, figure-eight, switch back. Straight to the right and around, arresting the swing and switching hands again. Straight to the left and round, feet gen-tly pivoting as they urged their weapons through the air, barely moving anything else but their arms from the shoulders.

Faster still, like a murderous, silent dance whose rhythm was struck out by the rush of their weapons, as only two master war-riors who have practised together for years can manage.

Now the increasing force and speed with which they moved their weapon-weights around moved them too. Wide swings round to the rear in their right hands, causing them both to jump-step smartly to stop the hammers tearing away. A mirror repeat, reverse step.

Then back to twin-palm grips, this time with the right at the base of the haft, left at the head, spinning the hammers before them like staves, practising the use of the haft for blocking. With each return, a grunt and a stamp forward. Block right, hilt upright. Block forward, haft cross-ways. Block left, haft upright. Repeat. Repeat faster. Repeat, repeat, repeat.

In the far shadows, Bruckner stopped his work and nodded his companions over to look. They all stopped, even the Wolves from Red Company. Though the most novice Wolf was an expert with the warhammer, few Templars in any of the noble companies could put on an exhibition drill of such perfect matched-timing as Einholt and Kaspen. It was always a pleasure to watch.

'Ulric's name!' Drakken murmured in awe. He'd seen the two Wolves practise many times, but never like this. Never with such flawless grace, never with such speed.

Gruber frowned, though he had seen it on occasions before. *They're pushing themselves. Like they have something to get out of their systems. Or one of them has, at least.*

'Watch them closely, and learn,' he told Drakken, who needed no encouragement. 'I know you can handle a hammer well enough, but there's no end to the mastery. See the way they switch hands? There's barely any grip there. They're letting the hammers do the work, using the force of the spin to carry them where they want them.'

'Like a horse,' Lowenhertz said beside him, clearly impressed. 'You don't force it, you guide its strength and weight.'

'Well said, Heart-of-a-Lion,' Gruber remarked, knowing there was little any could teach the saturnine Wolf about hammer-use. 'There's more skill in the controlled use of a warhammer than in a dozen sword-masters with their feints and nimble wrists and fancy prancing.'

Drakken smiled. Then his expression ebbed. 'What are they doing?' he asked, nervously. 'They're moving closer to each other!'

'Krieg, my lad,' Bruckner chuckled, 'you'll love this bit…'

Einholt and Kaspen now moved well into hammer-reach of each other, head on, their circling weapons and arms just blurs. The pace of the practice was marked out by the whistling chop of the weapons as they punched through the air. Each side-swing precisely missed the swing of the other, so that Einholt and Kaspen were like a pair of hurricane-driven windmills face to face, the sails of one slicing deftly in between those of the other.

There were impressed murmurs from the Red Company men behind them. *Now the switch*, Gruber thought, waiting for it.

Breaking his rhythmic swing out from the cross-swirling hammers, Einholt went low and swung at Kaspen's legs, as the red-head leapt over it and swung high through the empty space where Einholt's head had been. Without breaking speed, they reversed and repeated, Einholt leaping and Kaspen ducking. Neither was stinting on strength. If either faltered, if either connected, the blows were full-force killing blows. Mirrors, they swung at each other, each side-stepping to dodge the other's circling weapon, Kaspen left, Einholt right, then back again, across and repeat.

'Madness!' Drakken gasped.

'Want to try it?' Bruckner joked to the stocky young Wolf.

Drakken didn't reply. He was all but hypnotised by the dancing warriors and their whirling, deadly hammers. He wanted to rush out there and then and tell Lenya all about the incredible show he'd seen, though for the life of him, he didn't know how he'd describe it or make her believe it.

Left. Right. Under. Above.

Whooff! Whooff! Whooff! Whooff!

Drakken looked to Gruber as if he was about to applaud.

Above. Left. Under. Right.

Whooff! Whooff! Whooff! Whooff!

The hammer-spinning fighters circled each other, moving around, advancing towards the watchers under the awning.

Right. Above. Left. Under.

Whooff! Whooff! Whooff! Whooff!

Their turning bodies edged into the shadow of the canopy.

Lowenhertz suddenly grabbed Gruber's arm. 'Something's–'

Under. Left. Right. Right–

The hurtling hammers crossed together and struck. The powerful crack resounded across the yard. Einholt and Kaspen were flung backwards from each other by the impact, Einholt's hammer-haft splintering.

Curses and oaths broke the suddenly still air as the Wolves of White Company ran forward to their two sprawled comrades, the men of Red close behind.

Einholt was sitting up, clutching his armoured right forearm. His right hand was bruised and swelling. Kaspen lay on his back, unmoving, his left temple torn open, blood leaking down onto the flags.

'Kas! Kaspen! *Aghh!*' Einholt struggled to rise, the pain of his sprained arm knocking him back down again.

'He's all right! He's all right!' barked Lowenhertz, stooping by Kaspen, pressing the end folds of his wolf pelt into the head wound to staunch the blood. Kaspen stirred and groaned.

'Just a graze,' Lowenhertz insisted. He flashed a reassuring look back across to Einholt, as Bruckner and Gruber got the bald Wolf onto his feet.

Nursing his arm, Einholt pushed past his comrades to reach Kaspen. His face was as dark as Mondstille.

'Ulric damn me,' he murmured.

Kaspen was sitting up now, grinning ruefully, dabbing at his head and wincing.

'I must be getting slack, Jag. You caught me a good one.'

'Get Kaspen to the infirmary!' Gruber snapped, as men of Red Company helped Bruckner and Drakken carry the bleeding Wolf out of the yard. Gruber glanced round. Einholt was looking down at his broken hammer. He chafed at his swelling, purple wrist and hand.

'You too, Einholt!' Gruber snarled.

'Just a sprain…' Einholt murmured.

'Now!'

Einholt wheeled on the veteran Wolf. 'It's just a sprain! Some cold dressing and a herbal balm and it'll be fine!'

Gruber stepped back involuntarily. Einholt, quiet, self-mastered Einholt, had never spoken to him or anyone else like that Not ever.

'Brother,' he said, forcing calmness into his voice. 'You're a brave man–'

'And I'll stay out of the shadows!' Einholt spat, and strode away across the yard.

LOWENHERTZ EDGED quietly into the regimental chapel of the Wolves. The air was thick with incense, the rich perfume hanging heavy in the cold autumn air.

Einholt was kneeling before the empty plinth that for years had been the resting place of the Teeth of Ulric. His wounded forearm, stripped of its vambrace, the leather under-sleeve pulled back, was clutched to his chest, the flesh puffy and black.

'Einholt?' he breathed.

'You know me, sir?'

'Like a brother, I hope.' Lowenhertz was glad when Einholt looked up, the fury gone from his eyes.

'It was the shadow, wasn't it?'

'What?'

'The shadow of the canopy. It made you hesitate for a moment, made you mis-swing.'

'Maybe.'

'Maybe nothing. You know I was there. I heard what Shorack said to you.'

Einholt got to his feet and turned to face Lowenhertz. 'And I recall your advice. "Do as he says. Stay out of the shadows." Wasn't that it, Heart-of-a-Lion?'

Lowenhertz looked away. 'I know what I said. Ulric save me, I didn't know what else to say.'

'You're not like the others. Not like me. You take magicians and their kind seriously.'

Lowenhertz shrugged. 'Sometimes, maybe. I know they can often be right when they seem wrong. But Master Shorack was always a showman foremost in my experience. Full of cheap tricks. You shouldn't take his words so seriously.'

Einholt sighed. He looked away from Lowenhertz. 'I know what he said. I know what I dream.'

Lowenhertz was silent for a moment. 'You need help, brother Wolf. More help than I can offer. Stay here. Here, I say. I'll find Ar-Ulric. He will calm your mind.'

Lowenhertz turned to go.

'Kas is all right, isn't he?' Einholt asked, quietly.

'He'll not forget the lesson today, but yes. He'll be fine.'

'Been a long time since I taught him anything,' Einholt said sourly, looking back at the great Wolf Pelt on the wall. 'Twenty winters…' He coughed. 'Two pupils I've let down now.'

'Two?'

'Drago. Before your time with us.'

'Kaspen's no pupil any more,' said Lowenhertz. 'He knew what he was doing today. Practice accidents happen. I once broke a thumb in…'

Einholt wasn't hearing him.

Lowenhertz paused in the cage-door of the chapel. 'Brother, you're not alone, you know.'

'My hammer,' Einholt said quietly. 'I broke it. Funny, I've been wanting to ever since I used it to smash the Jaws. Didn't think it should be used for anything after that.'

'The weaponsmiths will bless you a new one.'

'Yes… that'd be good. The old one was… used up.'

'Stay here, Jagbald. I'll find the High Priest.'

Lowenhertz was gone and Einholt sank down in front of the Great Pelt again. His fingers twitched. His scar ached. His mind was flushed with images of Hagen Field over and again.

The greenskins, their tusks so white and sharp… the willows… Drago screaming. The impact. The shadows of the trees.

Stay out of the shadows.

'You are still not at peace, Wolf.'

The old voice crackled through the air behind him.

Einholt looked up. It was the ancient, cowled priest from the dawn before.

'Father?'

Einholt supposed Lowenhertz must have sent the old man to sit with him while he sought out Ar-Ulric. The fragile figure stalked towards him, one claw hand out to steady itself against the chapel wall. The thin form cast a long, brittle shadow in the candle light.

'Einholt. You broke the spell. You smashed the Jaws. Ulric is pleased with you.'

Einholt paused, looking down at his knees. 'So you say… but there's something in your voice… as if you are not, father.'

'This world has taught man that he must make sacrifices. For those sacrifices to be truly potent, that which is sacrificed must be valuable too. Things, lives, men. The same for all. I believe the most valuable Temple Wolf of all now is the one that shattered the Jaws of Ulric and dismayed the darkness. That's you, isn't it, Einholt?'

Einholt got to his feet. The throbbing pain in his wrenched forearm was terrible.

'Yes, that's me, father. What of it? Do you mean that somehow I have become more than I was before? That my action has bestowed some particular significance upon me?' Einholt fought to keep fear from his voice, but true fear was what he felt. Nothing in the holy shrine reassured him. The old priest's words disquieted him in ways he could not even begin to explain. 'You talk as if I am now invested with some power…'

'The history of our Temple, our Empire – even the world itself – is full of men who have become more than men by their deeds. Champions, saviours, heroes. Few choose such roles. Fewer still are ready to deal with what it really means. Your actions have made you a hero. That is your destiny. The blood of heroes is more holy than that of mortal men. In the invisible world, such men are luminous.'

Einholt opened his mouth to speak, but his voice died. He shivered, his breath shallow and fast. 'I-invisible world? Just this dawn past, in the Temple, I told you what the magician had said to me, told you he said the invisible world knew me too. Said it had told him my name. You told me to forget it. To dismiss it as nonsense. Now you… echo his words.'

'You misunderstood me, Templar–'

'I don't think I did! What is this, father? What game are you playing?'

'Calm yourself. There is no game.'

'In the name of Ulric, father, what are you saying to me?'

'You simply need to understand your destiny. More than most men. Seek that, and your mind will find peace.'

'How?'

The old priest paused. 'Ulric always amazes me, brother. To some he gives the question, while to others he gives the answer.'

'What does that mean?' Einholt barked, yet louder and angrier than before.

The old man in his cowled gown held up his arms in a calming gesture. His limbs quaked and shook, so very frail. 'Ulric has given the question to you. He has left the answer to others.'

Einholt grabbed the priest by the front of his tunic and held him tight so that the old man gasped inside his cowl. His breath stank of age and putrescence. Einholt tried to look into the darkness of the cowl, but light seemed to refuse to enter.

'*Which others?*'

'You're hurting me, wolf brother! My old bones!'

'Which others!'

'Morgenstern. Morgenstern knows.'

Einholt cast the old priest aside and rushed out of the chapel. Those Panthers, Wolves and worshippers of Ulric present in the Temple were perplexed to see a Wolf Templar, rushing from the regimental chapel and out towards the door, evading each pool of shadow and following the lances of sunlight shining in through the western windows.

EINHOLT ALMOST collided with Aric on the steps of the temple.

'Morgenstern! Where is he?'

'Einholt?'

'Morgenstern, Aric! Where is he?'

'Off duty, old friend. You know what that means…'

Einholt spun away from Aric, almost throwing the younger knight to the floor as he raced away.

THERE WAS NO sign of him in the Split Veil, or the Coppershiners. The Swan in Sail had last seen him a week Tuesday, and he had a tab to pay. The surly staff in the Drowned Rat said he'd been in early, supped a few, and then heaved his bulk out, saying he was heading down to the stews in Altquartier.

Altquartier, with vespers approaching and the sun heaving sideways in the sky. Einholt descended the steep streets and curling, mossy steps of Middenheim, past late-goers chasing homewards or barwards as the sun set. It became increasingly difficult for him to dodge the shadows. He hugged the eastern side of every curving street and alley, hungrily keeping to the last shafts of sunlight shafting over the roofs opposite. He avoided three streets completely because evening shadow had blanketed them entirely. But he kept on.

You are a brave man. Stay out of the shadows.

The Cut Purse. Its beckoning lamps shining. Early yet, late sunlight splashing the edges of the street. He kept to the light, a fever in his brain now, bursting in through the bar-doors so sharply that all present looked round at him.

'Morgenstern?'

'Here an hour since, now off to the Cocky Dame,' said a bar-girl who knew her employer didn't want any trouble with the Temple.

Einholt was running now, running like a lone wolf hunted by a pack of hounds. The pain in his dangling arm was forgotten, or blanked at least. He eked out every thread of sunlight in his path, skirting round the rapidly growing shadows of the early autumn evening.

Thunder, in the distant sky. Like hooves.

He hurtled into the Cocky Dame, lower on the city slopes, deeper in Altquartier. Einholt smashed two drinkers off their bench as he slammed in through the curtain door. He picked them up, tossing coins from his purse into cursing, scabby faces which bit off their snarls in alarm when they saw who had unseated them.

'The Wolf Morgenstern. Is he here?'

The chief barmaid was a powdered, dissolute sow with several black teeth, a stained balloon cap and a scent of week-old sweat not even a whole bottle of perfume could mask, though that's how much she'd clearly applied. She grinned a lascivious domino grin and propped her low-cut bosom up under her arms and pushed it out at him. 'No, my fine wolf, but there are more interesting things in the – *ow*!'

He had pushed her and her pallid frontage aside. 'Where's Morgenstern?' he snarled into the face of the barman, grabbing the startled bruiser by the collar of his patched jerkin. Einholt yanked the man off his feet and over the bar-top towards him on his chest, scattering earthenware jugs and pewter cups.

'Gone! Not here!' The barman stammered, trying to wrestle free from this mad Wolf, gazing up in true fear. The tavern all around fell silent. Brawls were common, but to see a Temple Wolf, in full armour and pelt, blood-mad – that was a frightening novelty.

'Where?'

'Some n-new place down in the old quarter! Opened just a few days ago! I heard him say he wanted to try it out!'

'What new place?'

'I forget–'

'*Remember*, Ulric damn you!'

'The Destiny! That's what they call it! The Destiny! Used to be something else! Now it's the Destiny!'

Einholt threw himself out of the Cocky Dame, and skidded to a halt. He had grabbed at the barman with his wounded arm, unthinking. Now renewed pain coursed in his limb like fire. He should have been calmer, taken Gruber's advice, had it seen to. There would have been time enough for this madness on the morrow. Time – and safety. Now the sun was done. Vespers had just struck.

The shadows were everywhere. Long shadows of evening. Black smudges of twilight. Dark stains of night. Daylight was a vague, departing twinkle above the glowering, blind roofline, far out of his reach even if his arm had been sound.

Einholt turned, panting hard. He reached up to grab one of the lamps hanging outside the Cocky Dame, then winced and pulled back with a curse. Spitting to clear his mouth, he reached out again more gingerly, now with his good arm, folding his damaged limb against his breastplate. He lifted the lamp off its hook and held it above him. Light surrounded him. He cast just the smallest shadow, a little pool under his feet. Raising the lamp high, he hurried down the Altquartier street, pulse throbbing, arm aching, mind tumbling.

After a while, he yearned to change hands with the lantern, but his bruised forearm was worse than useless. Sweat pricked his skin as he maintained the effort of keeping the lamp aloft. It was brass and lead glass, as heavy as a hammer. Twice he had to set it down on the cobbles and crouch into its light, resting his over-stressed arm.

By the twitching light, round the next steep corner, he saw the newly-painted sign: the Destiny. One of the festering, one-room stews in the grimmest Altquartier slums, changing hands and identities almost from day to day. *Destiny*. He chuckled at the irony despite himself. He had found his destiny, all right.

Einholt pushed in through the drape doors.

'Morgenstern! Morgenstern of the Temple!' he barked, swinging the lamp around. In the flickering gloom, various drinkers slid away from him and removed themselves from the attention of his questing light.

He pushed further into the stink, half-stumbling over a discarded wooden board in the gloom. The old sign board of the inn, its previous identity, taken down when the new management took over.

He was at the bar now, a row of lacquered barrels with a teak plank on the top. He slammed the lamp down on the teak, smashing a bowl.

'Morgenstern?' he gasped, out of breath, into the faces of the staff.

'No Morgenstern here, Templar... but if your name is Einholt, there's a fellow yonder waiting for you.'

Waving the lamp like his own personal totem, Einholt glanced around. At the end of the bar he saw–

The old priest. How in the name of Ulric had the old, lame man got here ahead of him? How had he known?

'Father? What is this, father?'

'An end to things, Einholt.'

'What?'

'Want a drink?' asked the barman, convivially, moving close. Einholt pushed him away roughly.

'What do you mean, father?'

The old priest's voice rose out of his robes, pungent and sallow. 'You were the Wolf that destroyed the spell. Broke the Teeth of Ulric. Saved your city.'

'Yes, father.'

'Good. It can be only you. You are the most... *guilty*.'

'What?'

'You are my truest foe. I could not touch you in the Temple, but now I have chased you out into the shadows where you are vulnerable at last.'

The skeletal priest slowly turned towards Einholt. The cowl flopped back. Einholt was appalled by what was revealed beneath. He was a Wolf Templar and a servant of Ulric, who had fought beastmen and things of the Darkness – and still he had never seen anything so monstrous.

Einholt backed away.

'Look,' said the unliving thing that had masqueraded as the priest. It gestured with a claw at the discarded sign board Einholt had stumbled over.

He saw what it said.

You are a brave man. Stay out of the shadows.

Einholt started to cry out, but the rake-thin creature under the cowl suddenly moved so very fast. A blur. Einholt knew what was coming. It was like... the moment. Like the point of the old dream. The moment that had always woken him, dry-mouthed and wet-skinned. Every night for twenty winters.

The impact.

Einholt saw his own blood spray the dark, dirty bartop beside him. He heard thunder outside, hooves of the riders come to carry him away to the invisible world where lost souls like Drago and Shorack had found their miserable destinies.

Einholt, life spilling out of him like water from a shattered flask, fell across the old sign board. His blood, hero's blood, more holy than that of mortal men, gushed across the faded lettering he had read: 'Welcome to The Shadows Drinking House'.

Stay out of the shadows.

The thing stood over him, blood dripping from its ancient, soot-blackened, sharpened finger-bones. The figures in the dim bar around it, patrons and bar staff alike, collapsed as one, like puppets with their strings cut. They had all been dead for hours now anyway.

Its eyes glowed once, twice... *coral pink.*

—

Mondstille

—

Hammers of Ulric

IT SEEMS TO me now, looking back on that fiercely hard winter, that the evil which swarmed over us was a long, long time coming. A destiny, for Middenheim perhaps. Destiny can be that cruel. I have seen the hand-marks of Destiny on the poor frames of countless men and women who have come into my care. Angry stab wounds, mindless battery, jealous beatings. In the service of Morr, I have been witness to the manifold unkindnesses of Destiny.

It has dealt me poorly too, back when I was a merchant, before I took the way of the dead. Death is cruel, but life is crueller. Hard, cold, unforgiving, like a bleak Mondstille at its most savage.

There are those that fight against it. Ganz, worthy Ganz, and his valiant crew. The servant girl, Lenya. The street-thief Kruza. Morr look to them, Ulric too. Sigmar. Shallya. Hell, any of them. Any of those feeble gods, high up in their invisible world, who claim to watch over us but who simply watch us.

Watch us. Watch our pain. Watch our discomfort. Watch our ends. Like the crowd in the Bear Pit on West Weg, cheering us to our tormented doom.

I've had my fill of gods and the invisible world. I've had my
fill of this life and any other.

I am a man of death. I stand at the brink of it all, watching
like the gods. And the daemons.

They all cheer, you know. Gods and daemons alike. They all
cheer.

— *from the papers of Dieter Brossmann, priest of Morr*

WINTER ARMED the city for war. Frost, as thick as a dagger's blade,
coated every surface and icicles as sharp as swords hung from
every eave and awning. Snow, like fleece under-armour, swaddled the rooftops tightly, under the plate-mail of ice.

War was coming. Far to the west, along the borders, the noble
armies of Bretonnia were chafing for the spring, anxious to
assault the Empire, the recent loss of Countess Sophia of
Altdorf a perfect excuse. Though rounds of ambassadors shut-
tled back and forth, no one really doubted that come next
spring, nations would be in conflict. News had also drifted in
that beast-packs were rising in the ice forests of the Drakwald,
making huge numbers, stinking the air with their scent, harry-
ing settlements and townships. They'd never risen in
Mondstille before. It was as if something, something huge and
dark and redolent with the reek of evil, was drawing them out
of their woodland haunts.

Armoured for war, shivering, nervous, Middenheim crouched
on top of the aching cold of the Fauschlag Rock and waited for
its suffering.

Only a very few, rare souls knew that the real war would be
fought within.

WATCH CAPTAIN SCHTUTT was warming his numb hands at a feeble brazier in the guard post on Burgen Bahn when he heard
distant wailing trickling down through the frosty Osstor district. It was past midnight.

'Sigmar spank me! Not now!' he hissed. Pfalz, Blegel and
Fich, his companions on the late watch, looked round at him
unenthusiastically.

'Pfalz, come with me. You two: stay in here,' he told them.
Blegel and Fich looked relieved. Yes, like they wanted to go outside.

Schtutt pulled on his mittens, placed his leather cap on his
bald scalp and took up his pole-arm and his lamp. He thought

about adding his barbute, but the idea of the cold cheek-guards against his face was intolerable. 'Come on, Pfalz! What are you buggering about at?'

Pfalz got his gloves on and picked up his pike. 'Coming, captain.'

'We won't be but a moment,' Schtutt told Blegel and Fich.

Like they cared.

He opened the door. The fierce cold of Mondstille cut down into him like a glass portcullis. He gasped. He heard Pfalz groan beside him.

The night air was clear and crystal-hard. Schtutt pulled the watch post door closed behind them and they shuffled out to meet the winter darkness.

The captain stopped for a moment and listened to the cold, hoping desperately that whatever the trouble was, it had died down, or had been his imagination, or had at any rate frozen solid. But there it was once more, the wailing – the fear.

'Come on! Let's see to it!' Schtutt said to his lieutenant, and they clumped off over the frosty cobbles and crisp patches of lying snow, leaving the only sets of tracks. They followed the sounds to the next turn in the road, where the street to the left dropped away steeply down a stairway flanked by snow-flecked, overhanging houses. There, the shivering sounds ebbed away for a moment.

'Up there?' Pfalz suggested, gesturing with his pike to the right. He wiped his watering nose on the back of his glove.

Schtutt shook his head. 'No… down there… down towards the college.'

They hurried down the steps as best they could, going gingerly because of the rime-ice under the snow. Last thing Schtutt wanted was to brain himself going arse-over-end on the Ostweg stairs in the middle of the night.

Ahead, in the slit of sky visible between the steep townhouses on either side, they could begin to see the noble, grey dome of the Royal College of Music, iced with snow that reflected the moons-light, so that it glowed like a small half-moon itself. The shriek came again, from an alley hard to the left of the foot of the stairs. Needles of ice hung from the low-arched gate of the alleyway.

'That came from the Wolf-Hole,' Schtutt said. There was a small street-shrine dedicated to Ulric a little further in that direction. The alley brought them into a small crossroads square, where five alleys met. In the centre sat the Wolf-Hole shrine, a font-like bowl of black stone, with a small graven image of a wolf's head raised on a plinth in the middle. Traders and local householders would leave lit candles, coins or votive offerings of flowers and herbs on the lip of the shrine as they went about their daily lives.

Tonight, in the coldest hour of darkness, someone had left another kind of offering altogether. Blood, dark as wine, spattered the snow around the Wolf-Hole.

The first body, a middle-aged man in his night shirt, was draped over the font so that his head, arms and shoulders were under the water level inside the bowl. Whether he had drowned before the back of his torso had been ripped away was not clear.

The second, a woman in a torn brocade surcoat, lay at his feet. She was twisted into a posture even the contortionists in the Mummer's Company would have found impossible to mimic.

The third, another man in the black doublet and hose of a merchant, lay on his back a few yards from the Wolf-Hole. He had no face left to be known by.

The snow was speckled in all directions with blood, and with bloody scuff-marks where heavy feet had moved and churned.

Schtutt and Pfalz stood together, speechless, viewing the scene.

The captain shivered, but for the first time that night it wasn't from cold. He forced his mind to think, his body to move. He was City Watch, damn it, he had a job to do!

'Left! Left!' he hissed at Pfalz with a curt swing of the lantern, as he himself stalked around the right hand side of the Wolf-Hole, pole-arm held out straight and ready in his left hand.

This was recently done. Steam rose from the wounds. Schtutt saw that the blood had been... used. Markings had been daubed on the font-bowl and on the statue of Ulric. Letters. Words. Others had been marked on the walls surrounding the little cross-yard.

Murder. Desecration. Schtutt swallowed hard. He thought about sending Pfalz back to the guard post to rouse the others so that they could investigate in well-armed numbers. A good thought, but that would mean being left here alone, which was a truly bad one.

Pfalz pointed. A trail of blood led down one of the adjacent alleys. They followed it, boots crunching on the frost. Another moan, a half-shriek, from up ahead.

'Gods!' Schtutt snarled and plunged down the alley at a trot, Pfalz at his heels. The doors of a house to the right, a well-appointed respectable townhouse, had been kicked in and splintered. More bloody words daubed the walls and wood. Inside, firelight, loose and spreading, danced. Someone was shrieking.

They pushed inside. The hall had been ransacked and defaced. Two more bodies, hacked beyond the point of recognition, were piled inside the door, spreading a lake of cherry-bright blood across the floorboards. A lamp had been smashed, and flames were taking hold of the newlpost and lower risers of the staircase and the tapestries along one wall. The air was full of acrid ash-smoke, and the firelight flared and flickered in Schtutt's vision. He didn't even think to notice how nice the warmth was.

A woman, her clothing ripped and bloody, was cowering on the floor by a door beneath the stairs. She shuddered and moaned and, every now and then, rasped out a thin shriek of pain and fear.

Schtutt ran to her, bending low. She was bruised and had a cut to her arm, but he could make out no greater injury than that. As he leant by her, she glanced up in surprise, and flinched in terror, pulling back from his touch.

'Easy! Easy! You're safe now! I'm a captain of the Watch. Who did this? Is he still here?'

Her pale, bruised, tear-stained face regarded him almost blankly. Her lips quivered. 'Ergin. Where's Ergin?' she asked suddenly, tremulously.

'Ergin?'

'M-my husband... where is he? Ergin? Ergin?' Her voice began to rise into a panicked wail.

Schtutt tried to calm her. Her screams were piercing his nerves. He glanced around, saw where Pfalz had set aside his pike and was trying to beat down the flames with a length of the tapestry he had pulled down.

Schtutt was about to call to him, and tell him to send out for the firewatch, when he saw the figure on the stairs, creeping down towards them. A man, or at least a shape of a man, covered in darkness and crouched like a wild beast. There were only three bright things about him, three things which flashed in the flamelight. His wide, white, staring eyes, and the steel hand-axe in his grip.

'Pfalz!' Schtutt bawled as the figure pounced, throwing itself off the lower landing of the staircase, down onto the fire-beating watchman. The woman shrieked, louder and more hysterically than before, probably prompted as much by the volume of Schtutt's roar as anything she had seen.

Pfalz looked up in time enough to raise his arms in defence. The figure flew into him and they both smashed over onto the floor. The slicing axe skidded off the mail-shirt of the cursing, struggling watchman. Pfalz fought to get the daemon off him, but both were now wrestling in the lake of blood from the corpses that covered the floor, and they slipped and thrashed, unable to get purchase, spraying red droplets into the air.

Schtutt charged in, his boots also slipping on the gore. As he closed, he realised why the figure seemed so dark. It was drenched from head to toe in blood. It soaked the clothes, matted the hair, stained the skin. *Not his own*, Schtutt thought.

He didn't dare risk a thrust with his pole-arm for fear of striking Pfalz. Instead, Schtutt brought the haft of it down like a flail across the attacker's back. The pole broke loudly, and the bestial figure convulsed with an animal yelp and tumbled off Pfalz. But it still had the axe.

Pfalz had taken a gouge to his ribs, and was clutching it as he looked round and yelled, 'Kill it! Kill it, in the name of Sigmar, captain!'

Schtutt had two feet of pole with the blade-head still attached. He faced the creature, low and set. The figure had turned its entire malevolent attention onto him.

'Put it down... put the cleaver down,' Schtutt ordered, in a practised, bass tone that had ended a good few tavern brawls before the body-count could escalate into double figures. He could hear Pfalz's pain-inspired urgings, but he still felt he had to try. A hand-to-hand fight with a maniac was the last thing anyone needed at this hour of the night.

'Put it down. Now.'

If the blood-soaked thing had any intention of putting the axe down, it was down through Schtutt's head. It leapt right at him, axe raised, howling a noise Schtutt would never forget.

'You idiot!' he managed to spit, just before the figure cannoned into him and knocked his breath out. The flailing axe smacked into Schtutt's temple and spun his head round as they went over. Simultaneously, the blade-head of Schtutt's pole-arm punched right through the killer's torso, driven as much by the figure's momentum as by Schtutt's muscle-power.

Schtutt landed on his back, the impaled killer thrashing out its death throes on top of him, wild and frenzied, like someone suffering a brain-fit.

Schtutt felt the body go limp at last. He felt the blood from his pain-wrenched head pouring down into his eyes.

Fine night to go leaving your barbute in the guard post, he thought, and passed out.

KRUZA WAS huddled in a corner of the Drowned Rat, wrapped in his velvet cloak. When frost actually began to form on his glass, he realised it was late enough. He tossed coins onto the table and shambled out into the painfully cold street.

The moons were up, winter moons, curled like claws. There was something about this winter that chilled him beyond the weather. Everywhere, talk was of bad omens and ill portents, of gathering war and rising darkness. The same talk as every day, every year, actually, but now it seemed different. It was no longer the doom-mongering of the gloomy drunks at the crowded bars, the nerve-jangled alarmists in the gaming-dens, or the crafty soothsayers working their business. It was… real. It was an ill time, and Kruza didn't like the feel of it at all.

There were stories doing the rounds, from the stews of Altquartier to the exclusive drinking halls of the Nordgarten. Spook stories: stories of vile murder, lunacy and strange phantoms in the snow. It was said a respectable butcher in the Altmarkt had run mad with a skinning knife the day before, killing two of his employees and three of his fellow traders before the Watch had cut him down. A novice sister at the Temple of Shallya had hanged herself from the hands of the water-clock in Sudgarten, stopping the mechanism forever at the hour of midnight. In the stables of the coach-runners on Neumarket, the animals had gone into frenzies the night before the first snows, and ripped and bitten at each other in the narrow barns; two had died and four more had been destroyed.

Moreover, luminous balls and arcs of green fire, like trapped lightning, had played around the towers of the Temple of Myrmidia for half an hour two sunsets past. People said shades had been seen to walk in Morrspark. A terrible smell of charnel corruption had invaded the Office of the City Clerics and driven the staff out, pale and bilious. Grotesque faces had been seen, for an instant, pressed to windows, or in household mirrors. In the Cut-Purse Tavern, a water-stain in the shape of a howling face had seeped into the plaster wall of the pot room, and no amount of scrubbing could wash it out. Three men known personally to Kruza had seen old relatives, long dead, standing over their beds when they woke, misty and screaming silently, before vanishing. Some even said there was plague in the Altquartier.

Certainly, winter-ague and influenza was rife. It was winter, after all. But plague? That bred in the hot seasons, in the stink and the flies. The cold was its enemy, surely? And death? Common currency in Middenheim. But even by the city's wretched standards, murder and violence was alarmingly common.

An ill time indeed. Kruza looked up into the darkness, at the twinkling, ominous stars. He wished sometimes he could read the wisdom others told him was indelibly written there. Even without such skills, he saw only threat in the faraway lights. Perhaps he should consult a star-reader. But did he really want to know what was coming?

He moved off, down the icy lane. Almost at once, although he had been sure he was alone in the side-street, he felt there was a presence beside him, a panting exuberance.

He looked round, his hand on his dagger-grip.

No one. His mind playing tricks. Too many scare-stories, too much imagination and far too little wine.

But… it was still there. Unmistakable. A breath. An invisibility that shadowed his movements, just unseen, always behind him.

It reminded him of–

Now that was just stupid. It was only because the boy had been on his mind of late.

But–

The breath again, just at his heels. He whipped around, suddenly very sober, his dagger drawn.

Wheezer?

'Come on, Kruza! It's there to be taken!'

Kruza started, but there really was no one there.

Just a winter wind, hissing through the arches and doorways around him.

He shuddered and headed for his bed.

AT THE GRAF'S Palace, high on the rock, ceremonial banners fluttered stiffly, weighed down with frost. Large, black iron braziers burned at the Great Gate and lined the length of the entrance drive. Two horsemen on war-steeds rattled past the guards without breaking stride and flew down that line of fire.

Inside the palace, Lenya was kneeling in a passageway near the main hall, warming her hands illicitly on a back-grate of the main kitchen chimney flue. She was resting, secretly, for a moment. The chief domestics had forced the staff to work flat out all evening, for some important, unnamed event.

She froze in the gloom as she heard a tik-tak tik-tak coming down the stone passage, and pulled herself into hiding behind a chilly suit of display armour. The chamberlain, Breugal, limped past her, not noticing the lowly servant girl far away from her business and area of the palace.

Breugal strode into the wide, cold space of the main entrance, his silver-headed cane chipping time in rhythm with his steps. He stopped. *He thinks no one can see him,* grinned Lenya from hiding. She had to stifle her laughter as she saw him adjust his ribboned wig and exhale onto a palm in front of his face to test his breath.

The riders drew up outside. One stayed with the horses; the other strode in, slamming open the great doors of the hallway.

Ganz, commander of White Company, paused for a moment on the threshold and kicked the ice off his sabatons, rowel spurs and grieves against the doorjamb.

Breugal observed this disdainfully, watching the ice-hunks skitter away from the Knight Templar's leg armour across the polished marble floor.

'Someone will have to clear that up,' he said snidely to Ganz as he paced forward, his cane-end clicking.

'I'm sure,' Ganz said, not really listening.

'The palace is honoured by a visit from the worthy Temple, but I'm afraid the Graf has retired for the night. He is expecting important guests early tomorrow and he needs his rest. You must return tomorrow… later tomorrow.' Breugal steepled his fingers together, his cane tucked under his armpit, bowing gravely.

'I'm not here to see His Highness. I was sent for. Find me von Volk.'

There was a pause. Breugal looked stiffly at the expectant Ganz.

'Find… you…'

Ganz stepped forward towards the chamberlain. 'Yes? Wasn't it clear enough? Find me von Volk.'

Breugal backed away from the huge knight. He looked like he was choking on something utterly distasteful.

'My dear… sir. You can't come in here at the dead of night and demand such things of the Royal Chamberlain. Even if you are a Knight of Ulric.'

Bruegal smiled his most courtly smile, the smile that said he was the true master here. A smile that had broken courtly love matches, ruined careers and terrified three generations of household staff.

Ganz seemed stunned for a moment. He turned away. Then he snapped back, fixing the chamberlain with a stare as hot as the sun itself.

'I'll tell you what I can do. I am charged with the power of the exalted Ar-Ulric to serve the Temple and Ulric and the Graf. I'll come in here any time I damn well please and all the Royal Chamberlains will scurry hither and yon until my will is done!

'Understand?' he added, for good measure.

Breugal's astonished mouth made several unsuccessful vowel sounds as he stepped back.

From her cover, Lenya grinned a triumphant smile. *I do believe Herr Breugal is going to wet his britches*, she thought. *This is priceless!*

'He understands all right, Wolf!' a voice rang out from the far side of the hall. Von Volk, flanked by two other Knights Panther, strode out across the marble to greet Ganz. Von Volk had his ornamental crested helm under his arm, his head bare, the other two were regally adorned with full close-helms rising a foot above their scalps into gilded panther icons and crenelated fans.

Ganz and von Volk met in the middle of the hall, armour clashing as they smacked gauntlets. Their smiles were genuine.

'Von Volk! It is good to meet you again under better circumstances! Gruber has spoken well of you.'

'Ganz of the White! And I have spoken well of Gruber!'

They turned together and both looked darkly at the waiting Chamberlain.

'Was there something?' asked von Volk.

'N-no, sir Knight Panther,' Breugal began.

Von Volk leaned into his face and snarled like a big cat. 'Then go!'

Breugal went. *Tik-tak tik-tak*, as fast as his cane could pace.

'I apologise for that self-important arse,' von Volk said.

'None needed. I've known many of his type. Now, why the summons?'

Von Volk breezed his waiting men away with a flick of his hand. They backed off. Lenya craned to hear.

'The ambassadors from Bretonnia are arriving in the next few hours. His Highness the Graf wants their visit to be as secure as possible.'

'None of us wants war with Bretonnia,' Ganz noted dourly.

'There's the point of it. There's sickness in the Panther barracks. An ague, a phlegmy fever. I've seventeen men down, bed-ridden. How's your Temple?'

'Healthy as yet. What would you have us do?'

'Support us. When the ambassadors arrive, security will be our foremost need. I haven't the men. I'm hoping the Temple Wolves will reinforce us.'

'Ar-Ulric has told me to provide you with everything you need, Panther. Consider it a pledge of strength.'

Lenya almost spilled out of her hiding place as she leaned to hear the last of this. *This is terrible*, she thought. *This is truly terrible. Plague, disease, foreign invaders…*

'I'll go and marshal my men,' Ganz said to von Volk, and saluted as the three Panthers exited. Ganz stood alone in the middle of the hall for a moment, then looked directly at Lenya's hiding place.

'I can see you, milk-maid. Don't worry, Drakken will be amongst the troops I send. Try not to distract him.'

Ganz turned and left through the main doors to his waiting horse.

Lenya sighed. *How the hell does he do that?*

BY THE TORCHLIGHT, Gruber looked down at the Wolf-Hole shrine. Abruptly he knelt and, head bowed, uttered a prayer of blessing in its direction.

'I didn't know what to do, sir,' said the Watch captain with the bandaged head, from behind him. 'I didn't know if I should clean it off…'

Gruber stood and turned, his gold-edged grey armour gleaming in the torch light. 'You did right, captain. And valiantly.'

'Just did my job,' Schtutt said.

'In exemplary fashion,' Gruber smiled. But the smile was hollow, Schtutt noticed.

'Schell! Kaspen! Hold that crowd back!' Gruber called sharply to the Wolves who edged the small yard of the Wolf-Hole, facing the gathering, anxious crowds. Gruber followed the bald Watch captain down the alley to the invaded townhouse.

'This is where you killed it?' he asked mildly.

'With my broken pole, sir!' Schtutt replied, holding his gore-caked weapon up.

'Very nice.'

'There is a matter of–'

'Of what?' asked Gruber,

'Of… jurisdiction.'

'A shrine of Ulric has been abominably desecrated. Can there be a question?'

Schtutt thought about the words, and then about how big and armoured the Wolves were, and then about how he'd had quite enough of fighting this night.

'All yours,' he said to the wiry veteran Gruber, and took a pace back.

Gruber stepped into the townhouse. He cast a quick glance at the mashed corpses in their lake of blood. The fire had been put out, and neighbours were consoling the weeping woman. The murderer lay in the middle of the floor, the hole Schtutt's weapon had made horribly visible.

'Ergin, my Ergin…' murmured the woman, inconsolably.

'Your husband?' Gruber asked, moving forward.

'Y-yes…'

'Where is he?' Gruber asked.

The woman pointed to the ruined killer's corpse in the middle of the floor. 'There.'

Her husband… did this? Gruber was amazed and appalled. The rumours of madness in Middenheim had seeped back to the Temple quarters of late: rumours of killing and insanity and shades. He hadn't believed a word of them until now.

A robe-shrouded figure entered the room behind him. Gruber was about to cast a question when he recognised the man's office and simply bowed instead.

'Gruber, of Ulric.'

'Dieter Brossmann, of Morr. I was about to ask the circumstances of Morr's work here, but I see it plainly, Wolf.'

Gruber moved close to the hooded priest. 'Father, I want to know everything about this act, all the details you can learn before you bury the shreds.'

'I will supply them. Come to me before nones and I will have searched out the facts, such as they are.'

Gruber nodded. 'These markings, the words daubed here and on the Wolf-Hole basin. They mean nothing to me, but I sense their evil.'

'And I too,' said the priest of Morr. 'I don't know what they mean either, but words written in fresh blood can hardly be good, can they?'

JUST BEFORE DAWN, the snow began to fall again, coating the city with a powder two or three inches thick. Up on the Palast Rock, the entire household staff had been working through the small hours. Already ovens were lit and water-barrels heating. Housemen in pink silk liveries were out with shovels, clearing the main approach drive and laying rock salt. Amongst them, Franckl paused, cursing at the starchy high collar of his new livery. All of the Margrave's staff had been seconded to serve the Graf during this critical visit by the Bretonnian ambassador. Like the Royal Bodyguard, too many of the palace staff were sick with the wretched winter ague.

Throughout the palace, servants were at work, changing linen, scrubbing floors, polishing cutler-ware, laying fires and wiping frost off the insides of the guest apartment window panes.

The staff had all been wondering what was afoot since the moment Breugal set them to work suddenly in the late evening as if it was early morning. A visit, that much was certain. When Lenya overheard Ganz and von Volk talking in the main hall, she became the only member of the domestic staff of a rank lower than chamberlain to know the details. And she had no one to tell. Even now she was working as part of the house-staff, she was alone and friendless.

In the palace, that was. As she hurried down the west gallery with two buckets of warm water to replenish the girls working on the main staircase with hog-brushes, she saw the snow out of the windows, settling down in the light of the braziers down the drive, and wondered how Kruza was faring on a night like this.

Just before the chime of vigiliae, a detachment of Wolf Templars rode up Palast Hill and in through the Great Gate, whipped by flakes, their thunderous hooves muffled by the snow. Aric led them, the Bannerole of Ulric held high in his left hand. Behind him, Morgenstern, Drakken, Anspach, Bruckner and Dorff in a tight pack, and then a dozen more Templars, six each from Red and Grey Companies. A Panther knight at the Gatehouse hailed them, and directed them around the inner courtyard to the Royal Guardhouse.

They reined up in the stone square before the guardhouse, the breath of their chargers steaming the air. The horses trod

uncomfortably on the unfamiliar depth of the snowcover.
Uniformed pages, their cold faces as flushed pink as their silk
coats, scurried out to grasp reins.

Aric dismounted smartly and, flanked by Bruckner, Olric
from the Grey and Bertolf from the Red, marched across the
doorway where a squad of Knights Panther in full armour,
torches raised high, waited for them under the portico. Aric
saluted the lead Panther.

'Aric, of the White, Bearer of the Standard. The Great Wolf
watch you, brother. Ar-Ulric, bless his name, has given me command of this reinforcement detail.'

The lead Panther had raised his ornate gold visor. His face
was stern and dark, and his flesh looked pasty and ill next to
the rich gold and reds of his steepled crest.

'I am Vogel, Captain, Graf's Second Own Household. Sigmar
bless you, Temple Knight. Herr Captain von Volk told me to
expect you.'

Aric sensed tension. The man seemed ill, and unlike von
Volk, he still seemed to harbour some of the stiff rivalry that
had become tradition between the Templars and the
Bodyguard. Relations between the Wolves and Panthers may
have thawed in von Volk's eyes, mused Aric, but the old preju-
dices are deep rooted.

'We appreciate the assistance of the Temple in this fragile
hour,' Vogel went on, sounding anything but appreciative.
'Border scouts report the ambassador's party is just a few hours
away, despite the snows. And the brotherhood of Panthers is...
unmanned. Many of us are bedridden with the fever.'

'We will say deliverance litanies for them. They are strong,
robust men. They will survive.' Aric sounded confident, but
Vogel seemed unsteady as he turned to lead them in. The Wolf
leader could see dark tracks of sweat on the Panther's exposed,
pallid cheek. And there was a smell. A smell of rank, sickly
sweat, of illness, half-cloaked in the pomander scent of the
courtly knights. Vogel was not the only Panther here who was
sick.

Ulric protect us too, Aric thought. It smells the way the city
air does when the plague visits. And hadn't Anspach reported
some loose rumour about plague in the stews and slums?

The Panther honour guard fell in behind Aric and Vogel, and
the Wolves followed en masse. They marched down a marble
colonnade into the draughty main halls of the palace, where
candles and – such luxury! – oil lamps burned in wall sconces,

for mile after mile, it seemed to Aric, in every direction down the tapestry- and mirror-lined promenades.

'Just tell us what you'd have us do, and we'll get to it,' Aric said. 'What duties would you have us perform?'

'I don't expect you Wolves to have a working knowledge of this labyrinthine palace. The layout can be disconcerting to strangers.' Vogel seemed to enjoy the word 'strangers', as it emphasised the fact the noble Wolves were on Panther turf now. 'Don't stray, or you'll get lost. We need patrols to sweep the palace, so I'll draw them up from the Panther companies. You Templars would do us a service if you agreed to stand watch on the guest apartments.'

'It will be an honour to serve,' Aric said. 'Show us the area and the places to watch.'

Vogel nodded. He waved up two of his knights. Their visors were shut and they seemed like automatons to Aric. He had never realised before how much he appreciated the Wolf custom of going to battle helm-less, hair flying. Faces and expressions communicated a lot, particularly in the heat of war.

'Krass! Guingol! Show the Wolves the layout of the guest quarters.'

'Aye, sir!' said Guingol. Or Krass. *Who in Ulric's name could tell behind those golden grilles?*

Vogel turned to Aric. 'Stand firm, Wolf. All of you. The watchword is "Northwind".'

'Northwind.'

'Repeat it only to your men. If any you meet can't provide it, detain them. Or slay them. No exceptions.'

'I understand,' Aric said.

Vogel saluted.

'May the day pass well,' he said. 'May none be found wanting.'

'As you say,' smiled Aric courteously.

Vogel and his men turned and clanked away down the gallery, armour jingling. Aric turned to Guingol and Krass. 'Let's get on, shall we?' he asked.

They nodded and strode forward. The Wolves followed.

'This place smells bad,' whispered Bertolf of the Red.

'Like sickness,' Bruckner agreed.

'Like plague,' Olric said dourly.

Behind them, in the ranks, Drakken glanced uneasily at Morgenstern.

'The Grey Wolf is right, isn't he? Plague?'

Morgenstern chuckled deeply, richly, stroking his vast, cuirassed belly as he stomped down the hallway. 'Boy, you're too much the pessimist. Plague? In this cold snap? Never!'

'Ague, maybe,' Dorff said sullenly from behind them, his directionless whistling drying up for once.

'Oh, ague! Yes, ague! Perhaps that!' Morgenstern chortled. 'Since when did anyone ever die of the sneezes?'

'Apart from the dozens who died last Jahrdrung?' Dorff asked.

'Oh, shut up and whistle something cheerful!' snapped Morgenstern. Sometimes morale was just too difficult to build.

'What's the betting,' said Anspach, who had been silent up until then, 'what's the betting that this is the worst mess we ever got into?'

The Wolf Templars slammed to a halt, the White Company men bottling the Red and Grey behind them. Aric, with his Panther escort, had gone on a few more paces before he realised they had all stopped behind him, squabbling and confrontational.

'I was only saying!' Anspach said.

'Keep it to yourself!' one of the Red Company snarled.

'He's right!' a Grey Templar snapped. 'Doom is coming to the Fauschlag!'

Others murmured agreement.

'Plague… it's true…' Drakken said, wondering.

'I've heard that!' said another Red Wolf. 'Thick and rife in the Altquartier stews!'

More agreement.

'We're on the brink of disaster!' said Olric, shaking his head.

Bertolf was beginning to explain something about ghosts walking the streets when Aric pushed past the bemused Panther escort and rounded on the gaggle of Templars.

'Enough! Enough! This kind of talk defeats us all before we've even begun!'

Aric had thought his voice was fierce and commanding. This was his first duty as a commander, and he intended to prosecute it with all the firmness and vigour of Ganz. No, of Jurgen. He was going to prove himself a fine leader of men. But he found himself shouted down by the arguing Wolves, comments blasting back and forth quicker than he could counter them. A boiling hubbub of voices filled the passageway. Aric had anticipated some trouble from the men of the other companies put under his command, but he had expected the men of White to follow him. Now there was nothing but mayhem, fierce conversation, disruption. And no discipline.

'Enough!' said a deep voice next to the increasingly frantic standard bearer. Silence fell, hard as an executioner's axe.

All eyes turned to Morgenstern. Very softly, he said, 'There's no plague. There's a touch of fever, but it will pass. And since when have we been afraid of rumours? Eh? Eh? This great rock-city has stood for two thousand years! Will such a place fall in one night? I think not! Doom on all our heads? Never! Not when we have armour on our backs, weapons in our hands and the spirit of Ulric to lift us!'

The silence was broken now as men of all Wolf Companies voiced their agreement with the great White Company ox.

'Let's do what we have to do and make the morrow safe for all good souls! And the morrow after that! For the Graf, for Ar-Ulric, for every man and woman in this beloved city!'

Morgenstern's throaty voice rose above the men's murmurings. Like the holler of a hero of old.

'Wolves of Ulric! Hammers of Ulric! Do we stand together, or do we waste the night with dispiriting rumour? Eh?'

They cheered. They all cheered. *Ulric take me,* Aric sighed. *I have a lot to learn.*

Guingol and Krass showed them the layout of the guest block. Aric appointed duties to all of the seventeen Templars in his command. He remembered, at a nudge from Morgenstern, to tell them the watchword.

He was left at the main doors of the guest apartments with the portly soldier.

'Thank you,' he hissed, a full three minutes after he was sure they were alone.

'Aric, Aric, never thank me.' Morgenstern turned to look at him, compassion in his huge, bearded face. 'I did as much for Jurgen when he was young.'

Aric looked at him.

'In panic, no one listens to a commander. They listen to those in the ranks beside them. They know the truth comes from the common man. It's a trick. I'm glad I could help.'

'I'll remember this.'

'Good. I remember when old Vulse used it, back when I was a pup. Who knows, in years to come, you'll be the old ranking veteran who can do the same for another generation of scared cubs.'

They both smiled. Morgenstern pulled a hip-flask out from under his pelt. 'Shall we bless the night?' he asked.

Aric paused, then took the filled cap Morgenstern offered. They drank a shot together, Aric from the cap and Morgenstern from the flask, clinking both together before sipping.

'Ulric love you, Morgenstern,' Aric whispered, wiping his mouth and handing the cap back to the big Wolf. 'I'll do a circuit of the men, make sure they're all in place.'

Morgenstern nodded. Aric slid away down the passageway.

As soon as the standard bearer was gone, Morgenstern sank back against the door jamb and knocked back a deep swallow from the flask.

His hands were trembling.

Plague, yes. Doom, yes, Death to them all, certainly. It had taken all his strength to speak out. To keep Aric's position as leader.

But in his great heart, he knew. He knew.

This was the end of everything.

KRUZA AWOKE IN the last hours of the night. His low, spare attic was cold as hell. His scar itched damnably.

He tried to remember what had woken him. A dream.

Wheezer.

He had been telling Kruza something. Wheezer had been standing next to the Graf and the Graf hadn't seen him.

Something about... the serpent, the self-biting monster. The world-eater.

Kruza shook so hard he had to crawl across the attic boards and pour a drink from the flask on the table. It was chilly, almost icy. Only the lead-weight of the liquor had kept it from freezing. He swilled it down, and the heat of the drink hit the back of his gullet.

Wheezer... what were you trying to tell me? What were you trying to tell me?

Nothing. Silence. Yet something was there.

The trinket? Was that it? The ceremonial necklace? Or something else?

Mist floated around him. His limbs felt hard and rigid with the cold. He took another drink. It warmed everything above his throat and everything else was rigid and dead.

Lenya. He remembered now. *Lenya. You want me to watch for your sister! She's in danger!*

That was no problem. Defending Lenya was something he didn't feel was an arduous task. Ranald take that Wolf of hers... Lenya...

Then he realised – or remembered, or simply imagined – what Wheezer had really been trying to tell him from the quiet world of phantoms. It wasn't just Lenya, though she was important.

It was everyone. It was Middenheim. It was the whole city.

He got up, pulling on his leather breeches and jerkin. His face was troubled, but he was not shaking any more.

FIRST LIGHT CAME, pale and clear, the sky a translucent blue. Snow lay a foot thick on the countryside and the city. Only the sheer black sides of the rock were free of it.

A train of gilt carriages and emblemed outriders churned up the southern viaduct, now just recently repaired, and flew in through the gate, puffing up sheets of snow. Holding the regal pennants of Bretonnia high, the vanguard of knights stormed up through the empty streets, leading the convoy of coaches towards the palace.

At the Great Gate, an honour guard of Panther Knights was mounted, and they turned to ride in with the speeding coaches. As the hurtling procession reached the entry yard, and pink-clad pages with torches ran out to form a fan of fire to greet the honoured visitors, housemen rolled out a velvet carpet to the foot-rest of the ambassador's carriage.

NONES WAS YET to strike as Gruber led Ganz in through the porch of the Temple of Morr. They looked up at the burned sections of the eerie temple, and the stretches that artisans were beginning to rebuild, many covered in tarpaulins against the weather. The day was clear and very cold, snow threatening again. Behind them, the escort detail of Schell, Schiffer, Kaspen and Lowenhertz.

Brother Olaf admitted them into the Factorum. The chamber was a cold, dank place, vaulted, smelling fiercely of astringent lavender-water and embalming fluids. Under the swinging ceiling lamps, Father Dieter looked up from the body on the cold slab as the Wolf Knights entered, rowel spurs clinking on the hard steps.

Gruber led them down the steps into the dark chamber. Even he was unnerved by the plinth slabs and the cold air. And the shrouded corpses laid out on those blocks. He had seen Father Dieter once before, in Osstor Street by the Wolf-Hole. Now Gruber saw him un-hooded. A tall, grim man, tonsure-headed, his eyes clear and cold, as if driven by some great, old regret.

Dieter looked up. 'Wolf Brother Gruber.'

'Father. This is Ganz, my commander.'

Ganz approached the priest of Morr and made a brief, respectful bow.

'What can you show us of this horror, father?' he asked simply.

Dieter led them across to the slab in the centre of the room where a male corpse lay, naked. The only distinguishing mark, as Ganz could see, was the wound through the white chest.

'The Wolf-Hole killer,' the priest said quietly, his hand flowing out to indicate the body. 'He was covered from head to foot in the blood of others when he came in. I have washed the corpse.'

'What has it told you?' Gruber asked.

'Look here.' The priest ushered Ganz and Gruber closer, indicating the sunken features of the dead man. 'When all the blood was gone, and despite the rigor, I saw a sallowness, a pale, sweaty pain.'

'Meaning?'

'This man was sick. Very sick. Out of his mind.'

'How can you be so sure?' asked Ganz.

'Because he's not the first like it I've had in here. Or the last. He was sick, Brother Ganz, death-sick. Madness was in him.'

'And is that why he attacked and murdered?' Gruber asked.

'Most likely.'

'And the desecrations? On the Wolf-Hole and the house?' asked Gruber.

The priest of Morr opened a small chap-book. 'Like you, I didn't recognise them, but I took them down carefully. I have since compared them to writings in our Librarium.'

'And?'

'They are names. The script is antique, and thus curious to our eyes, but the names are... common. The names of people. Citizens. Amongst them, the name of our killer here, Ergin. Also the names of his brother, his brother's wife, his neighbour, and three others who lived in the quarter nearby.'

'A roll-call of the dead,' breathed Lowenhertz quietly.

'Indeed,' the priest said, looking up sharply, as if surprised by the Wolf's insight. 'Or a roll of those that would be dead, if we assume they were written by the killer. A list then, almost a celebration of the sacred murder.'

Ganz frowned. 'Sacred? What was sacred about that act?'

The priest smiled slightly, though it reminded Ganz of the way a dog smiles before it bites. 'Not in our terms, commander.

I meant no blasphemy. But can you not see how this was a ritual thing? A ritual crafted by madness. The setting, for instance. It was more than chance that the murders desecrated a shrine holy to the patron deity of this city.'

'Have you seen this before?' Ganz asked.

'Yes, twice now. Twice in the last two days. A butcher ran amok in the Altmarkt, exhibiting similar signs of fever-madness. He had gouged the names of his five victims and himself in a side of meat hanging from his awning. Also, a scrivener in Freiburg, at the start of the week, just before the snows. Three dead there, stabbed with a quill-knife before the man threw himself from a window. Again, the fever-madness. Again, the names… the killer and his three victims, entered into a ledger the scrivener was working on, in a delicate copperplate hand.'

'Again the ritual,' Lowenhertz said, uneasy.

'Quite so. However, the incident at the Wolf-Hole last night was a little different in one respect. There were more names on the walls than victims at the scene.'

'You checked this?'

'I made… enquiries.'

'A priest with the instincts of an inquisitor,' mused Gruber, almost smiling.

'I can't be sure,' Father Dieter said, apparently ignoring the remark, 'if it was simply that Ergin was stopped by the valiant watch before he could reach his… quota. Or if the madness is causing the afflicted to enscribe other names down.'

'Other names?' asked Lowenhertz.

'A roll-call of the dead, you called it yourself. Who can say when the killing might stop?'

Ganz was pacing now, his hand to his brow in thought. 'Slow down, father. Let me try and take this in. Something you just said fills me with great alarm.'

'Has anything I have just said not?' asked the priest mildly.

Ganz turned to face him, pointing a finger as he locked onto the specific thought. 'You said if the madness is causing the afflicted to do this. I am no doctor of physic, but I know enough to realise a disease, an ague, doesn't direct purpose! That there is a brain-fever in Middenheim, so dire it can drive men to bestial rages, I can accept – but one that guides them on a particular course? Sets their agenda, their ritual, as you call it? Makes them perform the same way, makes them use the same old script? It beggars belief! No ague does that!'

'Quite so, Brother Ganz. But I never said it was a natural ague.'

The Factorum was quiet for a moment as this sunk in. The priest and the Wolves were as silent and unmoving as the dead around them. Gruber broke the still air at last with a low curse. 'Ulric damn me! Magic!'

Father Dieter nodded, pulling a shroud over the body of Ergin.

'I've had my fill of that this year already,' Gruber added.

'Have you?' the priest asked, suddenly and sharply interested. 'You're not alone. A dark undertow of the foulest sorcery has pervaded this city since Jahrdrung last. I have experienced it personally. And that is one of the clues for me. Another of the names, daubed on the wall near the Ulric shrine: Gilbertus. In the early year, just before Mitterfruhl, I had... dealings with one who called himself that. He was trying to pervert this holy Temple in the service of the darkest magic of all.'

'Where is he now?' Schell asked, not really wanting to know.

'Dead. Appropriately, as his name appeared in Ergin's list.'

'And the others?' asked Lowenhertz.

The priest consulted his chap-book again. 'Common names, as I said: Beltzmann, Ruger, Aufgang, Farber – I know a Farber, and he still lives, but it may not be him – Vogel, Dunst, Gorhaff, and another, curious, as it was written twice. That name is Einholt.'

All the Wolves froze. Ganz felt a trickle of ice-sweat bead down his brow. Lowenhertz made a warding sign and looked away.

'Does that mean anything to you? I see it does.'

'Commander!' the agitated Kaspen gasped, his face shockingly pale under his mane of red. 'We–'

Ganz silenced him with a raised hand. 'What else?' Ganz asked, stepping towards the priest and trying to master his own nerves. He wanted to stay circumspect until he had got the measure of this dour funeral cleric.

'Two more besides. Another name, but not a local one – Barakos. Anything?'

The Wolves shook their heads.

'And a symbol, or an indication of a symbol at least. The word "Ouroboros", in the antique script again.'

'Ouroboros?' Ganz asked.

Gruber looked round at Lowenhertz, knowing in his stewing gut that he would know.

'The wyrm that eats itself,' said Lowenhertz darkly. 'Its tail in its mouth, the universe consuming all that it is and all that has come before.'

'My, my,' Father Dieter said. 'I had no idea the Templars were so learned.'

'We are what we are,' Ganz stated flatly. 'Is that what you think this symbol means, father?'

The priest of Morr shrugged, closing his chap-book and binding it shut with a black ribbon. 'I am no expert,' he said, self-deprecatingly and inaccurately. 'The Ouroboros is an ancient sign. It means destruction.'

'No, more than that,' Lowenhertz said, moving forward. 'It means death defied. Undeath. Life beyond the grave.'

'Yes, it does,' said the priest of Death, his voice hard. 'It is the symbol of necromancy, and that was the self-same vile sin Gilbertus was guilty of. I thought that menace had vanished with Gilbertus when he pitched off the Cliff of Sighs. I was wrong. Gilbertus may have just been the start.'

'What do we do?' Ganz asked.

'Fleeing the city might be a good option,' the priest said phlegmatically.

'And those of us who can't? Those of us who are needed here? What do we do?'

'Fight,' said the priest of Morr, without hesitation.

IT WAS NEARLY midday, but the streets of the Altquartier were mournfully empty and thick with snow. No more had yet fallen and the air was glassy, but the sheer cold kept the population inside, around their hearths, desperate for warmth.

As he stalked down Low File Walk, wrapped in his cloak, Kruza wondered if other forces were keeping the streets quiet. Those rumours of plague. He couldn't believe them still, but there was a sickly smell in the cold, windless air. Of corruption, And of spoiled milk.

The thought hooked him, the memory. That smell, down in the pits of the tower house in the Nordgarten. The place he had last seen Wheezer alive.

It had been months since he'd last visited Wheezer's lonely home. In fact, Kruza thought, hadn't the final time been just after he'd last smelled that stink of spoiled milk?

He found his way up the dark stairs of the ruinous place, lighting a candle from his tinder box as much for the warmth it afforded his fingers as for light. Snow had blown in through empty window cases and drifted on the steps, and ice crusted the walls, like sheets of pearl.

He opened the door. It took a kick of his boot to free the ice around the jamb. Miraculously, almost painfully, the room was precisely as he had last seen it. No one had been here. Frost caked every surface, sheening the many mirrors and making the carpets and hangings crisp and rigid. It was as frozen as it was in his memory.

Kruza crunched across the rug, glancing around. He set the candle down on the low table, where the flame-heat melted the covering frost into great, wobbling beads. Kruza realised he had his short-sword drawn. Just like when he had burst in the first time, the very first time. His sword... drawn. *When had he done that? What instinct had made him unsheath his weapon?*

He looked around. *Now, where would it be?* He closed his eyes, trying to remember. Wheezer was in his mind. Wheezer laughing. Wheezer pulling a sack of bread and cheeses from the gable window ledge where he left them to stay fresh. Wheezer sitting by the fire, making up his tortuous, fairy-tale autobiography.

Kruza opened his eyes and looked again. He remembered taking a gilt mirror from the corner by the door at the end of his first visit. To make up his quota for Bleyden. The segmented wooden box where Wheezer kept his herbs sat there now. Kruza crossed to it. He reached out to open the lid and paused.

Here?

There was a noise behind him. Kruza spun like a cornered fox, blade out. Wheezer was there, nodding, smiling. *That's the place, Kruza, that's the place.*

But it wasn't Wheezer. It wasn't anybody. The candle stub Kruza had put on the table had slid off onto the floor, carried by the thawing drips of frost.

Kruza stamped out the feeble flames which were licking into the carpet where the candle lay.

'Don't do that, Wheez–' he said to the empty room, and caught himself doing it. Like he still believed Wheezer was with him.

Kruza went back to the herb-box and pulled open the lid. The scents from within were frail and thin in the cold. He rummaged inside with his numb fingers until he found the trinket and pulled it out.

The segmented metal band, the world-eater ornament with its sightless, ivory eyes. It was – damn it all – warm.

Kruza tucked the thing inside his jerkin and headed for the door. Ice crunched under his boots. He took one last look back at the frozen room. As sure as he was of anything, that Wheezer was a natural, that Wheezer was dead, as sure as he was even of his own name, he knew he wasn't coming back here. Ever.

He reached the street and hurried up the hill through the snow, slipping occasionally on the ice under the powder-cover. There was no one around, but somehow Kruza felt more guilty than he'd ever done in his life before. He, master of ten thousand thefts, all of them guilt-free, now felt the sting of shame for stealing a dead boy's trinket. *Stealing from the dead, Kruza!*

Worst of it was, he was sure Wheezer would have wanted him to have it. Or was the guilt in his mind because he was sure Wheezer would have rather Kruza never touched the sinister ornament again?

Before he could consider, he heard sobbing from his left; a side-lane. A woman, crying hard. Involuntarily, he went that way, into a jumble of ruins where a long burned-out stew-house stood. Snow clung to the blackened beams, and icicles hung like infernal defences.

There was something written on the sooty stone wall nearby. Words that he couldn't read. They were fresh, written in a dark liquid. *Tar? What is this?* And then as quickly, he thought, *What am I doing here?*

He saw the woman, a slum-mother, curled in a crotch of fire-black beams, sobbing. She was covered with blood. Kruza stopped abruptly. He could see a pair of feet, a man's, poking out from behind a heap of snow. The snow around the feet was dark red.

Enough. Not your business. Time to go, he thought, just as the man with the sword came out of the ruins behind him, shrieking from a foam-flecked mouth, death in his hideous, blazing eyes.

A MIDDAY FEAST was underway at the palace. Having rested briefly through the early part of the morning and then bathed in more warm water than the palace would usually raise for a week, the foreign ambassadors were being entertained by the Graf in the main hall. The air was thick with cooking smells from the kitchen, and delicious aromas from the platters the page-boys paraded out into the hall in series under Breugal's watchful eyes. Music, made by a bass-viol, a crumhorn, a psaltery, a tambour and a sackbut in the hands of the Graf's court players, filled the air.

'Quickly! Quickly now!' Breugal hissed in the side passage giving into the main hall, scurrying the platter-laden pages along. He tapped time with his cane and his eyes were as bright as ice. He had put on his finest two-horned periwig and an embroidered, broken-sleeve doublet under his houseman's coat, and his chisel face was extra powdered, white as the snow, or as the faces of the dead.

He cuffed a passing page as the boy made slow progress, and then clapped his hands again. He had heard many tales of the opulence of the Bretonnian court, and he would not have his own house found wanting in the eyes of these visitors.

Breugal stopped another page and sampled the goose-liver stuffed hog-trotters to make sure the cook was performing his duties. Excellent. Too much salt, but excellent all the same. *Let the haughty Bretonnians put on a feast as fine as this!*

LENYA WAS SERVING in the kitchen, one of several house-maids helping the undercooks decant mead and wine into the table jugs. The great, low-vaulted kitchens, with their steaming pots, roaring fires and bellowing men, were all but overwhelming. She thought she'd welcome the heat after the aching cold of the weather, but here it was too much. She was sweating, shaking, flushed, and her throat was burning and hoarse. Wiping her hands on her apron front, she looked round as she heard some-one call her name.

'Lenya! Lenya, girl!'

In the shadows of the back-doorway of the kitchen block, she saw Franckl. He was beckoning to her, pale and sweaty, his doublet front pulled open to expose a waxy, sweaty chest. His pink-silk livery-coat was dark under the armpits, big half-moons of sweat.

Glancing round to make sure she wasn't being watched, she crossed to him.

'Franckl?' The hierarchy of the Graf's palace had long since made them equals in status.

The Margrave's old houseman was mopping his pale brow, He looked as if his heart would seize and burst in another minute.

'Damn Breugal's had me shovelling snow since midnight,' Franckl gasped.

'You don't look well, sir,' she admitted.

'A drink is all I ask. Something cool but warming, if you understand me.'

She nodded and slunk back into the kitchen, dodging scurry-ing pages with armfuls of serving dishes.

She sneaked a stopped bottle of ale from a cooling bucket by the winery door and hurried back.

'Here. Don't say I never did anything for you. And don't let anyone see.'

He nodded, too busy breaking the stopper and choking down the cold ale. His face went pink with relief and delight. His eyes watered.

'What is this?' came a voice.

They both looked around. Franckl coughed out his last mouthful of ale in a spray. Leaning on his cane, Breugal stood over them, utterly disdainful and menacing, utterly composed... except for the trickle of sweat oozing out from under his wig and blotting the powder on his brow. Even he wasn't immune to the baking heat and chaos of the kitchen.

Neither Lenya nor Franckl spoke or even moved.

Breugal raised his cane and pointed the silver tip at Franckl. 'You, I will have whipped for this. And you...' The cane point moved slowly across at Lenya. Breugal smiled suddenly; a little, repellent, rat-like grin as an idea occurred to him. 'You I will have whipped also.'

'Is there trouble here?' asked a voice.

They all glanced round. A Wolf Templar stood, framed in the outer doorway, his hulking armoured form black against the snow outside.

Breugal frowned. 'Just a household matter, good Sir Wolf. I am dealing with it.'

Drakken stepped out of the door shadow. 'When you've so much to do? Sir, you're the Master of Ceremonies, the fulcrum on which this entire feast depends. You haven't time to waste chastising the indolent.'

Breugal paused. He had just been flattered, he knew he had. But it was not like any flattery he had experienced before.

'Captain von Volk of the Panthers has commanded my Templars to patrol the palace. Discipline and security are our duties. Charming the ambassador from Bretonnia is yours.'

'Quite so, but–'

'No buts,' Drakken said sharply. His commanding presence reminded Lenya of a hooded gladiator she had once seen dominate the action of the Baiting Pit.

Drakken leaned down and casually took the ale-flask from the speechless Franckl. 'I will take this man into the yard and break this bottle across his wretched skull. The girl I will beat with my fist until she knows correction. Will that serve you?'

Breugal smiled, without much fun in his eyes. 'Yes, Sir Templar, but I assure you I can easily deal with this infraction of–'

'You have work to do,' Drakken said, stepping towards the chamberlain. His spur chinked on the kitchen step. 'And so have I. All interlopers and malingerers are the guards' duty to punish.'

'No, this isn't right at all!' said Breugal, suddenly. 'You have the watch, of course, but–'

'Captain von Volk was very clear. All interlopers are the business of the guard. The watchword is Northwind, as I'm sure you know. We Templars prosecute that duty with a force fiercer than any north wind.'

Breugal knew he was out-ranked. He backed away. 'I am in your hands. Sigmar invest you with radiance.'

The chamberlain tik-takked on his cane away across the kitchen, cuffing pages and ordering staff about viciously to make up for his disappointment,

'And Ulric bite your bony arse,' Drakken muttered as the bewigged man departed.

He pushed Franckl and Lenya out into the snowy yard and closed the door. Lenya was laughing out loud and even Franckl was smirking. Drakken held the ale-flask out to the houseman, who flinched briefly, expecting the worst, and then accepted it.

'Leave some for me,' Drakken smiled and Franckl nodded, taking it and hurrying away towards the shelter of the timber store.

Lenya grabbed her Templar gleefully, ignoring the cold, hard bulk of his plate mail under her hands and forearms.

'You found me, Krieg!' she cried, delightedly.

He smiled and kissed her mouth roughly.

'Of course,' he murmured as their lips parted.

'Ganz said you would be here.'

'My commander is right in all things.'

Lenya frowned, leaning away from him, her arms still about him. 'But how did you find me?'

'I sneaked away.'

'From?'

'From my patrol. They won't miss me.'

'Are you sure?' she asked curiously. She had a bad feeling Drakken was taking a big risk.

He kissed her again. And again. He knew he was sure.

* * *

THEY HAD BEEN interrupted by a convoy of biers which had arrived at the porch of Morr's Temple from the Wynd district. Father Dieter went down to assist the watchmen and the other initiates of Morr as they unloaded the miserable burden.

The Wolf Templars went outside and stood together by their tethered horses, waiting.

'Why don't you tell him, sir?' Kaspen asked.

'Tell him?'

'About Einholt! Ulric's breath! He said his name was writ in blood!'

'I heard him,' Ganz said, his voice low.

'I agree with Kaspen here,' said Lowenhertz, his voice slow with considered thought. He looked up at Ganz. 'This priest of Morr is an ally, I'm sure. Gods, he knows what he's talking about! Tell him about Einholt. Fit the pieces together... the puzzle pieces you and he hold separately!'

'Perhaps,' Ganz said.

Gruber took the commander to one side. 'Lowenhertz is right. I think we should trust this man.'

'Do you trust him, Wilhelm?'

Gruber looked away, then right back at Ganz, straight in the eyes. 'No. But I know when a risk's worth taking. And I know it's now. You weren't with us in the tunnels under the Fauschlag. You didn't see what I saw, what Aric and Lowenhertz saw. You didn't see what Einholt did.'

'You've told me. That's enough.'

'Is it? Ganz, there was an evil down there like nothing I have felt before, or hope to do again. There was a... thing. It escaped. Ulric take me if this isn't part of this curse falling on our city. And from what the priest there says, he knows about it too!'

Ganz spun away, silent. His thoughts were broken by the priest re-emerging from the Temple. The man was wiping blood from his hands with a scrap of winding sheet. Ganz crossed to him. They stood face to face in the snow at the foot of the Temple steps.

'It's happened again,' the father said. 'Freiburg now. A wealthy merchant disembowelled his entire family and staff and then hanged himself. Twelve dead. Two hundred and eighteen names on the wall.'

'What?'

'You heard,' Dieter growled. He plucked a scroll of parchment from his belt and opened it out. 'My friends in the Watch wrote the names down. I haven't begun to cross-check them yet. But you can see the way it's building, can't you? With each act of murder, the list becomes longer. How many more before it numbers everyone in the city. You, me, the Graf...' His voice trailed off.

'Einholt was a beloved member of White Company. Three months ago, he was singular in valour and... saved this city. There is no other way to describe it. He saved it from some skulking darkness in the tunnels below. Then, a week later, he vanished. We haven't seen him since.'

'He is dead.'

'So we suppose,' Ganz said – and then realised it wasn't a suggestion.

'I know it to be true. It was a simple thing to check the records of the city and find the missing Einholt.'

Ganz glared at the priest, who held up calming hands.

'Forgive me that I knew. I have no doubt Einholt was the bravest of you. My... sources told me what he did.'

'What kind of priest are you?'

The priest of Morr looked darkly at Ganz. 'The best kind: one who cares. And one who knows.'

'What do we do?' asked Ganz, sighing in admission.

'Let's consider the facts. A force of dark necromancy threatens this city...'

'Agreed.'

'We have seen its mark. As I can conjecture, it has been with us at least a year. It has had time to take a firm toe-hold. To plan. To scheme. To build.'

'Again, agreed.'

The priest paused for a moment, his breath wiping the air with steam. Ganz realised for the first time how frightened the priest was behind his confident bearing.

'We have seen its sign too, the tail-eating snake, as I said. It inflicts upon Middenheim a distemper, a magic-fever that corrupts minds and makes them do its bidding, for some fell cause we are yet ignorant of.'

'Are we?'

'Maybe. Its curse is on us now, though, wouldn't you say? Its ritual menace is all around us.'

'Yes.' Ganz was grim. 'Do you know why?'

Father Dieter was silent for a moment. He looked down at his feet, half-buried in the snow. 'The last act? The finale? It's making ritual lists of the dead. Unless I'm a fool, those lists will soon number every soul in Middenheim. Necromancy is death magic. The greater the death, the greater the magic. It works, as I understand it – and believe me, Temple commander, I have made no great study of its vile aberrations – by sacrifice. A single death allows it to work some unholiness. A multiple death will work greater magic. The blood-sacrifice of a city–'

'Ulric take me! Could it be that much?' gasped Ganz.

'That much? That little! Ten thousand souls sacrificed here is nothing to the hundreds of thousands rendered up to the Dark Ones if Bretonnia goes to war with the Empire. Isn't that the point? This city-state hangs upon the cusp of conflict. What greater sacrifice to the foul hells of necromancy could there be than the heaps of the slain, murdered in open war?'

Ganz turned away from the priest. He felt as if he wanted to be sick, but choked it back. That would be unseemly in front of his men, in front of outsiders.

'You said we should fight?' he said, his voice thin, glancing back at the priest. 'Where do you suggest we make our stand?'

'Where is Bretonnia? What place is most vulnerable? Where does the *power* live?'

'Mount up!' Ganz bellowed at his men, running forward through the snow. 'Make for the Palast Hill! Now!'

'I'm coming with you,' Father Brossmann said. Ganz wasn't listening.

'Ganz!'

On his charger, Ganz cantered around in the snowy yard and saw the priest of Morr racing up behind him.

He held out his hand and yanked the man up behind him.

'I hope you know how to ride!' he spat.

'In another life, yes,' said the priest grimly.

They galloped out of the temple yard, kicking up divots of snow, heading for the palace.

KRUZA DUCKED the scything blade. The man was mad, that was clear enough from his eyes. It reminded Kruza of the intense determination behind a public executioner's hood. The sword whickered into a soot-flaking cross-beam and stuck. Kruza ripped round with his short-sword but missed his frenzied attacker.

The man was plague-sick, Kruza could see that. His skin was pallid and sweaty, cold and white with fever. He ripped his sword out from the beam and attacked again. The sword was a long, rusty broadsword, far longer in reach than Kruza's short blade. The sword whipped around again, trying to find Kruza's throat. He ducked and came up behind the swing, jabbing with his own blade.

The blade bit into ribs, through ribs, into organs and wetness. The fever-driven man went down, screaming and convulsing.

'Kruza! Kruza! Kruza!' The man ranted as he died.

Kruza was already running for the palace hill.

THE SNOW THAT had choked the sky's gullet all day began to fall heavily as the daylight faded. It was only mid-afternoon, but the snow-clouds added their bulk to the sky and made it like early night. Thick snow, at first, then as the temperature dropped, sleet and freezing rain came, driving hard across the city, fusing into the laying snow as it fell. Wilting slush became rigid and unbroken snow-cover began to glow like glass as it transformed into ice.

Lenya had escaped the kitchen after her meeting with Drakken. Her lips still tingling, she found shelter in the timber store where Franckl and a dozen other housemen, pages and domestic girls had escaped out of the rain. Someone had lit a small fire and Franckl's bottle obviously wasn't the only one stolen that day. Lenya slipped into the musty gloom, the rain pattering off the tiles like slingshots, and found a place beside Franckl, accepting a swig from his bottle.

'That's a good man you've found there,' he said.

'It is.' Lenya wasn't comfortable in this throng. She wanted to get back inside, but she was sure she'd be frozen alive by the time she reached the kitchen arch across the yard. Winter thunder rolled, hard and heavy above the city rock, like the hooves of god-steeds.

She crawled up a stack of timber until she could see out of the window-slit towards the main gates, blurry through the hail. Distantly, she could see watchfires, steaming out, Panthers pulling the braziers into cover, sliding the gates closed. Their decorative plumes wilted and sagged on their helmets.

She jumped as something banged off the roof. Then again, and again. Like fists. Outside, she saw hail the size of cannon-lead smacking down into the snow, puffing it up and fracturing the ice crust with their weight. A murder storm. The most lethal a winter in the Empire could unleash. In a moment, the banging got louder and more hasty as the strikes overlapped. Hail was lobbing down now, and thunder barked again. Through the pelt, she saw a Panther at the gate struck squarely by a stone and go down, his comrades running to him. Another dropped immediately, hit, his helmet torn off.

Lenya gasped. She'd seen storms of all force out in Linz, on the farm. Never like this. Never this fury.

GANZ PULLED his riders in under the sloping side-roof of a coaching inn as the deadly hail fell. Riding on into this would be madness. Behind him, on the saddle-back, the priest whispered, 'Just the start…'

Ganz made no answer. The palace gates were only two streets away. In this elemental assault, an impossible distance.

KRUZA REACHED the palace walls. He was cold through to the bones in the icy downpour and at least one hail-stone had smashed into his shoulder, leaving an aching bruise. Another ricocheted off the stones by his face, filling his eyes with ice-chips.

He ducked and sank down. The gates were shut. He had no idea how he was going to get inside.

IN THE PALACE, the guests were retiring. The feast had been a rousing success and now the ambassadors from Bretonnia asked for rest before the night's festivities. The Graf and his nobles were also returning to their quarters for a while. Hail drummed on the roof and thunder twisted the air.

Patrolling the guest apartments, Aric watched as Knights Panther and torch-bearing pages ushered the visiting dignitaries to their rooms. Already he could smell the kitchens as they stoked up the next round of entertainment. *Sleep well*, he thought. *You'll need all your strengths replenished come compline chime.*

He crossed into the corridor where Drakken was supposed to be on guard. Aric was standing by the doors into the guest rooms when the young, stocky knight appeared.

'Where have you been?' he asked.

'On duty–' Drakken began.

Aric's eyes quested into the young man's face. 'Indeed? Here?'

'I left for a moment…'

'How long a moment?'

Drakken paused. 'I suppose… half an hour…' he began.

'Ulric damn you!' Aric spat, and wheeled towards the doors. Thunder rolled outside, and a gust of wind breathed down the corridor, extinguishing all the lamps. 'How long did half an hour give them?'

'Who?'

'Whoever wanted to get inside!' Aric snarled, his hammer raised, kicking in the door.

Drakken ran after the Wolf, down a velvet-lined antechamber and into the first apartment. The carpet was on fire here from a spilled lantern. Two servants, in the tunics of Bretonnia, were dead on the floor. Words – names – had been daubed on the walls in their blood.

There was a scream from the adjoining room.

Aric burst through. A maid in waiting was pressed to the wall, on her haunches, shrieking. A hulking shape, almost a black shadow, backlit by the fireplace, had the Bretonnian ambassador held in the air by his throat. Blood dripped down. The ambassador was gasping out his last.

The hulking shape turned and looked at the sudden intrusion. It dropped the half-dead ambassador onto the ornamental rug.

Its one good eye glowed coral pink.

In a voice as low as the underworld, as dull as hoof-beats and as thick as tar, it said two clear words.

'Hello, Aric.'

THE BOMBARDMENT of hail was even fiercer than before. Under the stable lip, the Temple warhorses skipped and shuddered.

'We cannot wait. Not now,' said the priest, a shadow behind Ganz.

'But–'

'Now, or all is lost.'

Ganz turned towards the dimly lit faces of his men.

'Ride! In the name of Ulric! Ride!' he shouted.

Exploding out of cover, ice-chips shattering around their hooves, the thunder breaking above them, they rode.

KRUZA WAS half-buried in a snow-drift, his hands still flat against the aching cold of the stone wall, when the firelight throbbed over him.

He blinked and glanced up at the three Knights Panther standing around him.

'No weather for lazing out here,' said one.

'Not when the Graf is waiting to hear the sound of your voice,' said another.

'W-what?' Kruza asked, numb in almost every way.

Lenya oozed in between two of the Panthers.

'I was telling them that the great minstrel singer was late, and the Graf would be most displeased if he didn't arrive in time for the feast,' she said.

'Of course…'

'Come on!' she pulled him up. 'I saw you at the gate,' she hissed into his ear. 'What are you doing here?'

'Protecting you,' he murmured. He was sure there were icicles on the underside of his tongue.

'Great job you're doing!' she said.

The Panthers helped her into the gates with him as hail belted down around them.

There was a sound of thunder outside, like hooves.

'HE THWARTED me, so I chose him. He made me weaker than ever, so it was right I should take his form as my own.'

The thing with the pink eye was speaking, though Aric wasn't really listening.

'A thousand years, alone and buried within the Fauschlag. Can you imagine that, Aric? A thousand years. No, of course you can't, you're too far gone with fear.'

The impossible hulking shape paced around the candle and firelit chamber, circling the Templar.

'I took the form anyway. A good strong form. There was justice in it.'

'What are you?' asked Aric. 'You look like—'

'Einholt?' the thing sneered at him. 'I do, don't I? I borrowed his corpse. It was so full of zest and vigour.'

Einholt looked back at Aric with a blazing pink eye. The other was milky and dead, bisected by the scar, just as Aric remembered it. Einholt, pale, armoured, speaking, moving, alive. But not Einholt. No, that look. That penetrating, burning look…

'I am Einholt. He is me. It's amazing how his memories are preserved in this brain. Like inlay work on a good sword. My, these memories are mother-of-pearl! So bright! So hard! That's how I know you, Aric wolf-son. I know what you did. Not so great a crime as this Einholt, but party to it.'

'You have the face of my friend, but I know you are evil,' Aric said, raising his hammer hesitantly.

'Then go on! Crush this!' Einholt said, grinning and pointing at his own face. 'I dare you! Kill your long-lost comrade forever!'

Aric lowered his hammer. He sank to his knees.

'I wanted life again. Form, volume, bulk. You cheated me of that, just as the priest cheated me last Jahrdrung. But now, I am returned, renewed! Eager! Salivating for life!'

Einholt smiled down at the kneeling, weeping Aric. A warhammer was in his left hand, and he brought it up.

Drakken's flying hammer slammed him back across the room.

Einholt, or the thing that had once been Einholt, crashed into a side-table and shattered it under its falling bulk. It let out a raging snarl of anger that was entirely inhuman as it pulled itself upright. Drakken's fierce blow had dented its upper left breast-plating and torn the shoulder pauldron clean off.

Its one good eye throbbed like pink fire in time to its roar. Einholt's hammer was still in its hand.

Drakken pulled Aric up. The young Wolf yanked his dagger from his belt, his hammer too far away to retrieve.

'Come on!' he yelled.

'The pup has more spirit than you, Aric. Young Drakken has fewer qualms about striking his old comrade Einholt.'

Or a terrible guilt of dereliction to make up for, thought Drakken. We wouldn't be here... the ambassador wouldn't be vomiting blood on the floor, if it hadn't been for me...

Aric rose. It was as if Drakken's abrupt intervention had galvanised him anew, given him confidence. He looped his hammer through the air, circling the pink-eyed shade.

'Go!' he said to Drakken.

'But–'

'Go!' Aric repeated, his eyes never leaving the enemy before him. 'Get the ambassador out of this place. Sound the alarm! Go! Go!'

Covered by Aric and his looping weapon, Drakken dragged the gasping, semi-alive Bretonnian dignitary onto his shoulder and stumbled to the door. As soon as he was outside in the hall, he began to bellow at the top of his voice. By then, the maid had already run screaming from the suite. Cries and alarms filled the palace halls.

Aric and the thing circled.

'Shall we try it, Aric wolf-son?' asked Einholt-that-was, his hammer slowly whickering the air as it made lazy figure of eights.

'Try what?' Aric replied stiffly, his hammer held in a more defensive guard.

'Man to man, you and me...'

'You're no man.'

The thing laughed. The bottom edge of Einholt's laugh was stained with the inhuman rumble. Like thunder.

'Maybe. But I am still Einholt. One of the best hammer-arms in the Temple. Remember the displays I used to put on, me and Kaspen? What was it Jurgen said? "The art of the hammer lives in its best form as long as Jagbald Einholt is alive"? Guess what, little pup Aric –little starched-front, duty-bound Aric – Jagbald Einholt lives, and more immeasurably now than you could ever imagine!'

'No!'

'Oh yes, boy!' the thing hissed, its pink eye pulsing as it circled again, the hammer loops increasing in speed. 'Did you never think how it would be to face one of your own? Did you never idly suppose who in White Company could master who? Could you beat Drakken? Possibly, but the pup has fury. Gruber? Maybe with your youthful power. Ganz? Not him. Lowenhertz? Not him either. And… Einholt?'

It paused. It winked its dead, milky eye, slow and chilling.

'You don't stand a chance.'

Einholt's hammer snapped out deftly, hard, breaking the steady flow of Aric's returns, knocking the standard bearer's weapon out of true. Aric cried sharply as the snagged haft-loop tore into his fingers as he tried to arrest the knock. The pink-eyed thing smacked him in the chest with the butt of his hammer-head a second later.

Aric recoiled. His breastplate was dented and his breath was gone. He struggled to bring his own hammer round to deflect the next blow, but once-Einholt was already there, leering, circling round with a blow that shattered the upper vambrace of Aric's left arm and broke the bone.

Pain sparked like white stars, like snowflakes, across his vision. Aric kept the grip on the hammer with his remaining hand, pushing backwards, crashing into furniture.

'*You're not Einholt!*' he bellowed.

'I am!'

'No! What are you? What are you? The thing from the cellar?'

The shade's next blow took Aric in the right hip and spun him to his knees on the fire hearth.

Aric gagged. His vision already failing, his left arm dangling broken at his side, grinding agonisingly with every move. He struggled to stay conscious.

'The thing from the cellar?' said the monstrosity, the lowest register of its so-familiar voice twisted again by the thick, thunderous undernotes. 'I am all this city fears and more. I am the power that will blot Middenheim from the map and bleed the stars dry. I am Barakos.'

'Well met!' Aric snapped, smashing his hammer upwards in his one good hand.

The blow knocked the thing several yards back across the room, blood spraying from its broken jaw. It destroyed a lampstand and writing desk as it fell.

'Jagbald Einholt trained me well,' Aric gasped, and collapsed onto the rug, consciousness fleeing his pain-assaulted mind.

DRAKKEN SLID THE ambassador off his shoulder at a turn in the hallway, laying him down on an ornamental chaise. He couldn't get his bearings. There was shouting and confusion in the palace all around. He cupped his hands to his mouth and yelled 'Here! Here! To me! Send a surgeon!'

Two page boys appeared, side by side, took a look at the blood-flecked, comatose Bretonnian on the couch and fled, screaming.

'Drakken?' The young Templar look around. It was Olric of the Grey, racing up, sweaty and pale.

'What in the name of Ulric is going on?' he stammered.

'Murder! Evil! Magic! Here in the palace! Quick, Wolf brother! We must get him to a surgeon!'

Olric looked down at the crumpled man in his regal robes.

'Faraway gods! That's one of the foreign nobles! Come on, grab his feet. No, the end of the chaise, as a stretcher'

They took the ambassador up, on the chaise, each gripping the stunted legs of the piece of furniture. Olric, his hammer slung over his back, led the way, backing down the hall under the twitching lamp light.

'Panthers! *Panthers!*' he cried. 'Show yourselves! Show us to the infirmary!'

Struggling with the other end of the chaise, Drakken wanted to explain, wanted to tell Olric what he had seen back in the royal apartments. But the words choked in his mouth. How could he begin to tell this fellow Templar that Einholt, one of the White, was the assassin?

He was struggling with his words when six Panther Knights appeared, hurrying down the hall to them. Vogel, his visor raised, led them. The others, hidden behind their gilt faceplates, could all be Krass and Guingol, over and again, for all Drakken could tell.

Olric turned, fighting with the weight of the chaise. 'Vogel! Good! Look to us, man! Foul murder has been done!'

The Panthers paused, and Vogel slammed down his visor. He paced forward, and punched his broadsword through Olric's torso. Olric bellowed, his mouth bubbling blood as he went down, his end of the chaise smashing to the marble floor. The Bretonnian noble slumped off the makeshift stretcher and rolled limply across the floor.

Vogel pulled his sword out of Olric, ripping the backplate of the Wolf's armour away. Olric dropped on his face hard, falling into a lake of his own blood. The Panthers, Vogel at the lead, moved in on Drakken.

The young Wolf could smell the sickness smell again, riper and fuller than before. Spoiled milk. The smell of madness and the magic of the dead.

Vogel flew at him but Drakken was ready. He ducked under the sword arm and deflected the swinging blow with a lash of his armoured left arm. At the same time, he pulled out his dagger and slammed the blade deep into Vogel's neck, punching it up through the throat armour and through the madman's spine. Blood jetted out through the multiple joints of the Panther's gleaming, segmented helm. Vogel fell, pulling Drakken's buried knife away with him.

Unarmed now, as five more closed, swords ready.

A shockwave of stone on metal rang down the hall as Morgenstern and Anspach came in on the Panthers from the rear. Anspach sent his first foe face-down, the back of the ornate Panther armour splintered and bloody. Morgenstern decapitated another as easily as hoisting a turnip off a bucket-top. The helmeted head thukked off the ceiling and went clattering away.

The three remaining Panthers turned to face the onslaught.

Drakken could hear Morgenstern and Anspach yelling out the battle cry of White Company, and repeating the war-chant, 'Hammers of Ulric! Hammers of Ulric!'

Drakken snatched up Vogel's fallen sword and waded in, swinging the unfamiliar weapon like a hammer. A Panther was in his face, slicing hard with expertise.

Drakken blocked the strike as he would have done with a hammer haft, and sparks flew from the blades. He came around again, circling the sword around his head two-handed, as a hammer-man would turn his weapon, and cut the Panther through the shoulder, down to the belly. The sharp sword cut armour plate like a hot-iron through ice.

Morgenstern slammed a Panther into the hallway wall with his bulk, and killed him with repeated blows from his circling hammer. Anspach clove in the plumed helm of the last. They grouped, back to back, defending the fallen body of the ambassador, as dozens of other Knights Panther charged down at them from both sides.

THE HAIL CEASED. An oppressive stillness settled over the city and the night. The sky was an ice-haze of cold, smoky fumes, making the stars glint pink and bloodshot. Thunder moaned in the stillness, like distant packs of cavalry, turning far away for the next assault.

The palace gates were locked shut.

'Open!' Ganz bellowed, his steed bucking. The priest clung tight to the armoured warrior to remain seated.

'The palace is closed!' yelled a Panther Knight back from the gateway, behind the bars. 'Alarm has been sounded! No one may enter!'

Steadying his horse, Ganz looked further, and saw the lamps flashing in the windows of the great palace, heard the cries and bells and screams.

'Let us in!' he repeated, his voice a thunder all of its own.

'Go back!' returned the gate-guards.

Gruber slung his horse in around Ganz, and came up to the gates sidelong, hammer whirling. With celebrated precision, he smashed the padlock off the gate-bolt. Then he reared his horse and the front hooves crashed the gates open as they came down.

The six Wolves bolted down the main entrance yard through the gates as the Panthers rushed out to waylay them. The hurtling fury of Ulric's Temple Men at full charge. What could they do against that? Better they tried to stop a storm, a north wind, a thunderbolt. It was over in seconds.

Ganz's Wolves threw themselves off their steeds at the palace entrance, letting their chargers run free. With Gruber and the priest of Morr at their head, they crashed into the main hall, and had to stand aside as a gaggle of court musicians and domestics fled past them out into the night. Kaspen caught one by the throat, a lute player who clutched his instrument to his belly to protect it.

'Murder! Madness! Murder!' the man gagged, trying to tear free.

'Go!' snapped Kaspen, throwing the man out of the door. The six knights and the priest advanced across the great space off the hallway. The vast building beyond rang with screams and yells and incessant hand-bell alarms.

'We're too late,' said Ganz.

'We're never too late,' snapped Dieter of Morr. 'This way.'

'Where are we going?'

'The guest apartments.'

'And how do you know where they are?' Ganz asked.

'Research,' the priest of Morr smiled back at him. It was the coldest smile Ganz had ever seen in his entire life.

BACKED INTO A corner, sweeping at anything that came in range, the three great White Templars stood in a line, side by side: Morgenstern, Anspach, Drakken. Two hammers and one novice sword against twenty fever-maddened Knights Panther who bottled them in a back end of the corridor. Already, four more Panthers lay dead or dying. It was all the three Wolves could do to fend off the attacks now, to keep the weapons away.

Through the press, Drakken could see von Volk and a dozen more Panthers charging down from the end of the hall. This is it, he thought. *This is where the sheer weight of numbers–*

Von Volk cut a Panther knight down with a swing of his sword. Then another. He and his men hacked into the back of the insane press that had cornered the Wolves.

That first blow had been historic, unprecedented. The first time a holy Panther Knight had slain another of his kind. It didn't remain unprecedented for long. Drakken knew what he was witnessing was extraordinary. Panther against Panther. He thought of Einholt. *Had a Wolf ever killed a Wolf?*

He thought of Aric. The thought was too painful to keep in his head.

Morgenstern bellowed, and urged Anspach and Drakken up with him to crush the mad Panthers against von Volk and his relieving force.

Three fierce minutes, and nearly twenty-five noble Knights Panther lay dead or broken on the hallway floor. Von Volk pulled off his helmet and sank to his knees in horror, his helm crashing out of his loose grip and rolling away across the ground. His other, loyal knights also sank down, or turned away, horrified at what they had done. What they had been forced to do.

'In the Graf's name...' gasped von Volk, tears in his eyes. 'What in all of creation have we had to do here tonight? My men... my...'

Morgenstern knelt down in front of von Volk and grabbed the knight's clenched hands between his mighty paws. 'You have done your duty and may Ulric – and Sigmar – thank you. There is rank insanity in the Palace of Middenheim tonight, and you have kept your duty well and seen it off. Mourn these poor souls, yes. I will join you in that. But they were turned, von Volk. They were not the men you knew. Evil had taken them. You did what was right.'

Von Volk looked up into the face of the obese White Wolf. 'You say. They were not your own.'

'Still enough, you did right. Our loyalty is to our kind, but when evil strikes, our truest loyalty is to the Crown.'

Morgenstern pulled out his flask and von Volk slugged greedily from the offered bottle.

'It's only the start of the horrors we may have to face now,' Anspach advised, helping von Volk up.

The Knights Panther captain nodded, wiped his mouth and took another slug of the fire-water.

'Sigmar look to all those who have done this here tonight. For I will show them no mercy.'

THEY FOUND Aric face down in front of the guest room fireplace, blood matting his hair and seeping out of his armour joints. Dorff and Kaspen lifted him up and laid him on the bed, stripping off his armour. There was no surgeon to call, as the palace doctor was attending to the Bretonnian ambassador. The priest of Morr pushed in.

'I usually tend the dead, but I know about medicine, a thing or two at least.' With the help of Kaspen, who had been trained as White Company's bone-setter and wound-binder for the battlefield, Dieter began to dress the young knight's injuries.

'A madness befell my men,' von Volk was saying.

'A madness befalls this city,' Lowenhertz returned. 'We have learned that foul necromancy permeates this place, seeking its own ends. The fever is part of it. It is not a true plague, it is magic-born, bred to infect us all with insanity and killing glee. Is that not so, priest?'

Father Dieter looked up from his work splinting Aric's shattered left arm.

'Quite so, Lowenhertz. The sickness that afflicts Middenheim is magical in nature. A madness. You've seen the signs, von Volk. You've read the words on the walls.'

'A madness that makes those touched kill and kill again for the glory of blood-letting,' Ganz said, without life or spark in his voice. 'At any time, it could afflict us. It is spreading, pestilential, all around us.'

Drakken stepped forward. 'I know the evil,' he said.

'What'

'The thing you said you fought in the cellar,' Drakken said to Gruber. 'The thing with the pink eyes. It was here. But it wasn't a stick-form, a flimsy thing, it was…'

He couldn't say the name.

'What?' Lowenhertz snarled impatiently.

Gruber held him back from the pale young Wolf, who was still about to speak.

But it was the priest of Morr who finished the sentence. 'Einholt.'

They all looked around and then back at Drakken.

'Was it?' asked Ganz.

Drakken nodded. 'It said it was him, but it wasn't. It had borrowed his body like you might borrow a cloak. It wore him. It wasn't Einholt, but it looked like him.'

'And… fought like him.' Aric eased up onto his good elbow and looked at them all. 'It was Einholt's flesh, Einholt's blood, Einholt's skill and memories. But it was a hollow, evil thing inside. The thing said it had taken Einholt for revenge, because Einholt had somehow stopped it… in the cellar, I suppose. It wanted a body. It chose Einholt.'

Father Dieter had finished dressing Aric's injuries. He pulled Ganz to one side.

'I fear,' he said reluctantly, 'that we are not simply dealing with a necromancer here.'

Ganz looked round at him, feeling the ice-sweat trickle down his back.

'To possess a form, as your man Aric relates… this is something more.'

'It said its name was Barakos,' Aric said, leaning forward, listening to them from the bed.

'Barakos?' Dieter mused, his eyes lifted. 'Why, then, it's true.'

Ganz grabbed the priest of Morr by the front of his robes and slammed him into the hardwood panels of the stateroom. The Wolves and Panthers looked on in shock.

'You know? You knew?'

'Let me go, Ganz.'

'YOU KNEW!?'

'Let me go!'

Ganz released his grip and Father Dieter slid down so his feet were on the floor. He rubbed his throat.

'Barakos. The name appeared on the walls at Wolf-hole. I asked you all if you knew it – you did not. I cast it aside myself, hoping that it was just a coincidence. The name of some Araby merchant now in town who would fall victim to the plague-murders.'

'And what is it really?'

'Nothing. Everything,' the priest said. 'In the old books, it is written "Babrakkos", an ancient name even when Middenheim was founded. A dark power, deathless, necromantic. Also known as Brabaka, and in the nursery rhyme: Ba ba Barak, come see thee tarry! You know it?'

'I know it.'

'All those references refer to a pestilential liche-thing that threatened Middenheim in the earliest of days. Babrakkos. Barakos now, perhaps. I think it's back. I think it's living again. I think it wants the city of Middenheim dead so as to conjure enough death-magic force to make it a god. An unclean god, but a god never the less, as we would understand it, Ganz of the White.'

'A liche…' Even Ganz's voice was pale. 'How do we fight such a thing?'

Father Dieter shrugged. 'It has clearly already begun upon its work. Tonight is its hour. We have the men, but not the time. If we could find the foe, we might be able to thwart it, but–'

'I know where it is,' a voice from the door said.

The Wolves and the Panthers looked round. Lenya smiled at them as Drakken, humbly, led her in.

'Not me, actually. My friend here.' Lenya dragged the shabby figure of Kruza into the light behind her and Drakken. She held up the ornament, the world-eater, the biting snake. Lamp-light flickered off it.

'This is Kruza. My friend. My brother's friend. He knows where the monster dwells.'

SNOW, IN ICY pellets, had begun to fall out of the frosty pink night again. It was like riding down into Hell.

The dark cityscape was dotted with dozens of fires; numerous buildings blazed from Ostwald to the Wynd. Screaming and wailing and clamour rolled down the streets all around, where fever-maddened citizens brawled or fought in packs like wild beasts. Bodies littered the cold streets, the falling snow forming crusty shrouds over those that had lain longest. Names, written in blood, wax, ink and ice covered the street walls and the sides of buildings. The cold air smelled of spoiled milk.

The company rode out through the broken gates of the palace and down the steep Gafsmund streets into Nordgarten. Ganz led them, with Gruber at his side, carrying the standard. Kruza and the priest rode on stubborn palfreys taken from the palace stables, close at the lead knights' heels. Kruza had never been on a horse before in his life. But then again, every single thing that had happened to him tonight was new – and none of it was welcome.

Behind the lead four, Morgenstern, Kaspen, Anspach, Bruckner and Dorff, then Lowenhertz, Schell, Schiffer and Drakken. Next, in a close formation, the vengeful von Volk and six of his best Panthers, all men who had yet shown no signs of the fever. Bertolf, of Red Company, had ridden hard for the Temple, to raise the companies there in support. Aric, by necessity of his wounds, had been left at the palace, where von Volk's trusted Lieutenant Ulgrind was trying to re-establish calm.

Packs of feral citizens howled at them as they passed, some hurling stones, some even running out to dare the Templars in their insanity.

At the top of one of the sloping residential avenues, Ganz stopped them and looked round at the shivering cut-purse. The company leader mused for a moment that the fate of them all, the fate of the city itself, depended upon the sort of street-filth who would normally be invisible to him. The young man didn't seem much, rangy and lean in ragged clothes, his expression clearly showing he wished to be elsewhere. Any elsewhere. But he had come to them, so Drakken's girl had said. Come to the palace, braving the deadly storm, fired by some need to serve even he couldn't explain. Somehow, Ganz thought, in a moment of wonderful clarity, it seemed just. The foulness threatened them all. It was only right that the city stood to face it together, from the highest to the lowliest.

'Well, Kruza?' Ganz asked, making sure he remembered and used the ruffian's name. He wanted the young man to know he was an important part of the enterprise.

Kruza thought and then pointed down the hill. 'Down, and then the second turn to the left.'

'Are you sure, Kruza?'

'Sure as I can be,' the cut-purse replied. Why did the big war-rior keep using his name like that? He was scared enough – by the night, and the evil, and the simple fact of being here amongst this company of Wolves. Somehow, hearing his name on the lips of a warrior of Ulric was most terrible of all. He shouldn't be here. It was wrong.

'Come on, Kruza! It's there to be taken!' the priest muttered encouragingly, beside him.

Kruza looked round. 'What? What did you say?'

'I said, come on. Show us the place,' replied the priest, frown-ing. He could see the fear in Kruza's eyes. 'What is it?'

'Just ghosts, father, voices of the dead – but I guess you know all about that.'

'Too much, lad, too much.'

Ganz led them on, at a canter now. Kruza was having trouble staying in his saddle, but the big, elderly Wolf – Morgenschell, was it? – spurred forward and came alongside him, taking the palfrey's reins.

'Just hold on. I'll lead you,' he said, his voice rich and deep and encouraging.

The big Wolf winked at him and it made Kruza smile. It made the armoured giant seem human somehow, like the sort of man he would happily sit and sup with at the Drowned Rat. More than anything else, that wink steadied his nerve. But for it, he might have fled, leaving them all to their heroic doom. It was the wink that made him stay with them. Kruza grasped the sad-dle-front and clung on as the great Wolf dragged his steed down the slope into a gallop.

Rocks and abuse rained on them from a group of shadows at the street bend as they tore by. A house had been sacked and was ablaze. Bodies curled in the stained snow. One had been nailed upside down to a wall, and bowls set under it to collect the blood for more inscriptions.

'So,' Anspach considered out loud to those around him. 'What are the odds tonight, you reckon? I have a bag of gold pieces says we can take this monster down, even if it does look like one of our own! I'll give three to one! That's better than the Low Kings would give you!'

'And who'll be around to collect if you lose?' Bruckner asked sourly.

'He's right,' Kruza cried, turning to look back. 'You sell the wager sweetly, but those odds are just the sort of deal Bleyden would offer!'

The Wolves around laughed loudly. Ganz heard it and it cheered him that they could keep their spirits so.

'You know Bleyden?' Anspach asked, spurring forward, genuinely interested.

'Doesn't everyone?' the priest asked dryly.

'This is not for your ears,' Anspach said. He looked at Kruza. 'You know him?'

'He's like a father to me,' Kruza said, and even above the noise of the hooves, the Wolves could hear the acid irony in his tone. They laughed again.

'There's a matter of a tally,' Anspach went on, ignoring the jibes. 'If you could have a word…'

'You mean, if we live through this night?' Kruza asked, mildly, jolted by his steed.

'Oh, I'll make sure you live through this night,' Anspach told him seriously.

'There, lad!' said Morgenstern. 'You've Anspach as your guardian angel! You shouldn't have a fear in the world now!'

More laughter; more jibes and taunts. Ganz let them have their jokes. He wanted them ready when the time came. Full of jubilation, confidence, full of the strength of Ulric.

They turned into the next street. It was deserted, and the falling snow clung to every horizontal like a pelt. Ganz slowed his horse to a walk, and the others made double file behind.

'Kruza?'

Kruza looked around, though he knew exactly where it was. The tall, narrow, peculiar townhouse was just as he remembered it. It was fixed in his mind. The lean, slender tower with narrow windows and that strangely curvaceous spire, which rose up in soft waves to a tiny dome at its crown. The gallery of arrow slits under the base of the spire. The second circular tower fixed to the side of the main building, the breadth of perhaps two men passing, but with its own tiny dome and more of the strange slits for windows.

A place branded on his mind. A place of horror and foul magic and death.

He raised his hand. He pointed.

'*There*, Wolf,' he said.

HE WOKE, hearing distant fighting. Pain washed back into his body, like a tide. But it was softer now, as if he was floating.

Aric looked up from the bed. His broken arm throbbed. *Like the single pink eye had throbbed.*

In the flickering grate-light of the guest chamber, he saw the girl, Lenya, taking a glass of hot, brown liquid from a silver tray carried by a cadaverous old man in brocade, periwig and powder.

'Will there be anything else? The knight looks pale.'

'That will do, Breugal,' Lenya said, and the chamberlain nodded and left the room.

'You have no idea how much fun this is!' she laughed. 'The palace staff, even stuffed-rump Breugal, are falling all over themselves to help me as I tend the poor, brave knight who saved the ambassador's life!'

'S-so he's alive?'

Lenya started, almost dropping the glass. 'You're awake?'

Aric crawled up into a sitting position on the satin bolsters. 'Yes. Why, who were you talking to?'

'Um. Myself.'

'He's alive, the Bretonnian?'

'Yes... here, drink this.' She held out the glass and helped him sip. It was pungent and full of spices.

'What is it?'

'A tonic. From a recipe my brother taught me. The High Chamberlain prepared it by hand himself, if you don't mind!'

Aric smiled at her infectious good humour. The warmth of the balm was seeping into him. He felt better already.

'Your brother knows a good recipe.'

'Knew,' she corrected.

'He was this Wheezer, the boy the cut-purse was talking about?'

'His name was Stefan. But yes, he was Wheezer.'

'I will thank him when I see him.'

'But–'

'I know, I know. The cut-purse says he's dead. But for his courage, Ulric has surely taken him to his hall. I will thank him there, when I arrive.'

She thought about this for a moment, and then nodded. Her smile returned.

Aric was glad of it. He could see why Drakken loved the girl. She was so full of spirit and energy, it sometimes obscured her beauty. But that beauty was there. Her vivid, ice-light eyes, her hair so very dark.

'I heard fighting,' he said.

'The Panther, Ulgrind, is driving out the last of the fever-mad. It's got to the staff now. The chef attacked some pages, and a matron-lady stabbed a houseman with her embroidery needles.'

'Is the Graf safe? His family?'

'Sequestered by Ulgrind in the east wing.' Lenya looked down at him, holding out the glass for him to drink again. 'They say the city is running mad. Wild creatures, murdering in the streets. I never wanted to come here, and now I wish I never had.'

'You liked it back in Linz?'

'I miss the open country. The pastures and the woods. I miss my father and my mother. I visited their farm every week when I was serving at the Margrave's hall. I write to them each month, and put the missel on the Linz coach.'

'Has your father written back?'

'Of course not. He can't write.'

She paused. 'But he sent me this.' She showed him a cheap, tarnished silver locket that held a twist of hair, hair as dark as hers.

'It was his mother's. The clip is from my own mother's locks. He got the local priest to write my name and place on the wrapper. It was enough to let me know he had received my letters.'

'You're a long way from home, Lenya.'

'And you?'

'My home is down the hill, at the Temple of Ulric,' Aric replied quietly, sipping the warm tonic.

'Before that, I mean.' Lenya sat on a high-backed chair by the posted bed.

'There was no before that. I was a foundling, left at on the steps of the Temple just hours after my birth. The Temple life is all I've ever known.'

She thought about this. 'Do all Wolves join the Temple that way?'

He pulled up straighter, laughing, minding his splinted arm. 'No, of course not. Some are proposed as children, the sons of good families, or soldier lines. Your Drakken, he joined at eighteen, after serving in the Watch. So did Bruckner, though a little younger, I think. Lowenhertz was the son of a Panther. He came to White Company late in life. It took him a time to find his right place. Anspach was a cut-purse, a street boy, without connections, when Jurgen himself recruited him. There's a story there that Jurgen never told and Anspach refuses to relate. Dorff, Schell, Schiffer – they were all soldiers in the Empire's ranks and were sent to us on the vouchsafe of their commanders. Others, men like Gruber and Ganz, they are the sons of Wolves, following their fathers.'

'Are you the son of a Wolf?'

'I often think so. I like to think so. I believe that's why I was left on the Temple steps.'

Lenya was silent for a while. Then she said. 'What about the big one, Morgenstern?'

'Son of a merchant, who proposed him for admission when his father saw how strong he was. He's been with us since his teenage years.'

'So you are all different? From different places?'

'Levelled as one by Ulric, in his holy service.'

She paused. 'What about Einholt?'

He was silent for a while, as if wrestling with thoughts. 'He was the son of a Wolf, serving in the Temple since childhood. Old Guard... like Jurgen. He recruited and trained; Kaspen, for one. Myself, when the time came. There were others.'

'Others?'

'The fallen, the slain. Brotherhood has its price, Lenya of Linz.'

She smiled and held up a finger to silence him. 'Hush now, you make me sound like some high lady.'

'In Drakken's eyes you are. You should cherish that.'

'I fear for him,' she said suddenly. 'There was something in his face when he left. Like he had wronged and wanted to make amends.'

'Krieg has nothing to prove.'

She stood, looking away from Aric into the fire-glow. 'It was because he was with me, wasn't it? He came to me, did me a service, in fact. He left his post, didn't he? That's why you're hurt.'

Aric swung his legs off the bed and paused for a moment, fighting the pain in his arm. 'No!' he spat. 'No – he was true. True to the company over and again. Whatever he thinks he did, whatever wrong, I absolve him of it. He saved me.'

'Will he save the city too?' Lenya asked, gazing into the embers of the fireplace.

'I trust him to.'

She looked round at him suddenly, horrified. 'What are you doing? Lie down again, Aric! Your arm–'

'Hurts a lot, but it's splinted. Find me my armour.'

'Your armour?'

Aric smiled up at her, trying to keep the pain from his face. 'I can't let them have all the glory, can I?'

'Then I'm coming too!'

'No.'

'Yes!'

'Lenya–'

She grabbed him by the shoulders so hard he winced and then shrunk back, apologising. 'I need to be with Drakken. I need to find him. If you're going – and you shouldn't with your wounds – if you're going, I'm coming with you!'

'I don't think–'

'You want your armour? That's the deal!'

Aric stood up, swayed, and found his balance. 'Yes, I want my armour. Get it and we'll go.'

THEY WAITED outside for a moment, their horses in a wide semi-circle in the street facing the main arched doors. The moment was long enough for snow to begin to settle on their shoulders and scalps. Around them, the howls of the city rolled. Above them, snow-thunder, like the grinding of mountains on the move, shook the air.

'There was a small door to the rear,' said Kruza out of nowhere. 'That was where Wheezer and I got in...'

'It's long past time for sneaking, my friend,' Ganz said, looking round at him. He pulled his hammer from the saddle-loop and turned it once, loosening his arm.

'Hammers of Ulric! Knights of the Panther! Are you with me?'

The rousing 'Aye!' was half-drowned by the thunder of his hooves. Ganz crashed his horse forward and took the doors in with a massive up-swing of his hammer. Wood splintered and caved. Checking his steed's step for a second, Ganz ducked and rode right in through the front arch of the townhouse.

His horse stamped into a paved hall tall enough for him to rise upright again. Lamps in the wall brackets guttered in the sudden wash of air. Snow fluttered in around him. The chamber was bathed in yellowish light, and the stink of spoiled milk was unmistakable here. Gruber and Schell ducked in on their horses behind him. Ganz had dismounted, looking around.

'Kruza!' he yelled.

The thief appeared in the door, on foot, rubbing his sore rump, his short-sword in his hand.

Ganz gestured around. An arch led off the hall onto the stair-tower. Two other doors were next to each other in the left wall.

'The stairs,' Kruza gestured with his sword-point. 'We went down, two flights.'

Gruber had checked the other doors in turn by then, kicking them in. Empty rooms, cold and dark and layered with dust.

Ganz moved towards the stair-tower. The other Wolves and Panthers had entered on foot now.

'No welcoming party?' von Volk asked dryly, his blade glinting in the lamp-light.

'I don't think they were expecting us,' Morgenstern said.

'I don't think they were expecting anyone,' Lowenhertz corrected.

'Let's go and tell them we're here,' Ganz said, but a voice halted him.

The priest of Morr, cowled and stern, stood in the centre of the hallway, his hand raised.

'A moment more, Ganz of the White. If I can do anything tonight, any little thing, perhaps it is to bless those bound for war.'

The warriors all turned to face him, eyes averted from his gaze. He made a sign in the air with one elegant hand. His other, by his side, clutched the symbol of his god.

'Your own gods will look to you, the gods of the city you come to fight for. Ulric will be in your hearts to inspire you to courage and strength. Sigmar will burn in your minds with the righteousness of this undertaking.' He paused a moment and made another sign.

'My own lord is a dark shadow next to such awesome forces of the invisible world. He does not smite, he does not punish, nor even judge. He just is. An inevitable fact. We come to find glory, but we each may find death. It is Morr who will find you then. So in his name above all, I bless you. Ulric for the heart, Sigmar for the mind – and Morr for the soul. The God of Death is with you tonight, with you as you destroy that thing which perverts death.'

'For Ulric! Sigmar! And Morr!' Ganz growled, and the others caught it and repeated fiercely.

Anspach saw how Kruza stood back, saying nothing, his eyes dark with fear.

'And for Ranald, Lord of Thieves!' the Wolf said aloud. 'He has no Temple in Middenheim, no high priest, but he is worshipped well enough and he'll miss the place if it goes. Besides, he's played his part tonight too.'

Kruza blinked as eleven Templars of Ulric, seven Knights Panther and a priest of Morr volleyed the name of the thieves' dark trickster-spirit into the close air.

Then Ganz and von Volk led the party off down the stairwell, brisk and determined.

'Ranald was my lord for a long while, brother,' Anspach hissed to Kruza as he swept past, pulling him on. 'I know he relishes every little bit of worship he can get.'

The stairs swept down. Weapons ready, the pack descended. Intricate lamps shedding a white alchemical glow were looped down the walls.

Gruber pointed them out to Ganz. 'Just as in the cellar where we bested it last.'

'He's right,' put in von Volk. 'It was the same.'

The lower basement, circular, arched and dust-floored, was lit with the same white light from dozens of lamps. The walls were blank. Kruza looked around in confusion.

'This… this is not as it was. There were doorways, lots of them, and… it's changed. How can it have changed? It's only been… three seasons!'

Kruza crossed to the walls as the warriors fanned out. His trembling fingers traced the seamless stone. 'There were doors!' he repeated, as if angry with himself. 'All around! They can't have been bricked up – there would be some sign!'

'It's uniform and smooth,' Drakken noted, checking the far side. 'Are you sure this is the same place, thief?'

Kruza whirled angrily, but the steady haft of Anspach's hammer kept his short-sword from coming up.

'Kruza knows what he's talking about,' Anspach said calmly.

'We know magic is at work,' said Father Dieter from behind. 'Magic has done things here. You can smell it. Like rancid milk.'

Lowenhertz nodded to himself. Or like grave spices, sweetmeats, ash, bone-dust and death all wrapped up together. Just as he had smelled at the Margrave's hall in Linz, and in his great grandfather's solar, all those years ago. Had the wraiths they had fought this spring in the woodlands above Linz been part of this too? The priest had said the evil was old and great and had been planning for a while. And it was after power, strength, that much was also clear from everything he had heard. The old wet-nurse's amulet, the one Ganz had destroyed. Had that been a piece of this puzzle as well? A trophy, a powerful talisman their fell enemy had been trying to recover? Had they already thwarted it once before this year, without knowing it?

The irony made him smile. 'We've beaten you at every turn, even when we didn't realise it,' he murmured. 'We'll beat you now.'

'What did you say?' asked Ganz.

'Thinking out loud, commander,' said Lowenhertz, hurriedly. He glanced at the priest of Morr. The father had said something about defeating a necromancer called Gilbertus in the youngest part of the year; another part of it. Lowenhertz knew he would enjoy discussing this with the priest when all was done, putting the scraps together into a patchwork of sense.

Sharply, Lowenhertz realised he was imagining a time when it was over and they were all alive. *That was good*, he decided.

Kruza was busy searching the walls, fingertip by fingertip. His hair was dripping with sweat and melting snow. He would find it, he would. They had believed in him. He would not fail now.

Simply, unbelievably, the answer was there. Square ahead of the door from the stairs. Kruza didn't know where the other doors had gone, and he believed the priest when he spoke of magic. But here it was. Not magic at all.

'Ganz!' he called, in his eagerness, not caring about respect or rank. The Wolf commander crossed to him, apparently past caring either.

Kruza pointed to the wall, to the solid stones that matched the walls around, and pulled them aside.

Ganz started despite himself.

A drape of canvas, like a tapestry, painted perfectly to match the stones around, completely masking the archway beyond.

'We go to war, but the skills of a cut-purse show us where the war is,' chuckled Morgenstern.

Beyond the painted drape, a dark passageway, unlit and thick with warmth and smoke, led off into the unknown. Ganz marched through as confidently as he would through the doors of the Temple. The others followed.

Drakken was at the rear of the file. Kruza, holding the drape, caught him by the arm and glared into his face.

'You wanted me to look a fool in the eyes of your mighty comrades, Wolf?' he hissed.

Drakken shrugged off the arm. 'I didn't need to. You were doing well enough on your own.'

'She doesn't love you, Templar,' Kruza blurted suddenly.

Drakken turned back. 'And you'd know?'

'I know how she looks at me.'

Drakken shrugged.

'And I know you don't love her,' added Kruza, pushing his luck.

'We're here to save the city, and you think of her?'

Kruza grinned, almost triumphantly. 'You don't. That's why I know you don't love her.'

'There will be time for this later,' Drakken said, disconcerted, and passed under the arch.

Kruza let the drape drop back behind Drakken. Alone, he walked to the centre of the room and knelt in the dust, running the fingers of his left hand through the soft soil. This was the place. The place he'd last seen Wheezer. The place where Wheezer had–

Come on, Kruza! It's there to be taken!

Kruza started. There was no one there. Of course not. Wheezer wasn't outside him, he never had been. Kruza knew the ghost haunted secret spaces inside his mind.

'I'm coming,' he said, raising his sword and pushing in through the drape.

IN THE DRIVING snow, Aric's horse reared on the steps of the Temple of Ulric, and the Templar felt the girl behind him on the saddle hold tight as he fought the reins with his one good arm.

'What are we doing?' she gasped into his ear as the horse righted itself. 'Nordgarten, Kruza said! The place was in Nordgarten! You're as bad as Drakken, wanting to show me the Temple of the Wolf all the damn time!'

Aric dismounted. 'This is important. Come with me. I need your help.'

They strode in through the great atrium. Commotion filled the air. Bertolf had raised the alarm, and the stationed companies, Red, Grey, Gold and Silver, were martialling to support their White Company brothers.

With Lenya supporting him, Aric limped down the main aisle towards the great statue of Ulric. The cold air was rank with incense. The Wolf-choir was singing a hymn of deliverance into the night. Thousands of candle-flames shuddered as they passed.

Lenya was silent, looking around. She had never been in this great, pious place, and now realised why Drakken had wanted to show it to her. In a way beyond words, she understood what the Temple meant, what the Wolves meant. She was struck dumb, and surprised to find herself truly humbled.

They approached the great shrine of the Eternal Flame. Aric pulled off his wolf-pelt and began to wrap it around his hammer-head. With his one functioning hand, he made poor work of it. He glanced round. 'Give me strips off your skirt.'

'What?'

'Tear them off! Now!'

Lenya sat on the cold floor and began to shred strips of cloth from her skirt hem.

Aric had found a relic-bag and shocked Lenya by emptying out the dusty contents so he could pull free the leather thong. With the thong and the strips she gave him, the Wolf tied the pelt tightly around the head of his warhammer, using his teeth to brace against his one useable hand. She moved in, helping him to tie the bindings.

'What are we doing, Aric?' she asked.

Aric dipped the pelt-wrapped hammer into the Eternal Flame. The pale fire licked into it and Aric raised a torch of incandescent flame.

'Now? Now we're going to find the others,' he told her.

KRUZA JOINED Ganz and von Volk in the vanguard as the party pressed down the dark passageway. There was a dim light ahead, like a promise of dawn.

'This is not as it was before,' he told Ganz. 'It's utterly changed. I guess magic does that.'

'I guess it does,' said Ganz.

They reached the light and the passage opened out.

The chamber they looked out on was vast. Impossible. Immeasurable. The cold, craggy black rock of the Fauschlag arched up over them, lit by a thousand naked fires.

'Ulric's name! It's bigger than the stadium!' Anspach gasped.

'How could this be down here and we not know it?' breathed Bruckner.

'Magic,' said the priest of Morr. It seemed to be his answer to everything.

Ganz gazed down into the vast black bowl of the chamber, where flames flickered from hundreds of braziers, the firelight mingling with the white gleam of the thousands upon thousands of alchemical lamps roped along the rugged walls. There were hundreds of worshippers down there, robed, kneeling, wailing out a turgid prayer, the words of which punctured his soul in a dozen, evil places. The air was rich with the smell of decay and death.

At the far end, before the assembled worshippers, a raised dais, an altar. On it, a throne of rock, carved from the Fauschlag itself. On that, a cowled figure, soaking up the adoration.

Volcanic fire-mud belched and spurted in a pit behind the dais, and sulphur-smoke gathered in the upper spaces of the cavern. To the left of the chamber stood a great cage or box, as large as a Nordgarten mansion, shrouded in tar-treated canvas. It rocked and trembled.

'What... do we do?' Kruza stammered, knowing he wasn't going to like the answer.

'We kill as many as we can,' growled von Volk.

Ganz stayed his hand. 'A good plan, but I'd like to polish up the details.' He pointed his warhammer at the figure on the throne, far away.

'He is our enemy. Kill as many as necessary to reach him. Then kill him.'

Von Volk nodded.

Kruza shook his head. 'Your plan sounds no better than the Panther's! I thought you warriors were clever! Tactical!'

'This is war,' von Volk snarled back at him. 'If you've no stomach for it, go! Your job is done!'

'Aye,' sneered Drakken from behind. 'We'll call on you when we've done the work.'

'Ulric eat you whole!' Kruza spat back into Drakken's face. 'I finish what I start!'

'Then we're agreed,' Ganz said. 'The liche-thing is the target. Cut your way to it, by whatever means you can. Kill it. The rest is inconsequential.'

Ganz raised his hammer.

'Now!' he yelled.

But Kruza was already leading the charge, short-sword raised, bellowing a battle-cry from the seat of his lungs. The Wolves and Panthers followed him, bellowing too, weapons swinging.

The priest of Morr caught Lowenhertz by the arm.

'Father?'

'Could I trouble you for a weapon?'

Lowenhertz blinked and pulled his dagger out, handing it handle first to the priest. 'I didn't think you–'

'Neither did I,' said Dieter Brossmann and turned to follow the charge.

THEY FELL upon the worshippers of un-death from behind, slaughtering many before they could rise from prayer. Blood sprayed the dusty floor of the rock-chamber.

Three prongs: Ganz with Drakken, Gruber, Lowenhertz, Dorff, and Kaspen; von Volk with his Knights Panther, and

Schell and Schiffer; Kruza with Anspach, the priest, Morgenstern and Bruckner. They trampled the unholy congregation, chopping and hacking with their hammers and blades. The multitude rose and turned on them. Men and women and other, bestial things, throwing off their cloaks and hoods, raising weapons and raucous howls against the attackers. Kruza saw that each one wore a world-eater talisman round its neck, each identical to the one Wheezer had taken, the one now in his belt-pouch.

Von Volk's assault foundered as the enemy rose up around them, thickly, fiercely. A Panther fell, decapitated. Another spun back, gutted. Von Volk took a wound to his left arm and continued to hack away through the bodies that rose to meet him.

The thing on the throne stood up. It looked down in quiet wonder at the carnage below.

It tipped its head back up and rejoiced. Its unholy laugh thundered.

Death! More Death! Death unnumbered!

Kruza's party meshed into heavy fighting on the right side of the cavern. Cultists were all around them. Kruza stabbed out with his sword, ripping and turning. He had never known anything like this. The turmoil, the heat, the blood mist in the air, the noise. This was warfare, something he had never thought he'd experience, in his wildest dreams. A cut-purse, like him… waging war! At his side, Anspach, Bruckner and Morgenstern belted into the frenzied mob with their hammers.

A bestial, robed thing with ashen hide, glassy eyes and the snout of a goat, reared up at him. Kruza, his blade stuck solid in his last foe, flinched. A dagger tore out the thing's neck.

The priest of Morr looked down at the bloody blade in his hand. 'Morr is with me,' he repeated softly to himself. 'Morr is with me.'

Kruza spun and impaled a rabid woman with an axe who was about to shorten the priest by a head-span.

Morgenstern crunched a face nearby, chuckling. 'This reminds me of the fight at Kern's Gate.'

'Everything reminds you of the fight at Kern's Gate!' snarled the huge blond warrior, Bruckner, as he swung his hammer in the tight, stinking press.

'That's because he's senile!' Anspach barked, whistling his hammer down and over into a skull that flattened obligingly.

'I am not!' Morgenstern grumbled, rattling his hammer left and right, destroying bodies.

'No, he's–' Bruckner faltered. His mouth moved to finish the sentence, but only blood came out. A lance-head as long as a sword blade had impaled him from behind. He looked down at the steel jutting from his breastplate, blood jetting out around it. More blood found its way out of his mouth, foaming. He fell.

'Bruckner!' Morgenstern raged. Bruckner seemed to fall slowly in Morgenstern's mind, the long blond hair lank with gore as he struck the ground. White anger seared Morgenstern's brain. Like a bear, he shrugged off the cultists clawing at him, throwing them aside. One actually flew six or seven feet up into the air from the force of the Wolf's arms. Screaming as if insane, the Wolf flew into the thickets of the enemy. He was berserk. The dense enemy numbers recoiled and broke under his assault, smashed apart as they failed to get clear of him. Blood, meat and bone-shards flew out around his reckless frenzy.

Kruza looked down at the slain Bruckner in horror. He realised he had believed these Wolves to be invulnerable, man-gods who strode the battlefields of the world, denying danger. Despite everything, he had felt safe with them, as if the immortality was catching.

But Bruckner was dead. Just a dead man, not a wolf-god at all. They could all die. They were all only men. A very few men, surrounded by feral foe who outnumbered them five to one or more.

A hand grabbed him from behind, pushing him to the floor. Anspach blocked and killed two more cultists that Kruza, in his shocked daze, had been wide open to.

'Get up! Fight!' Anspach bawled. Kruza was shaking as he got to his feet. Robed creatures, stinking and yowling, were all around them. Kruza raised his sword and covered Anspach's back.

'I– I was lost there for a minute,' Kruza said, clashing blades with a cultist.

'Shock, fear, hesitation – they'll kill you quicker than any blade! Bruckner's dead! Dead! Hate them for it! Use the hate!' screamed Anspach. He said something else, but he was incoherent now. Tears of rage boiled down his blood-splashed face.

Kruza saw it, then, and the world turned upside down. Commotion and panic had pulled the canvas shrouds off the trembling cage close to them. The frenzied creature revealed inside the cage was an impossibility to Kruza. His mind refused to accept it.

A cultist pulled the cage open and the great snaking dragon streamed out to devour them all, and then the world, and then itself.

VON VOLK'S BLADE splintered in a cracking chest and he dropped it. Three of his Panthers were dead, crushed under the frenzy. Schell, the Wolf, howled out and threw him a captured sword. It spun end over end above the press. Von Volk caught it cleanly and laid in again.

Behind him, in a mob of bellowing and thrashing bodies, Schiffer was brought down, stabbed and pummelled into the dust by dozens of the enemy. His last act was to howl the name of his god up into the faces of the beasts that hacked and jabbed at him. A spear-point thrust directly into his screaming mouth silenced his oaths for all time.

Von Volk saw the lean Templar, Schell, turn back to drive the whooping carrion from Schiffer's smashed corpse.

He grabbed him. 'No! No, Schell! He's gone! We must fight onwards, to the throne! We must!'

'Hammers of Ulric!' Schell cried with fury as he turned back with the Panther leader to fight on. 'Drown them in blood! Drown them in blood!'

They fought on together, the other Panther Knights at their flank, cutting a swathe through the hectic mass.

GANZ BROKE FROM the mass first and charged the dais. Lowenhertz was behind him, with Drakken and Gruber. Kaspen was still caught in the vicious melee.

Dorff was dead. Kaspen had seen him fall a moment before, cut apart by frenzied cultists. His tuneless whistling would never haunt White Company again. Kaspen stood his ground, red mane drenched in blood, howling like a forest wolf, hammer whirling. He held ground and faced the rushing mob, partly to give his commander and the others time to reach the throne, and partly to make the bastards pay for Dorff's life, one by one.

Ganz reached the stone steps of the dais. Above him the hooded figure threw off its robes and laughed down at him. Volcanic flame-light from behind made the Templar armour it wore glow as if it were red hot. One pink eye gleamed.

'Einholt!' gasped Ganz. He had known what he was going to face, but still it fazed him. *Einholt, Einholt... Ulric spare my soul...*

'Oh, we're all friends here,' wheezed the one-eyed thing, beck-oning to Ganz.

The commander of White Company saw how the Wolf armour it wore was rusting and beginning to moulder. The flesh of Einholt's grinning face was greenish and starting to stretch. It stank of decay, of the grave. It held out its hand to him. 'Call me by my real name, Ganz. Call me Barakos.'

Ganz didn't reply. He flew at the monstrosity, hammer swing-ing in a wide, sidelong arc. But the decaying thing was faster – terrifyingly fast. It smashed Ganz aside with a fierce blow of Einholt's warhammer. Ganz fell hard, clutching at his dented breastplate and the cracked ribs beneath. He tried to rise but he had no breath. His lungs refused to draw. His vision went bright and hazy, and there was a coppery taste in his mouth.

Barakos took a step towards him.

Lowenhertz and Drakken leapt up the last few steps and ploughed in to attack the liche.

Lowenhertz was first and fastest, but the undead thing some-how dodged his first strike, blocked the return and then sent Lowenhertz flying clean off the dais with a hammerblow that took him in the belly.

Sweeping around, not even looking, as if it knew precisely where everything and everyone was, it reversed the swing and snapped Drakken's collarbone as the young Wolf came at him. Drakken shrieked out and dropped to the stone.

Barakos stood over the writhing Templar, as if wondering how best to finish him. It chuckled dreamily, its voice like syrup. Then it looked up.

At the top of the steps, Gruber stood facing him.

'You again, old knight.' said the thing with the face of his old friend.

'I should have killed you in the cellar.'

'You can't kill what has no life.' The liche's voice was hoarse and dry, but there was a depth to it, an inhuman grumble that curled the edges of the words, like age-mould curling the edges of old parchment.

Hammers whirled. Gruber met the liche's attack with unbri-dled fury. Two smacks, three, hafts and head spinning and counter-striking.

Gruber feinted left and landed a glancing blow at the thing's hip, but it seemed not even to flinch. It blocked Gruber's next swing with the centre of its haft, then kicked at the Wolf under the locked weapons. Gruber staggered backwards and the liche rattled round with a wide, devastating blow that slammed the warrior away down the steps. The old knight bounced once off the stone, his armour denting and rattling, and crumpled at the base of the flight.

The thing was laughing down at Gruber when Ganz's blow smashed it back across the dais. Rotting straps tore and the left cuisse flopped away. The mail beneath was rusty and oozing with oily black decay from the corpse beneath.

Ganz sallied in again, before the creature could right itself. It managed to raise an arm to ward off the next strike, but Ganz's weapon smashed into the hand, tearing off the tarnished gauntlet. Several fingers came off in a spray of stagnant fluid and shattered mail-rings.

Ganz roared, like a pack-sire wolf, bringing his weapon around. He could taste victory now, taste it like–

The thing recovered, unsteady but ferocious, lashing out with a poorly executed, frantic blow.

The flat-side of the hammer-head struck Ganz across the neck and ear. He felt his cheek crack. His head snapped round with the blow and he lurched away, taking two steps before falling onto his hands and knees. Blood drooled out of his mouth onto the stone between his hands. The world spun upside down, voices and fighting booming in his rushing head as if heard from underwater.

His face white with pain, Drakken pulled at Ganz with his one working arm, shrieking aloud as the effort ground his shattered collar-bone.

'Move! Move!' he gasped. Ganz was a dead weight, barely supporting himself on his hands. The liche moved towards them. It was not laughing now. Pink fury throbbed in the one seeing eye. It opened its mouth and pus-yellow fluid dribbled out around shrivelled gums and blackened teeth. It flexed its two-handed grip on the hammer, ignoring the missing fingers.

Lowenhertz was suddenly between it and the two wounded Templars. He was breathing hard, raggedly, and the armour on his belly was badly buckled. Blood ran down the armour on his legs at the front.

'You… will… be… denied…' Lowenhertz said, dragging the words out one by one.

'I will destroy you all,' the thing returned, thunder back in the edges of its voice. As it spoke the words, two maggots fell from its mouth and adhered to the front of its cuirass.

'Make… sure you… do,' Lowenhertz gasped. 'For… as long as… only one of us… survives… . you will be… denied.'

Lowenhertz swung at the thing, which dodged deftly, but the knight reversed the swing abruptly with a display of arm-strength that one in his state should not have been capable of. The reverse hit the liche in the side. Rusty armour broke and straps snapped. Ribs cracked like twigs, and brown, viscous matter spurted out, more maggots amongst it.

It faltered, setting the head of Einholt's hammer down and leaning on the weapon to support itself. Lowenhertz almost gagged at the stink coming out of it. It was the old smell, the death smell, rich with spices and decay, from his great grandfather's solar, from the hideous tombs of the far southlands. But a hundred, a thousand times worse.

Lowenhertz took a step forward to swing the hammer again, but the creature knocked him away with a backward smack of its free hand.

Kaspen screamed as he charged in, reaching the top of the dais at last, a trail of slaughtered cultists in his wake. His red hair streamed out behind him. He was drenched from head to foot in blood, as red as his mane.

'Einholt!' he bawled, wanting to bring his hammer down, wanting to slay the foul thing. But it was Einholt still, his old friend, 'For the love of all we have shared, comrades of the Wolf, sons of Ulric, please, Jagbald, pl–'

Kaspen's old friend killed him with a single blow.

THE DRAGON, the great serpent, the Ouroboros, slashed out into the cavern below, Death incarnate. Its long neck, as thick as a warhorse's girth and armoured in livid scales each the size of a knight's shield, curling back in a swan-throated S-shape as it coiled to strike. Its beaked, wedge-shaped skull with back-flared horns, was the size of a hay-cart. Its eyes were fathomless dark pearls, a mirror only of unknowable terror. Where it had come from could not be divined; all that was true was that it lived, writhing in its foul undeath. And it raged, screeching its eternal anger at all life.

Kruza stumbled backwards and fell over one of the countless corpses that littered the floor. 'No, no… impossible…' he stammered.

Hooked talons, each as big as a man's thigh, dug into the rock as the vast thing found purchase. Its tail, so very long and slender, sliced around, throwing screaming cultists high into the air or breaking them like corn stalks. The wyrm made a noise, deep in its vast throat, high and keening, like a blizzard wind. Its scaled flesh was gold-green, like tarnished coins, but its vast head was white as bone.

The neck moved in a snap, the great curve suddenly straightening like a whip, driving the head forward and down hard as a lightning strike. The beak clashed, rending and butchering cultists. It raised its head, gnashing at the shreds of bodies and limbs in its huge maw, then slithered forward and struck again. It was wild, uncontrollable, killing everything it saw.

'How can we fight that?' Kruza gasped as Anspach grabbed him.

'We can't! We don't! Run!' replied the Templar, white-faced with fear.

Morgenstern appeared from the milling confusion and panic. He said something, but it was drowned out by another blizzard keening from the wyrm. There was a further clack of jaws, and more screaming, as it struck again.

'I! Said! Run!' Morgenstern repeated, emphatically.

'My plan exactly,' Anspach said. The trio headed for cover amid the milling enemy, heading for the rocky alcoves and depressions along the great cavern wall.

Then the world disappeared. There was no ground. Kruza was flying, looking up at the sulphur smoke gathering in the roof of the cavern.

Abruptly, the ground came back, hard under him, and pain jolted through him. He rolled over, looking around. The wyrm's great tail had scourged through the crowd, sending him and the two Templars flying. There were broken corpses and wounded cult-beasts all around. Kruza couldn't see Anspach or Morgenstern now.

The keening cry of the wyrm came again.

Kruza could smell the vast monster now, a dry, clean smell like hide-oil or grain alcohol.

He got up into a crouch, preparing to run – and realised the wyrm was upon him.

Kruza looked up into the dark, pearl eyes of the world-eater, the Ouroboros. There was nothing there, no spark of intelligence or reason or life. It seemed to fix on him, though. The swan-neck coiled backwards, ready to strike, ready to bring the huge arrow-head skull down at him, beak wide open.

In the last second left of his life, Kruza thought of Wheezer, Wheezer who had innocently brought him to this place and time and doom. *I'm going to be killed by a dragon, Wheezer! How do you like that, eh? Who'd have thought it? It's so unlikely, it's almost funny.*

It seemed right, though. He had failed Wheezer and Wheezer had died, died saving him. It was time to pay for that.

I just wish, Kruza thought, *I just wish that I could be as invisible as you. I never did figure out how you did that. Except that you were a natural. Invisible, like you, yeah, that's what I'd like to be.*

The wyrm keened its rage at the whole sorry world. Its neck flexed and whipped. It struck.

AS IF KNOWING its end was upon it, the ancient city of Middenheim shook. The sky stretched and broke as the storm exploded down from the ghastly magenta sky. Snow and hail bombarded the roofs, shattering some, smashed windows and tore away chimneys and weather cocks. Lightning lanced the streets, exploding houses, shattering towers. Lurid green energies, writhing like serpents, coiled around the Fauschlag. The northern viaduct buckled and collapsed into the deeps, a half-mile stretch torn clean away.

The Temple of Morr, still only half-rebuilt, burst into flames spontaneously. The fire was pink, unearthly. It made a sound like laughter as it burned.

Lightning struck the Temple of Sigmar and brought the top of the tower down through the nave roof.

The chaos and killing in the streets was now overwhelming. Fever-madness and storm-panic drove the population into frenzied rioting. The Companies of the Wolf, heading from the Temple of Ulric to assist Ganz's men, were caught in a mass riot, and found themselves fighting for their lives as lightning skewered the night, hail hurtled down, and death burned out the heart of Ulric's citadel.

Shades and spirits were everywhere. It was as if the doors of death were opened, as if the invisible world had been permitted to get loose and roam the city. Phantoms, pale, gaunt and shrieking, billowed around the streets, dozens, hundreds of them. Some spewed out of the ground in Morrspark, like venting steam. Many came crawling and shimmering, stalking back up from the depths below the Cliff of Sighs. The dead were walking, free; the living would soon be dead.

Lenya thought she would surely go mad. She clung to Aric as they rode as fast as possible through the chaos. Skeletal, emaciated things made of smoke circled them, laughing and

beckoning. It was all Aric could do to keep the horse from shy-
ing. Thunder, so loud, and lightning, so bright, broke the sky
into pieces.

'Lenya? Lenya!'

She realised they had stopped. Lenya slipped down onto the
slushy street, soaked and bruised by the hail that still fell. She
helped Aric dismount. He held the hammer-torch aloft. It
blazed. Was that what was keeping the shades from touching
us? Lenya wondered. She could see them all around still, flickering, darting ghosts, transparent white like ice on a window's
glass.

'Where are we?' she asked over a crash of storm.

Aric gestured with the torch. There was a townhouse ahead,
curious and towered. Warhorses, Temple warhorses, roamed
the street around, trailing their reins, rearing at thunderflashes.

'Nordgarten,' he said. 'I can't say what we'll find in there. It
may be–'

'Worse than this?' she asked, pulling him forward. 'I doubt it.
Come on!'

The smoky things in the air around them were gathering,
growing in numbers, lighting the street with their ghastly lumi-
nosity. Lenya tried not to look at them. She tried not to hear the
whispering they made.

They reached the splintered doorway and Lenya helped Aric
to limp inside.

FUNNY THING, thought Kruza. *I'm still alive.*

He felt his body and made sure it was still in one piece. The
vast wyrm was slithering right past him now. It had struck, dis-
membering more squealing cultists just a few feet from him.

With this luck, I should go straight to the wager-pits right now, he
thought stupidly. He turned and gazed at the huge, sinuous
creature as it moved past, chomping and killing.

I'm invisible, he thought. *Ulric smile on me, I'm invisible! It can't
see me!*

He stooped and picked up a sword. Not his own; that was
long lost in the confusion. It was a long-bladed, basket-hilted
weapon one of the beast-things had dropped.

He could see Anspach and Morgenstern, raising their hammers to confront the wyrm as the cultists scattered around
them. *Brave, doomed,* he thought. *What can they hope to do
against this?*

What can I do?

The thought dug into his mind. Kruza didn't know how, but he was sure he had been spared thanks to Wheezer. The dead were walking free again tonight, and somehow Wheezer had come to him, and generously shared his talent for invisibility.

No, that's not it. He's been with me all along. In my head. He was waiting to be called upon.

He tried the sword for balance and then calmly walked towards the slithering beast. Blood and body parts were strewn, steaming, in its gory wake. It showed no sign of noticing him. He got right up close to its scaled flank, close enough to hear its rasping breath, close enough to smell its rich, clean scent. It was keening again, killing. Morgenstern and Anspach would be next.

Kruza lifted his hand and placed it flat against the scaled hide of the wyrm's flank. The armoured flank was warm and dry. His fingers found a space between the scales and directed the point of the sword there. All the while the cut-purse was almost calm, as if safe within some sphere of protection, or the eye of the storm.

He put his full weight behind the pommel and drove it in.

The wyrm shrieked. The braying sound it made echoed around the room, louder even than its keening. Hot, syrupy blood gouted from the wound, smashing into Kruza. The liquid pressure knocked him over.

He was flat on his back and soaked with sticky wyrm gore when the monstrosity went into convulsions. Its vast, serpentine form spasmed and lashed, crushing cultists under it or pulping them with its jerking tail. Morgenstern and Anspach leapt into cover.

Shaking the chamber and vibrating wildly, the wyrm keened again, three times, each one louder and more shrill than the last. Its claws ripped into the rocky ground, striking sparks and sending shards of stone in all directions. Its death throes killed more of the foe than the Templars' brave assault had done. But they were death-throes. One last, bitter wail, and the wyrm collapsed. The ground shook. The tail lashed round one more time and fell dead and heavy.

I've killed a bloody dragon, thought Kruza, as he blacked out.

DRAKKEN STRUGGLED with Ganz, who was half-conscious and far gone. Lowenhertz lay still on the rock of the dais, next to Kaspen's corpse. The liche, panting and ragged, slowly swung around to look at the youngest Wolf.

'I'll give you credit, boy...' Barakos sneered through his borrowed mouth. 'You Wolves did more than I thought you capable of. You hurt me. I'll need another body now.'

It limped towards them. Drakken tried to scramble back, tried to bring Ganz with him, but his smashed bones knotted and meshed and he passed out for a second with pain.

When he came to, Barakos was right in his face, leaning down and leering. The grave-stink of his breath was horrific.

'But it's all too late. Far too late. It's over and I have already won.' The dead thing smiled, and the expression ripped the decaying skin around its mouth. Its voice was low, resonating with that undertow of inhuman power. 'Middenheim is dead. Sacrificed upon my altar. All those lives, thousands of them, spent and spilled, feeding the great power that will grant me a measure of godhood. Not much – just enough to turn this world into a festering cinder. A thousand ages it has taken me, but I have triumphed. Death has given me eternal life. The last few moments pass now, as the city rises to murder itself. Then it will be done. I'll need a new form to inhabit.'

Barakos looked at the terrified Drakken. 'You're young, firm. With my power, I can heal that injury in a second. You'll do. A handsome boy – I've always longed for good looks.'

'N-no! In the n-name of Ulric!' Drakken gasped, reaching for a weapon that wasn't there.

'Ulric is dead, boy. It's high time you got used to your new lord.'

'Barakos,' said a voice from behind them.

The priest of Morr stood at the top of the steps. Gore soaked his robes, and he had taken a head wound that drizzled blood down his lined face. He opened his hand and the bloody dagger Lowenhertz had lent him clattered to the floor.

'Dieter. Dieter Brossmann,' Barakos said, rising and turning to face the priest. 'Father, in many ways you have been my fiercest foe. But for you, the stalwart Wolves would never have recognised my threat. And when you defeated Gilbertus, my! How I cursed your soul and name!'

'I'm flattered.'

'Don't be. You'll be dead in a few more moments. Heh! Only you saw – only you knew – dogged, relentless, hiding in your books and manuscripts, hunting out the clues.'

'An evil as old as yours is easy to find,' the priest stated dourly, stepping forward.

'And why did you hide in your books, I wonder?'

'What?' the priest paused for a second.

'Dieter Brossmann, the worthy merchant – if a little ruthless. Why did you turn to the way of Morr and forsake your life in Middenheim?'

The priest stiffened. 'This is no time for games.'

'But of course: your beloved wife and child,' the liche hissed, backnoted by the burr of distant thunder.

'They're dead.'

'No, they're not, are they? They merely left you, left you and ran away from you, because you were brutal and unscrupulous and harsh. You drove them away. They're not dead, are they? They're alive, hiding away in Altdorf, hoping never to see you again.'

'No, that's not–'

'It is the truth. In your mind, you made them dead, sent them to Morr! To avoid the bleak truth that you destroyed your own family with your cruelty and your greed. It was conscience and denial that made you pretend they were dead, made you take the path of Morr.'

Dieter Brossmann's face was as hard as the Fauschlag Rock. 'I will pay for my crimes in another life, Morr watch me. When will you pay for yours?'

The priest of Morr moved forward again, raising his hands. 'You're dead, aren't you, Barakos?' he said simply. 'Undead, passed beyond. That form you inhabit – poor Einholt of the White – he's dead too. You may be about to embrace god-like powers, but right now you're a corpse. And so you should be taken to Morr.'

Another step and the priest began to intone the funeral litany, the Nameless Rite. Dieter Brossmann began to bless the corpse that stood before him, bless it and protect it from evil and send the lost soul to Morr, the Lord of Death.

'No!' gasped the undead thing, quivering with rage. 'No! No, you shall not! You will not!'

The priest of Morr continued to chant, driving all his will and the full holiness of his duty back into the foul being before him.

Ritual, ritual as old as Middenheim, dug into the liche, slowly dislodging its being from the body it dwelt in. It convulsed, coughing, spewing brackish fluid. 'No, you bastard priest! No!' It began cursing in a babble of a thousand tongues.

It was a brave try. Looking on, clutching Ganz, Drakken believed for a moment it would succeed. But then the staggering liche reached Dieter Brossmann and, flinching, smashed him back off the dais with a vicious blow of his deathless hand.

THE STORM suddenly ceased. The last few pebbles of hail clattered across the streets. The pink night buckled and went dark.

A moment had come. The moment when a foul thing became a fouler god.

Every flame and candle and lamp and torch in the city went out.

Except one.

ONE STEP AT a time, Lenya supporting his weight, Aric mounted the dais. At the top, he faced the cadaverous relic that had been Einholt. A glance showed him the fallen Lowenhertz and Kaspen, Drakken clutching Ganz.

So much, so hard fought…

'You – again?' rumbled Barakos. 'Aric, dear boy, you're far too late.'

Aric, using his good arm, began to swing his hammer, turning it in great whooshing circles. The flame-head traced the circles with fire. The Endless Flame, the flame of the wolf-god. The hammer whistled round, the pelt lashed to it burning with unearthly radiance.

Aric let it fly, a perfect hammer release, just as Jagbald Einholt had taught him.

The burning hammer head struck the creature in the chest, knocking it onto its back.

Aric slumped, his strength gone out.

Lenya looked at the fallen liche, saw the tiny fingers of Eternal Flame crackling over its dented, decayed chest as it struggled to rise again. The burning hammer lay on its side, guttering out as if it were their last hope fading.

The one pink eye locked onto hers, as the Barakos rose like it was lifting itself out of the grave.

'I really don't think so…' it rasped, and it was too much to be endured.

Lenya rushed forward. It took all her strength to lift Aric's pelt-wrapped hammer. It took strength she didn't know she had to swing it up and bring it down on the liche-thing.

'For Stefan!' she snarled as the burning hammer smashed the dead monstrosity back into the rock of the dais.

The thing shook and ignited, blazing from head to foot with the Eternal Flame of Ulric. It jiggled and quivered, a living torch, issuing a keening shriek even louder than the great deathless dragon-thing, the world-eater, Ouroboros. The heat of the blaze was so great Lenya fell back. Barakos was incandescent, like a twitching firework, white hot and molten.

Undeath died. A clawing shade, frosty and steaming, tried to climb out of the torching body, tried to find a new home. But the sacred flames were too intense. The spirit folded back into the fire and was gone, shrieking out its last. Barakos, the endless, had finally found his end.

CAUTIOUS, TENTATIVE daylight filtered down across the city as prime struck.

A week had passed since the night of horror. Middenheim was rebuilding, burying its numerous dead, and getting on with life.

In a canopy tent erected in Morrspark, and duly consecrated to Morr himself, Dieter Brossmann conducted a funeral rite for five Templars of Ulric. Their names were Bruckner, Schiffer, Kaspen, Dorff and Einholt. It was unusual. Usually the High Priest Ar-Ulric would consecrate the fallen Temple men. But Ganz had insisted.

The priest spoke softly, as if he was recovering from some injury. In truth he was – the dressing on his brow showed that, but it wasn't the physical wounds that really hurt him. Dieter Brossmann would have scars inside him for a long while yet.

In the palace, healers attended Captain von Volk, the only Panther to survive the battle in Nordgarten. Bedridden, he asked the priests of Sigmar who treated him if, may they forgive him, a priest of Ulric might also attend.

In the Spread Eagle Tavern, after the solemn service in Morrspark, Morgenstern, Schell, Anspach, Gruber and Lowenhertz raised and clashed their tankards. It felt as it always did after a great battle. Victory and defeat mingled, bittersweet. They did their best to carouse and celebrate the victory and forget what had been lost. More worthy names for the walls of the Regimental Chapel. More souls gone to run with the Great Pack.

'To the fallen! May Ulric bless them all!' Morgenstern cried, chasing the tang of victory in their hearts.

'And to the new blood!' Anspach added dryly.

They clashed again.

'New blood!' they chorused.

'What new blood?' Aric asked, limping in, his arm bound.

'Haven't you heard?' asked Gruber, as if some great irony was at work. 'Anspach here has proposed a new cub for the Temple...'

SHE KISSED his lips and then turned from his bed.

'Lenya – I love you,' Drakken said. It sounded stupid, and he felt stupid, trussed up in bandages and splints to set his collar wound.

'I know you do.' She looked away. 'I have to get back. Breugal needs the maids to draw water for the feast. I'm dead if I stay.'

'You fear Breugal still? After all that has happened!'

'No,' she said. 'But I have a job to keep.'

He shrugged, then winced, wishing dearly he hadn't. 'Ow... I know, I know... but answer – do you love me?' Drakken looked up out of the infirmary bed.

'I love... a Wolf Templar, of White Company,' she declared emphatically, and left the room to get on with her chores.

THE GREAT STATUE of Ulric lowered over him.

Ar-Ulric, great Ar-Ulric, finished his intonation, scent-smoke from the altar burners swirling around him, and handed the newly forged hammer to Ganz, who took it carefully, mindful of his injuries.

'In the name of Ulric, I admit you to the Temple, bring you in to White Company,' Ganz pronounced soberly, 'where you may find comradeship and glory. You have proved your bravery. May you endure the long years of training keenly, and find a purpose and meaning to your life in the service of the Temple.'

'I take this as a blessing, as I take this hammer,' came the reply.

'Ulric look to you. You are a Wolf now.'

'I know it.'

The initiate lowered the hammer. The heavy pelt and the grey and gilt plate were unfamiliar and burdensome.

'How do you move in this stuff?' he whispered to his new master.

'You'll get used to it... beast-slayer,' Ganz smiled

Kruza flexed his armoured limbs and laughed.

IN THE ALTQUARTIER, down a filthy back-alleyway between stews, slum children were playing with a tight bound ball of cloth.

They threw the ball back and forth against the narrow, greasy, dingy walls.

And chanted.

Ba ba Barak, come see thee tarry!
Slow not, wait not, come and harry.
Ba ba Barak come and sup,
And eat the world and sky right up!

And at the end, they all flopped down, shamming death. This time.